IN

.16.99

Elizabeth Hawksley has been writing since she was six. As a child she had a free run of her grandfather's well-stocked nineteenth-century library and, as a result, has always felt at home in that century. She lives in London.

FROST FAIR

When sixteen-year-old Emilia Daniels elopes with charming ne'er-do-well Stephen Kirkwall, she is unaware that he is in debt to the sinister Balquidder, a man deeply involved in slave trading. Balquidder has an eye on the fortune Emilia will inherit when she is twenty-five — and will stop at nothing. Alone and desperate, Emilia turns to Colonel Noël Beresford, who has known her since childhood. But it is by no means certain that Noël will either believe her or help her . . .

Books by Elizabeth Hawksley
Published by The House of Ulverscroft:

LYSANDER'S LADY
THE CABOCHON EMERALD
CROSSING THE TAMAR
A DESPERATE REMEDY

ELIZABETH HAWKSLEY

FROST FAIR

Complete and Unabridged

ULVERSCROFT
Leicester

First published in Great Britain in 2001 by
Robert Hale Limited
London

First Large Print Edition
published 2002
by arrangement with
Robert Hale Limited
London

British Library CIP Data

Hawksley, Elizabeth
    Frost Fair.—Large print ed.—
    Ulverscroft large print series: general fiction
    1. Great Britain—Social life and customs
    —19th century—Fiction
    2. Historical fiction
    3. Large type books
    I. Title
    823.9′14 [F]

    ISBN 0–7089–4723–9

Published by
F. A. Thorpe (Publishing) Ltd.
Anstey, Leicestershire

Set by Words & Graphics Ltd.
Anstey, Leicestershire
Printed and bound in Great Britain by
T. J. International Ltd., Padstow, Cornwall

This book is printed on acid-free paper

Dedication

Dear Theo

When I was fourteen and you were ten, I wrote *Gideon de Triste* for you, a stirring mediaeval time-slip story, which had a print run of two. I still have my carbon copy. I thought it was high time I wrote you another book, so here it is.

With love from your affectionate sister.

Acknowledgements

I should like to thank Dr Lucy Peltz, Curator of Paintings, Prints and Drawings at the Museum of London, and Jeremy Smith of the Guildhall Library, Corporation of London, who were most helpful in finding me material on the 1814 frost fair in their several collections and in answering my questions.

A bibliography of all the books consulted for *Frost Fair* would take pages and, in any case, I believe that a historical novelist's research should be like an iceberg, mostly underneath and certainly not obtrusive. However, I must make an exception for *Crowns of Glory, Tears of Blood — the Demerara Slave Rebellion of 1823* by Emilia Viotti da Costa, published by Oxford University Press, which is a riveting, brilliant and horrifying account of early nineteenth-century slave plantations in what is now Guyana. I owe Professor da Costa a debt of thanks.

Finally, readers might like to know that the Museum of London holds a genuine piece of gingerbread from the 1814 frost fair. I confess I was thrilled to see it.

Elizabeth Hawksley
London 2001

1

It all started in December, 1813, on the day I realized that Balquidder wanted me dead.

I know that is a line worthy of the opening of one of my Gothic romances (published in three volumes by Messrs Robinson of Paternoster Row at three guineas) but, nevertheless, it is true. Indeed, in *The Mountfalcon Heiress*, the book I was writing at the time, my heroine Angelina flees from her home to escape the machinations of the evil Fra Bartolomeo, and finds herself, inevitably, in a ruinous castle on a crag amid the snowy Alps.

I've never been to Switzerland. I've no idea whether castles teeter on the edge of precipices there; but this is Gothic romance, and my readers expect such things.

I am digressing. Though as I, too, had to flee like Angelina, perhaps I'm not digressing too far. I'm also reluctant to mention Balquidder. Even now, I find it difficult to write about him. If, in the end, he failed to destroy me, there were others who were dragged down with him.

So, this is my story; of my youthful folly — stupidity rather — from when I was sixteen to when I was twenty-five, which ended one terrifying night on the frozen Thames during the Frost Fair of February 1814.

I'd better start at the beginning. I, Emilia Daniels, was born on 15 January, 1789. My mother was much younger than my father and I was an only child. She was very much a woman of her time — a Romantic to the core. She wept over *The Sorrows of Young Werther* and gloried in cultivating her sensibility. Poor Mama. I still miss her. I used to write her little stories and she would respond with hugs and kisses and tell me how clever I was. Neither she nor I ever received much affection from my father.

Tolley, my mother's maid, disliked my father. She never said so outright, but I could sense it. 'Your mother might have married a markess,' she was fond of saying. 'He begged her three times, on his bended knee.' I was always puzzled by this. Was this how men were meant to propose? I simply couldn't imagine my father ever doing such a thing. I think I had the confused idea that his knees wouldn't bend, or, if they did, they would creak. It was obvious that Tolley viewed plain Mr Daniels, however good his estate, as vastly inferior to the anonymous marquess.

Mama followed the ideas of Jean-Jacques Rousseau, and I was allowed to grow up almost in a state of nature. My fantasies were encouraged and my emotions unregulated. I can now see how unwise this was. God knows, I suffered because of it and there have been times when I've been torn between blaming her and trying to defend her. I've never quite resolved this, my love for her always wars with the 'but you should have known', or 'why did you let me'? But back to my story.

My father was a product of the Age of Reason, civilized, upright and, to me, impossibly remote. I rarely saw him. When I did, he would pat me on the head in an absent-minded kind of way and say, 'Well, Emilia, have you been a good girl?' barely waiting for my stammered reply before dismissing me back to the nursery. I wanted, desperately, to love him, but the only time I ever flung my arms round him and kissed him, he screwed up his face in distaste and said, 'A little moderation, please, Emilia.' It was one of the most humiliating moments of my life and I never tried again.

I see him now as a lonely man, covering up his emotions with a chilly reserve. He was inflexible where he believed himself to be right; just, and much respected, but warmth was beyond him — at least with his wife and daughter — though I've seen him jesting with some of his estate workers. That hurt. Little girls need to be loved by their fathers, but I always felt inadequate and awkward with mine. I never felt that my existence gave him any pleasure.

He must have seen that to bring me up as a child of nature was hardly a good preparation for life, for he insisted on chosing my governess himself. Doubtless he thought that Miss Chase's severity would counteract my mother's frivolity. Perhaps inevitably, I hated Miss Chase and avoided her whenever I could, and Mama abetted me.

'Emilia darling,' she would say. 'You don't want to be in the schoolroom on a lovely day like this. Come with me for a drive.'

Giggling, I would run off to my governess. 'Miss Chase, I have a headache. Mama is taking me out for some fresh air.'

There was nothing Miss Chase could do. I would stick my tongue out as we drove off and hope that she was looking out of the school-room window.

Would I have grown out of it in time? Possibly. But when I was nine my mother fell ill, as she did most winters, and the doctor tried all that bleeding and purging could do.

What can I say? Nobody tells a child what is going on. I knew they were hiding something. I began to have nightmares that something terrible was about to happen, but Miss Chase only scolded me for waking her up with my screams. There was nobody I could talk to about my fears. I would creep to the door of my mother's room — I wasn't allowed in — and sit there, huddled against the door, as close as I was allowed. I learnt then how time can freeze into an unendurable present — except that you must endure it, day after day.

One night, I crept in. Tolley was asleep in her chair. Mama was moaning and turning her head from side to side.

'Mama?' Her face was covered with beads of sweat. She didn't smell like my own mama any more. I was suddenly terribly frightened and whispered her name in increasing desperation.

'Mama!' I began to cry. What had happened to her? Why didn't she know me?

Tolley woke up. 'Miss Emilia, you shouldn't be here. Get back to bed at once.' She rose and began to mop my mother's face with a lavender-scented cloth and held some water to her lips. Mama quietened. Tolley turned to me and her face was full of pity. 'Here, child, come and kiss your mother.

Gently now. There. Now you must go back to bed.'

I kissed her clammy skin with reluctance. 'She will be all right, won't she?' I begged Tolley, but she didn't reply. I never saw my mother again. She died early the following morning.

A year later, my father remarried.

I hated my stepmother on sight, perhaps it was inevitable. She was brisk and practical, with no nonsense about her, and I saw her as a usurper.

'Mr Daniels,' I overheard her say to my father, 'Emilia must be taken in hand, or she will be quite ruined. She can scarcely sew a straight seam, she always has her nose in a book and her deportment is atrocious.'

'You must do as you think best, my dear,' returned my father. 'She is not a pretty child — too thin and beaky — but she will have her mother's fortune, and I should like her to make a good match.' Then he added, 'My first wife held some very trying ideas about female education!'

'An hour on the back board each day, and I shall regulate her reading,' promised my stepmother.

I didn't stop to think before rushing into the room. 'No!' I screamed, trying to pummel my stepmother with my fists, 'I hate you . . . I

6

hate you.' But I could go no further and burst into a storm of weeping.

My father mopped my eyes roughly and said, 'That will do, Emilia. Such behaviour is only for hoydens. Apologize to your mama and go to the nursery.'

'She's not my mama!' I shouted. I would never call this creature with her puffy face 'Mama'. I broke from my father's grasp and fled from the room. Even now I wince when I remember this. It is not my behaviour that hurts me, it is the bitter realization that my father had never cared about my mother, that all he saw was her imprudence. Her liveliness and laughter were unwanted and unregretted. I missed Mama desperately and nobody, not even my father, seemed to mourn her or understand how desolate I felt.

For many, many months I cried myself to sleep every night. For the first time in my life, I felt lonely. There was nobody to talk to. Tolley had left, though we still kept in touch; she wrote to me two or three times a year, bless her. This new Mrs Daniels was an interloper. I determined to fight her by every means in my power, but there was little I could do. Within two years I had two half-brothers and, inevitably, I ceased to be the centre of attention.

My mother's death made reality almost

impossible for me to bear. I'm still not very good at it. It has always seemed to me that if you stick your head above the parapet, some sharpshooter will come and blow it off. So, instead of becoming tractable, as my stepmother hoped, I retreated into my own fantasy world.

I've often wondered if many lonely children do the same. I discovered that a world of my own creation, peopled with knights and maidens, wizards and evil witches, could blot out the miseries of my outside existence.

I look back on this younger Emilia with pity. I had a loving heart. A little understanding on my father or my stepmother's part would have allowed me to come to terms with my grief and learn to live in the world as it is instead of some Gothic land of fantasy. But they saw it as their duty to suppress any show of 'unseemly' emotion.

I learned to hate my father and stepmother. Sometimes I felt quite eaten up with it. I could feel the bitterness corroding my heart. If only I'd been allowed to express something of what I felt, if I'd been understood . . . but, of course, that was impossible. I used to take it out on my stepbrothers and pinch them hard when nobody was looking. Their cries of pain momentarily blotted out the agony in my savage little heart. But then I felt guilty and hated them for causing it. And so it went on.

In the deepest recesses of the night, I have sometimes feared that Balquidder was a revenge for that hatred and bitterness.

As I entered my teens, I devoured the novels of Mrs Radcliffe, Mr Lewis's *The Monk*, Mr Walpole's *The Castle of Otranto* and scores of others. In them, I found the feelings and sensations for which I yearned.

When I was fourteen I started to write my own Gothic romances. Here, I could organize my world as I wanted it. My heroines usually had blue eyes; my own eyes were a curious grey with yellow flecks — one of my half-brothers said they were the colour of fog. I had long, straight, light-brown hair, which I had to remember to plait at night, if I wanted it to curl in the morning. I was small and almost flat-chested until I was sixteen and, even thereafter, not particularly well endowed in that direction. My mouth was too wide and my nose too prominent. Naturally, my heroines had pretty rosebud lips, straight noses and figures that would not have shamed a Venus.

Why am I going on about all this? Yes, I want to give you some idea of what I was like, but I am also delaying my story. The truth is, I am afraid to get back to Mr Balquidder.

Even now, the memory of him is enough to make my palms sweat with fear. He was such a big man. Huge.

I learnt from him how to depict villains all right. I am very good at villains. Angelina Mountfalcon has the sinister Fra Bartolomeo who pursues her through two and a half volumes. He has a yellow skull-like face, glittering black eyes and long bony fingers. Mr Balquidder was grossly fat with pale-blue eyes. I never depict him, just the terror he inspires. My publisher thinks Fra Bartolomeo is particularly effective, for various titled ladies have written to tell him so. However, back to my story.

I crowned the follies of my youth by eloping, at the age of sixteen, with Stephen Kirkwall.

He was a young advocate from Edinburgh, or so he said, on a walking holiday. I met him when my godfather, Mr Beresford, whose house, Ainderby Hall, was about ten miles from my own home of Tranters Court, invited Mr Kirkwall to fish in the river running through his estate.

I was staying with the Beresfords. Mrs Beresford knew how much my stepmother irked me and, though never directly critical of her, often invited me to stay for a few weeks. She had always wanted a daughter, I think, and whilst she gently corrected my wilder fantasies, she did so in a way which soothed even my prickles. I could be myself with the Beresfords and some of the happiest days of my childhood were passed at Ainderby Hall.

There was a pretty river which skirted round the top of the park. Overlooking it, on a little artificial hill, was a small folly, complete with carefully ruined turrets. I used to like to sit there and dream. I'd heard that a young man had been invited to fish somewhere along that stretch of river, and I was curious. Our first meeting was typical.

I soon saw him. The first thing I noticed was the informality of his dress. His fair hair was long enough to curl on the casually tied neckerchief he wore instead of a cravat. I found him very good looking. His rod was propped up by some stones and he was lying on his back, eyes shut. In a spirit of mischief, I picked up a small pebble and threw it into the water by his bobbing float. Plop! Stephen sat up suddenly and began to reel in. I giggled.

He turned round, saw me, dropped the rod and came over.

'Why, you little minx.'

'Lazybones,' I said. 'I don't believe you want to fish at all.'

Stephen laughed. I could see him looking

11

me over and I felt my colour rise. I was now sixteen, five feet and three inches tall and my figure, though not generous, had filled out enough to be described as slender rather than skinny.

'You are unchaperoned?' He looked around for a possible duenna.

'I am staying at Ainderby Hall. Mr Beresford is my godfather.'

Stephen sat down beside me and rested his arms on his knees. 'Kirkwall,' he said. 'And you are . . . ?' Our unconventional meeting did not seem to worry him and I, naturally, scorned conventional behaviour. Why should we wait to speak to each other until we had been introduced? I had no patience with such fusty notions. I was perfectly capable of introducing myself.

'Miss Daniels.'

We spent the rest of the morning together and when we parted he dropped a hint that he would come fishing again tomorrow, if I were there. His eyes said 'please come', and that he liked what he saw. He was the first person since Mama died to treat me as though I mattered.

I questioned neither his admiration, nor his sincerity. I told nobody. He told nobody. And I fell in love. I can remember the very moment it happened. We were sitting on the

12

grass. Stephen was making a daisy chain; I was throwing small pebbles in the river. We were talking about anything and nothing. I was feeling happy and the world had a special glow that morning. Then he turned and lightly dropped the daisy chain over my head and our eyes met. Suddenly, the entire universe stopped. A sweet warm pang went straight through me, I found I could scarcely breathe. Stephen was smiling slightly. I looked away and hastily began to hurl more small pebbles into the river. I was not sure what had happened, but I knew that everything had changed.

When I returned home to Tranters Court, we continued to meet. Mr Beresford, unsuspecting of treachery, gave Stephen an introduction to my father, who invited him to fish on our own land. Now, Stephen didn't even pretend to fish. We would walk up and down the river-bank, hidden by the trees, hold hands and talk. I poured out all my woes into his sympathetic ears.

'At least you will never want for the necessities of life,' said Stephen. He had already told me of his financial struggles to get a foot on the ladder in his chosen profession and of his hopes for the future. He was passionate and eloquent about doing good in the world.

'I shall have my mother's fortune of eight thousand pounds,' I said, 'but oh, Mr Kirkwall, I had far rather be poor and wanted.'

When Stephen first kissed me I thought I would die of delight. I still remember how the hairs rose all up my arms and at the back of my neck.

When he said, 'Will you marry me, Emmy?' I didn't think twice.

'Yes! Yes!' I flung my arms round his neck.

'Darling girl! But you're under age, you know. We'd have to elope. Do you love me enough for that?'

'How can you even ask?'

It never crossed my mind that an honourable man would rather insist on seeking my father's permission. I hated having to approach my father about anything; it seemed natural that a prospective husband would try to avoid it, too. Anyway, why did we need anybody's permission? Stephen loved me. One day he would be successful. I would be my own mistress, living with the man I loved and escaping from tyranny at home. Just like my heroines, in fact.

What I forgot was that, in your true Gothic romance, the hero must prove himself over three volumes — he doesn't simply make love to an inexperienced girl for a month or so.

Alas! sense had little to do with it. I was swept off my feet and I loved every minute of it. I had been half-expecting Stephen to leave me broken-hearted at the end of his holiday. I dare say I'd have enjoyed that, too.

I don't want to be unfair to Stephen. He was genuinely fond of me, I think. He had his weaknesses, but he was not vicious. His problem was that he found it difficult to separate a half-promise of work from somebody he'd met, from the success his imagination had already turned it into. He believed things himself so strongly that it was impossible not to be convinced as well. It took me many years before I was capable of disentangling his glittering fictions from the nugget of fact on which they were based.

Such was my animosity towards my stepmother that my first thought when Stephen suggested an elopement was, 'That'll teach her'. Stephen knew that my mother's fortune of £8,000 would be mine. He bemoaned his own straitened circumstances and promised to repay me as soon as they improved, which neither of us doubted would happen very shortly.

I left with him for Edinburgh in a hired chaise one Sunday when everyone else was in church. I prepared for it in a delicious mixture of excitement, longing to be alone with Stephen and experience all those intimacies which were so tantalizingly just out of my reach, and fear of being found out. I carried only a small valise and my mother's jewels. Naturally, I would live happily ever after. I knew nothing of the costs of hired chaises and it never occurred to me to wonder where the money had come from.

Stephen behaved impeccably during the flight north and his restraint only increased my ardour. I seized every opportunity I could to kiss and caress him, but he smiled and pushed me away. 'You're a passionate little thing,' he said, mouthing me a kiss, 'but you'll have to wait.' Very correctly, he placed me with a respectable widow while he searched for somewhere for us to live and organized our marriage.

'But I thought you had a house.' I was puzzled; he'd described a modern house in the New Town.

'It belonged to a friend,' he said frowning. 'I had to move out and, in any case, it was not suitable.'

'Oh.' He'd spoken as if the house were his, but I must have been mistaken.

'I've found us a couple of rooms in Cant's Close. It's less spacious than I'd like for you, Emmy, but once I'm settled, we can move. We shan't be there long. It has fine oak-panelled rooms. You'll like that.'

'I'm sure I shall.'

The first pangs of doubt struck me when I saw it. Cant's Close was a narrow, dark and dirty alley between the High Street and Cowgate. A malodorous gutter ran down the middle and the houses leaned crazily. There was a strong smell of ordure, drink and offal. Smut-flecked washing, stuck out on poles, flapped from some of the open windows. I scarcely dared look at Stephen. This was to be our home?

In the middle of the Close was a much larger building, with a fine gateway with square-cut pillars surmounted by large stone finials. An old coat of arms was carved into the gable end. A wide, curved forestair went up to the first storey, and this was where we had our rooms. As Stephen had promised, they were oak-panelled and had once been very handsome. I remember a hollow feeling in the pit of my stomach when the landlady showed us round, but I said nothing. I didn't know what to say and I didn't want to think too much. This was temporary, I reminded myself. We would soon move.

We were married in a side chapel in St Giles's Cathedral on 13 September, 1805.

My wedding night was a nightmare. For all my innocent ardour, when the moment came

17

I was tense and frightened. Stephen suddenly became a stranger.

'Open your legs, Emmy,' he ordered.

'Couldn't we just wait a little,' I whispered, longing for some reassurance.

'Come on. You want to be a woman, don't you?' He was breathing heavily and his grip on me tightened.

It all took so long. He didn't seem to care that I was crying with pain and fear and, when it was over, he slumped on top of me and went to sleep. The following morning, I awoke feeling bleaker and more alone than I have ever felt in my life. Stephen apologized. He was overwhelmed by passion, he said. I forgave him. But, however hard I tried to pretend, it was never the same again.

In the morning I wrote to my father and told him how happy I was.

My father refused to allow us even the interest on my fortune. It was in trust for me until I was twenty-five, he wrote, unless I married with his consent. I had not done so and he had no intention of allowing my husband to get his hands on my money a day before he had to. The rest of the letter was so cold and angry that I was physically sick with the horror of reading such words addressed to me. I couldn't burn it; I certainly couldn't reply to it. It lodged itself at the bottom of my mind like an incubus.

'Twenty-five!' echoed Stephen, when I read out the portion of the letter about my fortune. 'You never said.' He started to pace up and down, clasping and unclasping his hands. His face had paled.

'I didn't know,' I pleaded. 'But does it really matter, Stephen? You have this job coming up. We can manage, surely? You'll see how good a housekeeper I shall be.'

'Balquidder won't like it.'

I can no longer avoid mentioning Archibald Balquidder. It is difficult to disentangle what I know now from what I knew then. But, even at the beginning, I disliked and feared him. He was my husband's best friend. Stephen was bound to him by ties of obligation, the nature of which I could scarcely guess at, but, from the way Stephen spoke, they were heavy.

The first thing you noticed about Mr Balquidder was that he was grossly fat. Rolls of it swayed whenever he moved. His face was round and shiny with the consistency of lard and his piggy blue eyes peered out between the folds. He had a small mouth, too, which I dislike on a man, and he smelled of rose pomade. Reeked, I may say. I couldn't help wondering what he smelled of underneath that he had to disguise it so heavily.

He was a slovenly dresser. His clothes were

usually spattered with grease and stains from previous meals, for he was a messy eater, spattering food from his mouth in small explosions. He never bothered to close his mouth while he ate. He would walk into our apartment as if he owned the place and stand with his back to the fire, holding up his coat-tails to warm his backside.

The first time he saw me, he muttered to Stephen, 'Good God, man, couldn't you have found a wench with a bit more flesh? Not this skinny cockatoo?' It was an aside, but I could tell, from the way he glanced at me, that he meant me to overhear. There was something about the way he laughed which made me wonder if Stephen had told him about my inadequacies in bed.

I found him repellent. More than that, something in my very soul cringed whenever we were in the same room. I was frightened of him and unwilling to admit it. How could I fear a man who was my husband's best friend? I tried to view his personal habits as mere eccentricity, but it was no good.

I think, even early on, I sensed that he would not hesitate to remove anybody who was standing in his way.

He disliked women and I didn't know why. Things seemed to happen when he was around. Once he accidentally poured scalding tea all over my arm. Another time he trod heavily on my foot and I could scarcely walk for a week. He never apologized.

'I owe him five thousand pounds, Emmy,' Stephen confessed one evening, shortly after I had received my father's letter.

'Five thousand pounds!' It was an enormous sum of money. Whatever had he done with it?

'Of course, I'll pay it back. I have this new scheme that I'm working on with Jamie Kinross.' — What scheme? — 'But at the moment things are tight.'

'Mr Balquidder lent you five thousand pounds?' I was young and green, but even I knew that he would have needed some security for such a sum. The hollow feeling returned. 'Did you borrow against my fortune?'

Stephen looked away.

'Stephen, I love you. Everything I have is yours, you know that, but . . . '

'It's only a loan, Emmy. I wouldn't rob you.'

'Of course not.' But my heart sank. He had already pawned several pieces of my jewellery. How were we going to manage? 'Do you have any money on you at all?' I asked. Mrs MacLaren, our landlady, had approached me more than once about the rent.

Stephen rose. 'Now you're not to worry, Emmy. I can see from your face that old Slobachops' — Stephen liked giving people nicknames — 'has been on at you about the rent. Let the besom wait.'

'Won't she throw us out?'

'Nonsense! Don't you worry your pretty little head about it.'

There was a pause. I had about five shillings in my purse. Stephen had given me three pounds after he had pawned the first piece of jewellery, but that was the only money I had had from him, and he had pawned several pieces since. Mrs MacLaren was supposed to give us an evening meal, but it was a greasy stew which was quite inedible. I usually made do with a pie from the hot pie vendor or bread and cheese. Stephen often went out with friends.

★ ★ ★

Let me describe our apartment. I was there for eight years — until I fled. We had two rooms and a cubby-hole tucked away behind the stairs. The front room was panelled, with a fine oak fireplace. There was an elegant cornice and a large double window which looked out into Dickon's Close. The furniture, such as it was, had seen better days, but it was good.

Our bedroom was also oak-panelled and the bed was a fourposter with elaborately carved walnut posts and tattered silk curtains. Part of me quite liked all this faded grandeur, and I couldn't help thinking of Mrs Radcliffe's heroines and how it would just suit them. I even went so far as to tap the panelling in the hope of finding a hidden stairwell or sliding panel. Of course, there was nothing.

Jeanie, the landlady's skivvy, was meant to clean the place, but she rarely did. Every morning a bucket was left on the landing and I emptied the slops into it and Jeanie took it down and threw it into the open gutter outside. As we fell behind with the rent, the service got worse. Our coal scuttles weren't filled, or, if they were, it was with small, damp bits that made the chimney smoke.

I was far too proud to write home and tell them.

I tried to tell myself that things would be better with Stephen once he was settled. I couldn't bear to admit that I had made a terrible mistake.

I fell ill that winter. My chest ached with coughing and I had dreadful chilblains that were open and bleeding.

I don't know what Stephen did all day. He

would leave in the morning with a cheery, 'Bye, Emmy. Look after yourself now, and keep warm. Don't let old Slobachops vex you!' I could hear him clattering down the stairs, often with a few words for Jeanie. He would call her 'the nut-brown maid'. 'Her face is as dirty as the rest of her,' he told me. But Jeanie took it as a compliment, and I could hear her retorts. Stephen was often involved in some shady deal, whose nature I learned not to ask about. Occasionally, he would give me a guinea or so and I would struggle to keep us going.

It was the despised Jeanie who proved to be my salvation. She came into the apartment one morning to find me crying with the pain of my chilblains.

She came over and patted me roughly with one reddened hand. 'There, there, dinna greet. Shall I fetch ye a wee drink, maybe?'

I shook my head and blew my nose. 'Oh, Jeanie, is it always so cold in Edinburgh? I think I shall never get warm.'

'Mistress MacLaren thinks it's time ye were paying a bit of rent.'

I sighed. 'I'll ask my husband again.'

'Men!' Jeanie tossed her head. 'If I had their opportunities I'd manage better, I'm thinking.'

'Why? What would you do, Jeanie?' I'd

never associated Jeanie with any ambition.

'I'd be able to read and write and then, maybe, I'd get a better position.'

I jumped up, chilblains forgotten, 'I'll teach you to read and write.' I needed something to do. At the moment all I had was darning Stephen's hose and my stockings — not very well — and sewing on buttons. Reading and writing was one thing I could surely teach.

Of course I got it wrong. I was over-ambitious and wanted to introduce my pupil to the glories of poetry, but she got bored by knights and ladies. What she liked were tales of blood-curdling murders — the gorier the better. I learnt that, if I were to teach Jeanie to read, her own interests must come first and that each step had to be properly mastered before we could go on.

I bought some chalk and used a couple of old roof slates that Jeanie found in the road. Once she was proficient at the alphabet, she brought in a tattered copy of the *Newgate Calendar* and we pored over stories of appalling crimes and the last moments of condemned prisoners. Jeanie lapped it all up. 'Oh, it's grand!' she'd exclaim.

Her reading was much better than her writing, but she learnt enough to write a shopping list.

In return, she made sure that my coal

scuttle was full and taught me how to clean and dust properly. Under her direction, I made up some furniture polish with linseed oil, turpentine, vinegar and spirits of wine. I then set to with some old rags and began to do what I could for the oak panelling and our walnut bed. It took me weeks, but it kept me busy and warm and my spirits lifted. For the first time in my life, I learned about application and hard work. Miss Chase would have been proud of me.

★　★　★

One February day, in 1807, when I was just eighteen, I met the printer Mr Irvine, who lived in St Peter's Pend, just off Cowgate. I'd been out shopping. It was icy, and I slipped and stumbled along, not helped by my heavy basket. I stopped to rest and to admire a curious old house opposite. It was of obvious antiquity, timber-fronted, with each storey projecting out over the lower and a host of small windows with little leaded panes. There was an outside staircase which led up to a richly ornamented doorway with an inscription carved over the top which read: GIF VE DEID AS VE SOVLD VE MYCHT HAIF AS VE VOLD.

It took me a long time to work this out.

Eventually, I decided that it must mean, 'If we did as we should, we might have what we wanted'. I gave it a rueful smile; I was well aware how much I had failed to follow its precept.

Suddenly, I heard a crash behind me and a cry. An elderly man had fallen and banged his head against a hitching post. I hurried over. He looked dazed and a bump on his head was swelling rapidly. His hands were cut and grazed where he'd tried to save himself.

'I'll mend, nae doot,' he said, as I took his arm and helped him to rise.

'You are bleeding, sir. Allow me to escort you home.' I picked up a leather bag, which had fallen in his tumble. 'Why, books!' I exclaimed with pleasure.

'Aye, I'm a printer. Mostly religious books — too dry for 'ee, I fear.'

'I love books!' I cried, and my eyes filled with tears. I really couldn't help it. 'I had to leave my books behind when I married.'

'You married? You're nobbut a slip of a lass.'

'I am Mrs Stephen Kirkwall. I have been married nearly eighteen months.' We had crossed the road and Mr Irvine began to pull himself up the staircase I'd been admiring.

'You live here!' I cried. 'I was looking at the inscription.'

'Aye. In the old times it belonged to Mr Symson, the printer. It's come down in the world now.' He pointed to the sign above the shop front on the ground floor 'Fishmonger' and another on the first floor 'Shaving and Hair Cutting'. 'I live at the top and have my presses up there. Come up, Mrs Kirkwall, my wife will want to thank 'ee.'

The Irvines were simple, unpretentious people, living a quiet, industrious life and very fond of each other. The furniture was old, but obviously much loved, for the wood was well polished — I now had a connoisseur's eye about such things — and the carpets and curtains were carefully darned.

As I sat there, sipping tea from an almost translucent china cup, I felt a wave of homesickness so acute that tears began to pour down my cheeks before I could stop them. My pretence was over. My marriage was a sham. How rash and wilful I had been! How irretrievable the step I had taken.

'Dearie!' Mrs Irvine was all motherly concern.

'I'm sorry.' I was groping desperately for my handkerchief. Mrs Irvine tucked hers into my hand, rescued the cup and let me have my cry out. Of course, I confided in them; my stepmother's dislike, my father's coldness and my husband's somehow not getting on as he should. I couldn't bring myself to talk of my disillusion with my marriage, the loneliness and fears for the future.

'I don't mean to complain,' I said, sitting up and mopping my eyes. 'I know I've made my bed and must lie on it. It was just that being here reminded me of home.' It was not entirely true, for it was not the chilly propriety of Tranters Court I missed so acutely, but the quiet comfort of Ainderby Hall and the Beresfords. Mrs Irvine's motherliness reminded me of Mrs Beresford.

How unfeeling I'd been, I thought as I wept. I'd never once written to Mrs Beresford since my marriage and I knew, from the one angry letter my father had written, that she and my godfather had been deeply distressed at being the means of bringing Stephen into my life. I had had the foolish fantasy of writing to them all when Stephen had made his mark in the world. Then they should see how right I was.

The Irvines became my lifeline, the rock on which I kept my sanity. It was Mr Irvine who oversaw my first foray into print. I wrote a Sunday School story about frivolous Marjorie, who tore up her mother's Prayer Book to make curl papers and nearly went to Hell. Of course, this being a moral tale, she had to repent, but I allowed her to have some fun whilst being wicked. Mrs Irvine thought it had merit and persuaded her husband to publish it, suitably illustrated. He gave me three guineas for it and it sold well. Personally, I was on Marjorie's side every time, and I often wondered if my young readers secretly agreed with me.

Stupidly, I told Stephen of my success and he promptly borrowed the precious guineas.

'I wanted to pay Mrs MacLaren,' I said. 'We owe her six weeks' rent.'

'You'll get it back,' said Stephen impatiently. 'Don't fuss, Emmy.'

When Balquidder heard of my venture into print he threw back his head and guffawed, and his fat chins wobbled. 'A blue-stocking, by Gad! You've married a blue-stocking! Get her working, man! Crack the whip. Why, you can live off a scribbler.'

'Three guineas won't go far,' said Stephen sulkily, but he smiled too. He liked Balquidder's approval.

'Let her have that cubby-hole for a study,' said Balquidder. 'Lock her in, if necessary.' He was sprawled in our one easy chair, legs wide apart, his stomach bulging over his breeches. Every now and then he would thrust his hand down and scratch himself. A large slice of cake stood on the table next to him, which he devoured with huge, messy bites. When he laughed, crumbs spewed.

I was there throughout this exchange, but I'd learnt to button my lip. I sat there silently and hated him from the bottom of my heart. Balquidder didn't like interruptions by women and I knew that Stephen owed him £5,000.

He would probably stay the whole evening. I'd go to bed early and in the morning I'd have to clean up. The chamber pot on the sideboard would be full, with splashes everywhere. The carpet would be covered with little bits of food and our precious coals used up.

I'd been eyeing the cubby-hole for some weeks. It was full of broken lumber that Mrs MacLaren didn't want to throw away, but wouldn't remove. Jeanie and I took it up to the attics one morning when she was out. I whitewashed the walls, bought an old rug, a second-hand desk and chair and put a lock on the door. I did not want anybody prying, for I decided to have another look at the Gothic romance I'd started before I left home and see whether anything could be made of it.

After some hesitation, I showed it to Mrs Irvine.

'My dear Mrs Kirkwall,' she said, when I

next went to visit her. 'Your book! I don't know when I laughed so much.'

'Laugh! It was supposed to be serious.' But I couldn't help laughing myself. I was such a child when I wrote it and I was now well aware of its absurdities.

'But it has something,' she went on, patting my hand in her kind way. 'I think you should rewrite it. That sort of thing goes down very well now, you know. Mr Irvine doesn't publish such things, but I daresay he knows of a London publisher who might.'

I took a pseudonym. I turned my maiden name, Emilia Daniels, around and became Daniel Miller, whose first book, published by Messrs Robinson of Paternoster Row, London, and entitled *The Castle of Apollinari*, enjoyed a modest success. I sold the copyright for fifty guineas. That money changed my life. For the first time, I felt I had some control over my future. I was to have need of it in the days ahead. When the book was reprinted, Mr Robinson was gentleman enough to send me another twenty-five guineas. I got one hundred guineas for my second book, *The Doom of the House of Ansbach*. That, together with the money from my Sunday School tales, enabled me to support us both in modest comfort. I didn't tell my husband about the Daniel Millers. If he ever wondered how the sums added up, he never said. Money had always been easy come, easy go with him. He probably didn't think anything of it.

One evening, early in 1808, I overheard a conversation between my husband and Balquidder which was to have far-reaching consequences.

They'd returned to the apartment together and I knew they were set to make a night of it. I'd gone to bed with a cold. They'd left the door ajar and didn't bother to lower their voices.

'It's this damned Anti-Slave Trade bill,' Balquidder was saying. 'What the devil was Parliament thinking of? Merchants will be ruined and trade will collapse. If we don't ship slaves over, the Spaniards and Portuguese will. And the Americans! Pah!' He spat, and I could hear a hiss as it landed in the fire.

'You have money in it?'

'Of course. I've two slave ships and dammit, I need the money. There's my plantation in Demerara, for one thing. I want to move over to sugar and that's expensive. Then I need niggers to work it. No point in breeding them. Female niggers aren't productive enough and their brats take too long to become profitable, twelve years at least, and then, half of 'em are bound to be female. I tell you, Stephen, things are going to get sticky.'

'Is there no way round it?'

Balquidder had his mouth full. 'Oh yes. I foresaw this. I am re-registering my ships in Lisbon and I shall have to trade via Brazil, but it's a damned nuisance. I can buy slaves in Brazil, but they have to be transported to Demerara, and they die, or get scurvy and are no damn good. Until last year, I got them straight from the Gold Coast. I could pick the ones I wanted, make sure they survived the passage, and sell on those who weren't tough enough.'

'Isn't it illegal now to register slavers in Lisbon?'

Balquidder gave one of his fat laughs. 'There are ways.'

I sat up, my cold forgotten. Balquidder involved in slaving? I'd followed the course of the Anti-Slave Trade Bill avidly and the Irvines and I had discussed it many times. Mr Irvine was a keen supporter of the Society for the Abolition of the Slave Trade.

My feelings for the Africans shipped out as slaves were probably more romantic than anything strictly humanitarian, but the thought of slavery revolted me. When I was a child I'd been taken by Mama to visit a friend of hers who was taking the waters in Harrogate. She had a black boy as her page and I was fascinated by him. He was about my age, which was eight, and his skin was the colour of a burnished plum. His eyes were large and brown and his smile was the whitest I had ever seen.

He was petted, too. His mistress kept pulling him to her and fondling him. He wore a coat and trousers of crimson and gold and a gold cap with a tassel. It was only an hour or so later that I noticed his gold collar with his name *Caesar* engraved on it. Underneath was written *The Property of Mr Wells of Camworthy Park in the County of Somerset.*

I was terribly shocked. He must have seen my face. For a few seconds we stared at each other and then, simultaneously, we both looked away. He didn't look at me again for the rest of the visit.

Afterwards, my mother said, 'Yes, darling, it's very sad, no doubt, but you must remember that he was taken from a horrid pagan country and is now in a lovely home among Christians.'

Hearing my husband and Balquidder talk reminded me of Caesar and the pity and outrage I'd felt. But the conversation started again.

'I need that money, Stephen. You'd better write to old Daniels and suggest that Emilia be given her fortune. You've been married over two years, surely that's time enough?'

I hated him referring to me as Emilia. He had no right to make free with my name. But he did it with everybody. At first I thought it expressed some sort of democratic radicalism, but later I decided that he did it out of contempt. Nobody, not even Stephen, who counted him a friend, called him Archie or Archibald.

I didn't want my fortune to go towards Balquidder's slave ships, but how could I stop it? I had several times started to write to my father, but the thought of explaining, even in part, how we were living hand to mouth, was too much. How my stepmother would gloat, I thought.

No, I would write to my godfather and dear Mrs Beresford. They had always been kind to me. I would tell Mr Beresford of Balquidder's involvement in the slave-trade and he would persuade Papa not to release my money. It was probable my father would not do so anyway, but I couldn't risk it.

If I'd known what it would lead to, what misery it would cause the Beresfords — though no fault of mine — would I still have written? Useless speculation. What is done is done. We can only do the best we can, and in this case my motive was pure.

Balquidder financed no slave ships with my fortune.

Stephen said nothing to me about writing to my father. I wrote my own letter and Mr Irvine kindly got a friend of his to frank it for me. I ended my letter with a plea to be forgiven: *I now understand how thoughtless I was and how little I valued your goodness and kindness towards me. I can see that my actions must have hurt and distressed you both and I am heartily sorry for it. It would ease my heart if you wrote just one line to say that you forgave me.* Mr Irvine allowed me to use his address as a poste restante — I did not want to risk Stephen finding out what I had done.

I knew Balquidder harassed Stephen about my fortune on other occasions too, for I once overheard him say, 'Get her with child, man. Use your pizzle. Old Daniels won't refuse the ready for a grandchild.'

But I didn't prove with child. I had a couple of miscarriages in the early years and then Stephen lost interest in me that way. I cried over those lost babies — even in that, a woman's first duty, I failed. I put up a truckle bed in my study and usually slept there. There was no discussion about it. It just happened — to my relief. I still found the whole business distasteful, though I put up with it because that's what married women did. But I felt cheated, too; I didn't know why. I couldn't imagine how Angelina, or any of my heroines, would cope with the realities of married life. But then, they didn't have to. I left them at the altar, usually with the sun streaming in through a splendidly coloured rose window, and wrote FINIS.

★　★　★

I was to realize all too soon that Balquidder meant to write FINIS under my own life.

2

Rereading the first chapter of my story, I realize that I've made my life sound entirely disastrous. In one sense, of course, it was. I had left a comfortable home and a secure position in the world for an empty marriage and an apartment in a dirty and malodorous alley. Stephen gambled, and the last of my mother's jewels had long gone into pawn. I was left with little money and facing an uncertain future. Those first couple of years were very hard indeed. I was ignorant of the most basic things.

But I learned. I can truly say that, after the first two years had passed, I was not unhappy. I learnt how the poor managed, about scrimping and making do. I could cajole Mrs MacLaren into allowing another week's grace on the rent. I could coax a fire out of a few damp sticks and a couple of pieces of coal and haggle like any fish-wife in the street markets. Living where we did, I picked up a number of swearwords. This new vocabulary remained largely inside my head, though I could, if confronted by a drunk in Cant's Close, use it if necessary. I also learnt that some of the women actively enjoyed their bit of 'feather-bed jig' on a Saturday night — a new idea as well as a new phrase to me. They would talk with an earthy gusto which made me blush. But I thought about it and wondered what I had missed. It didn't seem very exciting to me.

Though Stephen gave me a few guineas occasionally, it was I who supported us, and this gave me a new self-esteem and my husband's respect. I had taught Jeanie to read and she found a new job in a chandler's shop. I felt pleased about my part in that. I then taught Eppie, the new skivvy, to read.

My friendship with the Irvines was a source of great pleasure. I owed my living to Mr Irvine, not to mention the introduction to Mr Robinson, who published my Daniel Miller romances. Mr Irvine also acted as my banker as any money I earned belonged legally to my husband. Mr Irvine, a most conventional man in many ways, was also a canny Scot and disapproved of my hard-earned money being frittered away in my husband's impractical schemes. I don't know how he settled it with his conscience, but any cheques made out to Miss E. Daniels (for I used my maiden name in my dealings with Mr Robinson) were cashed with no questions asked.

Dear Mrs Beresford replied — such a kind letter. I took it with me when I fled and have it still. She must have guessed that things were difficult with me, but she was tactful enough not to refer to it. Instead she cheered me up with bits of gossip from home.

I must tell you about the Beresfords because they are an important part of my story. They had all given me something very precious that had been lacking at home; a sense of security and a feeling of being valued. Mrs Beresford used to read the stories I had written. She was critical of any faults in grammar or syntax, but she gave praise, too.

I remembered her saying, 'Your description of the avalanche is truly thrilling. I was on tenterhooks lest the carriage should overturn.' She then added, 'My dear, if you write 'Donna Elvira stumbled past the ruined gatehouse on stiff legs', you will make it sound as though the gatehouse has stiff legs! Could you rephrase it, do you think?'

I never felt humiliated by her criticisms as I did when my father took me to task, or my stepmother.

I had been tempted to tell Mrs Beresford about Stephen — oh, how I wish I had.

Foolishly, I allowed myself to imagine introducing him as my husband, and her being charmed. In that, as in much else, I was self-deceived.

Then there were the Beresford sons, George and Noël. They were fourteen and twelve years older than I, and quite grown-up in my eyes. Such was my position as petted godchild, that I was allowed to call them 'George' and 'Noël' though, strictly speaking, I should not have done. They both had blue eyes and fair hair, but George was the better looking. He had the typical self-confidence of an elder son. As a child I worshipped him from afar and I still remember my feelings of jealousy and outrage, when he became betrothed to Aline de Doulaincourt.

Aline's parents had fled from France during the Revolution, but had returned during the short-lived Peace of Amiens in the hopes of regaining their estate. The price was to acknowledge Bonaparte and, being a high-minded child, I scorned this mercenary attitude and decided, most unfairly — for it was no decision of hers — that Aline was therefore unworthy of George.

She was a brunette with dark eyes and, in spite of their impoverishment in England, she always managed to look elegant. Both Noël and George were infatuated with her, and I knew that she favoured Noël. I once caught them kissing in a secluded corner of the shrubbery. I remember my shock at seeing a man and a woman so closely entwined. His fair head was bent over her dark one and his hand was pushed into her curls. I swallowed and crept away.

If she must have one of them, I thought, then I was happy for it to be Noël. I had privately reserved George for myself. But Aline, like her parents, knew on which side her bread was buttered. Her parents might not get back their inheritance. George was the heir to a good estate. She elected to stay in England and marry him.

George and Noël found her pretty imperiousness charming. She would pout and toss her head, weep careful tears — no reddened eyes for her — or throw a tantrum, to get her own way. She was quite transparent about it.

'Forgive, *chère Madame Beresford*,' she would say. 'I am *si méchante*.' She could speak English perfectly well, but she found that English of the broken variety was more effective.

I can see that I'm becoming waspish again. Of course, I was jealous of her. I adored George with all the passion of a lovesick eleven year old — and I knew Aline despised me. I once heard her referring to me as 'that little bag of bones' and it rankled.

Noël was stricken by Aline's marriage to George. The rest of his family seemed not to notice it, but I did, for I loved Noel, too, and I had seen that kiss in the shrubbery. He took to going for long walks, usually alone, but sometimes he would allow me to go with him. We didn't talk much and I took care not to interrupt his silences. For the first time I realized that grown-ups, too, could be unhappy.

Once, he bent and kissed my cheek and said, 'You're very sweet, Emilia. I'm sorry I'm such bad company.'

Even after her marriage, Aline continued to tease Noël in the same flirtatious way, as if she were half-promising something, and I resented it on his behalf. I forgot to be a silent witness and was foolish enough to speak my mind.

'Why do you let her treat you like a lap-dog?'

There was one of those awful silences when you wish that the earth would open and swallow you. 'I'm . . . sorry,' I whispered.

At last Noël said quietly, 'Aline treats me as she has always done, and what I do about it is my business.'

'She's very pretty,' I stammered eventually.

'But she's not kind.' She should let him go, I thought.

Noël stroked my cheek with one finger. 'You're very young, sweetheart. I'm afraid that life is not always simple.' He smiled down at me and I wanted to cry.

Two years later, Noël himself married Margaret Gilbert. I thought she was a pudding. There was nothing wrong with her. She came of a respectable family and her dowry was good (unlike Aline's which was non-existent). She was polite and well-bred and had absolutely nothing to say for herself.

George and Noël were the heroes of my childhood and I didn't see how either of them could be happy with the wives they had chosen. And though I have been blind in many aspects of my life, in this I think I was right. I couldn't believe that Noël loved Margaret. It wasn't exactly a marriage of convenience, for he had known her for years, but it was *for* convenience. I thought he had done it to escape from an increasingly intolerable situation at home. The woman he loved had married his brother, but she still liked to pull Noël's strings.

Marriage gave him a way out. He had a small estate of his own. His wife had money. He did the sensible thing. He settled her on his estate in Huntingdonshire, put the reins in her capable hands, got her with child and joined the army.

I couldn't blame him. To have to live with that mediocrity must have been unbearable. The last time I saw Noël was at the christening of his son, Richard, in the chapel at Ainderby Hall, shortly before I eloped. He looked older. His face was drawn and he had two deep lines going up from the top of his nose. He was as affectionate towards me as ever. He teased me a little and asked if I were writing a three-volume novel to rival *The Mysteries of Udolpho*.

In fact, I was. Eventually it would turn into *The Castle of Apollinari* and set me on the path to financial independence and allow me to escape from my husband eight years later.

'I wish you weren't going abroad,' I said. I was sitting on the sofa with him having a cuddle, something I always enjoyed doing — he made me feel safe.

Noël smiled. 'I must. I am a younger son. I can't live off my wife.'

And can't live with her, I thought rebelliously.

When he'd gone I noticed that a button had come off his jacket and was lying on the floor. I kept it.

Reading Mrs Beresford's letter, I realized that things had not been easy for the

Beresfords. Aline proved to be an extravagant wife and I guessed that Mrs Beresford found her an empty-headed creature though she was far too loyal to criticize Aline directly. There were no children of the union.

Noël's life was not as happy as he deserved either. In one of her first letters to me, Mrs Beresford wrote that Margaret had died of some complication following a still birth. *Noël is at Ainderby at present, sorting out Margaret's affairs. Poor man, he looks so drawn and tired. Dear little Richard can now walk very well and nothing delights him so much as climbing up on to his papa's knee and jumping up and down. Noël is too tired to cope with him, but he will get on better with Rickie when he is older, I daresay.*

This worried me. Noël had always played with me when I was little. I remembered being given piggybacks in the orchard. Noël was twelve years older than me and I'm sure that, when I was a toddler, I clambered all over him, too. Things must be very wrong if he were ignoring his baby son. I wrote to him to express my sympathy on his bereavement, though I had never cared much for Margaret. But then who had I cared for, self-centred child that I was?

I heard nothing from Noël. *He is finding it impossible to stay at home*, wrote Mrs

Beresford. *He is rejoining his regiment and will shortly sail to Portugal to join Lord Wellington's army in the Peninsula.*

One day, a couple of years later, I received a brief letter from Noël and a small packet. *Thank you for your kind letter of condolence, dear Emilia. It was a comfort to hear from you and I know my mother values your letters. I am enclosing a little present — I remember how you love surprises. There is not much to say about my present situation. I am writing this in a tent on a dusty plain with only a few stunted cork oaks for shelter. The tent is full of flies and my batman is busy trying to skin a hare for our supper and keep the flies off. An impossible task!*

Inside the packet was a couple of beautiful Spanish combs, such as the ladies there wear with their mantillas. They were made of ebony and decorated with mother of pearl. I had never mentioned my correspondence to Stephen, so I kept the combs hidden. In any case, I didn't want them to end up in the pawnshop.

In 1811 dear Mrs Beresford died, followed a month or so later by my godfather. I had a letter from George telling me. Of course, I wrote. Aline replied briefly and that was that. I missed that small contact with the Beresfords dreadfully. I wanted to write to

Noël, but I had no idea where he was. I felt as if my past life had all but disappeared.

★ ★ ★

On 15 January, 1814, I was going to be twenty-five and Stephen would be legally in control of my fortune, whatever my father did. It would be a tidy sum. It had been increasing at the rate of £400 a year ever since my mother had died sixteen years ago and there would be compound interest as well. My arithmetical abilities were small, but even I could see that my original £8,000 must have doubled.

My father never wrote to me after his first dreadful letter, but he was a just man. I was sure that he would try to arrange a proper settlement for me. I could probably count on the traditional widow's third, say five or six thousand pounds, I thought. But I hated the thought of Balquidder getting his share. Unless my husband had paid the interest on the loan over all these years, which I doubted, he could find that most of my fortune was owed to Balquidder.

It wasn't until one December evening in 1813 that I realized Balquidder had his eye on more than the £5,000 he was owed.

That December was a cold one and it

promised to be a very hard winter. The temperature was rarely above freezing, even during the day, and long icicles had formed on the leaky roof guttering. I could hear Eppie, the new skivvy, out in the yard breaking the ice round the pump.

Stephen and Balquidder were in our drawing-room, drinking. Stephen was drunk; I could hear his voice becoming slurred, Balquidder was reckless with our coals, flinging them on the fire with a crash.

'You'll soon be a wealthy man,' Balquidder was saying. He did not bother to lower his voice, though he must have known I was possibly within earshot.

'Eh?'

'Rich. Isn't it Emilia's twenty-fifth birthday soon?'

'January 15th.'

'Not long. Been in touch with old Daniels?'

'Wants me to settle a third on her. S'right. She should have something. It'sh her money. S'not Daniel's money. Came from her mother's family.'

Balquidder threw himself back with one of his guffaws. I could hear the chair groan. 'She might fall down the stairs,' he suggested. 'Break her pretty little neck. It happens.' Balquidder gave another of his fat laughs. I could hear him getting up and his heavy tread as he went over to pour out more claret. 'There are no children. If the money comes from her mother, it won't go back to old Daniels. You'd get it all. Must be well over sixteen thousand now.'

Stephen hiccuped and gave a cackle of drunken laughter. He had obviously decided it was a joke. Balquidder guffawed again and changed the subject.

I did not laugh.

Stone forestairs went down from our first-floor apartment to the entrance with its elegant pillars. The treads were worn, curved and treacherously icy just now. The wooden banisters were unstable and rotten in places. A quick push and I could be over the side with a broken neck on the cobblestones below. If it happened at night, anybody could be lurking in the shadows to finish me off.

It was no joke. Balquidder wanted me dead. Or rather, he wanted me to be twenty-five and dead. That way, Stephen would have all the money — no inconvenient widow's third — and doubtless Balquidder would get his sticky fingers on it soon enough.

If I were right, I had about five weeks to live.

I suddenly remembered something that had happened earlier that year. It was in late spring, for the window was open and a fledgeling sparrow had landed on the window ledge. It was cheeping for its parents and fluffing out its tiny feathers to attract their attention. It had obviously only just left the nest and I hoped it would be all right.

Balquidder came into the room and saw it. He walked over to the window, put his hand out and crushed it. I gave a cry of horror. He picked up the body, which was still fluttering, and stuffed it casually into his trouser pocket, turned round and laughed. All through that afternoon I could see the small, quivering bump in his pocket and a faint red patch.

When he left, Stephen and I saw him to the top of our forestairs, as we usually did. As he went down the stairs, he reached into his pocket and threw the baby sparrow down on to the cobbles below, where one of the alley cats pounced on it.

I shuddered as I remembered this. I knew suddenly, with absolute clarity, that Balquidder was a very dangerous man. To say I was frightened would be an underestimate. I was so terrified that I could scarcely breathe. Five weeks to live, I kept thinking, only five weeks. My throat dried up and I couldn't swallow. What could I do? Where could I go?

I was not wanted at Tranters Court. My father had not forgiven me and he certainly would not believe me. How could I blame him? If I went there I knew that his sense of propriety would lead him to send me straight back to my husband.

I couldn't go to the Beresfords. Mr and Mrs Beresford were dead; Noël was in Spain; I doubted whether George and Aline would welcome me.

There remained London. I'd only been there once in my life, when my mother and I had stayed with the Beresfords in their town house in the Adelphi. But my publisher was in London — and Tolley. When I was a little girl, I used to read her my stories of hobgoblins and dragons and beautiful princesses. She always exclaimed at my cleverness and I counted her as a friend. It was Tolley who had allowed me to say goodbye to Mama. My father had given her a pension after my mother's death and she lived with her sister in Somers Town. Tolley would never betray me.

I must confess that I felt a bit like Angelina fleeing from the evil Fra Bartolomeo. Angelina's bosom palpitated becomingly in moments of stress and I wished that I were as generously endowed — somehow I decided that beauty made misfortune easier to bear. She was headed for a ruinous castle; my destination was more humble. I would stay with Tolley until I found some respectable lodgings and then I would support myself by my writing.

If only I could get there.

The quickest, surest way was by mail coach. It was expensive, perhaps twice as much as the stagecoach, but it would be far speedier for it took only four passengers and stopped for nothing.

I had about twenty pounds from my last book hidden away. I also had a newly completed manuscript, *The Mountfalcon Heiress* — my support for the future.

Of course, in the morning, I decided I'd been exaggerating. Balquidder was an unpleasant man, but that didn't mean he would contemplate murder. This was 1813, not the Middle Ages. I must stop thinking I was living in the highly coloured pages of one of my own Gothic tales.

Stephen rose late and it was nearly midday before he went out. I was in my cubby-hole when he poked his head round the door.

'I'm off, Emmy. Don't know when I may be back. I've a meeting today with Jamie Kinross.'

I nodded.

'Oh, by the way, it's icy out. Don't slip on the stairs now, will you?' He closed the door and a moment later I heard him leave the house.

My fingers could suddenly no longer hold my pen and my heart began to pound in fear. In all these years, Stephen had never warned me about any hazards — and we had had some harsh winters. Why now, unless it was that he half-suspected some hidden danger?

For the second time in my life, I made plans to flee my home. As soon as Stephen had gone, I flung on my cloak, took my purse and went out. I discovered that the mail coach left Edinburgh each evening from the posting-inn in the Grassmarket. I managed to book an inside seat for that evening. I then went shopping. I bought bread, cheese, apples, a small bottle of brandy for emergencies and a leather water bottle.

It was odd getting out the old pigskin valise, the one I had fled with all those years ago. How naïve I had been! I remember taking my prettiest nightdress, but omitting my sensible boots. This time, I packed warm clothes and took my precious manuscript, my pens, my complimentary copies of my two books already published — bulky, but I couldn't leave them behind — Mrs Bereford's letters, the note from Noël and the combs. I had none of Mama's jewellery left. I took anything which might be useful, or which otherwise might give away my whereabouts.

I tried, and failed, to write to Stephen. I discovered that it was one thing for Angelina to pen a fluent missive before fleeing from Fra Bartolomeo, but quite another for me to write to my husband. What could I say? My clumsy attempts to explain my fear sounded merely pathetic on paper and I felt all the humiliation of spilling out my eight years of misery to a man who had long since ceased to want me. In the end, I just said that I was leaving, I would be quite safe and that the rent was paid until the end of December. I tried to make my pen add *forgive me* but it wouldn't.

Of course, I was frightened of the step I was taking, not so much of what lay ahead, but of what might happen if I stayed. I packed with a feverish haste and then hid the bag in my little study.

I spent the afternoon with the Irvines. I could not leave without thanking them for all their many kindnesses, but I did not like having to lie to them. I said that I was returning to my father's house; my husband's affairs were increasingly tangled and I hoped to effect some sort of reconciliation. I was taking the stagecoach the day after tomorrow to York and would hire a conveyance from there.

They were both concerned but wished me well, Mrs Irvine going so far as to press an old fur-lined muff of hers on me.

'The stagecoaches are shockingly draughty, dearie. Take it, do. I never use it.'

I kissed her, thanked them both and left.

With luck, I thought, Stephen would never think to ask them, and if he did, then the information would be misleading. I hoped that by that time I'd be safely in London with Tolley.

I was terrified lest Stephen come home early, though I knew he'd probably stay out most of the night. He wouldn't bother to check on my whereabouts. The mail coach left at six o'clock and waited for nobody.

I was not to know it, but I left Edinburgh just ahead of one of the worst winters within living memory. December had been cold, and as I stepped out into the frosty air, I could see in the yellow gaslight that the puddles in our filthy alley were iced over. A thin fog, heavy with a yellowish smoke, hung along the ground. Nobody stirred. The night closed round me.

In the inn yard all was bustle, with the four horses already harnessed. Luggage was being loaded on top — though I elected to have my valise by my feet. The post boy was putting the mail in the mail box. The coachman was stamping his feet, the steam from his breath puffing up into the air. The guard checked the tickets. His blunderbuss lay along his seat at the back.

'Best get inside, ma'am,' he said as I came up and showed my ticket. 'It's mortal cold out and we'll be off shortly.'

The other passengers were already inside. There was a portly man, who looked as though he were in business. He carried a black leather bag and wore a heavy greatcoat. He was sitting with his back to the driver. Opposite him sat an anxious couple, who introduced themselves as Mr and Mrs Stott; she was thin and pale and her husband nervy. They spoke together in low voices. The portly man indicated my seat next to himself and offered me a corner of his travelling rug.

I had already provided myself with an alias — I was not a romance writer for nothing. I was a Mrs Miller, going to meet my husband who was just returned from the Peninsula. I knew that women did not normally travel alone, without even a maid, and I needed to sound respectable.

I needn't have worried. Nobody cared. Married women, especially thin ones with beaky noses, are practically invisible.

The coach pulled out of the inn yard and set off at a smart trot. Peering out of the window, I could just see, high up, murky lights from the castle and, a short while later, the bulk of Arthur's Seat looming against the night sky. It was going to be a long cold night and I was grateful for Mrs Irvine's fur-lined muff.

Did I regret this second impulsive flight? Did it seem preposterous in the cold light of the following morning? No, I confess it didn't. I was convinced that Balquidder meant me harm, though I believed that Stephen would want no part in it. What I felt was a surge of release, as if a constricting iron band around my life had broken.

Most of my heroines have been shut up in dungeons — naturally. Of course, in my books, it is the hero who rescues them and I've always been more concerned with my heroine's emotions on seeing his manly form, guttering candle in one hand and a bloodstained sword in the other, coming to her aid, than in her feelings at being released. I now realized that I had underestimated that sense of liberation. It was like taking off a tight shoe. Whilst it was on, you could bear it. Once it was removed, you could never put it on again.

We travelled throughout the night and all the next day at a bone-shaking ten miles an hour, at a steady trot, stopping for nothing except to change the horses. The change was made in less than two minutes, but we were allowed time to relieve ourselves and there were two longer stops, with just enough time to grab a pie or some coffee.

On the second day we reached York and the countryside grew increasingly familiar. It was a strange feeling, stopping only briefly in a city I knew so well and then leaving it behind. Just out of York we passed the turning to Ainderby Hall and I felt a lump in my throat.

I thought about Noël and how unhappy he looked the last time I'd seen him. I thought of him sitting under a cork oak on some dusty Spanish plain and, childishly, began to snivel. There was no going back for either of us.

The mail coach swept on and I quietly mopped my tears. It was bitterly cold. The coach was draughty and even a portion of the portly gentleman's fur-lined rug did not stop my ankles and feet from feeling like blocks of ice. Mrs Stott's moans became audible and her husband grew impatient. He hunched himself away from her and stared gloomily out of the window. Not that there was much to see. The weather worsened as we went south and, as the countryside became flatter in the vale of York, so the fog rolled in from the east. Several times the coach had to pull up and the postboy clamber down to find the road. There were two oil carriage lamps, but their light was scarcely visible.

It was nine o'clock that evening, after an appalling twelve-hour journey, during which a wheel cracked, that we finally reached Grantham. We were forced to stay the night. The anxious lady, Mrs Stott, and I were to share a bed. I was so cold that I stumbled on alighting and Mrs Stott had to be carried into the inn. I could scarcely swallow the warmed-up mutton stew our landlady brought. Mrs Stott only sat and moaned.

The maid came in to show us upstairs and assured us that she had run the warming pan over the bed and given us each a hot brick, wrapped in flannel. Between us, we helped Mrs Stott upstairs. I noticed that Mr Stott was nowhere to be seen.

'My dear Mrs Miller,' said Mrs Stott, 'I can scarce speak for cold. How I shall sleep, I know not.'

My feet were still icy. I begged the maid to bring us up a bowl of hot water. Side by side, we put our white, numbed feet in the bowl and massaged them until they turned pink. We hung our clothes over the towel rail and put it by the fire. Mrs Stott pleaded for another scuttle full of coal.

'I daren't, madam.'

Mrs Stott offered her a shilling. I held up another.

The maid grinned as she pocketed them. 'I'll see what I can do.'

Ten minutes later she brought up four pieces of coal and a couple of small logs.

'Two shillings for that!' gasped Mrs Stott, when she had gone.

I was past caring. 'It should serve for an hour or so.'

It took me a long time to get to sleep after the jolting of the coach and, when at last I did, it seemed only minutes before the maid woke us with the information that the coach would leave in forty minutes and that it had started to snow. I went to look out of the window and the inn yard was quite white; it was not snowing very heavily, but the sky was leaden. Pray God we met with no mishap.

It was still dark when we went downstairs, though it was a fraction warmer. The snow had, at least, brought some cloud cover and the fog had lifted slightly. Our fellow travellers were in the parlour, neither in a good temper. They had been fleabitten and both gentlemen had red bites on their faces. I forced myself to eat what I could — some ham and a poached egg. The bread was good, freshly baked, and I broke a chunk off and hid it in my pocket for later, together with a piece of cheese. I saw Mrs Stott doing the same, and we exchanged a conspiratorial smile. The coffee was hot and warming.

We were supposed to reach London that night, though I thought it unlikely, on account of the weather. That meant the expense of another night in an inn. On the other hand, I did not want to arrive at the Bull and Mouth in London late at night. I wanted to arrive when we should, in the mid-afternoon, and have time to get to Tolley's before it got dark. I had had no time to write to her and she would not be expecting me. There might be problems and, for the first time, I felt a twinge of fear.

Everything depended on Tolley. Perhaps I should have written first and awaited her reply, but it was all too late.

Once we got out of town, the horses settled into their fast trot. The snow had the effect of making the road between the hedges of blackthorn and hawthorn easier to see. I tried to think of Angelina in the Alps. I mentally wrote a splendid new scene with my heroine, swathed in luxurious sables, going for a moonlit ride on a sleigh with her lover and the frost crackling and icicles sparkling like diamonds as they sped through the forest. But somehow, I couldn't help seeing that in reality Angelina's nose would be red with cold and her lover would probably be sniffing like the portly gentleman next to me.

It was another long, cold day. We were considerably delayed. The fog returned and it was past eight o'clock that evening when we arrived at the Bull and Mouth in London.

The inn was large, noisy and the servants patently uninterested in one shabby, lone female. I picked up my valise and went towards the cab rank. I didn't like the look of the first cabby, but the second was a mild-looking man whose horse was in reasonable condition. My years in Edinburgh had toughened me and I was able to ascertain the price, one shilling and sixpence, and give him the direction, without hesitation.

It was much later than I liked. Tolley would probably be in bed. People often went to bed shortly after it got dark. At Tranters Court and Ainderby Hall, of course, things were different. They could afford to have candles burning and to keep the fires going. Very often, when Stephen was out, I went to bed early to save the candle. Tolley doubtless did the same.

Tolley lived in Somers Town, in Ossulston Street. There was a lot of new building and the roads were bad. Just north of Woburn Place, it began to look like a huge building site to our left, and the gaslights petered out.

The horse picked its way carefully, stumbling once or twice. Fortunately, the houses began again and once we reached Euston Square, though it was half-built with houses on only two sides, at least there were lights.

At last the cab drew up. I clambered down. The house was dark, which I was expecting, but the downstairs window was boarded up, which I was not.

'Looks like your friend's gone, lady,' said the cabby. He obviously felt that my discreet knock was inadequate, for he went up to the door and banged loudly on the knocker. The upstairs window next door shot up and a night-capped head poked out and damned his eyes.

I had heard far worse in Cant's Close. 'I am looking for Miss Toller,' I said.

'Gone. And afore you asks, I don't know where.' He slammed down the window.

For a moment I was paralysed. She can't have, I kept thinking. I had had a letter from her not six months ago.

''Scuse me, lady,' said the cabby. 'Where to now? It ain't the night for standing around.'

What should I do? Should I ask him the name of a respectable lodging house? Or go back to the Bull and Mouth?

'Look, lady, if it's all the same to you, I

wants to get home. You don't want to be left here, I take it?'

'No.' I shivered and climbed back into the cab. It turned round and the horse began to plod its way back to London. Another shilling and sixpence, I thought. And five shillings or so for a respectable bed.

Then I remembered that the Beresfords had a town house in the Adelphi, in John Street. It would be closed at this time of year, no doubt, but there would be a caretaker to look after the place. The Beresfords were good employers who kept their servants. Would there be somebody there who remembered me, or, at least, my maiden name? Would they take me in? God knows, I did not have much of a reputation left. It was the only hope I had. I banged on the ceiling. The cab drew up and I opened the window.

'The Adelphi, please. John Street. I can't remember the number, but I think I'll know it when I see it.' There was a dolphin door knocker, I remembered, which I had admired, and the house was at the end nearest the river. I hoped to God that that would be sufficient to identify it. I'd only been there once as a child, but we'd stayed for a few days, and I had a good memory for places.

The Adelphi was a fashionable block in a not very fashionable area, just behind the

Strand and overlooking the Thames and the Adelphi Wharf. I don't know why my godfather had preferred it to a house in the more modish West End, possibly because he was not really a town man and liked the bustle of the river.

It took us a long time to get there. Fog had crept up from the river and the snow was falling more heavily now. I became aware that I was shivering with cold, fear and exhaustion. I was alone in a strange city and I didn't dare to think what I should do if nobody were at John Street to take me in. I knew I couldn't go on much longer and it was difficult to think clearly.

The horse plodded on. The fog became thicker, rolls of it drifted up from the Thames. Every now and then spidery glimpses of masts appeared and then vanished. But my memory had served me well. I directed the cabby to the river end and there it was, dolphin door knocker and all. And, thank God, there was evidence of occupation. Candlelight flickered in the basement and I could see a glow behind the fanlight.

'You will wait, won't you?' I said to the cabby.

He nodded. Stupid question. He wanted to make sure he was paid and doubtless expected a large tip. I was so cold that I stumbled and fell as I got out of the cab. There was now a large muddy stain on my cloak and my gloves were blackened where I had pushed myself up from the ground. I knocked.

Footsteps. The sound of a bolt being pushed back. I clutched my cloak more firmly around me.

A white face with a mobcap peered out at me suspiciously. 'Yes, madam?' She held the door open only a fraction. I could see her peering at the hired cab.

'It's Miss D . . . Daniels,' I stammered. 'Miss Emilia Daniels of Tranters Court. Mr Beresford's goddaughter. You remember me, I hope?'

I thought I recognized her. She had been a kitchenmaid at Ainderby Hall.

'Miss Daniels?' I could see her looking doubtfully at the mud and my shabby cloak. I noticed that she still held the door.

'Please, for the love of God, let me in!' I was nearly crying with cold and exhaustion. 'Is Mr Beresford here?' George would not refuse me shelter, I thought.

'Mr George Beresford died six months ago.'

'Died!' I tried desperately to hold on to this new information, to say something. George dead? How could he be dead? I began to shake.

'He was thrown from his horse. Mrs George is up in Yorkshire. There's only the colonel here and he's not up to visitors.'

'The colonel,' I said stupidly. 'What colonel?'

'Colonel Beresford. And he'll not thank me for disturbing him at this hour.' She began to close the door.

I grabbed it from her hand and pushed my way in. I could feel myself swaying and held on.

The cabby had come up the stairs and now said, 'That's three shillings, ma'am.' My valise was in his hand.

'Yes, yes, of course,' I said. I fumbled to open my reticule, but my fingers were so cold and wet after the fall that I couldn't undo the fastening. Then I dropped it and coins rolled out all over the floor. I began to weep with cold and exhaustion.

Dimly, I could hear a door opening behind me and slow, dragging footsteps.

A voice said, 'Good God, Emilia!'

I turned. All I could see was a tall, gaunt figure, leaning heavily on a stick. His hair was flecked with grey, his face lined and worn. Could it possibly be Noël? I would scarcely have known him. I opened my mouth to speak, but no words came out. I could feel the blood draining from my face and I crumpled in a heap at his feet.

★ ★ ★

I slept until late afternoon the following day. I remember nothing of being put to bed, or the cabby being paid off. When I awoke, I was in a pleasant room with a flowered Chinese wallpaper and pretty bamboo chairs. A fire was burning in the grate. I was warm for the first time in days, weeks even. It had been years since I was in such a room. All I wanted was to go back to sleep. I did not want to return and face the world. Somewhere at the edge of my mind was a bruise where George's death lay, still unmourned. But it was not George who filled my thoughts, but Noël. I could scarcely believe that the golden-haired, blue-eyed hero of my youth could have changed into this ill, care-worn man.

I stared up at the ceiling rose. Would Noël insist on sending me back to Stephen? Was there anything I could say to persuade him otherwise? Would he believe the truth? I still couldn't think at all clearly; after so much strain, my mind seemed to have taken a holiday. It was difficult to think at all, and think I must.

There was a scratch at the door and a fresh-faced maid appeared and bobbed a curtsy.

'Please, miss, Mrs Good says would you like something to eat?'

I sat up slowly. 'What is the time?'

'Past four o'clock, miss. You've slept nigh fourteen hours.'

'Good God.' The maid waited. 'Tell Mrs Good that I'd love some coffee and toast.'

The maid curtsied herself out.

Mrs Good, I remembered her now. When I had last seen her, she had been plain Tryphena Good, kitchenmaid. Now she must be the cook, or possibly the housekeeper, complete with her new courtesy title 'Mrs'. I should have to mind my p's and q's. She would have forbidden me the house last night if she could.

It was Mrs Good herself who brought up my tray. By that time I'd washed my face, brushed my hair and put on my dressing-gown. I felt more respectable.

'I am sorry for all the trouble I have caused,' I said.

Tryphena sniffed and turned to put an unnecessary piece of coal on the fire.

'Dinner is at seven o'clock, miss,' she pronounced. 'The colonel is in the drawing-room. Just ring the bell for Hannah if you need anything.'

'Thank you,' I said, meekly. I noticed that she had decided to ignore my married status.

Tryphena sniffed again and left. Noël must have made it clear that I was a guest, but his housekeeper was making her disapproval plain. I didn't blame her. I had been a selfish child. I'd probably been carelessly dismissive of Mrs Good when she'd been plain Tryphena the kitchenmaid. I daresay I deserved her disapproval.

The coffee and toast revived me. There was a small bowl of fruit, too, apples, pears and oranges. The orange was bitter sweet, but refreshing. My head began to clear.

The first question was how much should I tell Noël? I would play it by ear, I decided. If he were determined to send me back to Stephen, I would appear to acquiesce. I would try to find out what had happened to poor Tolley. I would take my new manuscript to Mr Robinson. We had developed a friendly epistolary relationship over the years. As Daniel Miller, I made him money. Perhaps he would help me to find respectable lodgings, if Tolley were not to be found. He knew I was a Miss Daniels, that was all. At least he wouldn't condemn me for fleeing from my husband.

I went to peer out of the window. It was dark again, and foggy — typical London dark-brown fog. But snow was falling too, and falling fast. With any luck, it would be difficult to travel in this weather. That meant no pursuit and, of more immediate importance, the post would be disrupted. If Noël thought to write either to my father or Stephen, the letter would probably not get through.

My next thought was what to wear. I had only two gowns with me. Hannah had whisked one away for cleaning and the other, a brown merino, which didn't really suit me, was hanging up, freshly pressed, in the wardrobe. I put on a fresh collar and cuffs and the white cheered it up a bit. I still had rings under my eyes, but it was not simple tiredness, I knew, but years of anxiety. I wore no jewellery save my wedding ring. Stephen had pawned the rest years ago.

All the same, I was clean, tidy, rested and safe, and I went down to the drawing-room with a certain confidence.

Noël rose as I entered, leaning heavily on a silver-handled, ebony cane. He limped forward and kissed my cheek. His lips were cool. As a child I used to hug him exuberantly. I didn't dare do that now. I was grown up and convention limited the ways I could express my affection for a member of the opposite sex.

73

He offered me a drink. We sat down, one on either side of the fireplace, he with his sherry, I with my lemonade. I apologized for the upheaval of my arrival. I offered my condolences on the death of his brother. If Noël heard my voice tremble, he gave no sign, but stared silently into the fire. I looked at him covertly; I could have wept for him. I remembered him twelve, fourteen years ago, before Aline came and the troubles started. Noël laughed often, and his spirits were infectious. He played the pianoforte well, or at least, with feeling, and he often used to entertain his parents with songs of their youth.

What had happened to all that?

He was thirty-seven now, but he could have been ten years older. He looked bent, prematurely aged and desperately unhappy. Perhaps I'm exaggerating, I thought. Noël always used to accuse me of that. 'You're either in alt, or in despair,' he used to say, teasingly.

Now, it seemed that as I had learnt moderation, Noël had learnt anguish. My heart bled for him. At thirteen, I'd have gone to him and snuggled up and cajoled his sorrow out of him. I could sometimes do that. I was the only person he talked to when his old spaniel died. But never about Aline, of course. There were always private areas with Noël.

He looked up and caught me staring. I flushed and looked away.

'Well, Emilia? What scrape have you got yourself into this time?' He smiled, but it was with an effort.

'It's a long story and I'm not sure I can tell it right.'

Noël gave a short laugh. 'If I know you, it'll be a 'story' all right.'

'I did not come four hundred miles in the iciest weather I can ever remember, because of some story I've invented!' It was unlike Noël to be so brusque.

'No, embroidered, perhaps. I'm sorry, Emilia, I've problems enough of my own. I'll hear you out and you can stay here and recover, though it's hardly proper with only Mrs Good as chaperon. Still, you're almost family and a married woman beside, so we'll have to make the best of it. But in a week or so, you must go back, if I have to take you myself. Do I make myself clear?'

I swallowed. 'Perfectly.'

'Well?'

I could see that things were going to be difficult.

3

It was obvious that I could not tell Noël the truth — that Archibald Balquidder wanted me dead. But he might believe that Stephen had wasted all my money and would do the same with my fortune as soon as I was twenty-five and it passed into his control. If I represented my flight as the result of a marital quarrel, an anxiety about my financial security, he would listen. He might even help.

'I hardly know where to start. It is a painful and humiliating story. You have no need to remind me of my capacity for fantasy, I am too well aware of it myself.'

'I'm sorry. I don't mean to be unkind, Emilia, I'm just worried by your sudden arrival. Your husband must be frantic with worry.'

I let that pass. 'You know what I was like, Noël. Yes, I lived in a world of my own creation. I thought Stephen was just like all the heroes in the books and it was wonderful that it was me he wanted.' I stopped. I hated having to confess the failure of my marriage, even to Noël, and I had to force myself to continue. 'I know I'm not a beauty, but I really did believe that he loved me. Of course, it was just the money.' I stopped again and looked at Noël. There was not a trace of 'I told you so', in his face. Encouraged, I went on, 'If you think I told stories, believe me, they were as nothing to the tales that Stephen could spin; his future prospects, his wealthy family, his gracious home . . . ' I swallowed.

'We live in a two-roomed apartment in Cant's Close, a filthy lane in the Old Town with an open gutter running down the middle. Stephen has no prospects, all he has is a smooth tongue. Somehow he manages to keep his head above water through various doubtful schemes. I have tried not to learn too much about them.'

'Emilia, my dear, I'm so sorry. I always suspected that he was a scoundrel.' Noël moved his injured leg to a more comfortable position and shifted a cushion behind his back.

'I have developed some unexpected qualities, Noël. I can clean and mend and polish. My buttonholes are a joy to behold. I also write professionally. An Edinburgh publisher, a Mr Irvine, pays me three guineas a time for moral Sunday School tales.' I saw Noël's eyebrows shoot up.

'Ironic, isn't it? I churn out stories of naughty boys or girls who are guilty of such

77

heinous sins as playing hopscotch on the Sabbath and I save them from hellfire and certain damnation with the aid of my much-derided imagination.'

Noël turned to face me. 'You don't have to be bitter, Emilia. I think you've coped with great courage — and some ingenuity!'

'I try not to be bitter. I know my elopement was selfish and thoughtless, but I wasn't deliberately wicked. Surely I have paid for it?' I pulled myself together. 'For the last six years, ever since I met Mr Irvine, I have supported us both.'

'And now?'

'I shall be twenty-five in a few weeks' time. My father does not write. I do not know what is being done for me, if anything, when I come into my fortune, and I am desperate for an income of my own, however small. I am so tired, Noël. So weary of mending and making do. I can never stop writing. I can't be ill or rest. I have to write to pay the bills.

'I've come to London because I want to see Papa's lawyers, to persuade them to tell me what is happening, to beg for some financial settlement. I don't mind supporting Stephen, if I must, but I'm frightened of this hand-to-mouth existence going on for ever, like the last eight years and . . . '

I could go no further. In spite of all my

efforts I started to cry. There was silence. All I could hear was the hissing of a wet log and the occasional muffled hooting from a barge on the river. I scrabbled for my handkerchief and hiccuped into it, trying to stifle my sobs.

I hadn't fully realized how I felt until I heard myself saying it. Even without Balquidder, it was so dreary and unending, like a life sentence. Whatever Noël said, I would never go back.

'Your father was deeply hurt by your elopement.'

Hurt? I found that difficult to believe. 'But after eight years . . . Could he not forgive me now?'

'Have you asked him? He has heard nothing from you.'

'I was ashamed. I didn't want him to know how bad it was.'

'My mother used to read out bits from your letters. Little stories of what you were doing. Lies, Emilia.' He spoke gently, but it hurt that I had lost his good opinion. 'They wouldn't have deceived a child. How do you think he felt that you asked forgiveness from my mother and not from him?'

Mrs Beresford loved me, I thought. That is the difference.

'Listen to me,' Noël continued. 'I, too, know what damage lies do. After George died, I found that he had mortgaged the estate heavily. Somehow, in the three years since our father died, George managed to cripple Ainderby. He was inveigled, God knows how, into buying a plantation in Demerara, which, needless to say, absorbs money like a sponge. Somebody had sold him a get-rich-quick scheme and he had never breathed a word to me, even though he knew I was his heir.'

'In Demerara!' Instantly, Balquidder came to mind. He, too, had an estate in Demerara. 'Why did George need to get rich quick? Ainderby is a good estate.' It was worth £4,000 a year, I knew.

Noël winced as he moved his bad leg again. 'He wanted to indulge his wife.' He tried to smile. 'And why not? Aline is worth it.'

So she is still the princess in the fairy-tale, I thought. I said nothing.

'You have never done her justice, Emilia.'

'I was jealous. She was beautiful and I wasn't.' It was plain that I could not say that I thought her manipulative and self-centred.

'You have changed,' said Noël, after a pause. 'I suppose that's inevitable; it's been eight years, after all. You used to be such a self-righteous little thing. Very high-minded!' He paused and considered me carefully. 'You've improved,' he said at last, smiling, 'certainly, in looks. You're too thin and you have black rings under your eyes, but you've grown into your face . . . '

'My nose, you mean,' I interrupted.

Noël laughed. 'You always were silly about your nose. I rather like it, myself.'

I was so unused to compliments that I didn't know how to respond and I found myself flushing in awkward embarrassment. I only just stopped myself putting up my hand to hide it.

There was the soft boom of the gong and Noël reached for his stick. He had been surveying my rising colour in some amusement, but all he said was, 'Let us go and eat, you must be hungry.'

Nothing more was said about my returning to Edinburgh, or, indeed, about Noël's own problems. He was not the sort of man to talk in front of servants as though they weren't there. Instead, I asked him about his son, Richard.

'He's upstairs. You'll see him in the morning.'

'Here!'

'Yes, but London smoke and fog don't agree with him. He's been ill and confined to the house.'

'Poor boy.' I'd only seen him as a baby. All I could remember was a square wailing mouth at the christening. 'Is he interested in learning, perhaps?' I ventured. 'I believe delicate children often are.'

'No. He hates reading. He's behind with his lessons, too.'

'Where was he while you were in Spain?'

'At Ainderby with George and Aline. She now hopes to return to France, as soon as circumstances permit. Her parents have got back part of their estate, so she has a home to go to. She has been looking after Richard since my wife died.'

There was a softness in Noël's voice as he spoke Aline's name. I noticed that giveaway tone years ago, when I first fell in love with Stephen. It was impossible for me to say 'Mr Kirkwall', without that tell-tale certain something in the voice. I have noticed it since. Jeanie, at Cant's Close, said the name of the local butcher's boy, Lachie, with just that same intonation. Noël would never acknowledge it to me, but he was still in love with Aline. I could not mistake it. Poor little boy, I thought. She was hardly a suitable foster mother.

'I should like to see Richard,' I said. 'Perhaps I could help him with his reading while I'm here. At least it would repay some of the bother I've caused you.'

Noël shrugged. 'If you wish. I should warn

you that he's backward.' He must have realized that he sounded dismissive, for after a moment he added, 'I'm afraid I find him a difficult child. I've tried, but . . . '

I had much to think about when I retired to bed that night. I had come into an unhappy household, that was clear. Noël seemed ambivalent about his only child. He was in mourning for his brother; his estate was mortgaged; he had an extravagant sister-in-law to support and one whom he could never hope to marry. The church did not allow a man to marry his sister-in-law. He would have all the trouble of either selling the Demerara plantation or making it profitable. I hoped it would be the former. I did not like the idea of Noël making money out of human misery.

I could see that his leg was troubling him for he was obviously in pain. Could anything be done about that? Was it a war wound? He hadn't said and I didn't like to ask. If I were on better terms with Tryphena Good I might have asked her but, as things were, I didn't think she'd tell me.

Thinking of Noël's problems, I found that my own had somehow shifted to a different perspective. Noël was right; I'd never written truthfully to my father, but then, it had never occurred to me that I might have hurt him. It seemed so unlikely. Perhaps I should write. But even as I thought of it, I knew I wouldn't. The letter from him after my marriage had been so icy, so unrelenting in its condemnation, that even now I couldn't bear to think of it. I would not risk another such, not yet.

My thoughts moved on to Stephen. If it weren't for Balquidder, I could probably have come to some arrangement with Stephen. With money of my own settled on me, we could have had a discreet separation. Plenty of couples did, I knew. Stephen would have a handsome income from my fortune and I would move to some spa town — for health reasons, of course.

But I couldn't ignore Balquidder and I wasn't sure if to mention him wouldn't do more harm than good. Noël had been more accommodating than I'd expected. How long would that last with Balquidder as an added complication? Noël would never believe it.

Nor had I mentioned my London publishers. It wasn't that I was ashamed of my Gothic romances, but I was wary of letting Noël know that I could support myself, especially as any money I earned belonged legally to my husband. If he summoned Stephen to fetch me, then I wanted to be able to flee again without Stephen hammering on the door of my publishers and demanding any money due to me.

My worst fear was that Balquidder would come to London in Stephen's place. Even the thought made my mind shy away in terror. I was pretty sure that Stephen would confide in Balquidder about my flight. Would Balquidder persuade Stephen to let him come instead? He could get rid of me with far less fuss in London, or he could hire a private carriage and arrange an 'accident' anywhere between London and Edinburgh — all 400 miles of it.

I fell into an uneasy sleep.

The morning dawned cold and grey. At nine o'clock one of the maids came up with hot chocolate, a delicious roll and butter and some fruit. She lit the fire. Luxury.

I sat up and took the tray. 'What is your name?'

'Hannah, Miss Emilia. You won't remember me, but I grew up at Ainderby. My dad is second gardener. I used to trot about behind him, when I was little.'

I recalled a bright-eyed little girl in a brown holland pinafore. I had envied the way she was allowed to help her father. I smiled and she smiled back. I remembered that I'd liked her. 'Of course I remember you. You used to pinch strawberries when you thought nobody was looking — but so did I. That makes us partners in crime.'

Hannah grinned. 'You never told on me, miss.'

'Nor you on me. Hannah, is there somebody who could take a letter for me to Paternoster Row?' I decided that I must see Mr Robinson as soon as possible and I felt that Hannah was to be trusted.

'Abel, miss. The boot boy.'

'I'll see him later. What day is it?'

'Why, Friday, Miss Emilia. Christmas Eve.'

'Good God, I'd quite forgotten.' I must buy a Christmas present for Richard at least.

'There's no decorations, nor nothing,' said Hannah sadly as she prepared to go, 'not with Mr George lately dead and the colonel ill. We're all proper worried about the colonel.'

'I, too,' I said. 'I would scarcely have recognized him and he looks so sad.'

Hannah left and I finished my breakfast. There was a davenport in the corner of the room with writing paper, quills, ink and a selection of wafers. I sat down at it and wrote to Mr Robinson saying that I was in London and that I had the manuscript of my new book, *The Mountfalcon Heiress*, which I would be glad to deliver. Could he spare me a moment later that morning?

Finding a small present for Richard would give me a good excuse to go out if Noël chose to question my movements. I would get Abel to hail me a cab and first try to find Tolley. I would then go to Paternoster Row. Mr Robinson might have a suitable book for an eight-year-old boy — a child's version of *Gulliver's Travels*, perhaps? If his reading wasn't up to it, I could read it to him.

When I came downstairs to give the note to Abel, I learnt that Noël had had a bad night.

'Mr Bagnigge's with him, miss,' said Abel, taking my letter. 'The colonel don't let anybody else near him when he's ill.' He looked anxious, his thin, sharp face creased with concern. Abel was about fourteen, I guessed, for he was an inch or so smaller than me, and still had a boy's smoothness of cheek and a voice which was teetering on the edge of breaking. He seemed pleased to be getting out of the house.

'I want you to wait for a reply,' I said, and promised him a shilling when he returned.

I wandered into the drawing-room. The other maid, Mary, was finishing off cleaning and she whisked her duster and polishing rags behind her back as I appeared. I was obviously not expected to put in an appearance this early.

'Don't let me interrupt you,' I said. 'Is Master Richard up?'

'He don't come down here, miss,' said

Mary, eyeing me with disapproval. Had she been talking to Tryphena Good, I wondered, or was she just resentful of my presence when she was working? 'He stays in his room with Miss Carver.'

'Is she his governess?'

'Oh no, miss. Master Richard don't have no governess. Miss Carver looks after him. He's not quite right in the head, see.'

I went upstairs, thoughtfully. Not quite right in the head? Noël had spoken of him being backward. Poor boy, if so. However, as Noël had raised no objection to me seeing Richard, I would go up now.

Richard's rooms were on the third floor. The front room, overlooking the street, was his day-room and behind that was his bedroom. I knocked at the door and entered on my knock.

No attempt had been made to make the room welcoming. There was a dreary patterned wallpaper in browns and yellows, a large oak table by the window with a couple of chairs and a threadbare carpet in the floor. An almost empty bookcase filled one corner and a nursery fireguard stood beside the fire. To one side of it was a Windsor carver chair and in it a dumpy woman with an untidy bun of wispy grey hair sat snoring. There was a bottle of what looked suspiciously like gin at her feet and a closed workbasket. I shut the door with a firm snap and she awoke with a jerk.

'I am Mrs Kirkwall,' I said with resolution, 'I am come to visit Master Richard.' One thing I had learnt over the last eight years of wheedling concessions out of landladies, was that confidence is everything.

Miss Carver put a hand over her mouth to cover a hiccup and carefully dropped her shawl over the gin bottle. 'The colonel said nothing about a visitor.'

I raised my eyebrows as I remembered my stepmother doing at some impertinence of mine. 'I spoke with him about it last night.' I moved over to the table and sat down.

There was a creak behind me. The bedroom door slowly opened and a small face poked round.

Poor child, he looks just like his mother, was my first thought. He had the same rather puddingy face and dull brown eyes. He was thin and pale and small for his age. He also looked apathetic. He dragged himself in, shook my hand politely and waited.

'I shall stay with Master Richard for a while,' I said. 'I'll ring when I need you.' I didn't like the way she was looking at me.

She nodded curtly, gathered up her things, and left.

Making conversation with Richard was uphill work. Nothing seemed to interest him and he had little to say for himself. It was as if all his vitality had been drained out of him. After about ten minutes I was wondering what on earth I could say next, when a chance reference to his father changed everything.

'I'm sorry your father has had a bad night.'

'It's his wound,' said Richard. 'He got it at Vittoria last year.' His eyes suddenly lit up. They stopped being dull and opaque and became warm and alive.

'Tell me about it,' I said. I meant the wound, for I was curious as to what had happened to Noël, but Richard launched into an account of the battle.

'It was on June 21st, which was very odd because it was the very day that Uncle George died. We had tremendous losses, five thousand men, though the French lost eight thousand.'

'Gracious!' Some comment was plainly called for.

Richard, eyes shining, rushed on. Words like Tres Puentes, the river Zadorra, the storming of La Puebla and the activities of various divisions and their commanders tumbled out of him.

I could make neither head nor tail out of what he said, but two things were clear: one was that Richard adored his father; the other was that if Richard were backward, then I was the Emperor of China.

The account of the battle of Vittoria took some time and Richard rushed into his bedroom and came out with a box of lead soldiers, which he set up excitedly on the table to show me exactly where his father had fallen.

'My father was with the third division under Sir Thomas Picton,' said Richard proudly. 'He was wounded in the attack on Tres Puentes. He got caught by shrapnel.'

'What is shrapnel?' Or should it be who?

Richard looked confused. 'It's lots of bits,' he said at last. 'He nearly lost his leg! In the end he told the doctor to go away. He wouldn't let anybody touch him, only Jem Bagnigge.'

'Jem Bagnigge is his batman?'

'Yes. He told me all about the battle.'

'So all these bits in the leg are still causing problems?'

Richard nodded. 'Every now and then another bit comes out and it's very painful.' He suddenly looked sad and I could see tears in his eyes.

'But you must remember that each time a

bit comes out, there's one bit less inside your Papa's leg.'

Richard turned to me and whispered, his lip trembling, 'I don't want Papa to die.'

Poor child, I thought. His life had been turned upside-down too often. His mother dead, his uncle dead and his father ill. If Noël died who would take him in?

'I don't think he'll die,' I said. 'I'm sure the most dangerous time is over. Just now it's too cold for your father to exercise properly and he has lots of worries on his mind. Once spring comes and he begins to sort things out, I'm sure his wound will improve.'

We were interrupted by Miss Carver returning with Abel, who had a note for me. I reached in my reticule and handed him a shilling. He grinned at me, sketched a mock military salute to Richard, and left. Richard gave him a small, scared smile and glanced anxiously at Miss Carver. He's frightened of her, I thought angrily. Why? What did she do to him when they were alone?

'I shall hope to see a lot of you, Richard,' I said as I bent to kiss him good-bye.

Richard's face had resumed its apathetic look. I could see that he didn't believe me. I smiled reassuringly at him and left the room. Behind me I could hear Miss Carver scolding him for having his soldiers all over the table.

I went to my room and opened Mr Robinson's letter. He would be pleased to see me any time that day which suited me, he wrote. They closed at four o'clock, it being Christmas Eve. Good, it was now just after half-past ten. I put on my travelling boots and warm cloak and took Mrs Irvine's muff, then opened my valise and took out the oilskin packet which contained my precious manuscript.

As I went downstairs I realized that I should have asked Abel to get me a cab discreetly but he had disappeared. Unfortunately, Tryphena Good was in the hall. She raised her eyebrows when she saw me.

'You're going out, miss?' For two pins I could see she'd like to stop me.

'Certainly,' I said. 'I wish to buy a small gift for Master Richard. Abel can escort me to the cab stand.' I stared her out.

'I'll call him, miss,' she said reluctantly at last. I could see her eyeing my parcel. Does she think I've stolen the silver? I thought.

I allowed Abel to hear me tell the cabby to go to Newsome's in Leicester Square and the moment the cab turned the corner I banged on the roof and redirected it to Ossulston Street in Somers Town.

It was a depressing journey, quite apart from the cold. None of the neighbours knew where Tolley had gone. The only information I gathered from a pâtisserie she patronized was that it had been in September and that she and her sister had moved to the seaside for her sister's health. I thanked the pâtissière, bought a bagful of delicious-smelling brioches, and left. How selfish I'd been, I thought ashamed. Childishly, I'd assumed that Tolley would drop everything to look after me; now I saw that I would have to fend for myself.

In one way, of course, I had been doing that for the last eight years, but even a day or so at John Street had shown me the unspeakable comfort of having a warm and secure roof over my head.

I climbed back into the cab. 'Paternoster Row,' I said.

Why were all cabs so filthy, I wondered, as I tried not to lean back against the grease-stained squabs. The straw on the floor was damp and the window glass so spattered with mud that it was almost impossible to see out.

I allowed my thoughts to drift, but this time not to some craggy Alpine pass with picturesque brigands waiting to capture my heroine, the leader of whom would be the hero in disguise . . . I contemplated my situation.

It was only now that I had left Cant's Close, that I could begin to realize how unhappy and lonely I had been all these years. I had had no real home, no hope for the future, nothing solid to build on. It had been simply existence from day to day, and that at almost the lowest level. What benefits I had gained I had truly earned; the friendship of Mr and Mrs Irvine; the small pleasures of teaching first Jeanie and then Eppie to read; the very real achievement of finding a way of earning my own living in the world.

Surely I could now forgive myself for my youthful follies? Was it not time to acknowledge my mistakes, to refuse to beat my breast over them any longer, and to look to the future?

But what future did I have? There was nobody to whom I mattered most in the world. Stephen, who should have filled that place, was fond of me in a mild way, but I doubted he cared whether I were there or not, except that some of his comforts would be lost.

Less than forty-eight hours at John Street had shown me that I wanted affection and purpose in my life. I wanted to be welcome. Hannah and Abel seemed disposed to be on my side, even if Mrs Good, Miss Carver and Mary were not. Richard needed me and I could help him, I was sure.

And Noël? What did I feel about Noël? I was now a grown woman, and my perceptions had changed. He was no longer the idolized hero of my childhood, but someone more human, with human frailties. I wondered whether he saw me any differently, or was I still an over-excitable, over-imaginative child to him?

The cab was now toiling up Ludgate and I could glimpse the bulk of Temple Bar through the dirty windows. I drew off my wedding ring and tucked it carefully into my reticule. Mr Robinson knew me as Miss Daniels who wrote as Daniel Miller, and Miss Daniels I must remain.

From Mr Robinson's letters over the years, I had imagined him to be an elderly businessman, dressed in black. I suppose I'd been thinking of an English Mr Irvine. In fact, he was middle-aged, with a nutcracker face, the most amazingly bushy eyebrows I'd ever seen, which ornamented the tops of his eyes like great furry caterpillars, and a plentiful black beard. The backs of his hands were hairy too, and I'm sorry to say that my first thought was that he'd make a splendid werewolf.

He, too, seemed surprised at my appearance. I'd have liked to have asked him what he had expected, but had the sense to hold my tongue.

He ushered me into his office, offered me coffee, which I accepted, took the manuscript and gave me a receipt for it. I remembered the brioches and opened the bag and offered him one before I remembered the vulgarity of such behaviour.

To his credit he didn't bat an eyelid. Being offered cake by strange women obviously happened to him all the time. 'Delicious,' he said, and accepted another. I liked him, bushy eyebrows and all.

He gave me a brief summary of my books' sales. *The Castle of Apollinari* was still selling. My second book, *The Doom of the House of Ansbach* was being reprinted.

'I was going to send a bill of exchange for fifty pounds to Mr Irvine's address for you, Miss Daniels, but perhaps, as you are here, you would prefer it direct.'

'I would rather have it in cash.' I wished, not for the first time, that women could hold bank accounts.

'Certainly.' He rang the bell and gave an order to the clerk. 'May I have your address? It may be a week or so until I can read *The Mountfalcon Heiress*.' The bushy eyebrows twinkled at me. 'Splendid title, by the way.'

'I rather like it myself,' I admitted. 'I do not

yet know where I shall be living. I had hoped to stay with my mother's old maid, but she has left London. I'll be in touch in a couple of weeks, when I'm settled.'

We began to talk about publishing and printing. Mr Robinson was a man of all trades and did everything. 'I prefer to keep things under my eye,' he finished. 'Some printers are awful rogues, Miss Daniels.'

'Criminal or just tricky?'

He laughed. 'There speaks the romance writer. May I expect a villainous printer in your next book?'

'I don't think they go with ruined castles and dungeons. Besides, it's hard to see printers as really evil.' I smiled at him.

'You'd be surprised. It is rumoured that a Mr Moxon now, who runs a small press off Three Cranes Wharf, has a nice line in forgery.'

'Forging what? Bank notes?'

'He has been arrested for forging false papers for the owners of British slave ships, to enable them to register their ships on the Continent.'

A chill went down my back. 'How . . . how horrible.'

'He was released for lack of evidence, or maybe rich friends bought him off, who can say.' He looked at me across the desk. 'I understand our mutual friend, Mr Irvine, is a member of the Abolition Society.'

'Yes. And I am with him.'

'I, too.'

'I heard,' I said hesitantly, 'of a Mr Balquidder in Edinburgh, who might have been involved in just such an activity.'

'Balquidder? Oh yes, I've heard of Balquidder. A dangerous man, Miss Daniels, not one to cross. Do you know him?'

'I have met him.' I couldn't help shuddering. What could I add? That he wanted me dead? That I was married and that my husband owed Balquidder an enormous sum of money? It was safer to change the subject. I switched the conversation to suitable books for an eight-year-old boy.

Mr Robinson directed me to another bookseller up the road and recommended a toyshop which sold lead soldiers and the like. The clerk returned with my fifty pounds, sewn up in neat cotton bags.

'They are heavy,' I commented, picking one up.

'Why don't you leave them with me, Miss Daniels, while you do your shopping? When you've finished, Henry here will escort you and the money to the cab stand over the road.'

'Thank you.' We shook hands and parted.

It was a relief to hand over *The Mountfalcon Heiress*. It was good, I knew that. I was getting into my stride with my books, becoming more confident. I could see no reason why Mr Robinson should not like it.

In the bookshop up the road, I found a child's version of *Gulliver's Travels* with crude, but pleasing, woodcut illustrations. I then went to the toyshop and bought a small cannon, which fired dried peas. Richard would like that, I thought.

When I came out of the toyshop, St Paul's clock said ten past one. Barely afternoon, yet already the day was closing in. The sky was a thick, yellowy grey. It looked as though it might snow. The temperature was scarcely above freezing, and the wind which swept down Ludgate Street was icy.

Paternoster Row was closed to traffic, so at least I didn't have to leap to avoid carts, cabs and other traffic. On the south side the shops were more elegant. I noticed several mantua-makers and haberdashers. I thought suddenly of buying a small fairing for Hannah, a pretty length of pink ribbon, perhaps. I could buy nothing for Noël — it would be most improper to do so. I rather wished I might give him a copy of *The Castle of Apollinari* or *The Doom of the House of Ansbach*. I realized that I wanted his approval of my writing, but I couldn't risk him knowing about them, not if there were the slightest possibility that he would tell Stephen. Anyway, he would probably despise them as frivolous.

I went into a haberdashers for the pink ribbon. Whilst I was there I saw a bale of oyster-coloured surah, which was reduced in price. All of a sudden I longed for it. I could just picture how I would make it up. I had noticed the dresses in London, with their new gores, beside which my old gowns seemed dowdy and old-fashioned. In the end, feeling guilty that I was spending money on myself, rather than paying Mrs MacLaren, I bought a dress length of the oyster surah and carried it back to Mr Robinson's in triumph.

Henry duly escorted me to the cab stand, gave me my fifty pounds discreetly wrapped and left.

'Where to, miss?' asked the cabby.

'The Adelphi. John Street.'

Home?

* * *

I ate a solitary luncheon served, with a barely disguised contempt, by Mary. The house seemed unnaturally silent. The servants had finished their morning's cleaning and were downstairs, doubtless glad to be in the warmth of the kitchen. The usual city sounds of rattling carts and the clatter of cabs and carriages were muted by the snow. The costermongers and street sellers had disappeared. Ice had formed along the shores of the river and various small boats, whose owners had not dragged them above the tide line, were now frozen in. The poor wretches who lived rough under the Adelphi Arches must be miserable, I thought.

Noël and the unknown Jem Bagnigge were, presumably, in Noël's room. Nobody stirred.

I was in that strange limbo between books. I can never settle to the next one until I know that the previous one is safely off my hands. It would be a week or so before I knew the fate of *The Mountfalcon Heiress*.

As there was nothing else to do and nobody to stop me, I decided to cut out the material I had bought. I found a workbox, presumably Mrs Beresford's, in one corner of the drawing-room, and inside were pins, tailor's chalk, scissors and everything I needed. It gave me a warm feeling to be using her sewing things, as if she were looking down and blessing my endeavours. I moved back the chairs and spread out the length of oyster surah.

I had, perforce, made my own clothes for years. At first, I'd unpicked old ones and used them as templates, but I had a good eye and was soon able to do it freehand. Since coming to London, I realized how old-fashioned my gowns were. Waists were now higher and bodices more shaped. My new oyster surah was a heavy Indian silk, suitable for evening wear. Noël, naturally, changed for dinner, and last night I had been ashamed of my shabby brown merino.

I was glad to be moving, even if only crawling about the floor pinning material. Away from the fire, the room was chilly, and I could feel a draught coming in from the window. All the same, it was much warmer than at Cant's Close, and at least I could put another coal on the fire, if I wished.

Time passed. Eventually, Hannah came in to light the lamps and candles and close the shutters. The heavy curtains cut out the draught. Soon, the room would warm up for the evening.

'Oh, Miss Emilia, isn't it lovely?' she exclaimed, bending to stroke the material.

'It's the most expensive material I've ever bought,' I confided. 'But it was reduced, so . . .'

'It's worth it, I'm sure,' said Hannah enthusiastically. 'I do love a bargain, myself.'

'Most females do, I think,' I said smiling. Hannah's approval gave me confidence.

When she had gone, I got down on my hands and knees and started cutting. The afternoon passed quietly and I hardly noticed the time. I was just marking the darts when the door opened. I thought it was Hannah checking on the coal scuttle and I didn't look up.

'What on earth are you doing?'

It was Noël. I rose and brushed myself down. Threads of oyster silk were clinging to my gown and I tried to pick them off.

'Dressmaking, as you can see. I went out this morning to buy Richard a Christmas present and I passed a haberdasher's on the way. I only brought two gowns with me, so my wardrobe needed replenishing. This is the result.'

'But, my dear Emilia . . . ' Noël seemed at a loss for words. He came in, leaning heavily on his stick, and sat down.

'I'm sorry to use your drawing-room floor. There was really nowhere else.'

'It's not that.'

I bent to pick up the pieces carefully, for I had pinned some of them together and I put them over a chair in the corner.

'I hope you don't mind my using your mother's workbox?'

'No, no. Not at all. Emilia, you mustn't do this.'

I laughed. 'Why not?'

'It's not fitting.'

'Really, Noël, every young lady has to be able to sew. Surely you should be pleased to see me so respectably employed!' I couldn't help teasing him a little. I could see what it was. He didn't like the poverty implied in my making my own clothes, but there was nothing he could do about it. A man could pay for the clothes of his *chère amie*, but he could never offer money to a lady.

'My mother left some clothes here, I think. They will still be in the wardrobe in her room. After her death, Aline dealt with the clothes at Ainderby Hall, but she hasn't been here. There won't be much, a London dress or two. You are most welcome to whatever you can use.'

'Thank you. That is kind. But won't Mrs Good see them as her rightful perquisites?'

'Nonsense. That's for the lady's maid and Céline has long gone to another post. Get Hannah or Mary to show you.'

I sat down and looked at him. He was drawn and pale and plainly in some pain. The two lines etched into his forehead above his nose were cut deeper. I wasn't sure whether Noël wanted his wound referred to.

'I met Richard this morning,' I said at last. 'He gave me a blow-by-blow account of the battle of Vittoria.'

'Good God, did he?'

'He's tremendously proud of you, Noël. He seems to know all about it and where you were on the battlefield. Your batman told him.'

'It was Jem who carried me off. God knows how he did it, for he's a small chap.'

I noticed that Noël did not comment on Richard's pride in him. Did he really not understand that his son looked up to him? That the child longed for some affection?

Perhaps he realized the omission, for he then said, 'How did you find Richard?'

'Lonely.'

Noël frowned. 'What else could I do? I'd send him away to school if he were stronger, then at least he'd have friends to play with. But he's so behind, I'm afraid he'd be bullied. I've been told he'll always be backward.'

I said nothing. Had he ever *talked* to his son?

Noël shifted uneasily in his chair.

'I scarcely know him,' he admitted. 'I've been on leave only once during the last four years and that was after my wife died. This last time, well . . . I returned home badly wounded to find George dead and the place in a mess. I haven't had the energy to deal with Richard. I'm not sure what I have to offer him, anyway.'

I couldn't help myself, 'At least you have a child!' I burst out. 'I miscarried with both of mine.'

There was a long pause then Noël said quietly, 'I'm sorry.' He reached for his stick and pulled himself to his feet. 'I'm not fit company today, I only came to see how you were. I shan't be dining downstairs, Jem will give me something in my room. I'll see that Mrs Good looks after you.' As he reached the door, he turned and said, 'I was worried when I heard you'd gone out, I thought you'd fled again. I was a bit crusty yesterday, Emilia. I apologize, and I'm glad you've come.'

When he'd gone I sat staring into the fire for some minutes. It warmed my heart that he was pleased I was there — my presence had been a pleasure to so few people in my life. All the same, I reminded myself that Noël would hardly be pleased to know that his guest was the author of two, possibly three, sensational novels full of murder and intrigue. I thought of one episode where the sinister Fra Bartolomeo pursues Angelina Mountfalcon which now struck me as almost scandalous.

Pray God Noël never found out.

4

I was used to quiet Christmases — in Scotland it is little celebrated, Hogmanay being the preferred festival, but this Christmas in John Street was almost funereal. True, Mrs Good, Mary and Hannah produced a side of beef and roast potatoes, followed by plum pudding, but everything else was missing. There were no decorations, not even a bit of holly.

Richard stayed upstairs and seemed genuinely pleased, not to say astonished, by his presents. Noël had given him a writing desk, which Miss Carter had placed on top of the bookshelf, where it would probably stay. It was so obviously a 'duty' present, that I was hard put to find a suitable comment. In the end, I simply said that it would be useful when he grew up. Richard accepted *Gulliver's Travels* politely, but the toy cannon was another matter.

'Oh!' he cried. 'Oh!' He jumped up and down in his excitement and hugged himself. Then rushed over and hugged me for good measure.

'Have you thanked Mrs Kirkwall?' asked

Miss Carver, sourly.

Richard looked stricken.

'Yes, he's thanked me,' I said, smiling at him. 'I couldn't ask for better thanks.'

Hannah was touchingly grateful for her ribbon. Mrs Good thought such things flighty, she confided, but she'd keep it against the time she returned to Ainderby. She had a young man in the village and she'd wear the ribbon when they stepped out together after church on her Sunday off. I was pleased Hannah had a follower; I hoped he was worthy of her.

Noël was largely absent. His wound was in the painful process of yielding up more shrapnel.

I spent the next few days going through Mrs Beresford's clothes with Hannah. There were a number of chemises and petticoats, which I pounced on, and some cotton stockings. There was also a length of printed cotton with pink flowers on it, which I gave to Hannah. 'So that you can dress up for your young man,' I told her. I had noticed that Mrs Good often picked on Hannah; she deserved something pretty to make up for it. Of the gowns, two were summer cambrics and I put them to one side. There were two warmer gowns, a walking dress in green merino and a day dress in a warm grey kerseymere. They were far too large for me, but I could alter them. There was also a dark-grey hooded mantle, rather worn, but certainly of a better quality than my own.

With Noël's permission, I had Richard downstairs for an hour at tea-time when we read together. He liked to snuggle up next to me and follow my pointing finger as I read. It was the cuddles he wanted, poor boy, even if he had to do some reading as well.

After some initial reluctance, the story of Gulliver in Lilliput began to fascinate him. Maybe it does all children. It's the pleasing notion that one might suddenly become a giant in a country where everybody else is tiny. Richard was small for his age; I could see that the idea might prove intriguing.

'The Lilliputians were silly, weren't they? Going to war over which way up you should eat your egg.'

'Perhaps people sometimes do go to war for foolish reasons.'

'Lord Wellington hasn't,' said Richard stoutly. He sat thoughtfully for a moment, leaning against me. 'Miss Carver won't let me go to sleep during the sermon in church. She keeps poking me awake. Now that's silly. If the vicar wanted me awake, then he should make his sermons shorter.'

I laughed. 'I agree with you. I used to feel

110

just the same. And just when you thought he was finishing, he'd turn the hour glass over and go on.'

Inside the house, icy draughts whistled down the landings in spite of the door curtains. I was glad of Mrs Beresford's warmer gowns. Outside the weather worsened. On 27 December the fog came down and stayed for several days. It was still bitterly cold, but now it was dark too. Looking out of the window, even at midday, was like looking into a brown soup. The fog was impenetrable, thick and heavy. Nobody went outside, for it was impossible to see more than a yard or so in front of one.

Gaslights remained unlit, for the lamp-lighters couldn't find them and, in any case, the fittings were frozen. Occasionally, you could hear the muffled hoot of a lighter on the river. Generally, though, all was silent and dark.

In the house, the lamps and candles were lit all day, for there was scarcely any difference between daylight and night-time.

At least, I thought, I must be safe from pursuit. It did not occur to me that other parts of the country might be fog free.

Fortunately, Noël's was a well-provisioned house. The coal cellar was full, so we were warm and we had enough to eat — unlike some of the poor wretches huddling in doorways outside.

Noël's wound yielded up another few bits of bone and shrapnel and he limped back into our lives. It was interesting to see how the household reacted to this. Mrs Good pursed her lips and said, 'The doctor told him he should have his leg off, but he wouldn't take advice and now see what happens. It'll end badly, you mark my words.' Mary and Miss Carver nodded agreement. Only Hannah and Abel seemed genuinely pleased that Noël was better.

As Noël was convalescent, Miss Carver wanted Richard to stay in the nursery for tea instead of coming downstairs. I wasn't having any of it. It was high time that Noël got to know his son, I thought. At first, I feared that I'd made a mistake, for Noël seemed uncomfortable having Richard in the drawing-room, but gradually he relaxed and I sensed a cautious enjoyment. Richard was plainly delighted and I noticed that he tried hard with his reading if he thought his father were listening.

We were now with Gulliver in Brobding-nag. Here Gulliver was a midget amongst huge people. Richard was very taken by Gulliver's fight with the wasp.

'I like the way it turns things topsy-turvy,'

he said, in his old fashioned way. 'You can be big and bad.'

I gave him a hug. 'What is important is what you are, not what size you are.' I wasn't sure how Noël would react to this heretical notion. Did he believe that children must be taught that adults always knew best? *Gulliver's Travels*, I thought, was a book that made you question things. That's what I liked about it. I had borrowed the original version from Noël's library and was reading it avidly.

'Teaching Richard to be a Radical, are you, Emilia?' asked Noël with a smile.

'I'm not,' I retorted. 'Dean Swift may be. But your son's quite bright enough to work it out for himself.'

Richard was looking from Noël to me anxiously. 'It's a good book, Papa,' he said earnestly. 'It's not a snare for the ungodly.'

We both laughed. Noël put out his hand and rumpled Richard's hair.

After the fog came the snow. I have never seen such snow. It came down solidly for days. Great drifts appeared in the streets and nothing could get through. Men appeared with shovels and cleared the pavements and a path down the middle of the road, but as fast as they cleared, more snow fell. The manholes to the drains were opened in an effort to get rid of it, but that only made things worse.

I read in *The Times* — some poor lad still managed to bring it — that the mail coaches throughout the country were struggling to get through. Many roads were impassable. The entire country seemed to be at a standstill. I hoped that poor Tolley, wherever she was, was warm and comfortable.

Stephen, I guessed, would spend his days in some tavern where the inn fire would keep him warm. Doubtless he would find some cronies to gamble with. I daresay he was fleecing them.

Noël sent Abel out to sweep the pavement in front of the house and to report on how things were outside.

'It feels like sending the raven out of the ark,' I commented.

Abel told us that the Thames was beginning to freeze over and that few boats could move. He was very excited about this. His granfer used to tell him tales of former frost fairs, he said, when there were booths on the ice and coaches could cross over from shore to shore. Abel obviously longed for the ice and snow to continue; he wanted another frost fair. The cold brought misery, too. I read in *The Times* that many watermen were starving now their livelihoods were gone. It was impossible to go out while it snowed so heavily and Noël and

I, perforce, began to talk.

'How bad are things with the plantation in Demerara?' I ventured one evening. Sound was muffled outside. Mrs Good had warned that we should economize on the candles and oil, so we sat in semi darkness with only a couple of candelabra on the mantelpiece in front of the looking-glass. It gave our situation a curious intimacy. Had things been normal I might not have asked the question.

Noël grimaced. 'Bad enough. It's all to do with growing sugar cane.'

'I don't know anything about growing sugar cane.'

'The processing is a complicated business. It is crushed, then boiled to a very high temperature and treated and the fire risk is high. Then there are all the associated trades, the milling, the cooperage, boat transport along the canals and so on.'

'Canals?'

'Yes. The Dutch first settled the country, it is linked by a most efficient system of canals.' He sighed. 'I wish George had never heard of Demerara.'

'What are you going to do?'

'Heaven knows. The devil of it is that it takes so long to communicate with the place.'

'Could you not just sell it?'

'Potentially, sugar is extremely profitable,

which is why George bought the estate, but it needs massive investment, not only in buildings and machinery, but in the extra slaves needed to work them. George borrowed heavily, using Ainderby as security. Bonne Chance the estate's called — God, how ironic. If I sell, it would be at a massive loss and Ainderby would still be heavily mortgaged with little hope of ever paying it off.'

'Do you have to grow sugar cane?'

'Unfortunately, yes. George's moneylender made that a condition. He wanted the highest possible return on his money, I suppose.'

'But that's outrageous!'

'It's not uncommon. But it means that I can't be content with a lower income and grow coffee, say, or indigo.'

'And the question of being a slave owner yourself?' I tried to keep my voice neutral. The Irvines and I had often discussed it and I had read articles on the treatment of slaves on the plantations. I found the whole idea of slavery repugnant.

'I've never really considered it. Beating Napoleon has taken up most of my thoughts. I can't honestly say that I have any great objections, though I wouldn't have chosen it. There have always been slaves, after all.'

'You . . . you can't mean that!' I looked at

him in horror. I had always thought of Noël as a good man, somebody on whose basic human decency I could always count. How could he possibly condone slavery?

Noël forced a laugh. 'Idealistic as ever, Emilia? People will always buy their coffee, cotton and sugar as cheaply as possible. If they don't get it from us, they will buy it elsewhere, from countries who do not have such tender scruples.'

'I don't care!' I exclaimed. 'To buy and sell other human beings is revolting.'

'I might be convinced by rational argument, Emilia,' said Noël, 'but not by such wild assertions.' There was an awkward pause, then he added, 'Ring the bell for Jem, would you? My leg's giving me trouble.'

Our moment of intimacy was over. When I went up to bed I realized I felt angry, upset and tearful. I knew Noël had his faults; he was ambivalent about his son, though he was trying; his wound could make him short-tempered, I could accept these, but I could not accept his apparent equanimity at being a slave-owner.

I was not going to leave it there. I would bring up the subject again when I had marshalled my arguments.

★ ★ ★

The year turned. It was 1814. In fifteen days I would be twenty-five. I had to get to Latimer and Briggs, my father's lawyers, as soon as possible. The snow fell only intermittently now, but it became even colder. On 3 January Noël reported that the temperature that night had been twenty degrees Fahrenheit, the coldest yet. It was to go lower.

I kept peering out of the windows trying to see whether the pavements were clear enough for me to pay a visit to Latimer and Briggs. I was worried about another thing: if the lawyers had to correspond with my father, would the letters have a hope of getting through? If there were no settlement, all my fortune would go to Stephen. I might shortly find myself with nothing, save what I could earn from my writing.

Rationally, I was fairly sure that my father's sense of justice would lead him to press Stephen for the traditional 'widow's third'. Would Stephen agree, or would Balquidder persuade him otherwise? I was desperate that something might be salvaged, for some safeguard against destitution, at least.

I was stuck indoors until 5 January, a Wednesday. I told Noël I wanted to see Latimer and Briggs and he offered to send Mr Bagnigge with me. I wanted to refuse, but

I didn't dare. Noël had reverted to seeing me as a tiresome schoolgirl and I didn't want to seem petulant and ungracious. It didn't cross my mind that Noël might be suffering from pangs of conscience after our disagreement about slavery.

I hadn't really met Mr Bagnigge before. He was a small, wiry man of about fifty, with a face like a walnut, all lined and brown. He had very dark, deep-set eyes, and his hair, or what was left of it, stuck up in two great tufts on either side of his head, giving him the look of a startled owl. He was astonishingly rude to anybody he didn't like — which included most women. I had overheard Tryphena Good saying she didn't know how the colonel put up with him.

He was devoted to Noël and had been with him ever since Noël joined up in 1806. It was Mr Bagnigge who had saved Noël at Vittoria, according to Richard.

Mr Bagnigge — I didn't dare call him 'Jem' as Noël and Richard did — had been to Latimer and Briggs's the previous day and arranged an interview for me. I had seen him stump off from the drawing-room window. From his demeanour as he stepped after me into the cab, he obviously thought I was nothing but trouble.

'Master Richard is very full of your account

119

of the battle of Vittoria,' I observed.

A grunt. Mr Bagnigge folded his arms and stared forbiddingly out of the window.

'Is the colonel's wound improving, do you think?' I tried next.

'It would, if he weren't worrited by things he hadn't ought to worrit about.'

'Meaning me, I suppose?'

'If the cap fits . . . '

'Look, Mr Bagnigge, this really won't do. I am here until this wretched weather eases, so you might just as well make the best of it.'

He turned to look at me, his tufty hair sticking up round the sides of his hat. He looked comical, but I knew better than to smile.

'I am not the colonel's problem, and you know it. It's this cursed Demerara business. Whatever can have possessed Mr George to do such a thing?'

'Mrs George buying all her fal-lals. I could see that one was trouble the moment she appeared.'

I made a face. 'Now there I agree with you.' It was most improper to be having this conversation with a servant, but Mr Bagnigge appeared not to notice. Did he speak to Noël like this?

'She wants to go back to France as soon as peace comes. Can't be too soon, I say.' Cross at agreeing with a mere female, he turned and glared out of the cab window.

Latimer and Briggs's offices were just north of St Paul's in Little Britain, a row of dirty houses which curved around from Aldersgate to the back of St Bartholomew's Hospital. Their office was slightly cleaner than the rest of the street, though still blackened by London dirt. There was a brass plate by the side of the door and a couple of window boxes, now piled high with snow. Long icicles hung down from the window ledges, giving the curious impression that the windows had grown hoary beards. Somebody had swept the front doorstep clear of snow.

Mr Bagnigge clambered out, let down the steps of the cab and paid off the cab. I saw him glance down the road to where the Saracen's Head stood invitingly.

'Why don't you return for me in half an hour?' I suggested. By sending Mr Bagnigge with me, Noël obviously wanted to keep an eye on me, but I wanted my business to be private.

Mr Bagnigge stumped off towards the inn, kicking the snow into the gutter as he went, and I went to the door with the brass plate and knocked. I was shown up to a handsomely appointed office where Mr Latimer greeted me with a brisk handshake and offered me a chair.

'I am sorry, Mrs Kirkwall,' he said without preamble. 'I can say nothing further to what I told your husband this morning.'

The blood drained from my face. Stephen here? But how? And where was he? I struggled to compose my features. 'Would you mind repeating what you said to him?'

'Your fortune passes straight into your husband's control on the fifteenth of this month. However, Mr Kirkwall, in arrangement with your father, has agreed to settle two hundred and eighty-eight pounds a year on you during your lifetime. Mr Daniels was not able to persuade him to allow you full control of your rightful third of the capital. Your whole fortune has, of course, increased considerably during your long minority and now stands at' — he consulted his notes — 'Seventeen thousand, four hundred and sixty-three pounds.'

'It's an awful lot of money,' I observed, shaken. Surely, Stephen should not begrudge me a third? That would be less than £6,000 and would leave him with nearly £12,000.

'The money comes from your mother's family, the Turnbulls. It was Mr Turnbull, your maternal grandfather, who drew up the original document. He doubtless envisaged a number of daughters to be provided for and assumed that your mother would have a longer life. He was a somewhat obstinate man, as I recall.'

'I don't remember him.'

'The result is that the entire fortune passes entirely to you and, naturally, as you are now married, to your husband. There was no marriage settlement and, legally, your husband cannot be forced to make one.' He sat back and surveyed me with a sort of gloomy relish.

'What happens if my husband dies first? After all, he is eleven years older than I.'

'Whoever is the main beneficiary of your husband's will must continue to give you your two hundred and eighty-eight pounds a year. You need not fear for that, Mrs Kirkwall.'

There was a knock at the door and a clerk entered. 'I am sorry to disturb you, Mr Latimer, but Mr Briggs begs a word with you urgently.'

'Excuse me a moment, Mrs Kirkwall.'

The moment the door had closed behind him, I jumped up and went round the desk to where I could see an open file and ran my eye down the page. Yes, thank God, an address: Mr Kirkwall, 12 Wych St, London E.C.

I heard footsteps coming back and hastily returned to my seat.

'Thank you for seeing me, Mr Latimer,' I said, drawing on my gloves. 'You have been very kind. I would be most grateful if you didn't mention my visit to my husband. Things are so . . . '

'I understand perfectly, ma'am.'

No you don't, I thought. 'One more thing, if you please. Was Mr Kirkwall alone when you saw him?'

He looked surprised. 'Yes, ma'am.'

I had much to think about as I went downstairs. I waited in a small office occupied by a couple of clerks perched on their high stools. They took no notice of me. I stood by the window and watched for Mr Bagnigge's return. Stephen staying at 12 Wych Street. Where was that? Had he come down with Balquidder? How had he got here in this appalling weather? Should I try and see him?

Mr Bagnigge returned in rather better temper; the attractions of the Saracen's Head must have cheered him up. This time in the cab it was I who was silent. I must find out whether Balquidder had come down to London as well, but that could be dangerous. I did not want to bump into him.

I wished I could confide in Noël.

I thought of asking Abel's help — I was pretty sure he would relish the adventure

— but decided that I couldn't risk it. If Noël learnt that Stephen were in London, then he would insist on my returning to him. For that reason alone, I couldn't risk telling Abel anything.

Then I thought, Mr Robinson! A bookseller would surely know where Wych Street was. I was due to be in touch with Mr Robinson on Friday, in two days' time. Abel could get me a cab. If questioned, I would say that I needed some trimming for Mrs Beresford's gowns, now altered to fit my smaller figure, and Mr Bagnigge would hardly be ordered to accompany me to the haberdasher's. I would find out the fate of *The Mountfalcon Heiress* and learn where Wych Street was. A returning cab could take me past it. I would look out for signs of it being a lodging-house or, as I feared, Balquidder's own.

The interview with Mr Latimer had clarified one thing: if I died first, then Stephen would get the entire fortune — with no strings attached. Any finger of suspicion on my sudden death would point at Stephen, not Balquidder.

But what if Noël found out? Latimer and Briggs dealt with the Beresford affairs as well, for old Mr Latimer had started business in Harrogate and had many clients in the North

Riding. Any number of casual remarks could betray me to Noël, however careful I was. I would look for lodgings as soon as I had my reply from Mr Robinson. God knows what I would do if he didn't want *The Mountfalcon Heiress*.

My respite from care and anxiety seemed to be over.

On my return, I found Noël and Richard in the drawing-room. Richard was sitting on the floor at his father's feet and demonstrating the cannon I had given him. I could see a number of dried peas on the carpet. He jumped up as I entered and Noël reached for his stick. I motioned them both to sit down.

Noël smiled at his son. 'Richard, ring for tea, please, and pick up all those peas.' The smile he gave me was cool. I couldn't help feeling that our conversation about slavery still rankled.

Hannah came in with the tea trolley. Richard had reached the age where he was always hungry and he eyed a plate of muffins hopefully. Noël put his hand on Richard's head for a moment and said, 'You look tired, Emilia. I hope everything was all right?'

'All very satisfactory,' I said brightly, busying myself with pouring tea. 'I can rely on an annual two hundred and eighty-eight pounds or so, which is considerably more than what I have been living on, so it is all something of a relief. Richard, sit down and I'll give you a muffin.'

Noël frowned. 'The whole fortune must be worth nearly eighteen thousand now, surely?'

'There's no point in dwelling on it.' I really did not want to talk to him about it. I had far too much to hide.

Noël opened his mouth to speak and then shut it again. 'It's a bad business,' he said at last.

I turned to look at Richard. He was sitting on a small stool as close as he could get to his father's chair. He, at any rate, was happy. Noël was making an effort with his son. He made some little joke about Richard's target practice with the dried peas and Richard grinned.

After tea I beckoned Richard over to hear him read. He had brought down a small book called, *Dame Trot and her Comical Cats* and slowly, with his finger pointing at each word, he read a page or two.

'You're improving,' I said, giving him a hug.

Richard looked across at his father, but Noël had picked up *The Times* and was absorbed. Richard blinked hard once or twice and shut the book. I longed to reassure him. I thought that Noël's withdrawal was probably more to do with his unease with me after our disagreement, than with Richard, but it was impossible to say anything.

Two days later, I crept out to see Mr Robinson. It was not too difficult to arrange. Noël never appeared at breakfast. He rarely slept well and it was understood that we met over luncheon at about two o'clock. I had my breakfast on a tray in my room and spent the mornings sewing or reading.

On the Friday, I dressed myself in one of Mrs Beresford's altered gowns, which was warmer than either of mine, and went down to the boot room to find Abel, who was usually cleaning oil wicks and filling lamps at this time of day.

'Abel, I need you to get me a cab again,' I said. 'I have to get some trimming.'

Abel put down his lamp with alacrity, reached for his cap and jacket and shot off. He was a lively lad and the enforced seclusion didn't suit him. When he returned with the cab, I gave him sixpence.

'The Thames is beginning to freeze over,' he told me, eyes shining. 'The cabby reckons there'll be another frost fair soon. It'll have stalls on it, Miss Emilia, and games and all sorts.'

'How exciting,' I said. I had no idea just how exciting and dangerous the frost fair would prove to be.

Abel went back inside and I climbed into the cab and gave the Paternoster Row address. Nobody was listening this time. If Mr Robinson's report were favourable, I would take the opportunity to return to Somers Town and look for cheap lodgings.

It would be a wrench to go, I realized. For the first time for years I was warm and fed and didn't have to worry about Mrs MacLaren's rent or persuading Eppie to smuggle up some inferior coal. My chilblains were healing. I was even putting on a bit of weight. I could still see all my ribs, but I noticed that my stays needed loosening a fraction.

I hadn't made an appointment to see Mr Robinson, but he didn't keep me waiting more than a moment or two. There was something immensely reassuring about seeing that nutcracker face and those startling bushy eyebrows again. Here, at least, was one man who took me seriously.

'I like *The Mountfalcon Heiress*,' he said, the moment we were in his office. He is probably used to anxious authors, I thought. 'I can offer you two hundred pounds for the copyright.'

I could manage on that. It would keep me for a year whilst I wrote another book. I

129

might even be able to save something, if Somers Town weren't too expensive. I realized that I would never be able to claim the £288 a year from my mother's fortune — not if I wanted to live.

'Thank you. I accept.'

After some discussion, Mr Robinson agreed to take over Mr Irvine's role as my banker. 'I shall get my clerk to draw up the agreement for your signature, Miss Daniels. Would you care to wait?'

'I shall return next week,' I said hastily. 'I hope to have a proper address by then.' I forgot to ask him about Wych Street — it was not the only mistake I was to make that day.

'Very well.' He ushered me downstairs and opened the door for me.

I had to cross the front of St Paul's to get to the cab stand on the other side. The cobblestones were treacherously icy, and I turned up my veil to see where I was going. I was just passing the statue of Queen Anne, when I heard a shout.

'Emmy!'

I pulled down my veil and tried not to quicken my pace.

'Emmy!' There was a sound of running feet and my arm was grabbed.

Stephen was alone. He looked wild, hunted almost. 'My God, Emmy, what are you doing here? I thought you were at your father's.'

'No, I'm here.'

He looked round and gestured to the coffee house behind him. 'Quick, in here.'

'I can't go into a coffee house, Stephen.' Only men went into coffee houses.

He pulled me up St Paul's steps and into the gloom of the cathedral. A bored verger was standing by the door. Stephen pushed past, dragging me after him. He manoeuvred me into a side chapel and we sat down in a far corner.

I untied my bonnet strings. 'What is the matter?' I knew Stephen well enough to realize that his personal interest in me was very small. He was far more concerned about his own problems.

'For God's sake, Emmy, you should be at Tranters Court.'

'Why?' Something was very wrong.

'Oh God, I wish I'd never seen you.'

'You didn't have to stop me just now.'

'No, I mean, I wish we'd never met. You just don't know ... ' Stephen lurched forward and buried his face in my shoulder. I patted him soothingly. 'I tell you, Emmy, things are so desperate, you don't know.'

'It's my fortune, isn't it?'

Stephen looked away.

'Come on, Stephen. It's the five thousand

you owe Balquidder.'

'Oh, Emmy! I'm sorry. I meant to pay you back every penny, truly I did.' I waited. 'It's that damned interest, Emmy. Balquidder charged me fifteen per cent — it's a lot less than some of the bloodsuckers charge. But I didn't realize how it would mount up. I thought he was my friend. Oh God, I owe him over seventeen thousand five hundred pounds and now he wants it, every penny.'

I was shocked. It was an enormous sum. Surely, with a friend, Balquidder should be content with regaining his capital? But even as I thought it, I realized I was being naïve. From the moment Stephen had told Balquidder about my fortune, and the fact that I was a minor, he was doomed. Balquidder had always meant to get his hands on all the money and he must have been furious at the eight-year delay until I was twenty-five. He certainly wouldn't want me to have a third of it. Even with all my fortune, Stephen would still be in debt.

'But Stephen, if you owe Balquidder everything I have, why have you settled money on me? You cannot afford it.'

'I could do nothing less, Emmy. It's your money. You are entitled to the income from your third, you know.'

Poor muddled Stephen. Appearances were

always important to him. He wanted to be seen as a man who did the right thing. Balquidder would never honour such a commitment, but Stephen would conveniently ignore that. Mr Latimer had doubtless said something pleasant to him and Stephen had been able to think of himself as being a gentleman.

'You know perfectly well that I shall never get a penny of it,' I said in exasperation. I was sick and tired of Stephen's fantasies.

'That's why you must go to your father, Emmy. I'm . . . I'm afraid for you.'

'You mean what Balquidder will do?'

'Of course, he's only joking when he says that . . . ' He stopped.

No, he wasn't, I thought. If Stephen were taking it seriously, Balquidder must have hinted several times that I should be got out of the way. 'But what about you?' Surely Stephen's own life was in almost as much danger as mine? If something happened to me, Balquidder would place no reliance on Stephen's ability to hold his tongue.

'What does it matter about me? I tell you, Emmy, I wish I had the courage to end it all. Then the whole damn lot would be forfeit to the crown.'

'You mustn't think like that!' I'd never

heard Stephen speak in so wild a fashion. 'Surely there's a way out?'

Stephen shook his head. 'No, I've signed things.' He paused and then said, 'Where are you staying, Emmy?'

I hesitated.

'I shan't tell Balquidder.'

'Oh Stephen, when did you ever not tell Balquidder everything?'

Stephen said nothing. Then he said sulkily, 'I suppose a man may ask his wife where she is living. Have you got a rich lover, Emmy, is that it? Someone who can give you all the things I can't?'

'Don't be ridiculous,' I snapped. 'Who would have me?'

'I don't recognize this gown.'

'It was Mrs Irvine's,' I lied. I could feel the tell-tale colour rise in my cheeks, I've never been good at lying. 'Look, you can see where it's been altered to fit me.' I should have given him a false address, I thought. Stephen's curiosity about me was rarely aroused, but he was quite capable of pursuing something like a terrier after a rat, if he thought it might be to his advantage.

'Is Balquidder here, too?'

Stephen shook his head. 'He's coming down next week. If he can get here, that is.'

In time for my birthday.

'I can't complain,' said Stephen despairingly. 'He's explained it all. He needs that money for his slavers. You know he has slavers, or did when it was legal. He now has false papers, a fellow called Moxon did them. The ships are registered in Lisbon or some such place.'

Moxon, I thought. Where have I heard that name before? It hovered infuriatingly just at the edge of memory and I couldn't retrieve it. Perhaps it would come back if I talked about something else. 'How did you get down here? The weather's appalling.'

'So was my journey.' Stephen shuddered. 'I came down on the stagecoach, the day after Christmas. It took nearly a week, I thought I'd die of cold. We were stuck for hours several times.'

I was thinking quickly. It would be best if Stephen and Balquidder (for I never doubted that Stephen would tell Balquidder of our meeting) thought that I was at Tranters Court.

'I shall go to my father's. Balquidder can hardly get hold of me there. And neither must you. I'm sorry, Stephen, but I think we should have a formal separation.'

Stephen looked up, opened his mouth to speak, and then closed it again. Finally, he nodded.

I knew what I had to do. I took out the small notebook I always kept in my reticule and a pencil, handed them to him and dictated:

I, Stephen Kirkwall, agree to separate from my wife, Emilia Kirkwall, née Daniels.

Signed 5 January, 1814

S. Kirkwall. E. Kirkwall.

★　★　★

'There,' said Stephen sulkily, when he'd finished and we'd both signed it.

'Not quite.' I stood up and went to the side aisle. Two cleaners were polishing the pews. I beckoned and they came over. 'Can you write?' I asked.

They shook their heads.

'Very well. If you make your mark here as witnesses and give me your names and addresses, you will get sixpence each.'

They looked at each other and with one accord put down their cloths and beeswax. When they'd done I folded up the piece of paper and tucked it into my bodice. Stephen was looking unhappy.

'We . . . we had some good times, didn't we, Emmy?'

Good times? My marriage portion had been poverty, neglect and unhappiness. But I had also learnt self-reliance. I leaned over and kissed his cheek. 'Yes, Stephen.'

'You haven't got a shilling or two on you, have you?'

I reached in my reticule, deducted my cab fare and gave Stephen the rest, which came to about twelve shillings.

'Thanks.'

'I must go,' I said. Suddenly, I was exhausted. All I wanted was to get back to John Street and peace and quiet. Too much had happened too fast. I stood up.

'I think I'll stay here for a minute,' said Stephen.

'Goodbye and good luck.'

'And you, Emmy.'

At the doorway I turned round, but he was out of sight in the chapel. I pulled down my veil and went swiftly down to the cab stand.

Stupidly, it never occurred to me to look behind.

5

All the way back, I was wondering whether to confide in Noël. It was all becoming more complicated than I liked and, with Balquidder coming to London shortly, positively dangerous. I was held back by several things: Noël's determination that I should return to my husband; his tendency to see me as an impractical dreamer — he had not really returned to his former ease of manner with me after I had made my views on slave owners so disastrously clear; and my fear that he would not believe me about Balquidder. Coupled to this was a dread that it was my letter to his father all those years ago, begging him to use his influence to keep my fortune away from Stephen and thus Balquidder's slavers, that put George in touch with Balquidder. Noël might well blame me.

I was also cursing the weather which made everything so difficult. Mounds of filthy snow were piled up in the gutters, together with horse and dog droppings and every sort of filth. Starved and pinched beggars huddled in doorways. It was the paralysing cold that was the worst.

As the cab turned down John Street and the Adelphi wharf was in front of me, traffic on the Thames was almost at a standstill. The edges of the river were frozen and small boats stuck in the ice. Great ice floes floated about. It would be hazardous using the river just now, a boat could so easily be holed.

Opposite, on the south bank, I could make out kilns from the potteries; their bulbous shapes protruding from the rooftops were still belching out smoke. That would last whilst they had coal. At least the workers there would be warm.

The cab drew up and I climbed down and paid the cabby. Thank God nobody had missed me, I thought. I was wrong. The moment I opened the door, Noël came out of his study.

'Where the devil have you been?'

'Out.' I was stung. Was I some sort of prisoner?

'Why didn't you tell anybody?'

'I asked Abel to get me a cab. There was no mystery.'

'But where were you going in this weather? For God's sake, Emilia, people have been freezing to death outside. Haven't you been reading the papers?'

'I didn't realize that I was on parole,' I

snapped. 'And it's none of your business where I went.'

'This is my house,' stated Noël. 'While you're under my roof, you'll behave like an adult.'

'So I'm a child now, am I?' I retorted. 'How do you think it feels never to be trusted?' I turned on my heel and ran up to my room. I'm afraid I slammed the door.

In Edinburgh I might do what I liked and nobody cared. That had its own sort of loneliness, I admitted, but being treated like a naughty child was intolerable. It was true that Noël had listened to me when I arrived and offered me shelter, but he hadn't wanted to know about the real difficulties of my position. The moment the ice melted, he would send me back to my husband.

How could I explain that, in my eyes, both my father and my husband had failed me? I've no doubt that I was an impossible child, but that was not entirely my fault. Had my father been more sympathetic, things might have been different.

I have often thought about my falling in love with Stephen. I have come to the conclusion that a girl who has a loving father is not going to make the mistakes I did. She would have a template, as it were, of what a loving and honourable man was like. I had

had no such template and that had made me very vulnerable to Stephen's persuasions.

I could not expect Noël to agree with me. However much I had loved him as a child, there was much about him now that I didn't like: his attitude towards his slave plantation, for instance. His relationship with Richard was improving, but he was still ill-at-ease. I knew that pain and anxiety must often make him tetchy, but Richard was his son. He had fathered him, surely he could love him as well? And I couldn't stand the way he assumed that my father's behaviour was faultless.

I would be glad to get away. I'd had enough of being on suffrance in everybody's lives. I was not wanted here any more than I had been either at Tranters Court or Cant's Close. I was an adult, a published author, whose works were accepted by a reputable printer. At least I was respected there. Stephen had agreed to a separation. Noël was no relation to me and I had every right to live where and how I chose.

I changed out of my outdoor things and went down to the dining-room in a mood of some defiance. I was half-expecting to be alone but, to my surprise, Noël was there, looking serious.

Our luncheon was the usual informal meal.

Food was placed on the sideboard and we helped ourselves, or rather, Noël helped me to some cold pork and salad. The moment we sat down, he spoke.

'I'm sorry,' he said. 'I spoke too hastily. I forget that now you are a grown woman.'

'Thank you.' I wondered how long that would last. 'In return I will tell you that I met my husband this morning, quite by chance.' Even as I spoke, I realized how unlikely that sounded.

'You mean you just bumped into him?' Noël put down his fork and looked at me.

'No. It was the other way about. I had no idea he was in London and I would much rather he hadn't seen me.'

'I see. And?'

'We had a short conversation and he gave me this paper.' I took out the note of separation and handed it to him. Noël scanned it and handed it back.

'You do realize that this has no legal validity?'

'Very likely.' Frankly, I didn't care. I would leave Stephen anyway.

'A document in pencil is invalid. It could be altered.'

'True. But what shall we say now, Noël? You wanted to know what I have been doing this morning. I have told you and have

142

brought the only evidence I can. I do not usually carry a quill and ink horn around with me.' I was not going to be bullied any more.

'What do you want me to do?'

'Nothing.'

'Nothing? But — '

'Will you please listen to me for once? I am not your responsibility. In due course I shall make my own arrangements. I would prefer to do so when this dreadful weather has passed, but, if you wish me to go sooner, I shall do that without fuss.'

'Of course you must stay. I never meant to suggest . . . but, Emilia . . . '

'There are no 'buts',' I said earnestly. 'Please understand me, Noël. I believe Stephen is willing to let me go and I have every intention of leading a sober, retired and respectable life without him.'

'But your father?'

My father again, I thought. 'Do you really think, in your heart, that my father cares what I do?'

'Yes, I do.'

'Well, I'm sorry, but I don't. I cannot think of a single occasion when he ever expressed any fondness for my society or a wish to understand me better.'

There was silence. Noël pushed a piece of

meat around his plate.

'I cannot deny that he is a remote figure and might well have intimidated a young girl, but I am convinced of his concern for you. I saw him after you eloped. He was beside himself with anxiety.'

'You should see the letter he wrote me,' I said acidly.

'I take it that you are thinking of taking some rooms somewhere?'

'Yes.'

'Wouldn't that be compounding your mistakes? I'm thinking only of your comfort. Have you thought how lonely it would be? Nobody of your own kind to talk to, only lodging-house-keepers and people of that sort. Besides, I'd miss you.'

I laughed. 'How on earth do you think I lived in Cant's Close? I associated almost entirely with 'people of that sort' as you put it, and, do you know, I found them quite human. The only 'gentlemen' I met were my husband's detestable friends.' All my bitterness came surging back.

'I see.'

'I doubt it,' I said. He didn't want to know my side of things. He had never asked me anything about my life in Edinburgh. I felt angry and misunderstood. It never occurred to me that Noël's failure to question me might be out of respect for my privacy.

Eventually, I mentioned that the Thames was beginning to freeze and Abel's hopes of a frost fair. The conversation turned.

Two days later, Richard was kidnapped.

It had stopped snowing and, for once, the day was bright, though still bitterly cold. Richard and Miss Carver went out for a short walk to look at the Thames. Richard, too, had heard stories of frost fairs and begged Miss Carver to take him down to see how the Thames was getting on.

Miss Carver arrived back alone and hysterical. I was sitting in my room working on the plot for a new book, when I heard voices. In no time, it seemed, the hall was full of people. I could hear Tryphena Good and a wailing Hannah, then Mr Bagnigge's voice and Noël's. I closed my book, locked it away, and went downstairs.

At last, some sort of story was prised out of Miss Carver. Two rough men had jumped out of nowhere by the Adelphi steps and bundled a screaming Richard into a waiting carriage and fled. Poor Miss Carver was still shaking.

'What could I have done?' she kept wailing. 'It all happened so fast.'

She had shrieked for help and two of the Adelphi watchmen came running, only in time to see the carriage turn into the Strand.

Children were taken, I knew, especially well-to-do ones. Usually, they were stripped of their clothes and money and set free. Here, the use of a carriage suggested something more serious. Whoever was behind this had planned it carefully — and that took money.

Had this anything to do with my meeting Stephen? For the first time, I realized that he might have followed me home. He could easily have hailed a cab and trailed me — after all, I had given him most of my money. But why on earth would Stephen want to kidnap Richard?

I knew why: Balquidder must be in London.

He could easily know Noël. If my fears were well founded, then George had acquired his Demerara estate through Balquidder's agency and it was Balquidder, therefore, who held the mortgage on Ainderby and to whom Noël now owed money. If Stephen had my address, it was inconceivable that he would not have told Balquidder, who would have recognized it instantly.

Of course, it was not difficult to buy a plantation in the West Indies. The country was full of men who had made their fortunes there — had I not read as much in the papers when Mr Irvine and I had discussed the Anti-Slave Trade bill? All the same, the possible connections between Balquidder and the Beresford Demerara estate struck me as being ominously coincidental.

Once Balquidder had got his claws into George, he would aim to squeeze him dry. If George had died owing Balquidder money, then Balquidder would screw it out of Noël. He would not scruple to kidnap Richard — but why?

It must be to do with me. I was quite sure that Noël would not be defaulting on the interest, whatever it cost him. No, Balquidder would keep out of the way. Stephen would use Richard to put pressure on Noël for my return.

All the same, it was a dangerous game for Balquidder to play. For a distraught husband to seek the return of his erring wife was one thing, for a businessman to indulge in kidnapping the son of a man in Noël's position in life, quite another. If his involvement became known, then he would be arrested within days.

But I had no proof.

What should I tell Noël? Would he even listen to me?

If I were right, then surely Richard would be at Wych Street? I didn't think that Balquidder would harm him, but the poor child must be very frightened. I couldn't bear to think of him fearing that he might never get home again.

The hubbub in the hall died down. Noël took Miss Carver into his study and the servants dispersed. Mr Bagnigge went off to call the officers of the law. I hesitated. Finally, I knocked on the study door.

'Come in.' Noël's voice was curt.

'I think I may know . . . ' I began.

'Not now, Emilia. Later.'

I left. I couldn't wait around to convince Noël. Whatever was going to be done would have to be done by me, and soon. If I'd been Angelina Mountfalcon, I'd have been noble and given myself up to Balquidder at once. I was pretty certain that that would have freed Richard. But it would be signing my own death warrant, and I am not the stuff of which martyrs are made. No, I had to try and see Stephen and find out if Richard were indeed at Wych Street.

The problem was that Stephen was as leaky as a sieve. He would tell Balquidder.

I needed some help. I thought of Mr Bagnigge. He would be a good man in a crisis, but I knew he had no time for me. Then I considered Abel, he was a bright lad and Richard liked him. Could he help? Would he be willing to do so without alerting the whole household?

Abel, at fourteen, was the youngest of the servants and I had heard Mrs Good bossing him about. He seemed to be at everyone's beck and call. Such a bright and lively lad must surely resent it. Yes, I would swear him to secrecy and confide in Abel. I daresay he'd enjoy it. I was well aware that the household had been awash with rumours about me. I didn't think I'd be telling Abel much about myself that hadn't already been discussed at length downstairs. It was the information about Balquidder that nobody knew.

I went down to the boot room. Abel spent most of his mornings there and, at night, slept on a mattress that was rolled up under the lamp table during the day. He was sitting glumly on his stool, staring down at a pair of Noël's boots he was supposed to be cleaning. He jumped up as I came in.

I closed the door. 'Abel, can you hold your tongue?'

'Yes, miss.'

I took a deep breath and told him what I feared had happened. 'Mr Balquidder is a creature of habit,' I finished, 'he never leaves his house until about midday, and my husband is certainly never up in the mornings. I think both of them will still be in Wych Street.' I sighed, for I realized that Abel had listened to me as Noël had never done and that hurt. 'The colonel doesn't take me seriously, and I could be wrong, but I am finding these coincidences come too pat.'

Abel thought for a moment and then said, 'I knows Wych Street, Miss Emilia. 'It's behind the Strand. Full of dirty books and prints it is. No lady could go there.'

'But I need to see Mr Kirkwall.'

'I could go, miss, if you told me what this Mr Balquidder looked like. I could wait until I knew he was out of the way and then slip a note to your husband.'

I shook my head. 'He wouldn't answer it until he'd consulted with Mr Balquidder. No, Abel, I must take him by surprise. Of course, he'll tell Mr Balquidder afterwards, but I hope that before that we could persuade Colonel Beresford to do something.'

'Tell you what, Miss Emilia, you could dress up as a boy, like, and come along o' me. I have a suit that belonged to Bill, who was here afore me, I daresay it'd fit you.' He grinned cheekily; he obviously found the whole thing an adventure.

'Dress up as a boy!'

I was pretty excited myself. My first thought was that it would be a wonderful idea for my new book, provisionally entitled *The Secret of the Drakensburgs*. My heroine, Erminia, with her raven-dark hair, black eyes

150

and adorably straight nose, was going to be abducted by the evil Count Drakensburg. I'd been wondering how he could do this. If he forced Erminia to dress as his page it would solve a number of problems. My readers could then have all the thrill of my heroine doing something really shocking, without feeling that they had to condemn her for her immodesty.

But in reality? If anybody ever heard of my doing such a thing, any shred of reputation I had left would vanish. If Noël ever found out, he would be quite justified in sending me back to my father instantly.

'It might work,' I said thoughtfully. I wondered what Balquidder's plan was. I suspected he'd prefer to wait a day or so — if only to make Noël sweat. There was a streak of cruelty in Balquidder — I had not forgotten the baby sparrow.

It was now just after eleven o'clock. If Balquidder were the same creature of habit in London that he was in Edinburgh, we must make haste. I told Abel that we'd meet in the boot room in about ten minutes, and ran upstairs with Bill's suit. If asked, Abel would tell Mrs Good that he was going out with me.

One thing about dressing up as a boy, I realized, apart from the shocking sight of one's legs, was that it gave one a kind of freedom. I could be somebody different — one for whom all the rigidities and constrictions of being female did not apply. I tied my hair in a knot and tucked it down the back of my collar, and then pulled on the hat Abel had given me. I put on my own boots, took my long cloak and my purse and crept downstairs.

Abel was waiting for me, hovering by the boot room. From Noël's room I could hear male voices, doubtless the Runners. Nobody else was about, they were probably all downstairs.

We crept out of the front door and walked swiftly towards the Strand, grinning at each other like truanting schoolboys.

Wych Street was a narrow road with very old houses, some of them Tudor, for the upper storeys projected out over the lower. They reminded me of the houses in St Peter's Pend, where the Irvines lived. They were almost all booksellers and, as Abel had said, the prints in the windows showed their clients' interests well enough. There was one print which, frankly, looked anatomically impossible.

Poor Abel was squirming with embarrassment beside me. At least, I thought, Erminia wouldn't have to put up with this lewdness, though I could probably indulge in a hint or two as to the dark proclivities of Count Drakensburg.

I had described Balquidder to Abel and it was only fifteen minutes or so after we arrived (a couple of smutty young men looking in the print shop windows was ample disguise) that Abel nudged me.

'That your cove, miss?' he whispered.

I glanced round. There was no mistaking the huge rolling figure. I shuddered; just to see him made my mouth go dry with fear.

I nodded.

'Should we follow him?'

'You could,' I said, as Balquidder walked away from us, elbowing aside anyone who was in his way. 'Be careful, Abel. Don't be deceived — he is dangerous.'

Abel grinned. 'Don't fret, miss. I can tag him so as he won't notice a thing.'

I was left alone in Wych Street. Now what? I moved along to another print shop and studied a print satirizing Prinny. His mistress, could it be Mrs Fitzherbert? was sitting on his knee twiddling his epaulettes in a very suggestive manner. Eventually, I came to a decision. Balquidder was out. I would lose nothing.

I crossed over to number 12 and went down the basement stairs. I remembered just in time that I couldn't go to the front door

— it would be slammed in my face.

I was expecting there to be a number of servants and thought that I'd have to persuade or bribe a maid to take a message to Stephen, but there was only one grim-faced man. He was obviously drunk; I could smell it on his breath. He stank, too, of unwashed linen, and worse.

I dropped my voice and put on a Scottish accent.

'May I be speaking with Mr Kirkwall, if you please?'

''E's out.' He belched in my face.

'Where will he be?'

'Dunno.' He slammed the door. Through the small basement window I could see him sinking back in his chair and picking up a glass.

Odd, I thought. Surely, if Richard were here there'd be more than a drunken manservant? Was he drugged upstairs? Perhaps he wasn't here at all? I'd imagined Balquidder to have a comfortable home, with servants and good food. I'd never been invited to his home in Edinburgh but, from Stephen's description, it was very well appointed.

I felt depressed and turned to go. I crossed over the road and stood for a minute looking up at it. It was a tall, thin house, one of the few in the street that didn't have a shop on the ground floor. The windows were clean, the front doorstep free of snow; I couldn't puzzle it out.

The man's reply had indicated that Stephen had been there and it was certainly the address he'd given Mr Latimer.

I then remembered the coffee house Stephen had tried to pull me into near St Paul's. Stephen had always liked his local tavern or coffee house. Would he be there? Somewhere I heard a clock strike half past the hour. I had the time. I would go and see.

I set off up the Strand towards Ludgate Hill. The main roads had been cleared, after a fashion, and snow was piled high in the gutters, but it was possible to walk, with care.

I was extremely conscious of my legs but, of course, nobody noticed me. Young boys, I realized, like old women, are practically invisible — indeed far safer, because pickpockets assume they are nimble and they have no money beside.

The coffee house was called The Palm Tree and, as I peered cautiously through the windows, I could see no sign of either Stephen or Balquidder. It looked respectable enough. There were a number of tables and benches and gentlemen were sitting quietly, some reading newspapers, others chatting.

155

Then I noticed a man going up a narrow flight of stairs to the left of the bar, where a handsome wench distributed drinks and coffee.

What was upstairs? God forbid it was a bawdy house.

Pulling my hat well down, I sauntered in and over to the bar. A couple of men looked at me curiously — I must have been the youngest customer they'd ever seen — but then they resumed their conversation.

'I've been sent to find a Mr Kirkwall,' I said, trying to deepen my voice and wishing that it didn't tremble. 'Is he here?'

The barmaid shrugged, 'You could try upstairs. Only don't disturb him if he's playing. Gentlemen don't like that.'

Gambling, I thought. I might have guessed. Upstairs, I found a long room with a polished oak floor and green baize-covered tables with lamps on them. There was the concentrated hush of the gamblers' den. I wandered round quietly and kept a wary eye open for Balquidder. I would not risk meeting him, even to see my husband. Then I spotted Stephen. He was in a corner with a bewigged man in an old-fashioned skirted coat. I stood and watched. Stephen was giving the game the sort of concentration he rarely had for anything else. There was a small pile of

156

guineas beside him and he was obviously doing well. Cheating, I wondered?

He looked up and blenched.

'What the devil are you doing here?'

'I've a message for you.'

'Well, sit down and be quiet. We've nearly finished and I don't want to be disturbed. Your turn, sir.'

Typical Stephen. He did not notice that I wore trousers underneath my cloak, nor that there was anything odd about my being in The Palm Tree at all.

The game ended. Stephen scooped up his winnings, shook his opponent's hand and came towards me.

'I need a drink,' he said. 'Let's go downstairs.'

We found a vacant table in a corner and Stephen hailed a waiter. 'A pint of beer.' He glanced towards me.

'Coffee,' I said. I had no idea what to ask for, but at least in a coffee house I ought to be able to get coffee.

'Why did you follow me the last time we met?' I demanded.

Stephen laughed. 'What else did you expect me to do?'

'That's no answer.'

'Oh, come on, Emmy. You're my wife. Besides . . . '

'Besides?'

Stephen picked up his beer and drank thirstily. 'If you really must know, I knew Balquidder wanted to know where you were. Dammit, Emmy, I was concerned for you.'

'So what can I expect?' I asked. 'A morning visit?'

'Balquidder wants to surprise you. Don't know what he has in mind. Maybe he's planning something for your birthday.'

Stephen seemed to have forgotten any warning he'd given me.

'So what's Balquidder doing in London, then?'

'I don't know. I hardly see him. He has dealings with this printer fellow he knows. He doesn't talk much about his affairs. You learn not to ask.'

He doesn't know anything about Richard, I thought. I knew Stephen. If he'd known Richard was in Wych Street, he'd be trying to hide it from me, but I could always tell when he was being evasive. He had this habit of pulling at his ear when he was lying. There was no ear-pulling today.

'Look, Emmy.' Stephen leaned forward. 'Come back with me, eh? You're my wife. A wife's place is by her husband. I'll see you right with your fortune. We'll move out of

Cant's Close.' He gripped my wrist. A strong grip.

Belatedly, I realized my danger. Stupidly, I had assumed that I could handle Stephen, but if he chose to make it a show of strength, there was no doubt who would win. I thought of Erminia. What would she do? Faint probably. My readers expect my heroines to faint — it shows their sensibility. As a tactic in The Palm Tree coffee house, however, it would be completely useless.

I looked up at Stephen from under my lashes in a way I hadn't done for years. 'I've missed you,' I said softly. I touched his foot with mine under the table.

'Of course you have.' Stephen released my wrist and sat back, smiling. He mouthed me a kiss, just as he used to do when we first met.

'I couldn't bear to go back to Cant's Close.'

'We'll look for something else the moment we get back,' Stephen promised.

Balquidder didn't mean me to get back — a fact that Stephen was conveniently ignoring. I had to get out of there. Just then a couple of men came up, weaving their way drunkenly through the tables. Stephen obviously knew them, for he raised his glass.

I stood up. 'I'm just going to pluck a rose,' I whispered. 'I'll be back in a minute.'

Stephen nodded. I walked over as casually as I could towards the barmaid, who directed me towards the privies in the yard. When I got out there, I found several doors, but the yard was enclosed. There was no outlet. As I was frantically wondering what to do, a man with a small handcart came through one of the doors. Surely that led somewhere? Anywhere. He went into the back entrance of the coffee house and I darted to the door. I found myself in a small alley, took to my heels and fled. Fortune was with me, I came out in Little Bridge Street, and eventually picked up a cab by Temple Bar and fell back against the squabs, my heart racing.

Back in John Street, no one was on hall duty and I slipped up to my room without being seen. Once I'd changed back into something decent, I went downstairs and found Abel in his boot room. He was relieved to see me and he was big with news.

'I think I've found him, miss!' he said, grinning from ear to ear.

'Where?'

'It's a printers in Crane Alley, behind Three Cranes Wharf.'

Moxon's, I thought. I'd suddenly remembered the name Mr Robinson had told me. 'Go on.'

'I followed the fat cove and that's where he went. Squalid sort of place. I could hear him talking with this other geezer, some name like Oxen. I couldn't hear much but the fat cove said, 'I want the boy kept out of sight', so I knew he was there.'

At least he's alive, I thought thankfully.

'Whereabouts is Master Richard, Abel? Did you find that out?'

'I don't exactly know, miss, but I guess he's upstairs. Downstairs is just the printing press and an office and I could see a ladder going up. It'll be a storeroom, seemingly.'

'Will somebody be there overnight with Master Richard?'

'I should think so, miss. He's only little.'

I recounted my adventures briefly, then said, 'I think this Oxen you heard is probably Moxon.' I told him how I thought he knew Balquidder. 'I wonder if this Moxon lives there?'

Abel shook his head. 'I asked a couple of lightermen down by the wharf and they said he has a house in Holywell Street, next to Wych Street, Miss Emilia.'

I wouldn't put it past Balquidder to deal in obscene prints as well, I thought.

'There's an apprentice lad and an old biddy who comes, though I don't know whether she sleeps there.'

161

'I daresay she would for a shilling or two,' I said.

'So now what, miss?'

'We tell the colonel. What else can we do? We can't rescue Master Richard ourselves. Any attempt has to succeed the first time.' Abel was only fourteen and I was a female. Neither of us would be any match for a full-grown man. We couldn't risk failure.

Abel looked disappointed, but said, 'The colonel's had a fall, miss. He slipped on the stairs when he was seeing off the officers.'

'Good God, is he much hurt?'

'He fell on his bad leg. Mr Bagnigge's with him.' He paused. 'It'll have to be Mr Bagnigge, Miss Emilia.'

'Oh, God!' I contemplated this in some dismay, but there was no help for it. There was nobody else. We decided that after luncheon I would ask Mr Bagnigge for a word. Abel would back me up. I was not looking forward to it. The prospect of facing Mr Bagnigge reminded me forcibly of awaiting the summons of my old governess, Miss Chase. My luncheon turned to ashes in my mouth and the palms of my hands were wet with nerves.

So, for the second time that day, I told my story. The three of us were in Noël's study, where we would not be disturbed. Mr

162

Bagnigge sat, arms folded, with a forbidding expression on his face. At least he listened. Every now and then he threw in some question. Finally, I finished and there was silence.

'Why didn't you say all this before?' Mr Bagnigge's tone was accusatory.

'I tried. The colonel wouldn't listen.' I was equally terse.

'Humph.'

Another pause. Abel and I looked at each other. Was Mr Bagnigge so shocked by my revelations of going out dressed as a boy, that he would refuse to believe a word I said?

Eventually, he spoke. 'The colonel said as you were a handful, Miss Emilia, and he was right.' His voice was stern. 'All the same, you're a plucky wench and no mistake.'

I looked up, startled. His features were still set sternly, but there was an amused twinkle in his eye.

'I know it was disgraceful,' I said humbly, 'but what else could I have done? I had to do something.'

'So you want me to rescue Master Richard?'

'I want you to help us,' I corrected.

'Not you, Miss Emilia. You'd be more trouble than you're worth.' He saw my look and added, 'You'd be dead meat. No, it must

163

be Abel and me and maybe a couple of useful men I know. And it must be tonight.'

'What do we do, Mr Bagnigge?' asked Abel eagerly.

'I'll have to think. I'm not doing anything hasty.' Again his face took on its forbidding expression and he stared into the fire for about ten minutes. Neither Abel nor I dared move.

'We must aim to be there at about three in the morning,' he said at last. 'The body's at its slowest then. Best time for a surprise. Seen it with the watch in Spain.' He glanced at the clock on the study mantelpiece. 'The colonel's asleep now so I can leave him for a couple of hours. I've a couple of old army mates who work in the stables at the Bell and I reckon they'll join us. We'll need a carriage nearby; Master Richard can't walk back and we may have to leave fast.'

'Is there anything I can be doing?' I asked. I was impressed by his quiet efficiency.

'You can see that Abel brings a warm coat for Master Richard. I'll get the colonel's brandy flask. Abel, go to bed dressed in something dark and warm and I'll wake you up when I need you. Until then, behave just as usual. Get some sleep if you can. It's going to be a long night.'

'What about the colonel?' I asked.

'I'll give him as much laudanum as he can hold tonight, he needs it anyway. But I'll leave him a note in case he wakes telling him to ask you.' Mr Bagnigge fixed me with an an ironic gleam. 'I daresay you'll cope with his crochets.'

Mr Bagnigge was out for most of the afternoon. I tried to continue normally, but it was impossible to settle to anything. I couldn't concentrate on *The Secret of the Drakensburgs*, I read half a chapter of a book and tossed it aside in disgust, I couldn't even do a small darn in the heel of my stocking without running the needle into my finger. In the end, I gave up. I sat in the drawing-room and stared into the fire.

Poor Richard, I kept thinking, how terrified he must be. He had such faith in Noël, but he was an intelligent little boy, he must also know that his father hadn't wanted him. I just hoped he believed that we would never leave him. I couldn't help thinking of myself at his age. If I'd been kidnapped, I'd have had very little faith in my father's bothering to recover me.

I dragged myself up to bed at the usual time, but, of course, I couldn't sleep. I think Mr Bagnigge must have gone out again, for I heard him returning shortly after midnight and later the creak of a floorboard as he and

165

Abel came into the hall. I got up, put on Mrs Beresford's dressing-gown and went downstairs.

'I just came down to wish you good luck,' I said.

'You go back to bed,' said Mr Bagnigge, eyeing my bare feet with disfavour. 'Come along, Abel.'

They left and I crept back to bed. I knew I wouldn't sleep, so I lit a candle, put some more coal on the fire and lay watching the flickering shadows on the walls, thinking about the day. Thank God I hadn't mentioned Richard to Stephen, I thought, otherwise he'd have run with it to Balquidder.

I heard a church clock strike one o'clock. It sounded muffled. There must be fog outside. As I listened, I heard a creak as of a door slowly opening. I sat up in bed, my heart pounding. Silence. I listened to the night sounds, old houses always made noises, I told myself. Then there was another creak and then, a quiet tap at my door. I shot up in bed.

'Who is it?'

Noël, face grey with pain, limped in. He held a candle in one hand and the shadow flickered over the wall as he came in. He shut the door and set the candlestick down on the mantelpiece.

'You shouldn't be up,' I said crossly, to hide my relief. 'And you certainly shouldn't be in here!' Mrs Good's room was on the floor above, I hoped that she was a heavy sleeper.

Noël ignored this. 'What the devil have you been up to, Emilia? Jem's left this note and I can't make head or tail of it. He says you've found out where Richard is.' There was a raw note of anxiety in his voice. 'For God's sake, tell me!'

I got out of bed and put on Mrs Beresford's dressing-gown and my slippers.

'Sit down, Noël.' If he had decided to ignore the impropriety, then I would, too.

For the third time that day, I told my story. I skated over my wearing boy's clothing and fortunately Noël was too tired and in pain to notice any inconsistencies. At last, I thought, he's listening to me.

'Let me get this straight,' said Noël. 'Abel heard Balquidder talking to Moxon saying that Richard was being held there, in Crane Alley?'

'Yes.'

'But why would Balquidder take Richard? He's only a little boy.' Noël's voice was raw with anguish.

'I can't be sure, but I think he wanted to use Richard as a bait for me. It was sheer chance which led Abel to follow him to

167

Moxon's — he must have thought the connection would never be known.'

'I'll see him rot in gaol for this.'

'If you could prove it,' I said quietly. 'Abel's word against Balquidder's? Which would the courts believe? I don't doubt that he has friends in high places.'

'We shall see.'

There was a long pause.

'Come here,' said Noël. I rose and moved across. He took hold of my hand and raised it to his lips. 'Thank you,' he said, simply. 'I haven't been fair to you, and I know it. It's this cursed leg. When the pain is bad I can't think straight; I know I get crochety, for Jem tells me so.'

I smiled at him. My world had righted itself. I wanted to take his face in my hands and kiss away those lines of pain and anxiety. I wanted to hold him close and give him what comfort I could. The longing was so strong that I had to hold on to the back of the chair to stop myself. Gently, I freed my hand and sat down again.

I knew well enough what I wanted and he must never know.

6

It was not easy for me to admit to myself that I was in love with Noël. If it hadn't been in the middle of the night, when one's feelings are less under control, I'd have tried to bury it again. I'd been in love before, and the results had been disastrous. Part of me longed for Noël as a lover but another part shied away from the shame and awkwardness I had felt with Stephen. Long-suppressed passions shot up to the surface. I wanted him, but I was also afraid. My emotions were a tumultuous tangle of desire and remembered humiliation from the past.

There was nothing I could do about it and I didn't know how to begin to sort it out. It was the wrong time and the wrong place. I was married to another man and Noël, unless I were mistaken, was still infatuated with Aline. It was all completely hopeless.

I remember at one point hearing three o'clock strike. Mr Bagnigge and Abel should be at Crane Alley now.

'It's the waiting,' said Noël.

'I know.'

'I'm so damned useless nowadays. Makes

me wish sometimes that the shell had put an end to it all.'

'Is it getting better? Your leg, I mean?' The dark allowed confidences.

'Very slowly. This weather doesn't help. I was lucky not to have lost it. For months I couldn't walk at all. It keeps throwing out splinters of bone as well as shrapnel, and that sets up an inflammation. It's not a pretty sight.'

'And the pain? Is it better or worse?'

'Depends. I take the edge off it with laudanum, but I don't like to use that too much. It makes me drowsy and I can't think straight. One becomes used to the stuff and then one needs more of it. It's a fine balancing act between relief from pain and a clear head. It doesn't help if one is so stupid as to fall as I did this afternoon.'

There was a pause, then I said, 'Noël, I'm sorry about bringing Balquidder among you. I didn't mean to.'

'It wasn't your fault, don't think I blame you, but I wish you'd told me earlier.'

'I didn't think you'd believe me — that he might want me dead, I mean.'

'I haven't been very fair to you, have I, sweetheart? We should have talked about it more, but I didn't want to intrude. For what it's worth, I believe Balquidder to be capable of anything. When Briggs heard that George had borrowed money from Balquidder, he told me some hair-raising stories.'

Noël hadn't called me 'sweetheart' for years, and to hear it now made me want to fling myself into his arms. Stop it, Emilia, I scolded myself, he's just being kind. 'Briggs?' I said, in as disengaged a voice as I could manage.

'Of Latimer and Briggs. You know I have the same firm of lawyers as your father? George had done it all independently — hadn't mentioned a thing to Briggs.' He sighed. 'I loved George, but I tell you I could have wrung his neck over all this.'

From Mrs Beresford's letters, I guessed that it was Aline's extravagance which had caused George to take this disastrous step, though a less besotted man could surely have put his foot down. Noël had been in Spain and I wasn't sure how much of this he knew and I certainly was not going to mention her name.

Then Noël said, 'I had a letter from Mrs George this morning. She's coming down to London as soon as it's safe to travel. I must tell Mrs Good to prepare her room.' I could hear the warmth in his voice and my fingernails dug themselves into my palms.

'I'm sure she'll be delighted to see you

171

again after so long,' Noël continued. 'It certainly solves the chaperonage problem.'

I could think of nothing suitable to say, so I held my peace.

When I had got ready for bed earlier, I had plaited my hair in a long braid, as I usually did. My hair is long and fine — so long that I can sit on it — and it is a question of keeping it out of the way during the night. If I plait it tightly, by the morning it has enough curl to enable me to put it up more easily. I had not realized, until Noël reached out and touched it, that my plait had come undone. Noël had taken off the ribbon and was gently spreading out the strands.

'I'd no idea it was so long or so silky,' he said wonderingly, twisting a strand round his fingers.

Scarcely daring to breathe, I turned to look at him. He smiled and, for a timeless few seconds, our eyes locked. His face held a look of surprise, as if he'd just discovered something. Then a coal clattered down and broke the spell. Noël dropped his hand and I began to replait my hair with unsteady fingers.

I got up to put on some more coal and Noël made some random comment about the time. I didn't dare to think about what had just happened. I banished any lingering enchantment and switched my thoughts to Stephen and Balquidder. I had been truthful there with Noël, and it was a relief to have it out into the open, but I had said nothing about my novel writing. Most men disapproved of ladies earning money. I remembered my father once saying that it coarsened ladies to have any traffic with the rough male world of commerce. Our new understanding was precious to me and I did not want to jeopardize it. There were other forbidden areas, too: Aline, Richard, Noël's marriage.

I did not believe that he had loved Margaret but, after all, many successful marriages were based on mutual respect, suitability and affection. They had had a son together. Why had Noël been so indifferent to Richard? He was a dear boy and an engaging one. All he wanted was a little affection. I couldn't understand why Noël, who had come from a happy and loving family himself, could have failed to see that this was what his son needed. Richard was not a difficult child to love.

Suddenly there were noises outside, steps going down to the basement. We both started up.

'For God's sake, Noël,' I said, 'get out of my bedroom. We have enough problems as it is.' My ears had caught another noise, this time from upstairs, the sound of a door.

'I'm in no condition to threaten your virtue,' said Noël ruefully.

I smiled, but it was with an effort.

'You go on.' Noël reached for his stick. 'It'll take me some time.'

I left the room and raced down the stairs to the basement, leaving Noël to follow. I reached the kitchen just as Mr Bagnigge and Abel returned. Abel was as white as paper and could scarcely drag himself in. Mr Bagnigge was carrying an unconscious Richard.

'Thank God,' I cried. 'Is he all right?'

'He's been stuffed full of syrup of poppies, or some such stuff,' said Mr Bagnigge worriedly. 'Can be dangerous for so young a lad. I'd best get him up to bed, Miss Emilia.'

Abel had slumped down on to a chair and I could see blood seeping through his jacket.

'You go on, Mr Bagnigge. The colonel's on his way down. I'll see to Abel. I know what to do.'

Mr Bagnigge, after one concerned look, left. I could hear him talking to Noël on the stairs. I turned to Abel and began to ease off his jacket, fortunately it was a loose one, or I'd have had to cut it off him. I then took off his shirt. He'd been stabbed in the shoulder at the back.

There were some jugs and bowls waiting for the morning on the kitchen table. I dumped them unceremoniously on the draining board and helped Abel on to the kitchen table, laying him face downwards. He promptly fainted.

The cut was narrow, but deep. A single stab, I guessed. I needed a bread and water poultice in case of any matter in the wound and then lint or oiled silk. It should be kept clean and dry. Mr Bagnigge had left his coat draped over a chair and I put it over Abel to keep him warm while I went to prepare the poultice. Inside Mr Bagnigge's coat was a flask of brandy and I poured some of it on to the wound and then spooned a little into Abel's mouth and felt his pulse. It was faint, but steady. His eyelids fluttered open.

'Master Richard?' he whispered.

'Everybody's safe,' I said. 'You've been stabbed and you've lost some blood, but I think you'll be all right.'

Abel's eyes closed again.

I went on with my work. I coaxed up the fire and swung the kettle over, found the bread crock and crumbled some bread into a clean bowl. Whatever I thought of Mrs Good, the kitchen was scrupulously clean. The kettle began to sing and I poured water on to the crumbled bread and left it to soak. I found some clean teacloths in a drawer and tore one into strips.

By the time Abel's wound was clean and bound, Mr Bagnigge and Noël had returned. In fact, when I turned round they were both watching silently from just inside the kitchen door.

'Bread and water poultice to draw out any inflammation and then clean bandages,' I said crisply. 'He should have a proper bed, though. The mattress in that draughty boot room won't do.'

'I'd best take him up to Master Richard's room then, Miss Emilia,' said Mr Bagnigge. He didn't argue with my orders. 'He can sleep in the truckle bed next to Master Richard and Miss Carver can keep an eye on them.'

'That will do,' I said. I had every intention of watching over them both myself — I had no opinion at all of Miss Carver's abilities, but I didn't want a quarrel about it.

Mr Bagnigge picked up Abel carefully and left the room. I busied myself with tidying up. Anything to stop me throwing myself into Noël's arms and bursting into tears of relief. The longing was so strong that I wished he'd go.

'Leave that,' said Noël. 'Mrs Good can clear it up in the morning.'

'I shouldn't dare,' I said lightly. 'There's blood all over the table and the floor. If I leave it, it will stain. Go to bed, Noël. This won't take me a minute.'

Noël took no notice and sat down. 'The sawbones in Spain bled me and gave me a mustard poultice,' he said. 'I nearly died.'

'The doctor bled my mother again and again, and she did die,' I replied. 'I only use what I know is safe. They use bread and water poultices for horses, so I know they're all right.' I'd often noticed as a child that the methods used in the stables at Tranters Court to treat cuts and strains were remarkably effective. I had scant regard for doctors. I'd always blamed the family doctor for my mother's death.

'You've treated Abel as though he were a horse!'

'Why not? It's still blood and torn muscle.'

I scrubbed down the table, washed the bowl and threw out the rest of the bread poultice, then found the mop and bucket and cleaned the floor. Noël watched me with a curious expression on his face, but he said nothing.

Eventually, Mr Bagnigge returned and sat down at the other end of the table. I put away the mop and bucket and pulled up another chair.

'Come on, Jem,' said Noël. 'How did you do it?'

'I got the help of John Baxter and a couple of mates of his,' began Mr Bagnigge. 'You'll remember them, sir, I daresay, invalided out after Salamanca. John now works at the Bell. Always good with horses was John. I arranged with him to hire a carriage. A couple of his mates joined us, men who wouldn't mind a bit of a fight, if it should come to that. Bull and Smithson, good men, though not in our company.

'At about three, we were at Moxon's in Crane Alley. We weren't anticipating trouble. We thought Master Richard would be upstairs and there'd be only one old biddy guarding him and maybe a printer's boy, but we went prepared for trouble all the same. Just as well, for it turned out two of Mr Balquidder's bully boys were there. They'd been drinking and were asleep when we rushed in, but one of 'em had a knife and got Abel before Bull could deal with him. I dealt with the other and he won't be going nowhere for a while.

'We tied them up and went upstairs and the biddy set up a screech you could have heard a mile away. We tied and gagged her as well, took Master Richard and escaped. Bull carried Abel.

'John Baxter drove us back and here we are. I promised them five guineas apiece on your behalf, sir.'

'And they shall have it,' said Noël. 'You've done well, Jem. Thank you.'

'Not as well as Abel and Miss Emilia did earlier.'

'Don't,' I said quickly. 'It was nothing.' I had skated over my wearing boy's clothing and I certainly didn't want the story repeated.

Noël looked from Mr Bagnigge to me and said, 'Mrs Kirkwall's been wonderful, but all the same, Jem, you tackled a couple of armed men at some danger to yourself, and I am in your debt.'

Mr Bagnigge's eyelid drooped at me in a suspicion of a wink, and he allowed the subject to drop. I heaved a sigh of relief. He helped Noël upstairs and I went up to Richard's room.

As I suspected, Miss Carver was fast asleep in her chair, snoring loudly. I shook her awake and sent her off to bed. 'I'll wake you at seven,' I promised.

She seemed thoroughly resentful at having been woken. 'You didn't have no call to do that,' she accused me. 'It's not my job to look after boot boys. As for Master Richard, he's not right in the head, and the sooner he's packed off somewhere, the better. Mrs George always thought so, and all this teaching him to read and whatnot is a waste of time, it seems to me.'

'Fortunately, it's not up to you,' I said tartly.

As she left she muttered, 'When Mrs George gets here, things'll be very different, you mark my words.'

I wondered how she knew of Aline's impending arrival for I had only just heard of it myself. I dismissed her from my mind and went to check on Richard. He was deeply asleep, but his pulse rate was steady and his skin not unduly cold. I tucked his blanket more securely round him and dropped a kiss on his cheek. I thought he'd be all right.

I moved across to Abel and put my hand on his forehead. He was not running a temperature, though he was slightly hot. I thought that was probably normal. Time would tell. Sleep would probably do as much for both of them as was needful.

I replenished the fire and sank down on Miss Carver's vacated chair and set myself to wait.

I began to think about Noël's wife, Margaret. Usually, I was content to stigmatize her as a pudding and dismiss her. Now, different thoughts entered my head. I remembered her at Richard's christening, looking pale and dumpy and wearing an unattractive gown in a dull green. Aline was holding Richard at the font, for she and George were his godparents, and Noël was gazing at Aline with a look almost of anguish.

How must Margaret have felt? She must have known that Noël loved Aline — she probably married him knowing it. What a dreadful position for her to be in, even if she didn't love him herself. But if she did? It was not her fault that she was dumpy and that she couldn't compare with Aline's delicate prettiness. I thought of my own feelings for Noël and, for the first time, I pitied her.

★ ★ ★

In spite of the fright we had all received, things were better on a number of fronts. Richard slept off the syrup of poppies without ill effects, but the emotional shock was harder to recover from. It became obvious that he felt safer having company, so Abel was allowed to use the truckle bed in Richard's room until his own wound had quite healed. I couldn't help feeling that Abel's presence protected Richard from Miss Carver.

'He has these nightmares, miss,' Abel told

me. 'He says he's always had them but she only scolds him for waking her up.' He jerked his head towards Miss Carver. 'All he needs is a bit of reassurance, if you know what I mean. Poor little man,' he finished kindly.

Abel's wound healed as it ought and he thoroughly enjoyed his new heroic status. I had to warn him not to mention our earlier escapade.

Noël went out with Mr Bagnigge and duly rewarded John Baxter, Bull and Smithson. To my quiet amusement, Jem Bagnigge was favourably impressed by the bread and water poultice, and he used it on Noël's wound, with similarly beneficial results. Not that I heard of it from him, no, it was Hannah who confided the information. All the same, I could see that Mr Bagnigge now regarded me with more approval than he accorded most of my sex.

Noël was determined to bring Balquidder to justice and he and I went up to the nursery to talk to Richard, for his evidence would be crucial. Miss Carter was sent downstairs and Noël pulled up a chair and sat down. I took Richard on my knee.

'Your papa wants to make sure that the bad man who took you goes to prison,' I said gently. 'Can you tell us what happened, Richard?'

Richard went white. He shook his head.

'It's important, Richard,' said Noël seriously. 'Did you see a very fat man while you were there?'

Richard shook his head vehemently. 'I don't remember anything, Papa,' he whispered.

I could feel him trembling. A pulse in his temple throbbed. The child was terrified.

'He may have been threatened,' I said quietly to Noël. 'I think we should leave it for now. Maybe in a day or so.'

We tried to encourage Richard to talk, but he became so upset that it was impossible. He'd been made to drink the syrup of poppies in the carriage and could remember very little after that.

'I can't put him through the ordeal of being a witness,' sighed Noël. 'Poor little chap, he's being so brave and I hate to put this pressure on him.'

'He's worried about failing you,' I said.

'I'm concerned about your reputation as well,' Noël continued. 'You would be bound to be called as a witness and how would it look, with you living here, apart from your husband?'

I wanted to say that I scarcely had any reputation to keep up, but I remained silent. It did not take much imagination to see that being in the witness box, at the mercy of Balquidder's lawyer, would be a most unpleasant experience — and one which would not help Noël's case.

Noël dropped the idea of prosecuting Balquidder. However, his relationship with Richard continued to improve. He went up to the schoolroom for half an hour or so every morning and expressed an interest in what Richard was doing. He would watch while Richard set up his lead soldiers for the battle of Vittoria, and suggested one or two improvements. As soon as he had recovered enough, Richard came down to tea as before and either I read to him, or he to me and Noël listened.

I could see that Noël still wasn't entirely easy with his son, but he was trying and Richard was blossoming. All this gave me a very real, though silent, pleasure. My own feelings for Noël had to remain unexpressed.

I had grown up a lot since I had met Stephen fishing all those years ago. It had never occurred to me then to hide my feelings — I was not a child of the Romantic Movement for nothing. Now I had learned restraint. Noël was a far worthier man than Stephen in every way, but he was also an honourable one. Even had he been attracted to me, I was quite sure that he would never

184

have allowed anything to develop between himself and a married woman. He held my position as guest in his house and daughter of a family well known to him far too seriously for a dishonourable entanglement, and nothing else was possible.

I decided that, whilst he liked me as a person, I didn't interest him as a woman. Being thin and bony was a cross I had had to bear all my life, but that didn't make it any easier. At least I could make Erminia beautiful and voluptuously endowed.

I returned to *The Secret of the Drakensburgs*. I noticed that Erminia, who was much more spirited than my earlier heroines, seemed to have taken on a life of her own. For one thing, she refused to faint at the crucial moment, as I had intended. When the evil Count Drakensburg carried her off, she amazed me by seizing a stone (they were in a mountain pass) and hurling it at him with a splendid speech beginning, '*Fiend! Cur! Dost thou think that I, Erminia FitzUrse . . .* ' etc. etc.

If I couldn't tell Noël how I felt about him, at least Erminia was expressing herself passionately.

On Monday, 10 January, five days before my birthday, Aline arrived in a hired post-chaise with a mountain of luggage, accompanied by her maid, Jeanne, and a couple of outriders. The whole must have cost her at least eighty pounds. Private travel was not cheap.

Mrs Good, wreathed in smiles, bustled out to greet her and I could hear her solicitious enquiries about the journey, the state of madam's health and would she like tea or coffee sent up to her room? Naturally, as a daughter-in-law, she was entitled to the best room, the one that had been Mrs Beresford's.

The last time I'd seen Aline was the summer of my elopement. I'd been sixteen, scarcely grown-up, and Aline had been a beautiful young married woman. She was very much a man's woman and resented other women receiving male attention that was due to herself alone — even gawky girls like myself. She must have seen that I adored George and Noël, and she was determined to put me in my place.

She had succeeded. She made me feel gauche and clumsy and, as I listened to the hubbub of her arrival, those feelings rushed back. When I looked at myself in the glass, my eyes looked the colour of the fog outside and my nose stuck out like a parrot's beak. I would keep out of her way. I had my tea upstairs with Richard.

'Aunt Aline has arrived,' said Richard gloomily.

'I know. I thought we'd have tea up here today to give her time to talk to your father.'

'Do I have to see her?'

Miss Carver was sitting in her chair by the fire and she now interrupted, 'Indeed you do, Master Richard. Shame on you for talking so. Didn't she look after you all those years while your father was away?'

Richard looked down. I said nothing. I wondered what Aline had said to Noël about Richard, for she must have written to him in Spain. Was it she who had set Noël against his son?

'I understand that Mrs George hopes to return to France as soon as hostilities have ended,' I said at last.

Miss Carver dabbed at her eyes. 'Such a beautiful lady. I don't doubt that she'll be the toast of Paris. And it's what she deserves.' She flung me a glance as if to say, 'and you don't'.

I didn't know what I'd done to incur Miss Carver's dislike, for it was plain that she resented me. Perhaps it was simply that I'd taken an interest in Richard when she had decided that he was a hopeless case.

I stayed in the schoolroom with Richard until it was time to go and change for dinner. I had recovered some of my fighting spirit. I

187

might have been thin and scrawny, but that didn't mean that I was not going to do my best. I wore my new oyster surah gown and pinned up my hair with the ebony combs that Noël had sent me from Spain. I looked at myself critically in the glass. I had put on a little weight since I'd been in London and I looked less gaunt. In fact, Hannah had complimented me only the other day on my improved looks.

'You've got ever such nice hands and feet, Miss Emilia,' she'd said. She giggled and added, 'Abel thinks you're like a fairy princess!'

'Good God!' I exclaimed. 'Does he really? But he's partial, bless him.'

All the same, such championship cheered me up. If I had had a daughter, I thought, I'd never have told her that she was stick-thin, bony and unattractive. These things etch into one, like acid on a copper plate.

When I reached the drawing-room, Aline was sitting by the fire, talking to Noël. She did not rise to greet me, just inclined her head as I came forward to shake hands. 'Mrs Kirkwall.' She touched my hand briefly.

Noël frowned. 'I expected you down for tea, Emilia.'

'I thought that you and Mrs Beresford might like some time to catch up on family news,' I replied smoothly. I'd prepared this earlier.

'You should have brought Richard down. I have been telling Mrs George of his improvement and, of course, of the terrible ordeal he has been through.'

'I was up in the schoolroom with Richard. If there had been a request to see him, of course I'd have brought him downstairs.' And there was no such request. Already I was feeling defensive.

'Dear Richard,' sighed Aline. 'I long to see him.' She made no mention of Richard's kidnapping, which I thought strange, but then I'd always thought her self-centred.

She had obviously decided that I was invisible. She made no enquiries about me. She turned back to Noël and resumed her conversation as though I did not exist.

I looked at her. She was in mourning for George, of course, and black did not really suit her; however, she was wearing a really pretty jet and pearl necklace, and a fine black mantilla was arranged with careless artistry over her shoulders. Her hair was done up in the antique roman style, with ringlets coming down from a classic knot at the back of her head. I happened to know that Aline had straight hair and that those ringlets were a triumph of her maid's art — not to mention the curling tongs. I also decided that her neck looked decidedly scrawnier since I had last seen her. Miaow. I felt a little better.

I couldn't help asking myself why she was here. Why travel in the middle of the worst winter for a quarter of a century? Why go to the trouble and expense?

Noël was looking like a man who has been in a desert and now sees an oasis. His eyes were warm and tender as they rested on her and he was laughing at some observation she made. I couldn't bear to watch it. Aline was being very French, using fluttering hand movements and prettily accented broken English. For heaven's sake, I thought, she'd come to England as a small child, she could speak perfectly fluently if she wanted to. I was horribly jealous of her effect on Noël.

I thought suddenly of Erminia. I'd give her a false friend. She would be called Alienora, probably Italian and maybe given to poisoning. Yes, she could have a poisoned ring. I could do a lot with a poisoned ring.

I stopped feeling threatened and began instead to feel amused. I would watch Aline winding Noël round her little finger and note how she did it. It was an art that I had never acquired.

'But, Noël,' she pouted, 'you are so much man that you do not understand how the woman feels about this.'

Overacting, I thought sourly. All her 'ths' were 'zs'.

'About what?' said Noël, smiling.

'These little trinkets. I am only asking to borrow.'

Ah, I thought. She wants the family jewels and doubtless she would skip off to France with them as soon as peace was declared and they would never be seen again. She would have worn the Beresford jewels as George's wife, but they were not hers to keep. In due course they would go to Richard's wife. There were some very pretty pieces, I remembered.

'You know you can't wear coloured jewels while you are in mourning, Aline.'

'But why must they be locked away, like I am *un bébé*. You are unkind, Noël.' God knows how, but her eyes actually filled with tears.

I cringed in embarrassment, but Noël noticed nothing amiss.

'Safety reasons, Aline. Ah, there goes the gong. You must be hungry after your journey.' He rose to his feet, took his stick and limped over to offer her his arm. I followed them into the dining-room.

★　★　★

I realized over the next day or so that Aline was trying to undermine me — with the willing collusion of Tryphena Good.

The following morning I came down in one of Mrs Beresford's gowns and I saw Aline eyeing the lace at the neck. I don't know whether she said anything to Noël, but I did overhear her discussing me with Mrs Good.

'Men have no idea,' Aline was saying, crossly. 'Brussels lace, too, Mrs Good.'

'I always thought she was encroaching, ma'am. Why, when she arrived she was practically in rags and she almost forced her way in.'

'Disgraceful.'

'The colonel is too kind-hearted, ma'am. And where is her husband, pray?'

I turned away and went back upstairs. I always seemed to be overhearing something unpleasant about myself. Why did I never hear, 'Emilia, such a charming girl?'

Noël had asked me to bring Richard down to tea that afternoon, so I went upstairs to check that he was tidy and took his hand comfortingly as we went down. The poor child was pale with nerves and his hand clutched mine so tightly that it hurt. He tried, but he was awkward. His bow was ungainly and he dropped his bread and butter. Worse, he could see that he was disappointing his father.

Aline's behaviour was a disgrace. She raised her eyebrows at the bow and dropped bread as if she expected nothing better, said a few cold words to Richard and then ignored him.

'And this is the improvement?' she murmured to Noël, but not so low that Richard couldn't hear.

I wanted to shout at both of them. Did they not remember what Richard had been through? Of course, he was going to react badly to any extra stress. Noël, I knew, had decided that Richard was not to be subjected to more questions, but he might at least have defended his son from Aline's insinuations.

I smiled reassuringly at Richard and we sat down together. She pointedly ignored us both and, picking up a volume from the little table by her side, began to read. Noël, perhaps wanting to avoid a scene, absorbed himself in the paper. I hoped Aline's bad manners made him feel uncomfortable, but, if they did, he wasn't saying.

I glanced over at the book — the other two volumes were lying on the table — and noticed, to my horror, that she was reading *The Castle of Apollinari*. My heart began to hammer loudly. Had she sneaked into my bedroom for them? Surely not? I kept my copies locked away in my valise. I hadn't dared to take them out.

I looked again. No, they weren't my copies. Mine were a presentation set, bound in blue leather. Aline's were cheaper, in brown.

Noël looked up. Richard was slowly eating a slice of cake. I had picked up my sewing and was darning the heel of my stocking — I was always going through heels. I wasn't doing it very well. Before Aline had arrived, there had been cheerful chatter, now there was total silence. Maybe even Noël, besotted though he was, realized that the atmosphere was strained.

'What are you reading, Aline?'

She told him.

'A Gothic romance by the sound of it,' observed Noël. 'Is it any good?'

Aline stifled a yawn. 'Passable.'

Nonsense, I thought crossly. I'd been watching her and she was quite absorbed.

'Who's it by?'

Aline flicked to the front. 'Daniel Miller.'

I held my breath and looked fixedly at the heel of the stocking. Surely Noël would guess? He was quite acute enough to put two and two together. I could feel him looking at me and I forced myself to continue darning.

'I haven't heard of him.' Noël returned to *The Times*.

I relaxed.

Time passed. Richard went up to bed. We had dinner. After dinner, Noël apologized — his wound was troubling him — and retired to his room. Aline and I sat in silence in the drawing-room, Aline taking care to demonstrate how little she relished my conversation, by becoming completely absorbed in my book. Several times she even turned back a page or two to reread some passage. I longed to ask her what she thought.

At half past nine, she laid the book aside and rang the bell for tea. When it came, she did the honours and I went to get my cup.

'Did you actually marry Mr Kirkwall?' she asked. 'Or is Mrs Kirkwall just a courtesy title?'

Colour flared up in my cheeks. She had meant to insult me and she had succeeded.

'I am married,' I replied, in as even a voice as I could manage.

'Really?' She did not sound convinced.

I am not playing this game, I thought. What does she want me to do? Present her with a copy of the entry in the parish register? She was nothing but a grasping little bitch. I was almost sure that I could detect burnt cork where she'd darkened her eyelashes. I resented her hold over Noël; I would do everything possible to protect Richard from her slights and innuendoes, and I would no longer allow her to hurt me. I sipped my tea.

Aline bit her lip. 'Forgive me, Mrs Kirkwall,' she continued, making it clear by the way she emphasized the 'Mrs' that she didn't believe it, 'I don't understand why you are living apart from your husband. Are you widowed? I hadn't heard of it.'

'I am not widowed. And my marriage is none of your business.'

'Oh, but it is,' returned Aline, as sweet as honey. 'I want Colonel Beresford to give a dinner party for me while I am here. Just a small affair, nothing I may not do whilst I am in mourning, but I cannot expect my guests to meet a woman who is separated from her husband.'

'I am sorry for your disappointment.'

Aline's eyes flashed. 'I think you should go. You have trespassed on the colonel's kindness long enough.'

I put down my cup and rose. 'You had better discuss that with the colonel,' I said quietly. 'Good-night Mrs Beresford.' I dropped her a brief curtsy and left the room.

I hoped this was not going to be a portent of battles to come. Was she simply using me as a scapegoat to vent some of her anger at being thwarted over the family jewels? I had no financial claim on Noël, so it couldn't be that. It was illegal to marry one's brother-in-law and I could see no symptoms of love for him, which might have made her jealous of my presence — though without cause, alas, as I well knew. So why all this hostility?

The following day, I kept to my room in the morning and got on with *The Secret of the Drakensburgs*. In fact, the addition of the false Alienora gave a welcome boost to the action. I've often noticed that if a plot is sagging, the best remedy is to throw in a problem, and Alienora was all set to provide Erminia with some very nasty moments indeed.

When I went downstairs for luncheon, only Noël was in the dining-room. Aline, I was told, was resting upstairs with a headache.

'What on earth have you been saying to Mrs George?' demanded Noël, almost as soon as I sat down. 'You have upset her.' He was looking grim. I had hoped that we had reached enough of an understanding to stop him instantly prejudging me, but it seemed not — at least, where Aline was concerned.

'We have exchanged the merest common-places,' I replied.

'That's not what she said to me. She said that you had been most uncivil, suggesting that she was unwelcome here and asking why she had come. Really, Emilia, you are thoughtless. She is always welcome. You might have considered that she has just lost her husband.'

I ate my ham and salad in silence. I wasn't at all sure how to counteract this new ploy, when Aline's word would automatically be believed and mine would not.

'Have you nothing to say?'

I put down my knife and fork. 'I will say what I have to say,' I said at last, 'though I can see that it will not be of the slightest use. Mrs George cast doubts on the validity of my marriage, and it was she who suggested that *I* had outstayed *my* welcome. I gather that she wants you to give a dinner party for her which my contaminating presence makes impossible.'

'Nonsense. She has told me that she wants absolute quiet. Her nerves are far too shattered to allow her any social activities.'

So why has she come to London, I wanted to ask, but I could see that it was hopeless. 'Perhaps you'd better ask yourself why she says one thing to you and another to me.'

'Are you suggesting that Mrs George is lying?' demanded Noël.

'Are you suggesting that I am?' I snapped. I felt angry and upset. Suddenly our mutual understanding had vanished. I could have killed Aline.

I finished my meal in silence and then left the room.

★ ★ ★

That afternoon was sunny and I longed to be out of the house. Would it be safe, or was Balquidder having it watched all the time? It was not that I had forgotten the threat of his presence these last few days, but that Aline's arrival had pushed it to the back of my mind. Abel's shoulder was still bandaged and he was confined to the house. Richard would not be allowed out after his recent fright. I was just wondering whether I dared to put on Bill's clothes again, when I saw Mr Bagnigge, hat in hand and with his coat on, going towards the back stairs.

'Oh, Mr Bagnigge! Are you going out?'

'And if I am?' The owl look was there.

'I need some fresh air and I want to see how the freeze on the Thames is coming on. May I go with you — if you think it's safe?'

'I'm delivering a message to Latimer and Briggs for the colonel. You can come with me if you want. You'll be safe enough; it's daylight and Mr Balquidder's not the type to take foolish risks. Leastways, he wouldn't do it more than once.' Mr Bagnigge indicated the knife in his belt. 'I'll give you five minutes.'

I darted upstairs to change into my boots and to grab Mrs Beresford's cloak, my bonnet and Mrs Irvine's fur-lined muff.

Mr Bagnigge was standing at the bottom of the stairs, turnip watch in hand. 'Four minutes,' he said sourly. 'Not bad for a woman.'

'It's good to get out,' I said, as we turned up the Strand. The atmosphere in the house was so oppressive and Noël so cold and distant, that I was beginning to feel desperate.

'Mrs George up to her tricks, is she?'

I made a face. 'Spreading lies about me to the colonel,' I said. 'I'll survive, but it's hurting him and I don't like that. I can't help wondering why she has chosen to come down now. It's not the weather for travelling, if you don't have to.'

'Humph.' He shot me a surprisingly understanding look, but said nothing further. We walked as briskly as possible up the Strand, given the state of the pavements. Even though we were walking fast, I could feel my toes becoming chilled and my breath came out in puffs of steam. The rooftops were covered with snow and the dome of St Paul's, from the bottom of Ludgate Hill, looked as though it had been covered in icing. Not clean, white icing though, for it was streaked with black from the thousands of coal fires.

We went to Little Britain and Mr Bagnigge delivered his message, then we turned down Creed Lane and then St Andrew's Hill to Puddle Dock. The ships there were frozen in their moorings and there was no sign of activity. On one of the ships a ship's cat mewed dismally. We walked along Earl Street, behind the row of docks fronting the river and thence on to Blackfriar's Bridge.

Mr Bagnigge pointed out Three Cranes Wharf. I could see that the river between Blackfriar's Bridge and London Bridge was far more iced up than the stretch in front of the Adelphi.

There was still black water to be seen in the middle of the river, but it was flowing sluggishly and on either side the ice was piling up. I'd imagined that it would freeze in a smooth sheet, but in fact it was very uneven, as if small icebergs had joined up at random, come unstuck and then piled up again. By the shoreline it was five or six feet thick and some boats were almost submerged.

'It's London Bridge,' explained Mr Bagnigge. 'The arches are so narrow and the starlings project out, which impedes the flow further.'

'Starlings?' I said. I'd thought they were birds.

'The protective piles under the piers, see. They stop the arches from being swept away, but they also block the river. You need an experienced waterman to take a boat under London Bridge, the flow's so fast.'

'Do you think it will freeze over?'

'Bound to, if we don't have a thaw.'

'Abel would love it. He wants a frost fair.'

'I remember the one in the winter of '88–'89,' said Mr Bagnigge. 'Lasted for weeks, it did. There were puppet shows, bear-baiting, all sorts of amusements.'

'I was born in January '89,' I replied. 'I remember my mother saying that it was a hard winter.'

'Frost fairs only happen three or four times a century,' said Mr Bagnigge. 'Abel shouldn't set his hopes too high.'

★ ★ ★

I hadn't realized that Noël had written to my father, and I was considerably alarmed to see a letter addressed to Colonel Beresford in my father's distinctive hand, sitting on the hall table. I knew that Noël would not now send me back to Stephen, but he might well think that I'd be safer at my father's. I did not want to return there as the disgraced daughter.

I went up to see Richard in the schoolroom before settling down to my writing, and it was there that Noël found me.

'I'd like a word with you in my study, if it's convenient, Emilia.'

'Of course.' We went downstairs.

'I've had a letter from your father about your fortune. He has given me power of attorney to deal with your affairs. I understand that he has specifically requested that your fortune revert to you in its entirety in the event of Kirkwall's death. Or, at the very least, the widow's third. He has heard nothing.'

'It's hopeless,' I said. 'We both know why.' I would predecease Stephen and the money would go to Balquidder.

'It's outrageous. There is little I can do — I did not know the full story when I wrote to your father. We both know Balquidder's a scoundrel and will cheat you out of your inheritance if he can. All the same, I think we should have one last try.'

'It's very good of you to take the trouble,' I said. I was conscious that Noël had still not forgiven me for my supposed cruelty towards Aline.

'Not at all. I'll arrange to see Kirkwall at Latimer and Briggs.'

'My birthday's on Saturday. It'll have to be tomorrow or Friday.'

★ ★ ★

The following morning, Hannah brought me up my usual breakfast on a tray, opened the curtains and shutters and replenished the fire — she had come in an hour or so earlier to light it, but I had been half asleep. I sat up and took the bed jacket she held out.

'What is it, Hannah? You look worried.'

She was standing twisting her hands awkwardly in her apron.

'Is it something about Mrs George?' I ventured. Hannah was a pretty girl, perhaps Aline had been unkind to her. I certainly wouldn't put it past her.

'I don't rightly know how to say this, Miss Emilia, and it's really not my place, but . . .'

'It is about Mrs George, then. I can promise that anything you say will go no further.'

'She means to make trouble for you, miss.'

I sighed. I already knew that.

'I overheard her talking to Mrs Good. Mrs Good heard you and the colonel talking during the night that Master Richard was kidnapped.'

'Ah!' In my bedroom, and doubtless she'd put the worst construction on it. I remembered now that I'd heard a door opening or closing. 'Does Mrs Good imagine that the colonel and I are . . . er . . . entangled?'

'I don't rightly know, Miss Emilia, but Mrs George said she'd make sure that your name was dragged through the mud.'

7

That afternoon, whilst Noël, Aline and I were having tea in the drawing-room, a letter arrived from Stephen agreeing to meet Noël at Latimer's on Friday afternoon at three o'clock. Silently, Noël passed it over to me. It was suspiciously well written. *It is unnecessary to trouble my wife with this. We can settle any small adjustments that are required between ourselves.* Stephen would never write like that — the language was far too formal and precise. I couldn't help wondering whether Balquidder had dictated it. As I handed it back, I caught a knowing expression on Aline's face.

'Tomorrow at three,' I said. 'I wonder whether I ought to come with you.'

Something about the tone of the letter worried me. I had loved Stephen once. In spite of all his faults and weaknesses, I still had some fondness for him — or at least some concern. I would be leaving him in Balquidder's toils. God alone knew what would happen to him. I did not want to continue living with Stephen, but neither did I want him thrown on the dunghill once

Balquidder had bled him dry.

'My dear Mrs Kirkwall,' put in Aline, 'I am hoping for your company tomorrow afternoon, I want your advice on altering my violet silk — Jeanne has made such a mess of it, and I know what taste you have.'

Noël smiled at Aline, as if to say, 'I knew you could not be traducing Emilia' — and flashed a 'your sins have found you out' look at me.

'How very kind of you, Mrs Beresford,' I said. I was thinking furiously, why did she want me at home at the very time of Noël's meeting with Stephen? I simply couldn't believe that Aline desired either my company or my sartorial advice. The only thing I'd be likely to do when helping Aline with her violet silk, would be to stick a pin into her.

'So that's settled then.' Aline gave me a condescending nod and looked under her lashes at Noël.

No, it isn't, I thought. Something is up. I didn't believe that Aline wanted my company so much as not wanting me to go to Noël's meeting with Stephen. I had nothing more than a suspicious dislike of Aline to go on, but I wondered whether she could be involved with Balquidder? I found him so physically repellent myself, that it was difficult to see Aline being romantically entangled, but there might be a financial connection.

I said nothing more, but I was determined that I would be at that meeting.

The following day, I came downstairs for luncheon, picked at my food, and declared that I had a headache.

'I am so sorry to disappoint you, Mrs Beresford,' I said, 'but I believe I must lie down this afternoon.'

Aline looked unconcerned. So long as I was not at the meeting, she didn't care where I was. I gave what I hoped was a wan smile, left the dining-room and went upstairs. Shortly afterwards, I heard Aline go up to her room and call for Jeanne. At quarter past two, I heard Abel go out for a cab. At twenty-five past two I was dressed and waiting.

The moment I heard Abel come back, I crept downstairs. Noël was in his study with Mr Bagnigge. I went outside and climbed into the cab.

'Colonel Beresford will be here in a moment,' I said. I sat back against the squabs and tried to be invisible in case Aline looked out of the window.

Noël and Mr Bagnigge came out. Noël climbed inside and Mr Bagnigge clambered up on to the roof beside the cabby.

'What the devil are you doing here?'

demanded Noël. I noticed, sadly, that ever since Aline's arrival he had become shorter with me.

'I am coming with you,' I said firmly. 'Stephen is my husband. I believe that I may see my own husband?' I was not going to voice my suspicions about Aline.

The cabby closed the door on us, climbed up and shook the reins. We moved off.

'What is all this, Emilia?' Noël was seriously annoyed. 'You told me that you had both agreed to a separation. Have you now changed your mind? And what about Mrs George? Have you no consideration for her?'

'I am uneasy about Stephen's letter, that is all.' I ignored the bit about Aline.

'It seems perfectly straightforward to me. It's a man's business dealing with financial settlements.'

I thought about my dealings with Mr Robinson. I'd never had any problems, though a mere female.

'I believe that Balquidder dictated that letter,' I said. 'It just didn't sound like Stephen. And if Balquidder doesn't want me there, then that seems an excellent reason for me to go.'

'I certainly don't want to meet Balquidder,' replied Noël. 'I didn't like the man the one time I met him. Since then I've always dealt with him strictly through Briggs. If I met him now, after what he tried to do to Richard, I'd probably put a bullet through him.'

'I doubt whether he'll be there,' I said. 'Would he really want his connection with Stephen known?' I knew it was unwise, but I couldn't help a small probe. 'I wonder whether Balquidder ever visited at Ainderby?'

'God, no!'

'How would you know? You were abroad?'

'Mrs George never said anything about it in her letters to me.'

'She wouldn't though, would she?' So it was Aline who wrote, I thought.

'Are you suggesting that Mrs George has anything to do with all this?' demanded Noël furiously, but I could tell that he was uneasy.

'It was not I who brought up Mrs George's name,' I protested. 'I was only wondering, but I shall do so no more.' Or not aloud, at any rate.

When we reached Latimer and Briggs's office in Little Britain, Stephen was already waiting. He had spruced himself up a bit. His hair had been trimmed, he was freshly shaved and he wore a cravat instead of his usual knotted scarf. Somebody had polished his boots and given his clothes a press.

He was also extremely disconcerted to see me.

'Emmy! I was not expecting you!'

I put my muff down on a chair. 'Why not? How are you, Stephen?' I came forward and offered a cheek.

Stephen kissed me briefly and then pushed me away.

'It's damned awkward . . . why are you here?'

'Why shouldn't I be?' A clerk had brought up three chairs and we sat down. 'Pray take no notice of me. I know this is gentlemen's business.' I hoped I didn't sound too ironic.

'Beresford,' said Noël, coming forward.

Stephen nodded irritably in Noël's direction and bit the side of his thumb as he always did when he was upset.

Mr Latimer had been going through his file and now looked up. 'It is all quite straightforward,' he said. 'By the terms of the original settlement, Mrs Kirkwall stands to inherit her mother's fortune and all the interest accruing on her twenty-fifth birthday, which is tomorrow. It will then pass absolutely under the control of her husband, unless there is a settlement to the contrary.' He looked up over his spectacles.

'Yes, yes,' said Stephen impatiently.

'Mr Kirkwall has agreed to Mrs Kirkwall receiving the income of two hundred and eighty-eight pounds, per annum for life.'

'Yes,' said Stephen, more sulkily this time. He seemed agitated. He kept flinging me little glances and tugging at his ear.

'Mr Daniels has pointed out that the capital from that, some five thousand eight hundred pounds, should be Mrs Kirkwall's absolutely,' put in Noël. 'It would be usual, especially considering that Mr Kirkwall is some ten years older than his wife and, in the normal course of things, must be expected to predecease her.'

'Then my executor will see that she is paid, of course,' said Stephen. 'I don't want to go over all this again. If old Daniels doesn't like it, he should have come himself — I can't see why you should be involved.'

'Mr Daniels is an old man, and you must be well aware that the weather is treacherous. I am a long-standing family friend.'

'Family friend, ha!'

'May I ask the name of your executor?'

'No, you may not, sir. He is a gentleman at any rate.'

Stephen seemed to be working himself up into a passion.

'Let us get back to the settlement in question,' put in Mr Latimer, smoothly. 'I am sorry you cannot be persuaded to allow Mrs Kirkwall control of her share of the capital, Mr Kirkwall. However, I have the document drawn up, and if you will wait a moment while I ring for one of my clerks, we can have it signed and witnessed at once.' He reached out and rang a bell that stood on his desk.

Stephen, after another fulminating look at Noël, subsided. He avoided looking at me.

The clerk entered. Mr Latimer pushed two documents across the desk and handed Stephen a pen. Stephen dipped it in the ink and scrawled his signatures impatiently. Noël followed suit. The clerk and Mr Latimer witnessed the signatures. Mr Latimer then handed one of the documents to Stephen.

'The other will remain here, on Mr Daniels' instructions,' he said. He rose. 'If you will excuse me, I have other business to attend to.' He bowed and left the room.

'Now, Emmy,' said Stephen, 'this has gone on long enough. You're my wife and you're coming back with me.'

'No, Stephen,' I said, quietly. 'I am not returning to you.'

'I order you!'

'No.'

'You are staying with that damned fellow there?' He indicated Noël.

'What on earth is the matter with you, Stephen? Colonel Beresford is here as my father's representative. If you are worried about propriety, the colonel's sister-in-law,

Mrs George Beresford, is also staying.'

'Ha! it don't fool me,' said Stephen, his face twitching. 'But you shan't hear a word of blame from me, Emmy, if you come back with me now. I daresay you needed a canter elsewhere. I may have neglected you, though all my business has been in care of you.'

'Nonsense,' I retorted. 'You've never cared a scrap for me. It was always my money.'

'Of course I care about you,' Stephen's hand was tugging at his ear. 'You're my wife, dammit.'

'I'm sorry. I wish you well, indeed I do, but we must remain apart. You have already agreed that we should separate.' Why was he in such a temper?

Stephen's mouth went tight. 'All right, if that's the way you want it, I'll see that you're dragged through the courts until your name's mud — and your precious colonel with you.'

I went cold. 'What do you mean?' It came out barely as a whisper.

'That changes your tune, doesn't it, eh? Think of it, Emmy. I'll divorce you for adultery. And I'll make damn sure that it'll be a juicy crim. con. case that'll be in all the papers — '

'I think you've said enough!' Noël interrupted furiously.

'I daresay!' Stephen gave a mocking laugh.

'But . . . this is absurd!' I said, desperately trying to collect my thoughts.

'Is it? Well, let me tell you I have a sworn affidavit that Beresford here was seen coming out of your bedroom on the morning of January 8th. You'll find it very difficult to explain that away. And there will be more evidence, don't you worry.'

'But . . . I've never been unfaithful to you, Stephen, I swear it.' I was scarlet with embarrassment and humiliation.

Stephen laughed. 'I daresay you haven't. Frankly, Emmy, I don't care whether you have or not. But, if you don't come back with me now, you'll find that I'll turn into an outraged husband.'

I didn't dare look at Noël. I felt too ashamed. I couldn't let Stephen do that to Noël, it would ruin him. I wasn't concerned about my own reputation; as Aline had made plain, it was in shreds already. But to go back to Balquidder's house with Stephen was to go to certain death. My heart began to pound with fear.

'Do your worst, Kirkwall.' Noël's voice was cold with anger. 'You must know perfectly well that Mrs Kirkwall is innocent. Your so-called evidence won't stand up in court — if you dare bring it so far. This is blackmail and if one whisper of it gets out, I shall have great pleasure in suing you for libel.'

Stephen leapt to his feet. For a moment I feared that he was going to attack Noël, then he rushed out of the room, ran down the stairs and the door slammed behind him. Almost immediately outside we heard a crash, a neighing of terrified horses and shouting.

I ran to the window. Outside, a crowd was gathering. A heavy brewer's dray was in the gutter with one wheel broken. The shire horses were trying to rear up and Stephen was lying at an odd angle underneath the dray. Beneath him, the snow was turning red.

'Oh, my God!' I ran downstairs and outside.

Stephen was still alive. One of his legs had been crushed by the heavy wheel and a horse shoe had caught him in the chest. His right arm was lying twisted underneath him.

People were very kind. Stephen was lifted into the office and a storage room cleared on the ground floor. Somebody found a straw pallet and a couple of blankets and a clerk went to fetch a doctor. I asked for water and clean rags and did what I could to staunch the bleeding and to make Stephen comfortable but I could see that it was only a matter of time.

Noël came in and looked down at him.

'He's dying, Emilia.'

'I know.'

'Is there anything you need? Shall I send for some laudanum?'

'That would be kind.'

Noël dealt with things with a quiet efficiency. Jem Bagnigge was sent off for laudanum. Noël found me a chair. He made no attempt to interfere, but sat himself down behind me and kept vigil. I was glad of his presence.

Stephen's face was grey with pain. He lay with eyes closed and mouth clenched. All I could do was sit beside him and hold his hand. When the laudanum came, I spooned it into him. Stephen's eyes flickered open with an effort.

'This solves your problems, Emmy,' he whispered.

Tears were running down my cheeks. 'I never wanted you dead, Stephen.'

'Doesn't matter . . . wasted . . .' He closed his eyes.

Time passed slowly. It grew dark. A clerk came and replenished the fire, brought in an oil lamp and some candles and whispered to Noël, 'Mr Latimer says you're not to worry about being here, Colonel. The nightwatchman's in the back room should you need him.'

'Thank you.'

Stephen drifted in and out of consciousness. Once the laudanum had taken effect, he seemed in less pain, but he was sinking. He kept hold of my hand and whispered, 'You'll stay till the end, Emmy?'

'Of course.'

'Bless you.' His palm was colder now, and damp.

Behind me I heard Noël go to the door and talk to someone outside and later some bread, wine and cheese arrived. He made me eat something and saw that I drank my wine and then resumed his seat.

I heard St Paul's strike midnight. My birthday, I thought, without feeling. I felt numb, as if frozen in time. My fortune was now Stephen's or rather Balquidder's. Stephen would not live to enjoy it.

There was a knock at the front door and Noël went out. He came back with a doctor, who smelled of drink, had dirty hands and made only a cursory examination.

Stephen's eyes opened. 'Don't bother yourself. I'm done for.'

The doctor shook his head and went over to talk to Noël.

'Emmy,' whispered Stephen. 'Can't see you.'

'I'm here.' I knelt down.

'Balquidder . . . watch out for Balquidder . . . He'll kill you.'

'I know.'

'Sorry, Emmy . . . never meant it.'

I leaned over to kiss him. When I drew back I saw that he was dead.

I don't remember much of what happened after that. I was in a state of shock and nothing registered. I folded Stephen's hands gently across his breast and drew up the blanket. Noël helped me to a chair and it was he who made arrangements with the doctor; I remember hearing the clink of coin. Later, Noël took my arm and helped me into a cab. He climbed in beside me and put his arm around me as he used to do when I was a child. I lay quietly against his shoulder and some of the numbness went.

'I heard St Paul's strike midnight,' I said. 'I'm sorry all your trouble had been for nothing, Noël. Balquidder has won.'

'No, he hasn't. Kirkwall officially died at eleven forty-five p.m. on Friday, January 14th. I suggested to the doctor that, as today was your birthday, it would be less painful for you to have your husband die the day before. He agreed, for a suitable sum.'

'I can't say I care very much just now,' I said, 'but thank you.' I closed my eyes and Noël held me.

I remained in a curious state of limbo for the next few days. I slept enormously, scarcely waking to swallow a mouthful of something brought up by an anxious Hannah. Sometimes, I roused myself enough to put on my dressing-gown and sit by the fire, but the effort was too much for me, and after forty minutes or so, I went back to bed and slept again. Grief and shock are exhausting states to cope with.

It was as if my mind could not take in so violent a change all at once. I wept for Stephen. I forgot his faults. Instead, I kept thinking about when we first met and us walking along by the river holding hands and exchanging shy kisses. He had been the love of my youth, however foolish, and we had been wed nine years, over a third of my life. I mourned the tragedy of his wasted life. He was a good-looking man, intelligent, but all his talents had been frittered away. He had been ruined by bad company and a lack of self-discipline.

I also felt guilty. If I had not gone to Latimer's against Stephen's wishes, he might have been alive today. I knew that this was illogical, but I still felt it. My guilt was compounded by the fact that I would now be rich — again illogical, the money should always have been mine, I knew it, but that didn't stop me feeling like a swindler.

At last, on the Wednesday, 19 January, I woke up with a clear head. I cried a little, blew my nose and felt better. When Hannah came in with my breakfast tray, I sat up and sniffed the chocolate gratefully.

'You're back with us, Miss Emilia,' said Hannah, smiling at me. 'We were all proper worried. The colonel asks after you all the time.' She went to open the curtains.

I took a roll and buttered it. I realized suddenly that I was ravenous. 'I must speak to him later,' I said. As I spoke, the realization hit me that I was now a widow. I felt a burst of elation at being free, free to love Noël, followed by guilt. How could I be so lost to all proper feeling? Stephen was barely cold in his grave. Noël would be disgusted with me, if he knew.

My self-respect demanded self-control. I was in mourning and Noël was not interested in me. I had to face up to it. I wasn't going to behave like Aline, all ostentatious woe. Whatever my grief, for Stephen, for my own wasted youth, for the pain I had brought on people like the Beresfords who wished me well, for the love I had for Noël, I would acknowledge it quietly. I would try to repair things. This time I really would write to my father. I owed him thanks for his efforts over my inheritance, if nothing else.

I dressed in the most sober gown I had, the grey kerseymere that had been Mrs Beresford's, and went downstairs to face my future.

Noël was in his study and he came out as I descended the stairs. He took hold of my hand, kissed my cheek and looked carefully at me.

'I'm back in the world, Noël,' I said. 'I shall be all right. I'm sorry if I worried you.'

'Hannah said that you hadn't eaten anything.'

'I daresay that was true. But I had a good breakfast this morning, you may ask her if you wish.'

'Come into the study.'

I did so and sat down in the leather armchair opposite Noël's desk. 'Please tell me what's been happening. The funeral?'

'The funeral took place yesterday afternoon. Kirkwall was buried in St Bride's church. I asked Mr Latimer to place a notice in *The Times* and I've written to inform your father.'

'What about the debts?'

'You are not responsible for Kirkwall's debts.'

'But the five thousand he borrowed from Balquidder?'

'Especially that. You were not married to him when he incurred that debt and you cannot be held responsible for it. As for any other debts, he died before you were twenty-five, so your money cannot be used to clear them.'

'Does Balquidder know?'

'Almost certainly. The Times notice is there precisely to inform him. Fortunately, Kirkwall's accident was widely witnessed, so there should be no repercussions there. The Times gives Latimer and Briggs's address and Mr Latimer will deal with any enquiries.'

'Balquidder won't let it go.'

'There is nothing he can do,' said Noël with some satisfaction.

'He is a vindictive man,' I said worriedly. 'If he thinks that you have been instrumental . . .'

'My own business dealings with him are scrupulously observed. Interest is paid promptly and I make sure I get a receipt. He has nothing with which to get me.'

I couldn't bring myself to mention Stephen's accusations of adultery. The very thought made me blush — with anger at the accusation and with shame at my longings. Noël did not mention it. Had he forgotten it?

Or did he wish to spare me any embarrassment? Guiltily, my mind went back to that moment of shared intimacy in my bedroom. Perhaps I was mistaken. I must have been.

'There is something else that you should know, Emilia.'

'Oh?' My heart lurched.

'Whilst we were at Latimer's, there was an intruder here in the house.'

Shame made the blood surge into my face. Stupid, stupid Emilia. How dared you imagine . . .

'A man was discovered creeping up the stairs. Hannah gave the alarm and Abel tried to catch him, but he escaped. We don't know how he managed to get in. Mrs Good and Mary were in the kitchen and heard nothing. Nothing was missing, which is a blessing, as the silver was in the dining-room.'

He came for me, I thought. An ordinary burglar would have surely looked in the dining-room. Stephen had been disconcerted to see me, perhaps he knew, or guessed, that Balquidder planned to have me kidnapped, just as he had kidnapped Richard.

I would wager anything that Aline had opened the front door to him. There had probably been an accomplice outside, ready to bundle me into a waiting cab.

'I do hope Mrs George was not hurt,' I

said, mendaciously. 'How frightened she must have been.'

'Mrs George was lying down in her room with a headache. She didn't know anything about it until it was all over.'

How convenient, I thought. Her room was at the front. She had probably waited for the man's arrival, crept down, let him in and given him directions to my room. The servants would be downstairs at that time of day. Unless somebody heard the door-knocker, there would be no reason for anyone to go into the hall.

It was impossible to voice my suspicions to Noël.

'I daresay one of the servants was careless and left the door unlocked,' said Noël. 'God knows there are plenty of poor wretches around the Adelphi wharves, any one of whom could be our man.'

'You must be right,' I said. I hoped my survival would give her a permanent head-ache.

Back in my room, I sat down by the fire and scolded myself. Was I allowing my dislike of Aline to prejudice me? She might dislike me, but would she deliberately assist in a plot to have me kidnapped? Surely not? All the same, I was uneasy. From now on I'd keep my door locked if Noël and Mr Bagnigge

225

were out of the house. Abel alone could not be expected to protect me against an intruder.

I felt a desperate urge to confide in somebody. Tryphena Good, Mary and Miss Carver were on Aline's side. It did not seem proper to discuss Aline, not to mention Noël's affairs, with Abel. I did not want to frighten Hannah. That left only Mr Bagnigge.

He had a curious position in the house. As Noël's batman, he had the run of the house in a way that even Mrs Good did not. By terms of his rank in the servants' hall, he would have been entitled to sit with Mrs Good in her parlour, but he rarely did so. He acted as butler as well and, when he wasn't attending to Noël's needs, he would often be found in the pantry.

Noël did not keep a lot of silver in the house — most of it was locked away in the silver cupboard at Ainderby — but there were a few pieces, of course, cutlery for everyday use in the dining-room and some vegetable dishes and the like. Mr Bagnigge kept them clean and polished and, when he was not doing that, Noël employed him in his office as his clerk.

He wrote a good clear hand and, as Noël couldn't sit for long without discomfort, he wrote Noël's letters for him and kept notes of the transactions. I didn't doubt that he knew all about Noël's business with the Demerara estate.

Mr Bagnigge might not take what I said seriously, but I believed that he would keep my confidence. I found him that afternoon in the study.

Noël was upstairs in the drawing-room with Aline and I really did not want to join them. I hated seeing them together. Every time she looked up at him through her eyelashes and gave a soft little sigh, I wanted to kick her. Noël would give a painful half-smile. I could see him struggling not to look at her, to keep the conversation general. I saw that part of him wanted to be free of her toils, but something made him succumb every time. She gave him nothing but pain, there was no future in it and yet he could not help himself. I hated her for torturing him so and, at times, almost hated Noël too for allowing it. I kept out of their way as much as possible.

I went downstairs to the study and knocked politely — one always remembered one's manners around Mr Bagnigge.

'Oh, it's you,' he growled. 'You'd better come in.' He looked me over carefully and indicated the leather chair in front of Noël's desk. 'You've lost weight again. It doesn't suit you. But I'm sorry about Mr Kirkwall. He was a no-gooder, but he was your husband when all's said and done.'

'Yes,' I said. 'Thank you.' I drew a breath. 'Mr Bagnigge, I want to consult you in confidence.'

'Fire away.'

'As I understand it from the colonel, Mr George bought the estate in Demerara through Mr Balquidder's agency and, by terms of the loan, has to turn it over to the production of sugar, of which Mr Balquidder will take a share. Do I have that right?'

'More or less.'

'I know Mr Balquidder's reputation. I'm sure he wants far more than the interest and his percentage of the profits. I think he hoped, maybe through exploiting Mrs George's extravagance, to persuade Mr George to take on an even bigger loan so that, in the end, he was owed an enormous sum. Much as he did with my husband.'

'That seems a fair assessment.'

'I want to know what part Mrs George is playing in all this? She is now a widow on a much-reduced income and yet she has the money to hire a post-chaise and come to London in the worst weather for twenty-five years. Why? And how did she afford it?

'Then she tells me that my presence here is

228

a disgrace. I should return to my husband. At the same time, she tells the colonel that I have been unkind to her.' I was careful how I phrased this. The last thing I wanted was for Mr Bagnigge to get the smallest hint of my feelings for Noël.

'Finally, my husband writes forbidding me to go to the meeting at Latimer and Briggs about my inheritance. That same afternoon, when I should have been here, a strange man gets inside the house, ignores the silver in the dining-room and comes upstairs in the direction of my bedroom.'

'Are you saying that Mrs George is being bribed by Mr Balquidder? That she may have let the man in?'

'It is a possibility. Remember, my husband was staying with Mr Balquidder. He stood to gain a fortune on my twenty-fifth birthday and Mr Balquidder would want us under the same roof. After that . . . ' I stopped.

Mr Bagnigge folded his arms and stared into the fire. The two tufts of hair stood up like alert, intelligent ears.

'But now you're a widow, that little plot is blown.'

'There is something else. Something I blush to repeat, but I must.' Careful, Emilia, I thought. I told him, as dispassionately as I could, of Stephen's threat to cite Noël as my co-respondent in adultery.

'The colonel never mentioned it to me.'

'My husband is dead. The case cannot be pursued. On the night you rescued Master Richard, the colonel woke up, found your note and came down to ask me what was happening. Somebody heard him come out of my room and informed my husband. I would dearly like to know who signed the affidavit he spoke of.'

'Hm.' Another long pause.

I stared at the desk. Who could have heard us that night? Mrs Good? Miss Carver? Mary? It could be any of them. My eye caught a small pile of books. Idly I reached out and turned them towards me. They were the three volumes of my second romance, *The Doom of the House of Ansbach*. They were new, for only the pages of the first volume had been cut. Noël must have bought them.

There was a note lying by them and, when Mr Bagnigge wasn't looking, I inched it round. *My dear Aline, I know that you are enjoying* The Castle of Apollinari *so I hope you will allow me to* give you *offer you the* author's next book The Doom of the House of Ansbach. Your affectionate brother-in-law, Yours ever, *Yours affectionately* — Noël seemed to be having trouble with his letter.

Mr Bagnigge was looking at me. I wrenched my eyes away from the note and pulled my thoughts together. 'I don't see what Mr Balquidder can do,' I said, 'but, whatever it is, I fear that Mrs George may be willing to assist him — possibly for financial reasons.

'I'm worried about the colonel's reputation, Mr Bagnigge. My husband could be indiscreet and I know how Colonel Beresford would hate to be the subject of malicious gossip. I've thought about leaving, but the weather makes it impossible. This is not the season for getting lodgings and I doubt whether I could get the mail or the stagecoach back to Tranters Court, even if my father would have me.'

'Not to be thought of,' said Mr Bagnigge. 'You're too thin and pale to go off and live in some lodgings and freeze to death. The colonel wouldn't hear of it. I take it you don't want me to discuss all this with him?'

I thought briefly of Noël and Aline in the drawing-room, and them laughing softly together.

'It would be no good,' I said, tersely.

Mr Bagnigge shot me a look of understanding. 'Aye. Let's hope it'll pass, but for the moment we'll just have to manage without him.'

'You could talk to Abel, Mr Bagnigge. He

tried to chase the man out of the house. He may have some useful information.'

'It's a pity the colonel won't listen to you.'

'He thinks I have too vivid an imagination,' I replied. 'My childhood reputation dies hard.' If he's guessed that I am the author of *The Doom of the House of Ansbach*, I thought, he's probably decided that anything I say about Aline is an invention.

It was an enormous relief to unburden myself to Mr Bagnigge — to know that I had one ally in the house who took me seriously.

The next week or so passed without incident. I thought about Stephen a lot, not so much grieving for him, as absorbing his death. I needed time to adjust. I found myself thinking about my father, too. Several times I started to write to him, but I kept getting stuck. I was sorry if he had suffered because of my actions, but I, too, had suffered because of his. Every time I sat down to write, I felt tearful and angry. In the end, I gave up. I was not going to write a lie. The post went two ways, after all. If he really cared about me, he could have offered me a small olive branch in a letter. I'd have been happy with the merest twig.

The weather did not let up; if anything, it got worse. The icicles outside my window lengthened and Abel reported that birds were falling out of the trees, frozen solid. According to *The Times*, all mail was now at a standstill. Even if I did write to my father, nothing would get through. It was a good excuse, at any rate.

I was worried about Richard. He had stopped coming downstairs for tea. Aline never asked for him and Noël seemed to have forgotten his existence. I went up to the schoolroom every morning and his reading continued to improve, but it was plain that he was not happy. He looked pale and had black rings underneath his eyes. Abel had told me that he was scared of the dark and when I asked him if he had been sleeping badly, he gave a frightened glance towards Miss Carver and nodded.

'Could Master Richard not have a night-light?' I asked Miss Carver.

'Oh, no, miss,' she replied, with a thin, triumphant smile. 'Mrs Beresford says that we must not make a Miss Molly out of him.'

I hated the idea of Richard being frightened at night; he was only eight years old, and had been the subject of a terrifying ordeal. Why should he not be given a night-light, if it made him feel safer? Unfortunately, Abel was now better and back sleeping in his boot room. I wished that I could appeal to Noël over Aline's head, but I knew that it was impossible.

Noël, too, seemed tense and unhappy. Aline had not given up about the jewellery. Every now and then she mentioned it and each time, it seemed to me, Noël's refusal became less absolute.

He could scarcely take his eyes off her and I must admit that she looked beautiful and pathetic. She had a number of elegantly cut mourning dresses and I noticed that Jeanne continued to curl her hair. So much for the inconsolable widow. Noël pretended to read *The Times* in the evenings, but it was plainly only an excuse, and I was sure Aline could see that as well as I did myself. Every now and then she would catch his eye, give her tremulous half-smile and flutter her eyelashes. Sometimes, she'd dab at her eyes with a wisp of lace-edged handkerchief. She even had a different tone of voice when talking to Noël, softer and a little deeper.

There was a tender expression in Noël's eyes whenever he looked at her that made me want to cry inside. I wanted him to look at me like that, and I knew he never would. There was one point in *The Mountfalcon Heiress* where Angelina nobly renounces the hero. '*Shall I stand in thy way?*' she asks. It is a rhetorical question, naturally. '*If thou dost love another then go, be happy with her, and I shall rejoice in thy happiness.'* What nonsense, I thought. Yes, I would suffer anything to give Noël his heart's desire, but rejoice? I was not so high-minded.

I could see perfectly well that Aline was acting, and that made it worse. When Noël wasn't there, her voice was harder and she certainly never bothered with the handkerchief routine. She would go back to *The Castle of Apollinari* and ignore me completely. She was now into volume two.

'Your book seems to be absorbing you,' I said. 'As you have read the first volume, do, pray, allow me to read it.'

'I have lent it to Colonel Beresford.'

Oh Lord! I wondered whether I had written anything in it which might possibly give me away. I didn't think so. I had had to be careful of my anonymity because of Stephen.

I didn't pursue the subject and returned instead to *Gulliver's Travels*, which I was now reading for the second time. I admired it tremendously. I liked the way one was led to consider how one's moral perspective changed with Gulliver's changing size.

Eventually, Aline put down her book.

'Perhaps, as soon as it stops snowing, you

might like to accompany me to Madame Gérard in Bond Street.'

'That's very kind of you,' I said cautiously. Why would Aline want to introduce me to her dressmaker?

'After all, what you are wearing can hardly be called mourning.'

I saw now what she would be at. We would go out together in a hired cab — and only Aline would return.

'True, but until Mr Latimer settles my affairs, I have no money for clothes. It hardly matters, anyway. I see nobody.'

Aline waved this aside. 'Madame Gérard will not ask to be be paid at once,' she said. 'So that's settled.'

'No, I'm sorry, it isn't,' I said. 'I am deeply grateful for your offer, but I am not yet two weeks widowed; it would be most unbecoming in me to go shopping.'

'Fiddle.' I could see that she was getting cross.

'I must do the right thing in memory of Mr Kirkwall,' I said piously. I, too, dabbed at my eyes with my handkerchief, though I fear that it did not have the same effect. 'The end was so awful, so sudden, that I really cannot face going out.'

Aline bit her lip. 'I can't see that it matters, as you had already separated.'

'You yourself pointed out how my reputation might suffer,' I continued. 'Of course, you were right. I must take the greatest care to do everything that is proper at such a time.'

Checkmate, I thought.

8

Aline did not give up, though I noticed that she only mentioned it when Noël was in the room.

'I do think you might accompany me to Bond Street,' she said crossly one tea-time. 'It's not much to ask — one little morning.'

Noël looked up.

'Wouldn't you like to go out, Emilia? It cannot be thought improper with Mrs George to accompany you.'

'I'm sorry,' I replied. 'With my husband so lately dead, I really could not . . . Surely you can understand my feelings, Mrs Beresford?'

'Naturally, I grieved dreadfully when my husband died,' declared Aline, 'but I have a special sensitivity. Your case is different. Come, Noël, persuade her.'

Noël looked uncomfortable, but said, 'I must leave it to Mrs Kirkwall's own judgement.'

Aline tapped her fingers impatiently on the arm of her chair.

'Why do you not take Jeanne?' I suggested.

'She always wants me to try on twenty

different things and insists on everything being just so.'

'Is that not what a lady's maid is supposed to do?' I asked innocently. 'Surely, her trained eye and familiarity with your wardrobe must be far more useful than my poor company.'

Aline bit her lip — she did not like being contradicted. 'She dawdles so.'

'Then what about Abel, if he can be spared? His wound has healed and he could carry your parcels. Besides, I know he finds the forced inactivity galling.'

'I suppose that would be better than nothing,' Aline pouted.

I wanted to kick her.

'Of course you may have Abel, my dear Aline,' said Noël. 'Pray, do not tease Emilia to go, if she does not feel up to it.' He smiled at me reassuringly.

I resisted the temptation to put out my tongue at Aline. I could see that Noël didn't like her persistence, for this was not the first time the conversation had come up, but he seemed unable to do anything about it other than looked pained.

After all that, Aline did not go. I didn't think she would.

I kept to my room as much as I could and got on with *The Secret of the Drakensburgs*. I had uncovered a new problem — love. In my previous books, *The Doom of the House of Ansbach*, for example, only the readers guessed that Bertram was in love with Fidelia. She, herself, was too modest. Even after his proposal (on bended knee, naturally) she only blushed and whispered, '*Pray, sir, talk to Papa.*' This, in spite of the fact that he has rescued her from brigands, left elegantly written sonnets in her chamber and heaved enough sighs to extinguish any number of candles.

I now saw that this would not do. Loving Noël had made me acutely sensitive to his changing moods and feelings. I treasured every word or look and searched it for meanings that, alas, were not there. If Fidelia had truly loved Bertram, she could not possibly have been oblivious to his affection — it simply was not credible.

Erminia must behave differently with Sir Godfrey de Roussillon. I would allow her to weep into her pillow when she thinks he cares for the false Alienora. I hoped that Mr Robinson would not find such an innovation so shocking that he would turn down the book.

I had another worry. I was running out of paper. I wrote my romances in blank leather-bound books and each novel took about two of them. I had only a couple of dozen pages left and would shortly be forced either to stop writing, which was unthinkable, or to go out and buy a replacement book, which would be awkward. However could I explain it? If I could go out shopping for one thing, why not to Bond Street with Aline?

On 25 January, there was a slight thaw, which continued for four days, though it still froze at night. Abel was gloomy.

'There won't be no chance of a frost fair now,' he said sadly.

'Never mind, Abel. At least you'll be able to get out again.'

Oh, for some warmth, I thought, and to get rid of this dreadful snow. I could hear the drip of melting icicles. The whole country seemed to be obsessed with the rise and fall of the thermometer; it was chronicled every day in *The Times*. On the Thames, the ice began to crack up and huge unwieldy floes detached themselves and started to move downstream.

At the end of the week Abel sneaked out and went down to the Adelphi wharf. He returned, eyes shining.

'You can hear the noise, Miss Emilia,' he exclaimed. 'A cracking and a grinding, like giant's teeth. They say it's all moving downstream and it'll be gone in a few days.'

'The damage left will be dreadful,' I

observed. I'd seen the boats frozen and crushed in the ice. There were many poor people who would be ruined.

It looked as though the freeze was over and soon the roads would be clear again. Post and carriages would get through once more. I would have to make a move.

Where should I go? Where would I be safe? Rich widows were always vulnerable to predatory men, and Balquidder was ruthless. He knew where I was, but at least in John Street there were people who would protect me. In Somers Town, say, I could live more freely in that I would not have to explain my comings and goings, but if Balquidder ever tracked me down I would be at his mercy. There would be no Noël to turn to.

Then it struck me: I did not have to live in Somers Town, where it was cheap, nor did I have to return to Tranters Court. When Mr Latimer had sorted out my affairs, I would be a rich woman. I could live where I liked, I would have nearly £900 a year, quite enough to enable me to hire a burly footman or two to protect me.

Mrs Irvine had once told me of a friend of hers who had inherited a fortune and was paralysed with fear for six whole months and quite unable to enjoy her new wealth. I had laughed and thought that I would never be so foolish. Now I understood. My imagination was used to dealing with hair-raising adventures amid the Alps — which I had never visited — but when it came to the reality of having my own house and sufficient servants to protect me, not to mention freedom to live my life as I saw fit, I could scarcely envisage it, let alone act.

I was now wealthy. I need no longer make my own clothes. I could travel if I wanted to, see the Alps for myself, spend the winter in Rome, anything. None of it seemed real; Count Drakensburg's castle, towering on its precipice, had more reality for me than my fortune.

Leaving John Street meant leaving Noël. I couldn't bear the thought of not seeing him even though, since Aline's arrival, it cost me more pain than pleasure. I dreaded saying a final good-bye.

My mind went round and round my new status like a squirrel in a cage, unable to rest anywhere. Eventually I decided to make an appointment with Mr Latimer and talk over my financial situation. Perhaps that would make it more real.

On Saturday, the temperature dropped suddenly. The ice floes froze together in an unwieldy mass and jammed against the narrow arches and projecting starlings of

London Bridge. Upstream of the bridge, everything froze solid from shore to shore.

On Tuesday, 1 February, *The Times* reported that it was safe to cross the Thames. In spite of the snow, once again piled high in the gutters, hundreds of people flocked to the stretch between London Bridge and Blackfriars Bridge to see the astounding sight.

I confess that I, too, was longing to see it. I told myself that it was research. I had often described my heroines and villains fleeing over the ice, now I could see, even walk on, something similar.

Abel and I hatched a plan to sneak out the following morning. We would tell nobody, and I would wear Bill's clothes again. We decided to go out early, at about nine o'clock. Abel would have finished his early morning tasks and was usually undisturbed in the boot room, cleaning lamps or shoes. I mostly stayed in my room in the mornings, so nobody would wonder where I was.

I didn't think that Balquidder would be watching for me at an hour when he probably knew, from his spies, that I would be upstairs. All the same, I took precautions.

'I'm feeling tired, I didn't sleep well,' I said to Hannah, when she came up with my breakfast tray. 'Please see that I am not disturbed.'

The moment she'd gone, I bounded out of bed, put on Bill's old clothes and bundled up my hair under his cap. I wolfed down my roll and butter, swallowed my chocolate and put an apple in my pocket for later.

I crept past Noël's room to where Abel was waiting in the boot room, his eyes bright with excitement. The most difficult bit was getting out of the house. The front door was too visible — both Aline's and Noël's windows faced the front. In the basement was the kitchen, the scullery, the larder, the wash-room and Mrs Good's parlour. The door to the basement area was at the end of a short passage to the right of the kitchen. Outside was the privy and the coal hole.

There was no help for it. That was the way we must get out. Abel had been down earlier and unbolted the basement door.

We negotiated the back stairs safely and crept past the kitchen and scullery. We had just reached the larder when Mr Bagnigge came out of the privy. He stopped still and looked at us both, his arched eyebrows mirroring his tufts of hair.

'Oh, Mr Bagnigge,' I exclaimed breathlessly. 'You won't tell on us, will you? We'll only be out for an hour or so.'

'And where might you be going?'

'We want to see the river.'

'Ah.' He pulled us both inside the larder and looked me up and down. I was relieved to see a twinkle in his eye. 'So this is Master Daniels, is it?'

I blushed.

'Very well, then. Be off with you. I'll say I sent Abel out with a message.'

We ran.

People were gathering all along the shores of the Thames and crowding on to the bridges. The watermen, who had been unable to ply their trade for some weeks now, had placed planks down to the ice as a safe passage and were charging twopence per person. I could see one man energetically trying to break the ice on either side of his plank to ensure custom. An increasing number of brave souls were already down on the ice, one small boy turning cartwheels in his excitement.

Abel and I stood on Blackfriars Bridge.

'I thought it would be all smooth-like,' said Abel, disappointed.

'It does look rough,' I agreed.

All the same, it was an astonishing sight. The river had completely vanished. In its place was what looked like a white field with dips and hummocks, and every now and then a boat frozen into it, its masts laden with snow. I could see huge icicles hanging down, as sharp as knives, from the bridge arches. One man was bashing at them with a pole and, as they fell, they shattered with a noise like breaking glass.

'You're going to get your frost fair, Abel,' I said, and indicated the rows of tents which were already springing up on the ice. Somebody was strewing cinders from a bucket to form a path. We pointed things out to each other; swings with a small queue of children by them; donkey rides, with the donkeys' hooves tied up in makeshift sacking boots; a number of printing presses and numerous tents advertising drink.

'Do let's go down, miss,' urged Abel. He was stamping his feet to keep warm.

'I'd like a closer look at Three Cranes Wharf,' I said, pointing to the huge ungainly building on the left. There was a row of tents quite close. 'Put your muffler round your chin, Abel, you don't want to be recognized.'

I did the same with my own scarf. I was taking no risks.

We decided that it would be quicker to walk up Upper Thames Street and get down to the river by Queenhithe Stairs. On the way, I passed a stationer's and bought a new book to write in. The shopkeeper tied it in a neat paper parcel and made a loop with the string. I put it round my wrist. Dozens of people were heading for the river. In spite of the cold, the snow and the muddy pavements, there was an air of holiday. Faces were pinched with cold and starvation, but eyes were sparkling.

Queenhithe itself was fairly quiet. All the ships in the dock were frozen in and a few disconsolate sailors were sitting on the quay warming their hands around a brazier. At the bottom of the stairs was a man with a plank. We could perfectly well have jumped down without his assistance, but his face looked gaunt, so I paid our twopences, and he handed us down on to the ice.

Sharp Cockney enterprise was already beginning to take over. A woman with a tray round her neck was selling mutton pies for twice the price they would normally fetch. 'Pies on the ice! Fresh pies on the ice! Pipin' 'ot!' There was a sign hanging from her tray which read, *Fresh Lapland Mutton*.

The row of tents was right in front of us now. Most were for drink and had gaily coloured pennants flying from the tent pole. *Moscow* said one — I suppose in ironic reference to Napoleon's defeat in Russia the year before. Someone had set up a charcoal brazier on the ice and was selling roast chestnuts. He seemed quite unconcerned about the icy water somewhere beneath him.

''Ot chestnuts! 'Ot!' he cried.

Abel tugged at my sleeve. 'Look, miss.'

One of the tents bore the legend *Jack Frost's Printing Press*. There was a small queue outside it. What on earth were they selling? We wandered over. Outside was a notice, which read:

Copperplate print done in the best style by Jack Frost, Esquire, 3d.

You that do walk here and do design to tell
Your children's children what this year befell
Come buy this print and it will then be seen
That such a year as this has seldom been.

In memory of the Great Frost, February 2nd, 1814

A man was collecting money and another was working the press so that each customer got his own, freshly printed.

'Shall we go, Abel? Would you like a print?'

'Oh yes, miss.'

Threepence was a lot of money for a flimsy piece of paper but I reckoned, as doubtless did everybody else in the queue, that it did not happen often. We had to queue for about ten minutes.

I could see the Moscow tent more clearly now. *City of Moscow*, said the sign, *Fine Purl, Good Gin and Rum*. There was another tent close by which read *Wellington for Ever. Good Gin. Shave Well* read a third. Shave? On the ice? They must be mad, but I noticed he had some customers. I gave Abel sixpence.

'I'd like some gingerbread,' I said, nodding towards a sign which read *Gin and Gingerbread Sold Here*. 'And get whatever you want.'

Abel darted off. I shuffled up the queue until it was nearly my turn. There was a charcoal brazier just outside and I was grateful for its warmth, for standing about, even for ten minutes, had frozen my toes and my fingers were bloodless inside my gloves. Hot cinders fell on to the snow and hissed. I could see inside the tent now.

There was the press, with several packets of paper resting on an upturned box. A man was working a lever which pressed the plate down on to the paper. Behind him were a couple of chairs and there, sitting like some huge malevolent toad, was a figure I recognized. My mouth went dry with fear and I could feel the hairs prickle on the back of my neck. He had his back to me and he was smoking a cigar and talking to another man.

As it neared to my turn, Abel came back. I nodded towards Balquidder. Abel's eyes widened. 'That's one of Moxon's coves with him,' he whispered.

''Ow many?' demanded the man by the press.

I couldn't speak. It was Abel who said, 'Two.'

Fumbling, I handed over sixpence. Crunch, crunch went the press and two prints, still wet, were handed over.

'Next!'

We left. My knees were shaking. Abel handed me my gingerbread, but I couldn't eat it. I thrust it into my pocket.

It wasn't until we were a good twenty yards away that a thought struck me, 'I wonder what he wants with Moxon's?'

'I don't know, miss,' said Abel. 'And if it's all the same to you, I don't want to stay to find out.'

★　★　★

On the way home, we decided that Abel would inform Mr Bagnigge of our seeing Balquidder. We got back without mishap and I was able to sneak in unobserved and go up to my room and change. I was relieved to have my new book to write in.

At luncheon, I noticed that Aline was looking unusually animated. Her eyes were sparkling and she was dressed with more than her usual elegance in the violet silk — she had evidently decided that it was time she went into half-mourning.

'I am 'at home' this afternoon,' she informed us. 'I do not know who will venture out to see little me in this dreadful weather, but one must try and keep up with one's friends.' She raised her eyebrows coquettishly in Noël's direction.

He said nothing.

'I am sorry that you will not be available, Mrs Kirkwall,' continued Aline, darting me a look that would not have shamed Medusa.

'Are you going out, Emilia?' asked Noël.

'No.'

'Mrs Kirkwall has informed us frequently of her recent widowhood; I know she does not want company,' said Aline, with a thin, triumphant smile. 'But I hope that you will look in, Noël.'

'I fear not. I have work to do.'

Aline left the table early, doubtless to put some more burnt cork on her eyelashes.

'You must forgive her, Emilia,' said Noël, when she'd gone. He looked uncertain and unhappy. 'She cannot know how unkind she sounds.'

'It doesn't matter. I shall have a comfortable afternoon up in the schoolroom with Richard.'

'It's very good of you to take so much trouble with him.'

'It's no trouble. I'm very fond of him.'

I went upstairs to my room. I would write for an hour or so first. At half past three I heard the front door knocker. I would wait until whoever it was had come upstairs to the drawing-room and then I'd go up to the schoolroom. I could hear Mary's voice in the hall as she welcomed the visitor, the heavy tread of feet — surely masculine feet (I might have guessed) and the sound of the drawing-room door opening and closing.

I locked *The Secret of the Drakensburgs* back in my valise and pushed it under the bed and then went upstairs. Miss Carver was snoozing by the side of the fire and Richard was sitting at the table with his model soldiers in front of him.

'You poor thing!' I exclaimed. 'It's so dark in here.' I bustled round lighting the candles and the oil lamp. 'That's better. What is it today, Richard? Still Vittoria?'

'It's a battle of my own,' Richard confided. 'I wanted to build a fort with my bricks, but

253

Miss Carver says that's it's too noisy when I knock it down.'

Did she indeed? I was outraged. She was supposed to be there for Richard, not the other way about.

'Why don't we build a fort on the carpet?' I suggested. 'That will be quieter.'

Richard climbed down from his chair, ran to get his box of bricks and was soon animatedly explaining about bastions and redoubts. I understood (more or less) what he was saying, it was when he got to ravelins that he lost me. I spent a happy hour or so with him, and whatever noise we made, it certainly didn't disturb Miss Carver. I said as much.

'I daresay it's the gin,' said Richard unconcernedly.

'Gin!' I remembered suspecting as much the first morning I had met Richard.

'Yes, she keeps it under her mattress. I'm not supposed to know.' He saw my look and added, 'I don't mind, truly I don't. It's better when she's asleep.'

What was Noël about to be employing such a woman?

Richard and Miss Carver usually had their supper at six o'clock.

'Oh, she always wakes up for meals,' he said, as we began to clear up at about twenty to six.

I could hear faintly the closing of the front door downstairs. Whoever it was had gone. A long visit, too; certainly not the correct twenty minutes or so. Was this visitor an admirer, I wondered? It would explain why she was wearing the violet silk gown. Of course, Aline would remarry, she was far too pretty and pleasure-loving to stay single, and it would have to be to somebody rich, either here or in France. Possibly she was already encouraging potential suitors.

I wished I had her confidence.

I kissed Richard good-night and went downstairs to change for dinner. I could not hope to emulate the violet silk, but at least my oyster surah, although home-made, was cut in the latest fashion. In any case, I knew well enough that Noël would scarcely notice me beside Aline.

The moment I opened the drawing-room door I smelled the rose pomade. Balquidder had been. I have known fear several times in my life, and it's always the same. I am plunged under an icy waterfall which goes straight down from my head to my toes, leaving me cold and shivering. I had to clutch at the door jamb for support. I could see Noël and Aline staring at me, but I couldn't move.

'Balquidder's been here!' I whispered.

Aline flushed. Noël looked from her to me. 'He's been in this room. I can smell him.'

Aline gave a light laugh, but she was disconcerted. 'Mrs Kirkwall is envious of my male visitor, *peut-être*.' She gave Noël a sideways glance.

'Has Balquidder been here?' demanded Noël.

Aline pouted. 'Why should he not? He is a charming man and he was a friend of my husband's. Surely, I may see my friends? He is most attentive.' She looked down and fiddled with a button on her dress.

'It was Balquidder who had Richard kidnapped,' said Noël. 'You knew that, and yet you let him visit you?'

Aline dabbed at her eyes. 'You told me that Richard was discovered at a common printers. What have they to do with Mr Balquidder? I asked him and he said he knew nothing of it. In any event, Richard was not hurt.'

'What do you mean, 'not hurt'?' I put in. I was so furious that my voice shook. 'Richard has had nightmares ever since. You must know that, since I understand from Miss Carver that you have forbidden him a night-light. How could you be so cruel to such a loving little boy?'

'How dare you!' Aline tossed her head. Part

of me was very angry, but another part was wondering how she managed to get away with gestures which, in anybody else, would be seen as melodramatic. 'Who are you to tell me how to look after Richard? You, who are little better than a trollop. Noël, how can you sit there and let her insult me so?' I noticed that her English had suddenly improved.

'Did you really forbid him a night-light?' asked Noël.

'You don't want a Miss Molly, do you? Good heavens, is this creature to say what shall happen in this house?' She indicated me. 'Mr Balquidder says that your precious husband never cared two straws for you.'

'But I might have cared for him,' I said quietly. 'To lose somebody you have loved when you have not been loved in return is a double pain.' I realized that I was not talking only of Stephen.

'I have always been able to attach men,' replied Aline. She smiled at Noël from under her lashes.

'You are fortunate,' I said drily. 'But you should not have been discussing me with Mr Balquidder.'

I looked at Noël, I had never seen a man fall out of love, but I recognized it at once. He looked shocked, angry — and relieved. When he spoke, his voice was perfectly calm, but resolute.

'In future, Aline, you will have nothing to do with Richard's upbringing. Secondly, Balquidder is not welcome in my house, and lastly, I think you should apologize to Mrs Kirkwall.'

'Apologize! To that doxy? Did anybody think to check that she really was married? I'd be very surprised myself.' She shot me a venomous look.

There was a short silence, then Noël said, 'Why did you come here, Aline? What did you want? You regularly overspend your jointure and yet you went to the expense of hiring a post-chaise and outriders to come here in such unseasonable weather for no very good reason. Or was there another purpose? One to do with Balquidder, perhaps?'

Aline drew several shuddering breaths, which agitated her bosom in a way which I daresay she had practised in the glass, and then said, 'I shall not stay here to be insulted. Lady Forres has begged me to consider her house as my home. I shall leave tomorrow.'

The gong went.

I was most impressed by her timing. All it needed was for Aline to remember her cue and sweep out.

She did not fail me. She rose to her feet. 'I

258

cannot face a morsel of food,' she announced. 'Pray ask Mrs Good to send a tea-tray up to my room.' She left in a swirl of skirts.

I nearly clapped.

Noël rang the bell for Mrs Good and gave the order for Aline's tea-tray and then said, 'Mrs Good, under no circumstances is Mr Balquidder to be allowed into the house. Please make sure that everybody knows and you will see to it that the front and back doors are secured at all times.'

'Yes, sir.' She darted a malevolent look at me and left.

We ate our dinner almost in silence. When Noël did speak, it was about Richard.

'Emilia, could you please tell Miss Carver that Richard may have his night-light?'

'It must come from you,' I replied. 'Miss Carver has already snubbed me once on the subject.'

Noël sighed. 'It is natural that she should take her orders from Aline, I suppose. She has been responsible for Richard for so long.'

Interesting, I thought. Noël may be disillusioned, but unpicking the threads of love is a long business. He must acknowledge that Aline was never a proper person to look after Richard, and he will feel guilty. It reminded me of Gulliver on Lilliput, tied down by hundreds of tiny threads. That's what love was like — there was no clean cut, and you were free. It was the painful undoing of all the small threads that bound one heart to another.

My own heart was soaring. I could almost hear it singing. It was not just that Noël was no longer Aline's dupe, it was the prospect of her going.

There was more: Noël was free — and I wanted him myself.

I did my best to dampen my singing heart. I was thin and beaky, and Noël had been seriously annoyed with me. Why on earth did I think he might ever want me? It would be stupid — no mad, to hope for anything. It made no difference.

We finished our meal and moved back to the drawing-room.

'I heard from dos Santos, my agent in Demerara, this morning,' said Noël, suddenly.

'Oh?' My heart sank. I had not forgotten Noël's views on owning slaves. I still felt very strongly about it, but I wasn't sure that I was up to another full scale argument just then.

'He writes of small fires breaking out in the sugar mill. He can't be sure whether it is accident or sabotage.'

'Are sugar mills especially vulnerable?' I guessed that Noël did not want to discuss

Aline and this new topic was as much a diversion of his thoughts as anything.

'Yes. After the cane is crushed, the liquid has to be boiled several times to a very high temperature for the sugar crystals to form. Fires are a constant risk. A bad fire at the mill would be financially disastrous.'

'Why should the slaves care whether the mill burns down or not?' I observed. 'I'm sure I shouldn't.'

'I have written to dos Santos to say that, apart from essential maintenance, the slaves are to have Sundays free. There is a law to that effect anyway, but I gather it's honoured more in the breach than in the observance. I also ordered fewer floggings than he sees fit to hand out at the moment.'

'Do you have any way of checking whether he does as you ask?'

'No,' Noël admitted.

'You are keeping the estate, then?' I could feel my temper rising. Noël to be making money from the degradation of other human beings? I nursed my anger jealously — it would save me from too much regret and heartache.

Noël looked across at me. 'I listened to what you said when we talked about this before. You pricked my conscience. I don't want to be part of the rampant cruelty that I know goes on. I can't change the world, but I can try to make the lot of the slaves I do have easier.'

'Slavery is uneconomic, you know,' I said. 'Certainly it will be from now on, when no more slaves can be imported.'

'How do you work that out?'

'It's not me. There have been pamphlets on the subject. Most of your slaves are male, I take it?' Noël nodded. 'Female slaves are less valuable in terms of work and children are a liability until they are about twelve. Then somebody has to look after the babies, the children, the ill and the old. Your slaves will grow steadily older, the reproduction rate will fall and then what?'

'True, I hadn't thought of that.'

'Quite apart from the hideous cruelty, it will be uneconomic to run an estate using slaves in about twenty years' time, even if we don't manage to get a law against it by then.'

'Then a lot of people are going to be ruined,' said Noël. 'Not only the plantation owners, but people in this country, the sugar merchants and cotton manufacturers, for example. There are whole towns in Lancashire which depend upon cotton.'

'Is that a valid reason to have one man's prosperity on the back of another's misery and degradation?'

'Emilia, life isn't that tidy — '

'Noël!' I burst out. 'I can't bear it that you are involved in slave-owning. I know that things aren't easy, that of course you cannot just wave a wand to free your slaves like in some fairy-tale. I know that if you sold the plantation, then somebody else would buy it and perhaps be a cruel taskmaster. I know that it's none of my business what you do . . . it's just that I find the idea of slavery so repellent, so degrading, like some loathsome disease that I can't bear to think that you could be associated with it.'

I stopped, appalled at what I'd said. It wasn't that I didn't mean every word, but that I should betray how deeply I hated Noël's part in it. If the issues around slavery weren't easy, I thought, neither were the processes of loving a man who was, however unwillingly, involved with it.

There was a pause, then Noël said, 'Did you know that there is at least one ex-slave, maybe several, who have bought plantations of their own in Demerara?'

'That cannot be true?' It came out as a whisper. I had never heard anything so horrible in my life.

'It is. Human nature is not always reasonable and consistent. I have to cope as best I may with the situation as it is. There are very strict laws about freeing slaves out there. Look, Emilia, I promise that I will do what I can.'

I drew a deep breath. 'Thank you. I am sorry to be so melodramatic. I'm sure you've had enough of it for one day.'

Noël smiled. 'Let us change the subject then. Tell me, have you read the book Mrs George has been reading? *The Castle of Apollinari?*'

I felt my colour rise. 'No . . . no, is it any good?'

'I've been enjoying it. In fact, I bought another one of his, *The Doom of the House of Ansbach*. I had thought to give it to Mrs George for her birthday but, in the circumstances, I think I shall keep it myself.'

I began to feel like a mouse being played with by a cat. I didn't dare to look at him. Had he guessed?

'I am enjoying *Gulliver's Travels*,' I said desperately. 'My father would never let me read it as a child. He thought it was lewd and immoral. I can see why he thought it lewd, but not immoral. It's one of the most seriously moral books I've ever read.'

The dangerous moment passed. Noël allowed the discussion to move to the safer subject of the satire of Jonathan Swift. I glanced at him only once. His eyes held a look of amused understanding. I hoped it was about Gulliver.

★ ★ ★

There was much to-ing and fro-ing the following morning. Aline had obviously written to Lady Forres, for a footman wearing the Forres livery arrived with a letter. Then there was all the to-do of packing her things.

I spent the morning writing in my room and trying to ignore the bustle along the corridor as Aline complained and her maid trotted to and fro. I was well into my chapter, when there was a creak and my door began to open stealthily. I looked up. It was Jeanne, Aline's maid.

'Yes, Jeanne? What is it?'

She looked horribly guilty. 'I am sorry, *madame*. I didn't think ... I must have mistaken ... ' She beat a hasty retreat.

I went to the door and locked it. I could hazard a good guess as to what Jeanne was after: the lace on those gowns that had been Mrs Beresford's.

Aline left later that morning and I felt obliged to be civil and go downstairs to say good-bye. Mrs Good was in the hall mopping her eyes on her apron as was Miss Carver, who had brought Richard down. Aline was smiling bravely. She clasped a stiff Richard to her bosom, murmured a few words to Miss Carver and patted her eyes again with that ridiculous handkerchief. She was obviously generous with the servants' vails, for Mary and Hannah were curtsying up and down like a couple of jack-in-a-boxes. I got the merest touch of two cold fingers and a slight inclination of the head. Mr Bagnigge looked sour. I caught his eye as he went out to Lady Forres' carriage with her luggage and an eyelid flickered at me.

Noël limped out from his study and said all that was proper. He insisted on handing Aline into the carriage and stood politely on the steps until it had rounded the corner. I turned to go back upstairs and found Mr Bagnigge beside me.

'He won't be himself for a while, I'm thinking,' he said, in a low voice, 'but I don't doubt that eventually he'll come to his senses.' He gave me an enigmatic smile and went into Noël's study.

I stared after him. Did he mean . . . ? I floated upstairs as if on wings. I had existed on such short rations of happiness for so long, that even the faintest encouragement was heady, like drinking champagne on an empty stomach. The simile is appropriate, for

I relaxed my guard and made a catastrophic mistake.

That afternoon, Richard, Noël and I resumed our tea-times. Miss Carver came down with Richard and said, 'Excuse me, Colonel Beresford, might I have a word with you, if convenient?'

'Certainly, Miss Carver.' Noël put down his paper.

'Master Richard needs some new clothes. He is growing so fast that he is shooting out of his jackets and trousers. Mrs George used to get his jackets made at Stammers in Bond Street. I have the measurements to hand. I wonder if Mrs Kirkwall would come with me to choose the materials? She will know best what is needed.'

'Of course, I will,' I said at once. 'We'll go tomorrow. Would you like that, Richard?'

'Best not take Master Richard, madam,' said Miss Carver. 'This cold weather doesn't do his chest any good.'

We arranged to go the following morning at ten o'clock. I was stupidly gullible and naïve. I even looked forward to getting out.

We did the first bit of shopping amicably enough, discussing the best materials and how much turn up should be allowed. I argued successfully for some military-looking brass buttons for the jacket. Richard would like that. It gave me a painful pleasure to be ordering things for Noël's son.

Having settled that, we went to Grafton House, where one could buy practically anything. Socks were socks, we decided, Richard would grow out of them. They need only be of serviceable quality. Miss Carver left me to buy the socks and went off to see about some linen for his shirts.

Even then I didn't suspect.

The crush in the shop was indescribable. At first I didn't realize that the pressure was anything out of the way. Then I felt hands on my neck. There was a sudden squeeze. Too late, I tried to cry for help but no sound came out. Fool! I thought. Then the darkness closed in and, after that, nothing.

The next thing I remember, I was being bundled up some stairs by a couple of men and thrown roughly on to a bed. The room was icy cold. Then there was the creak of heavy steps and the smell of rose pomade. I didn't need to open my eyes to know who it was.

9

I kept my eyes closed. I still felt dizzy and my neck ached unpleasantly from where it had been squeezed. Balquidder made no attempt to wake me. He stood for perhaps two minutes which felt like two hours. Then he left. I heard the key grate in the lock and his heavy footsteps going down the stairs.

I opened my eyes cautiously. I was in an attic room somewhere, probably Wych Street. There was a steeply sloping ceiling, a window with very small windowpanes and a fireplace which had obviously been unused for many years, for a jackdaw's nest had fallen down into the grate. I was lying on a lumpy mattress on a narrow wooden bed. Beside it was a rickety wooden chair and beyond that an old chest of drawers with a large book propping up one leg.

I got up carefully and went to the window. My head was still swimming and it hurt whenever I swallowed. I peered out. I was indeed in Wych Street, at least the houses opposite overhung in the way that I remembered. I wasn't in Crane Alley, at any rate.

I cursed myself for not being more suspicious of Miss Carver asking for my company. I should have guessed. I had allowed myself to be flattered when she said, 'She will know best what is needed'. Stupid, stupid Emilia! Why on earth should you know best? You have no children. You know nothing of what a small boy needs.

How long would it take for anybody to raise the alarm? Probably not until luncheon. Would Abel guess that I was here? At least Balquidder didn't know that I knew he lived here. Was there anything I could do? I was frantically trying to block out my fear. I could feel panic just underneath the surface — and terror — but I couldn't, mustn't, give way to it.

I had a spare handkerchief in my reticule. Could I fix it somehow outside the window so that Abel would see it? If he came. On the other hand, Balquidder might see it as well. I would wait. Maybe after dark — I tried to quell the thought that I might not be alive then.

It was freezing in that attic room. Whenever I breathed out, I could see a cloud of steam. I went back to the bed and lay down, pulling the thin blanket round me. Thank God I was wearing my warm cloak. I felt cold, ill and wretched. This time the walls had closed in and there was no escape.

I forced myself to think about Balquidder. He wanted my money, I was quite clear about that. What would he do? Getting me to write a will in his favour was one way but that, surely, would arouse suspicions, especially if I then conveniently died. There would have to be a body, my disappearance would not be enough. Besides, Noël would surely take steps to see that questions were asked?

I knew enough of Balquidder to know that he never did anything which would cast suspicion on him directly. He always hid behind somebody else, like Stephen, or George. He was the arch puppeteer who pulls strings. So long as I did not sign away my money, I would be left alive — probably.

What should I do? The only thing I could think of was to buy time, even twenty-four hours would help. At least in London I had friends; Noël would not desert me: he knew how dangerous Balquidder was.

I tried to think of what Erminia would have done, but it was hopeless. That was a Gothic fantasy — this a terrifying reality. My readers knew that she would somehow gain freedom, fortune and love at the end. Wretched make-believe!

I turned my mind back to Balquidder. He didn't like women — I certainly didn't think he was after my body. Would it be better to be calm and dignified, as Erminia would surely have been, or weepy and hysterical? Which would buy me the time I so desperately needed?

Many years ago I had had a nightmare about Balquidder. He had turned into a monstrous baby with a huge gaping mouth, which sucked everything into it. I knew that whatever he swallowed would never be enough to satisfy him. I had often thought of that dream and had used versions of it many times in my books. The next morning I had asked Stephen if he knew anything about Balquidder's childhood and he told me that he was an orphan brought up by a stern Presbyterian aunt.

'Don't mention it to him,' he warned. 'He doesn't like it known.'

It echoed in my mind like a warning. I must not awake that baby. Balquidder's opinion of women was low, let me keep it low. I would be cringing and weepy, everything he despised. It was not much, but acting a part took away the feeling of total helplessness. My intuition told me that a pathetic woman would serve my turn better than a defiant one.

Time wore on and it began to get dark. I was just wondering whether I dared risk putting out my handkerchief on the window ledge, perhaps wedging it under the window-frame, when I heard footsteps. I fled back to the bed and found that I didn't have to act trembling. It was his bulk that was so terrifying, and I am a small woman.

He came in, holding a candlestick.

I gulped, tried to speak, and couldn't. I pulled my cloak closer.

'Good,' he said. 'I expect you've worked out why you're here.'

'I'll give you my money,' I quavered. 'I don't want it. Truly, I don't. Only, please, let me go.'

He laughed. 'Let you go? No, my dear Emilia, I have another plan for you.' My heart began to pound so loudly that all I could hear was drumming in my ears. 'I've decided I need a wife.'

I went numb with fear; it was a sort of physical horror that made the bile rise up in my throat. If I were his wife then my fortune would automatically become his. No need for an instant disappearance. The law would allow him to do anything to me: beat me, lock me up, have me put away as mad. Nobody could do a thing. A woman was, as Mr Latimer had explained *une femme couverte*, she had no legal existence outside her husband. I would prefer death.

'No!' it came out as a whisper.

'My dear Emilia, you really must be more co-operative.' He reached out and took hold of my chin and jerked my face towards him. I winced as he crushed the bruises that were already painful. 'You are fortunate. I can assure you that there are many women who would love to become Mrs Archibald Balquidder — Aline Beresford amongst them.'

'Mrs George!' I echoed, stupified. Had he promised marriage to Aline?

'Now there's an attractive woman but, alas, she has no money. No, Aline is going to be disappointed. And furious.' He laughed. 'See how I care about you, Emilia? Aline has made her feelings about you very plain. Think how you will enjoy putting her in her place.'

Somehow, in my terror, a solution occurred to me. 'I . . . I cannot marry you, Mr Balquidder,' I said. 'I have resigned the control of my fortune to my father. He would never allow it.'

'You've what?' The grip tightened cruelly. He threw me back roughly and there was a crack as my head hit the wall. I gave a cry of pain, which he ignored. He strode to the window, his bulk filling the frame, so that the remaining light was blotted out. I could see his fat, bull-like shoulders clenched. Had I gone too far? Would he believe me? He must be well aware that my father had not allowed me a penny during my marriage to Stephen.

Then he turned round. The look on his face was murderous. 'I have a way round that,' he said. 'Even now, as we talk, your precious friend Noël is tied up and under guard. When I have your written word that you will marry me, he will be released, and not a moment before. I do not recommend that you keep him waiting. You know what the temperature is like outside. Once I decide that he is no longer of any use to me, he won't last long. You will marry me and I can assure you that I shall find a way to persuade your father to release your fortune.'

I began to cry. It was partly genuine; I was horrified by Noël's capture — if it were true — and partly because I didn't know what else to do.

'You can't have got Colonel Beresford.' I hated the way he gave everyone their Christian names, as though he were intimate with them.

Balquidder laughed, reached into his pocket and brought out the broken-off silver handle to Noël's stick.

'Next time I shall bring something more personal. An ear, perhaps.' He saw my look of horror, and added, 'My dear Emilia, the reason for my success in life is that I dare do many things that deter lesser men. Well? Which is it to be? Marriage, or Noël's life?'

My sobs grew louder and this time they were genuine. I felt trapped, desperate and almost paralysed with terror. I could feel Balquidder shaking me, hear him saying something, but it made no sense. For the first time in my life, I had hysterics.

Eventually, he dropped his hand and said, 'I can see there's nothing to be got out of you now. My servant will be up later — he'll enjoy that, even if you don't. You'll see reason in an hour or so. Good-bye for now, my dear.' He turned to go, then turned back and said contemptuously, 'Perhaps you'd like the candle?' There was barely an inch of it left and he put it on the chest of drawers beside the bed and left the room. The key turned in the lock and the stairs groaned under his weight as he went downstairs. I heard him shout to somebody and then the front door slammed.

The moment I heard it, I got up. My hysterics had gone and in their place I felt a cold rage. I knew precisely what I had to do. I was going to get warm. The icy cold made it difficult to think, and I needed a clear head. Somehow, under the paralysis of terror, my mind had been at work. Incongruously, I remembered my moral tale of Marjorie and the curlpapers.

I pulled the heavy book out from where it was propping up the chest of drawers and began to tear out the pages, twisting them into fire lighters. If they could be used for curlpapers, I thought, they could certainly light fires. Soon, all that was left of the book was the bare boards. I took the candle over to the fire and began quickly arranging the twists of papers among the fallen twigs in the grate.

Then I took hold of the rickety chair and forced it apart. It broke with a loud crack. Soon it was a mass of sticks. If there was one thing my years in Edinburgh had taught me, it was to light a fire in the most unpromising circumstances. At least here the twigs were dry. The candle was beginning to gutter. There was about half an inch left.

I applied a twist to the candle, lit the other firelighters and blew gently. I used the boards of the book cover to help the draught. The fire caught. Soon it would need more fuel. I would burn everything in the room, if necessary. Maybe I could burn my way out. That, however, was more risky.

My brain was working again. I had stopped shivering with cold. I fed the fire with sticks from the chair then went over to the window, pushing it up a fraction — it was very stiff. I secured my handkerchief by one corner underneath it and then closed it. With a bit of luck it would just be visible.

I took the remaining bit of candle to the door. I wanted to see if there was a weak bit, a cracked panel, perhaps, but it looked and felt solid, but there was a gap of about half an inch at the bottom. I could see a faint light, presumably from a lamp on the landing below. Balquidder had locked it but the key was still in it on the other side. The candle was guttering.

I took the book cover, now reduced to two boards, and pushed it under the door. Then I went to find a sliver of wood from the broken chair. There was a piece that I thought might do to poke into the keyhole. If I could only push out the key then it should fall on the board and I could draw it into the room. I tried and tried, but the wood was too thin.

The candle went out.

My hands were slippery with desperation. There was only the flickering firelight and I could barely see. The key didn't want to budge. I tried the other end of the sliver, which was thicker, feeling for the keyhole with my fingers. It shifted. I tried again and there was a heavy clunk. Had it fallen on the board? I lay face down, but could see nothing. Stealthily, I began to draw the board in. It felt heavier, but I wasn't sure how secure it was. Eventually, after what seemed like hours, I felt the key and gently eased it in.

I had just picked it up and retrieved the board when I heard footsteps, lighter ones. Abel? Could Abel have come for me? I held my breath.

There was a rattle at the door. Then a jerk.

'Dang it!'

Who was it?

A kick. Several kicks.

'Dang and blast it. Promised me a bit of fun and now he's gorn and removed the blasted key.' A few more savage kicks, then, cursing, the man stomped back downstairs. I could hear him going down several flights and then, a long way below, another door slammed.

I sat down abruptly on the bed. I remembered the dirty, drunken servant I had spoken to when I'd asked for Stephen before. Was that what Balquidder had meant by my seeing reason in the morning? He didn't want me himself, but he'd allow his servant to have his 'bit of fun'. I had to get out, and quickly. The servant was down in the basement and I didn't think he'd bother to come all the way up again, but I couldn't be sure.

I hoped the front door wasn't locked. I had noticed that there were no front areas to the houses in Wych Street. If necessary, I could get out of a ground-floor window, though that would be conspicuous.

Then what? Respectable females were never out alone after dark. If I couldn't get a cab, then I had a long, possibly frightening, journey back to John Street in front of me. However, I couldn't allow myself to dwell on that. First, I had to get out of the house.

The fire was burning away merrily now and I could see reasonably well. I picked up my bonnet, which my captors had flung on the bed, put it on and fastened my reticule to the belt of my dress for safety and tucked a guinea into my bodice. Then I picked up the key and cautiously opened the door.

All was silent. I locked the door behind me, wincing at the noise it made, tucked the key into my reticule and tiptoed downstairs. On the second floor landing all was quiet. It seemed safe to go down again. On the first floor landing was a peg-top oil lamp and again all was silent. I was just about to put my foot on the next tread, when a monstrous shadow elongated itself up the wall.

Opposite me was a door, slightly ajar. I slid in and stood just behind it, between it and a large bookcase. I could feel my heart pounding so heavily, that I was sure it must be audible. The footsteps went into the room next door, I could hear the floorboards creaking. I had no choice but to stay where I was and pray that nobody would come in.

I was in a biggish room with two leaded windows at the end, through which shone a gaslight from the street outside. Was this Balquidder's office? There was a heavy desk underneath the windows, and what I had thought was a bookcase turned out to be a sort of cabinet with dozens of pigeon-holes, each one full of papers. There was the faint, elusive scent of rose pomade. A fire burned in the grate behind a brass fireguard, and that alarmed me more than the rest. Balquidder meant to return — and soon.

Whatever should I do? Should I leave now — and risk the servant catching me? Or should I wait and hope that he would go back downstairs? Suddenly, the footsteps got louder and my door crashed open. I barely suppressed a cry as it hit me and I was squashed right behind it. A man lurched in, bringing with him a powerful smell of brandy. It wasn't Balquidder, the footsteps weren't heavy enough. It must be the servant who had tried the attic door earlier.

I couldn't see him because of the door, but I could hear him. He lurched over to the fire and I heard coals from the scuttle being thrown on. Then he crossed to the window. There was a creak of shutters closing and bangs as the bars slid into place. The curtains were jerked shut. More banging and curses as he hit the desk. Now I could smell tobacco as well as brandy. He sounded in something of a temper.

Finally, he lurched out, slamming the door behind him and crashed down the stairs. I stayed until I heard a basement door shut and then I crept out.

The room was much darker now, but the fire had flared up and was spitting at the fireguard. There was a branch of candles on the mantelpiece. I lit them and returned to the pigeon-holes. I took out one of the contents and read the front cover. *Alexander Max*, it read. Inside were columns of figures on the right and writing on the left. Suddenly, it dawned on me that this must be where Balquidder kept records of all his shady transactions. This Mr Max was obviously one poor wretch who was in his clutches. Strange name, Max, I thought. I replaced it and pulled out the next one. *Alistair Came*, it read. Yes, I must be right. Mr Came — odd name again — must be another client. But why did C come after M?

Then I realized: it was Balquidder's little

habit of referring to people by their Christian names. When I first met him, I had assumed that he called me 'Emilia' because I was his friend's wife, though such familiarity was quite wrong. Later, it occurred to me that maybe he did it as a way of expressing his contempt. Could it be that Mr Max was really a Mr Maxwell, say, and Mr Came, Cameron? Had he pigeon-holed them alphabetically under their Christian names?

Would there be anything under George? There were a lot of Georges, but no George Beresford. I tried Bonne Chance, the name of the Demerara estate. Nothing. Ainderby. Nothing. Had I got it wrong?

In desperation, I looked under Noël and yes, there it was. I opened the file and spread it out on the desk. Letters, receipts for interest — I noticed that Noël had indeed had them all witnessed. Ominously, there was a page listing Noël's own assets and inheritance, as if Balquidder had his eye on those as well. Lastly, there were two parchment documents with seals dangling from them; one was the deeds of Bonne Chance, the other the deeds for Ainderby. Dear God, I thought, no wonder Noël was worried: George must have been mad to risk Ainderby.

What should I do? I ought to remove them,

283

but how? I only had my reticule and that was not nearly big enough.

My eye fell on a cushion. I stripped it of its cover and stuffed the folder inside. Then I returned to the pigeon-holes and looked for Stephen K. It was crossed through in angry black ink and underneath were the ominous words, 'see Emilia', I didn't bother to check my folder beyond confirming that it was indeed mine.

Then I looked up Aline — oh yes, quite a full one there. I flicked through it. At the bottom I noted that money had been paid to Tryphena and Maria C. Miss Carver, perhaps? That too went into the cushion cover.

There were now three suspiciously empty pigeon-holes. I took other folders out at random and filled them, but it would still be easy enough for Balquidder to see where the sequence was wrong. Should I destroy the lot? All I had to do was remove the fireguard and put a couple of burning coals on the hearthrug. The house was an old timber-framed one, it would catch in no time. But there were neighbours to be thought of. In a street like this, fire would spread quickly.

A noise from outside — shouting. It was only some drunken quarrel, but it reminded me that I must get out. Taking the bulging cushion cover, I left the room and crept downstairs. Not a sound. There was a heavy curtain over the front door to keep out the draughts. I lifted it aside and, praise be, the key was in the lock. The servant must have locked it after Balquidder left. I unlocked it and put the key with the other one in my reticule — God knows why, I certainly had no intention of returning.

Once outside and after the warmth of Balquidder's office, the cold made me shiver. Then something struck me. Cold though it was, it was distinctly warmer than it had been. I looked down at the pavement. The paving stones were uneven and there was a puddle of water. The thaw had begun.

As I started off down the road towards Newcastle Street, the church of St Clement Dane's struck seven. Not so late then, but night all the same. I wanted to get to the Strand as soon as possible. It would be more crowded and I'd feel safer. Maybe I could get a cab. Clutching the cushion cover awkwardly, for it was bulky and difficult to grasp, I hurried on.

I was just turning left when I heard quickening footsteps behind me. I began to run. Then a voice, 'Miss Emilia!' I spun round.

'Abel!' Rarely have I been more pleased to see anybody.

'Oh, Miss Emilia, I been waiting. I was going to try to get to 'ee when it was safe. I saw your handkerchief,' Poor Abel's teeth were chattering.

'How long have you been here? Did you see Balquidder?'

'No, miss. I only been here twenty minutes or so. Oh, miss, the colonel's been taken.'

I closed my eyes. Balquidder had told me, but I had hoped it wasn't true. But, of course it was. I had seen the broken-off top of his stick to prove it.

'What happened?' We had turned into the Strand. 'Quick, Abel, get that cab.'

There was a dank old carriage with a bony horse in the cab rank. The cabby spat as Abel ran up, removed the rug from the horse's back and opened the door. Abel made as if to go up on the roof with the cabby.

'For God's sake get inside,' I said. This was no time for social niceties. 'I need to know about the colonel.'

The horse shambled along at a slow trot, but at least we were out of the cold, even if the cab stank of mouldy straw and as if somebody had relieved themselves inside. I told Abel what had happened to me.

'The colonel was that worried when you

didn't return, Miss Emilia. Miss Carver said she must have missed you in Grafton House. She went all weepy.'

Abel managed to put so much disbelief in his voice at the last statement, that I laughed. She was acting, I thought. I remembered the entry in Aline's file. 'Maria C.' Surely that was her?

'What is Miss Carver's Christian name, do you know?'

'Maria, miss. Why?'

'No matter. Go on.'

'Then somebody came and said that you'd been taken in custody for shop-lifting . . . '

'What!'

'That's what they said, miss. The colonel just grabbed his cane and went with them and that's the last we've seen of him.'

I had to force myself not to burst into tears. It was all too much. I seemed to have been rocketed between extreme fear, anger and relief all day. All I wanted was to get back to John Street, be cared for and cosseted and relax. That was impossible, things were far too serious. I must keep calm, I told myself. I pushed my own experiences to the back of my mind and tried to concentrate on what Abel had just told me.

'Is Mr Bagnigge at home?'

'Oh yes, miss. Pulling his hair out, what's

left of it. Sorry, miss, shouldn't laugh.'

I thought of Tryphena and Maria C. I couldn't risk them knowing that I had escaped, not if they were in Balquidder's pay. 'Abel, can you keep quiet?'

'In case someone grasses, miss? Don't worry. I have my suspicions and I know how to hold my tongue. You didn't need to ask.' He was obviously affronted.

I apologized, then said, 'Somehow I've got to get into the house without being seen. At least, I don't mind Hannah knowing, but nobody else. I must see Mr Bagnigge urgently.'

'Better stop the cab at the top of the road and let me go first, miss. Nobody will question it if I go in by the basement, then I can let you in the front door.'

We had turned down off the Strand. I banged on the cab roof to stop it and we got out. I paid the cabby. Abel darted off and I could see his head disappearing down the basement stairs. I walked slowly to the front door and stood quietly.

It was a clear night and the moon had floated up, turning everything a bluey-silver. The masts of the small boats sparkled with drops of water and the light cast strange shadows, different from daylight ones, bluer. There were few people about. Down towards the Adelphi Wharf I could hear the occasional voice. Under the wharf arches, men were sleeping rough. Poor beggars, I thought. As I listened, I could hear a new noise, a sort of groaning and a cracking; the ice was beginning to break up.

If I were right in my suspicions, Noël was in deadly danger.

There was the sound of a turning key and the door behind me opened. It was Hannah.

'Oh, miss,' she breathed. 'We heard you'd been arrested.'

'No such thing,' I said tartly. 'Kidnapped. But not a word, Hannah. I need to see Mr Bagnigge at once.'

'He's in the study, miss. Shall I fetch you something to eat? You must be starving.'

'Yes, please. Anything, whatever you can get hold of, but do it discreetly. I'm serious, Hannah, the colonel's life may depend on it.'

Gracious, I sound melodramatic, I thought, like something out of one of my own romances. Hannah, however, seemed to enjoy it for she crept back downstairs with exaggerated stealth.

The moment I entered the study, Mr Bagnigge came over, shut the door behind me, pushed me into a chair and handed me a small glass of brandy.

'I'll be drunk if I drink all this,' I said, but I

took a sip and felt the warmth spreading inside me.

I told him my adventures as briefly as I could, indicated the cushion cover stuffed full of documents. 'I think you should look at this,' I said. I opened the folder marked Aline and pointed to the two names Tryphena and Maria C. Mr Bagnigge whistled between his teeth. 'They must go in a safe place for now, we haven't got much time. Oh, and these.' I removed the two heavy keys from my reticule and handed them to him.

Mr Bagnigge opened the cupboard where the brandy was kept and locked them inside. The keys went inside an old tobacco jar. There was a soft tap at the door and Hannah entered with a tray with two cups of coffee, a bowl of soup and a couple of slices of bread and butter.

'It's all I could manage, Miss Emilia,' she said breathlessly. She was enjoying herself immensely.

'Don't worry. That's just what I need. Thank you, Hannah.'

'Is that all, miss?'

'I shall be going out again soon. And not a word, Hannah.'

'Oh no, miss. Wild horses wouldn't drag it from me.'

When she'd gone, Mr Bagnigge turned to

me. 'What do you mean, going out, young lady?'

'I believe I know where the colonel is.'

'Moxon's?'

'No. I doubt whether Balquidder would risk that twice, but Moxon's have a printing press on the ice in front of Three Cranes Wharf, Abel and I saw Balquidder there. It's called Jack Frost or some such name.'

'You won't go another step!'

'You need me, Mr Bagnigge. The fair is full of printing presses. I counted at least half a dozen and there may be more. I'll recognize it.'

'And Mr Balquidder will recognize you.'

'No he won't. I'll wear Bill's old clothes and bundle up my hair. Anyway, he won't be expecting to see me ... Besides, time is running out, you know that, Mr Bagnigge. The freeze is over.' My voice faltered and I could say no more. I had a vision of Noël, trussed up and hurt, knowing it was only a matter of time before he sank beneath the icy waters of the Thames. Even as I spoke, I could hear the soft drip, drip from outside the window as the ice melted.

Mr Bagnigge ran his hands over his face. He looked grey and strained. He knew as well as I did that, if Noël were in that tent on the ice, if the cold didn't kill him, then the icy waters would.

'Very well, Miss Emilia. But you'll do as I say. The colonel would never forgive me if I let you come to harm.'

If only that were true, I thought. 'I should think he'd be pleased to be rid of me! I've been nothing but a worry to him.'

Mr Bagnigge gave me a strange look, but said, 'He's probably being held as a hostage for your good behaviour, though it's difficult to see what he could do to stop a marriage between you and Mr Balquidder. You are free and of age. I suppose Mr Balquidder could demand a ransom from the colonel for your freedom.'

'I could never consent to that!'

'The colonel would pay anything to see you safely back.'

I shook my head. I'm sure he meant it kindly, but it was cruel.

'What do we need?' I asked,

'What I took campaigning,' said Mr Bagnigge, holding up a rucksack. 'I had this in the Peninsula, useful when you don't know what lies ahead: knife, rope, flask of brandy, tinder box and lantern.'

'Do you have a spare knife?' I asked. If anything happened I wouldn't surrender without a fight. Indeed, I wouldn't surrender at all. Odd, I thought, my heroines never thought to carry a knife. *In extremis*, they fainted — well, that would be of no use to me. While we were speaking, I had been wolfing down the soup and bread and butter and I began to feel more human.

I put down my soup spoon. 'If the coast is clear, I'll go up now. I'll be about ten or fifteen minutes. And I mean that about a knife, Mr Bagnigge.'

He went to the door and opened it quietly. Noises came from the basement, but otherwise all was silent. He lit me a candle.

'Off you go then,' he said. 'I'll see about your knife.'

I crept upstairs to my room and locked the door behind me. Then I lit a branch of candles, put them on my dressing-table in front of the mirror and set to work. Warmth, I knew, was essential. I had already learned how cold could paralyse. I put on two pairs of stockings under the trousers, and a warm bodice under Bill's coarse linen shirt and corduroy jacket. I wound my muffler round my neck, bundled up my hair under Bill's cap and put on my warm gloves. Then I took my old cloak and, after opening the door carefully and locking it behind me, crept back downstairs.

Mr Bagnigge raised his eyebrows when I came in. I put my hand on my hip and swaggered about the room.

He gave a brief laugh. 'You're a baggage, Miss Emilia, and no mistake.' But at least he didn't tell me that I was a disgrace. He handed me a small dagger.

'Careful, it's sharp. Put it in your belt. That's it. Now, our main job is to get the colonel off safe — without getting you captured. In this exercise, I'm the one who's expendable.'

I opened my mouth to protest.

'Military orders,' he said. 'Come along.'

$$\star \quad \star \quad \star$$

It was a strange scene, the frozen Thames, that night. The sky was clear and a deep midnight blue, almost black, and studded with stars. The Milky Way was flung like a gauze veil almost directly above us. The silhouettes of the houses and churches were etched sharply against the sky. I could see Orion just above the dome of St Paul's, and Cassiopeia over London Bridge. The moon was a brilliant yellowy-orange, like a bright new penny — far too bright for what we needed.

We got onto the Thames at Queenhithe Stairs and, thank God, we were not the only ones out that night. There were a number of glowing braziers on the ice, with huddled shapes around them. The frost fair was far larger than it had been when Abel and I were here only a few days before, though some people were packing up; several tents towards the centre of the river were being dismantled.

It was definitely warmer. There were ominous creaks under my feet. Towards the middle of the river the ice sheet heaved slightly, as if about to give birth.

'Where's this press, then?' asked Mr Bagnigge.

'In front of Three Cranes Wharf. There's a gingerbread hut not far away and a tent that says *Moscow*. Look!' I pointed. The Moscow tent still had its pennant bravely flying.

'It's a long way out.' Mr Bagnigge frowned. Once the ice started to break up, it could disintegrate with frightening swiftness. We did not have much time.

'Come on,' I said. Surely Balquidder would not be here? Surely he would not risk his weight when the ice was beginning to melt? On the other hand, if he had gone home and discovered that I was missing . . .

We followed a group of young lads out on the ice for a lark. There was much pushing and shoving and rough horseplay. Fortunately, they seemed to be heading the same way, down towards London Bridge. I hoped their noisy presence would draw attention away from us. I kept my eyes peeled.

'There!' I tugged at Mr Bagnigge's sleeve and gestured with my head. *Jack Frost's Printing Press*. We were further out than I liked. I could feel the ice moving slightly underneath my feet.

There was a man sitting on an upturned crate outside the entrance, warming his hands at a brazier. Every now and then he reached down to the bottle by his side and took a swig.

'Odd that he's alone,' muttered Mr Bagnigge. 'Of course, he could be guarding the press. Expensive things, presses.'

'Or guarding something else,' I added.

We walked past and, as I did so, I glanced at the tent flap. It was shut.

'We need to see inside that tent,' said Mr Bagnigge.

I felt my dagger. It was razor sharp and the end was pointed. 'He's been drinking,' I said. I looked across at the Moscow tent, which was open. Raucous voices were singing inside. 'If you get a bottle from Moscow, you could engage him in conversation while I slit the tent at the back and have a look inside.'

'You'll be seen from the shore.'

'Can't be helped. I'll lie down. The ice is very uneven and I'll be less visible. Anyway, we don't have a choice. You are the only one who can engage our friend there in drunken banter!'

'Cheeky baggage.' Mr Bagnigge was plainly not happy with this arrangement, but could suggest nothing better.

We parted company. I wove my way behind the tent as if looking for a place to relieve myself. I found a small ridge of ice which would help to conceal me. After a swift glance round, I lay down and edged towards the tent. It was made of thick canvas and, though the point of the dagger went in well enough, it was a struggle to cut through the thickness.

I removed one of my gloves and felt for a tent seam. It might be easier to cut the stitches there. As I moved my hand down, I came across something giving, but inert. A body? Noël's? I pressed slightly. It moved. I didn't dare speak in case the guard heard me, so I gave the lump a reassuring pat, then took the dagger and pushed it into the seam. Each stitch gave way reluctantly. It seemed an age until I had a hole big enough to look inside. Of course, it was dark and I could see very little, in spite of the moon, but enough to know that there was a body trussed up.

'Noël?'

A low groan answered me. I cut some more and reached inside. He was gagged and his hands and legs bound.

'Keep quiet,' I whispered. First, I cut the gag. That was the easiest, then the ropes that tied his hands. They were worryingly tight and his hands were icy. I sawed away as gently as I could until at last the rope fell away. I wanted to kiss his hands warm again, to cry, to shout with the horror of what he must have been through, but I did none of these things. When I spoke, I was relieved to hear my voice coming out quietly and matter-of-fact.

'I need to get to your feet. Can you move up a bit?'

Noël bent his knees and shifted slightly. Outside I could hear Mr Bagnigge and the guard talking. Mr Bagnigge had obviously cracked some lewd joke, for the man spluttered and guffawed. The rope around Noël's ankles had been done in haste, for it was looser and easier to deal with. Noël managed to pull himself into a sitting position and began to massage his hands. It must have hurt him dreadfully. I could see a tear glistening on his cheek and hear his indrawn breath. I turned my attention to the hole and widened it as much as I could.

'Crawl out,' I said.

'I'm not sure I can, my dear.'

Then I heard a familiar voice, 'Drinking on

the job, Ned?' Followed by a blow. The guard screamed. Then, 'Who the hell are you?' This presumably to Mr Bagnigge.

'Jusht passing the time, guv,' came Mr Bagnigge's slurred voice.

'You clear off . . . Hang on a minute, don't I know you . . . ?'

'Get out, Noël,' I hissed. 'I don't care if you crawl, just get out.' I peered round the edge of the tent. Mr Bagnigge was running drunkenly towards the Moscow tent, the guard was lying flat on his back and Balquidder, his back to me, was turning this way and that, hesitating as to what to do.

Mr Bagnigge could take care of himself. My job was to get Balquidder away from Noël. I crawled round, got hold of one of the brazier's legs and jerked it over. Burning coals hissed on the ice, the brazier fell against the tent and fire began to lick upwards. Noël was now half out of the tent and I clambered to my feet, hauled him out and pulled him behind a hummock.

Balquidder spun round. At first I thought he hadn't seen me, for he kicked at the guard as though he were to blame for overturning the brazier. Flames were now shooting up the canvas. There were shouts from the Moscow tent and Mr Bagnigge and a load of customers spilled out and began to run towards the burning tent.

Then Balquidder saw me.

I ripped off my cloak so that it wouldn't impede my movements, flung it over Noël and ran. I headed straight towards the middle of the river and, as I ran, I noticed that an uneven, thin black line of shimmering water had appeared. The ice under my feet was rocking and every now and then I could feel water. As I neared the middle more cracks appeared.

I glanced over my shoulder. Balquidder had stopped and was beginning to turn back. He must not. Noël was in no state to escape.

I cupped my hands to my mouth and yelled, 'Archie!' He spun round. I did a little dance of triumph on the ice and cocked a snook at him. If he hadn't known it was me before, he did now.

With a roar of anger, he came after me — and he could run.

Stephen told me once that Balquidder had won prizes for running at school. I hadn't believed him. Now I did. In spite of his bulk, he was light on his feet and he was gaining on me. I was tiring, my head and my neck were bruised and aching and my limbs felt like lead. I knew they would not carry me much further.

My only advantage was that I was light and

he was heavy. I must lure him to where the ice was thinnest. It was a risk but there was nothing else.

The crack down the middle of the Thames was more visible now. I could see the reflection of the stars in its inky blackness, and it was widening all the time.

Balquidder was closing the gap. I could feel his heavy tread reverberating behind me on the ice. My lungs were aching and my heart pounding as I reached the black ribbon of water and, with all the remaining energy I possessed, jumped.

10

There was a crack. I had landed on a small outcrop on the far side, but the crack was behind me. I reached for my dagger and turned. If I had to, I'd sell my life dearly.

Balquidder now realized his danger. The ice had broken around him and he was standing on a small, unstable ice floe. He could not jump — it would upset the floe's fragile balance. He could go neither forward nor back, for all around him the freed river was widening. There was a grinding and a splintering as his ice floe collided with the ice sheet behind. Then, as if in slow motion, it began to tilt. Balquidder moved to redress the balance. Too late. The ice floe gained momentum and keeled over. There was a horrible scream and Balquidder, arms and legs flailing, plunged into the water. The floe slid over him, righted itself and he was gone.

I stood frozen with horror and then the dangers of my own position struck me. My own small hummock was preparing to leave the pack. I looked round to the south bank of the Thames. Perhaps it was the way the current ran underneath, but the ice to the south was far more unstable than to the north. I had to get back to the north side to where the ice looked more solid. And the gap was widening fast.

My terror was such that it took me some time to hear the shouts. I swung round. In the distance, I saw the smouldering remains of the Jack Frost tent — and two men running towards me with a plank. As they neared I recognized Mr Bagnigge.

I could see what they wanted, but would it work? Was there time? As they got closer they slowed down and chose their route carefully, going further downstream. Mr Bagnigge gestured frantically and I stumbled towards them to a place where the crack was narrower. They edged the plank across.

'Hurry, there's not much time!' Mr Bagnigge's face was strained.

I tried to grab the other end but my hands were frozen and could not hold things properly. The plank kept slipping.

'Come on, lad,' urged the other man.

The ice underneath heaved and groaned. Finally, my red and swollen fingers caught it. The plank fitted with only an inch or so to spare, it looked desperately unsafe.

'Quickly, lad. Don't stop to look. It's breaking up fast.'

There was a crack behind me. I didn't

hesitate: I ran across and was caught on the other side as the plank tipped and fell into the water.

Somehow we got back to the burning tent, though at times they had almost to carry me. My leg muscles were shaking and I felt dizzy with reaction and exhaustion.

As soon as we reached safety, I sank down on the ice, too spent to go further. Mr Bagnigge unscrewed the brandy flask and handed it to me. I gulped it gratefully. I heard him thank my fellow-rescuer and then the clink of coins.

'The colonel?' I managed, when he returned.

'He's all right. We carried him to the Queenhithe Stairs and he's getting a cab. Can you manage a bit further?'

I stood up shakily. 'Yes. For God's sake, let's get out of here.'

Noël was waiting at the Queenhithe Stairs. He was seated on an old piece of sacking, a couple of men by his side. One of them whistled as we came up, and an ancient cab appeared. Noël was wearing my cloak and, as I came up, he stood up, unsteadily, and put it round my shoulders and clapped Mr Bagnigge on the arm. 'Well done, Jem.' He turned to the two men and shook hands. Again the clink of coin. The men touched their caps and left.

Noël gestured to me to get into the cab.

'What about Mr Bagnigge?' I protested. Cabs only held two people inside, and Mr Bagnigge was not young.

'Best I go with the cabby, Miss Emilia. Probably safer that way — he seems rather the worse for wear.' The cabby was indeed swaying perilously and every now and then he reached into his greatcoat pocket and refreshed himself from a leather bottle.

'You'd better have this.' I handed him my cloak and got inside.

Noël climbed in after me, grasping at the door for support. I noticed, with relief, that his hands appeared to have recovered. He tugged at the fastenings of his cloak and put half of it over my shoulders, before pulling the door shut. The cab jolted up the hill towards the Strand.

I felt more exhausted than I can ever remember in my life. It was worse, even, than my flight from Edinburgh. It was partly delayed reaction; my heart was beating erratically and I couldn't stop shivering. Noël put his arm around me and pulled me to him. I sank back against his shoulder and closed my eyes.

'Are you all right?' I managed to whisper.

'Shh!' Noël bent his head and kissed me.

I went rigid with shock.

Noël had kissed me before, of course. He used to kiss the top of my head when I was a child or, more recently, a decorous salute on my cheek. There was nothing decorous about this kiss. He kissed me with an intensity, a passion, that rocked me to the core.

Noël, who was always so well-bred, so polite, so . . . so controlled! He couldn't know what he was doing. My mind was in a turmoil. A thousand thoughts whirled through my head.

Then he raised his head and said roughly, 'Come on, Emilia. This takes two, you know.'

I kissed him back. If this be madness, I thought, it was a madness I wanted to share. Perhaps, I, too, was unhinged. I forgot my bruises and the bump on my head. My careful self-control had disappeared. There is a sort of shock at that first touch of an unfamiliar mouth. Noël kissed me as though he were starving for a taste of me. A hot bolt went straight through me and I kissed him back as I had long wanted to do. After a timeless moment, he raised his head and growled, 'That's better,' before resuming.

There is one thing about kissing on a freezing winter's night in a draughty carriage: you get warmed up. When I entered that cab I was shivering and my toes and hands felt like blocks of ice. Ten minutes later, I was as warm as toast. If I trembled, it was not from cold. I was also aware, with a mixture of triumph, desire and incredulity, that Noël was as eager for me as I was for him.

The cab turned into John Street and stopped. Noël let me go.

Mr Bagnigge paid off the cabby, opened the cab door and let down the steps. I climbed down. He wrapped my cloak decently around me and went to help Noël. I suddenly remembered that I was wearing Bill's clothes and clutched my cloak together as firmly as I could. Somewhere that night, my cap had fallen off and was probably now under the ice. My hair was half way down my back. The chill touch of reality began to return. I must look like a hoyden, I thought.

Great were the exclamations at our arrival. Mrs Good, hand over her heaving bosom, declared that she had been worried sick. Hannah clapped her hands together, grinned from ear to ear and then burst into tears. Abel and I exchanged conspiratorial glances. The hubbub eventually died down.

'Emilia,' said Noël, 'you look exhausted, you should be in bed. Hannah, take Mrs Kirkwall upstairs. I daresay she needs a hot brick and maybe something to eat.' He turned back to me. 'We must talk,' he said, 'but we'll do it in the morning.'

I felt as though I had been slapped in the face. Did what had happened in the cab mean nothing to him? Had he forgotten it already? My eyes suddenly filled with tears and I had to blink hard to stop them from spilling over. I nodded and followed Hannah. I could say nothing. What was there to say?

The moment I saw myself in the glass, I realized that I was filthy.

'For God's sake, Hannah, bring me up some hot water,' I cried. 'Don't bother with anything to eat.' I felt too tired for food; all I wanted was to be clean and warm.

As soon as she'd left, I tore off my boy's clothes, bundled them into the wardrobe and hastily pulled on my nightgown. I didn't want Hannah to notice how shockingly I was dressed. Perhaps that was it, I thought. Noël believed I was a wanton, lost to all vestiges of shame dressing in such a fashion. He must have seen me running over the ice, showing my legs like some trollop and decided that I was no better than I should be.

The worst of it was that I had kissed him back as greedily as he had kissed me.

I was too exhausted to think clearly. Hannah returned with a ewer of hot water and a hot brick wrapped in a flannel, balanced precariously on top of a warming pan.

'The colonel says you're to have your sleep out, Miss Emilia.' She began to run the warming pan over the bottom sheet.

When she'd gone, I washed as well as I could, climbed into the wonderfully warmed bed, snuggled up to the hot brick and tried to go to sleep.

I did not sleep very well. Too much had happened that day; there was too much to take in and pictures kept flashing in front of my eyes and I couldn't banish them: the darkness engulfing me as my neck was squeezed; the menacing figure of Balquidder in that attic room; the pigeon-holes filled with so much human misery; cutting open that tent and not knowing if Noël were alive; the awful shriek as Balquidder slid under the ice and lastly, that miraculous time in the cab . . .

A cold, clear dawn was beginning to break before I finally drifted off to sleep.

It was half past ten the following morning before I woke up. I had been vaguely aware of somebody coming in earlier, but had gone back to sleep. When I finally awoke, there was a fire burning brightly in the grate and, outside, sounds that the thaw was continuing. The long freeze was over.

Somehow, as is so often the case, things

had sorted themselves out in the night. Balquidder must be dead. Nobody could survive in that freezing water for longer than a few minutes. There had been no sign of him after he had fallen in.

It was a horrifying end. That last image would stay with me for a long time. It was difficult to see Balquidder as anything other than a grotesque monster, but even he must have once needed to be loved, just as I had. How dreadful then, that his death would only come as an enormous relief to many people. As I lay and thought, I could feel a heavy burden being lifted. Ever since I had first met him when I was sixteen, he had frightened me, and over the last few months, it had grown into terror.

His tentacles had reached everywhere. He must have caused untold anxiety to George, perhaps even made him reckless whilst out riding. Aline had been in his power and, through her, he had bribed Tryphena Good and Miss Carver. He was partly to blame for Stephen's death.

Lastly, I allowed my thoughts to turn to Noël. The morning had brought comfort — and the return of some rationality. I took out what had happened and examined it carefully. For the duration of the cab ride at least, Noël had wanted me as much as I had wanted him. I still could feel his heart thudding against mine and his hands holding me to him. My lips were slightly swollen with the remembrance of his kisses. Whatever he might have to say this morning, I must not be deceived about last night. For once, it was not my fault.

There was a gentle tap at the door. It was Hannah.

'You're awake, miss. I'll bring up your tray.'

She closed the door softly and disappeared again. I pulled myself up and pushed a pillow behind my head, wincing as it touched the bump where Balquidder had banged my head against the wall. Hannah returned, put the tray down on my bedside table and went to fetch my dressing-gown. Then she caught sight of the bruises on my neck.

'Oh, Miss Emilia! Why didn't you say last night?'

'I was too tired,' I said truthfully. 'Do they look very dreadful?'

'They're all black and blue.' Hannah bent over me with concern. 'I'll bring up some arnica. And there's a message from the colonel, Miss Emilia. He'd like to see you in the study at noon, if that's convenient.'

'Pray tell him it's quite convenient, thank you.' I busied myself with the coffee pot to hide the tell-tale colour that had surged up over my cheeks.

It took me twice as long as usual to get dressed. I had been too exhausted the previous night to plait my hair, and it now hung straight.

'I could get the curling tongs for you, Miss Emilia,' said Hannah, seeing my despairing look. Her gentle fingers had already anointed my bruises and the bump on my head.

'No,' I said. 'I'll manage.' I could not bear for Noël to see that I'd gone to extra trouble if he wanted only to apologize for his behaviour. The humiliation of being thought 'on the catch' was too awful to contemplate. I coiled my hair into a neat bun on my neck. At least it hid some of the bruises.

I took down Mrs Beresford's green merino. I would wear that. It suited me and, if it did not denote the proper degree of mourning, that was too bad. Aline was no longer here to make some barbed comment.

I looked at myself in the glass and sighed. My eyes seemed even more fog-like in colour this morning and my nose jutted out like a promontory. I must be mad to think that Noël could ever feel for me what I felt for him.

I went downstairs just as the grandfather clock in the drawing-room struck midday and

312

noticed that the palms of my hands were damp with nerves. I felt more apprehensive than I have ever felt in my life.

Noël was sitting at his desk as I entered the study, all the documents from the cushion cover spread out in front of him. He rose unsteadily and limped towards me. I remembered that his stick had been broken.

I had prepared some platitude, designed to salvage my pride, but I never uttered it. Noël had caught sight of the bruising on my neck. He pulled me into his arms, lifted my hair and began kissing wherever the bruises flowered. As he did so, I saw the angry red weals on his wrists and I, too, began trying to kiss them.

The whole thing threatened to become absurd. In between kisses, we both started to laugh.

'For God's sake, kiss me properly!' said Noël. He abandoned my neck and turned my face towards him. It was just as wonderful as the evening before. Much later, he said, 'Marry me, Emilia.'

'Oh yes, Noël. Please.'

As a proposal, it fulfilled none of the requirements of a true Gothic romance. It was far too short, for a start. But I had no complaints. We stood in each other's arms for a long time. I felt as if I'd come home.

Eventually we moved ourselves to the window seat, which was the only place, uncomfortable though it was, where two people could sit together.

'I should have gone down on one knee,' said Noël.

'With your bad leg?'

'My dearest Emilia, I have read *The Castle of Apollinari*. I am well aware that there are occasions in life when a man is expected to kneel!'

'You . . . you know about my writing?' I looked at him in alarm. 'Are you very shocked?'

Noël laughed and stroked my cheek with his finger. 'Good heavens, no. I am full of admiration for your talent.' He saw my look of incredulity. 'I mean that.'

'My father would be appalled. He would think it very unladylike for a woman to be earning money in that fashion.'

'I sometimes think you have confused me with your father. I am really not such a fuddy-duddy as you seem to believe.' Those blue eyes held a most disturbing expression.

I thought of the cab last night and coloured. 'Last night, in the cab, might just have been reaction,' I said. 'I knew you loved Aline. Then, I am not pretty and I have this awful nose.' I put my hand up to hide it.

'Ah, Aline,' said Noël ruefully. 'I admit that I wasted many years over Aline. I knew I was in love with you the night that Richard was kidnapped; there was a moment when . . . '

'I remember,' I said softly. 'It was the same for me, too.'

'But you were married — and then Aline arrived and things became muddled. These last few weeks have been like struggling to get out of a jar of molasses.' He sighed, then turned and saw that my hand was still hovering over my nose. 'And I love all of you, including your nose!'

'You're joking!' The thought of anybody liking my nose seemed incredible.

Noël laughed. 'It's true that when you were little you were a bit beaky, but even then it had charm. Now you've grown into it, I think it has real elegance.' He removed my hand and kissed my nose. Then he looked at me. 'Are you sure you want to marry a battered old soldier?'

'Oh, Noël,' I cried. 'I love you whatever you are.'

Some considerable time passed, but eventually normality returned and we began to discuss Balquidder and the folders I had brought back.

'I shall have to go to Bow Street,' said Noël. 'The attempts at extortion are serious matters and there may well be many victims. Besides, from what I heard in that tent, extortion wasn't the worst of it.'

'I wondered if he were forging documents to register slave ships in Lisbon or somewhere similar.'

'At the very least. He was an evil man, Emilia. We do not have to mourn his passing.'

'Aline seems to be mixed up with him as well,' I ventured.

'Yes, so I read.' Noël gazed into the fire for a moment. 'I should have guessed, of course. Balquidder paid for her chaise here and supplied the wherewithal to bribe Miss Carver and Mrs Good. They will have to go.'

'Miss Carver is not good for Richard,' I said, and told him of her drinking.

'Poor Richard. I have neglected him as well and I don't deserve such a loving and forgiving little son. It is all my fault.'

'Why, Noël?' I asked gently. 'What is it about Richard?'

Noël sighed. 'I resented him. Before his arrival, I managed to deceive myself that my marriage was merely a convenient arrangement; then I became a father and I felt trapped. I know I behaved badly, and I'm sure I hurt Margaret. I should never have married her, but after Aline chose George, I felt it didn't matter whom I married. I was honest with her; she knew I didn't love her, but she was a good woman and deserved better.'

Poor Margaret, how dreadful to be married to Noël and to know that he loved another woman. I was sorry for Noël's pain, but I couldn't help being cheered by the knowledge that I was not the only person to get herself into such an emotional mess.

'I always thought that Aline preferred you to George.'

'She told me that she loved me, but she felt it was her duty to marry George for her parents' sake.'

Nonsense, I thought. Her parents had nothing to do with it. When did the de Doulaincourts ever come to Ainderby? No. Aline wanted to have her cake and eat it.

Noël saw my look of scepticism and said, 'You don't believe it, do you?'

I shook my head.

'You are right. I cannot believe how stupid I was.'

'Not as stupid as I was with Stephen.'

'More stupid. You were only sixteen and, later, you had the sense to put your fantasies into your books. I, on the other hand, held on to this sickly dream.'

I leaned over and kissed his cheek. 'You must learn to tie a knot and go on.'

'Wellington used to say that, whenever there was some hitch.'

'So Richard told me. I think it very good advice.'

The conversation moved to our future.

'This time, Emilia, we shall do things correctly. I shall write to your father and ask for your hand and you will write and ask for his forgiveness.'

'Do I have to tell him about my books? He'll be horrified.'

'It'll be worse if he finds out accidentally. 'Daniel Miller' is easy enough to guess at.'

I made a face. 'Very well. And do we have to wait a year to be married as well?'

'Ah, that is another matter. We'll have to wait six months, certainly, but I hope I can persuade your father that a quiet wedding in, say, July, would be acceptable.'

'I shall leave that to you: I have no power to persuade him.'

I was not looking forward to this. I didn't think I could stand going back to Tranters Court, even if my father would have me, which I doubted.

'I think you misjudge him,' said Noël.

'We shall see.'

Both of us wrote to my father. I received a cool acceptance of my apology, an expectation that I would thenceforth desist from

318

writing ill-judged romances and an invitation to pass my months of mourning in the proper seclusion of Tranters Court. Noël's letter expressed barely hidden astonishment that he wished to marry me — together with the requisite permission. Personally, I didn't give a fig for his permission and the tone of both letters made me resentful, but Noël only laughed and said that that was just my father's way.

'He is of a more formal generation,' he said. 'He expects things to be done according to the proper form.'

'Of which he is the only arbiter,' I retorted. I looked down at my own letter. 'I have no intention of stopping writing. Why should I? Read it, Noël! I'm not making this up!'

Noël saw that I was seriously upset. He removed the letter from my hand and took me in his arms.

I struggled free. 'Read it!'

Noël did so. Then he put down the letter and said gently, 'I can understand your indignation, but you must not allow him to trouble your mind. You are the only proper judge of what is right for you.'

I hugged him gratefully. 'Oh, Noël. Why can't Papa ever say that?'

'He is who he is, Emilia. You cannot change him.'

We had several such conversations over the next few weeks and it was an enormous relief to be able to talk to somebody who both knew my father well and who loved me. In fact, I've never talked so much in my life; all my years of enforced silence in Edinburgh, when I had to measure every word, now burst open. Noël talked too, about his marriage, about Richard and about Aline. It was a sweet release, being able to be open.

The thaw continued, but slowly. Spring came very late that year and it was several weeks before the roads were even reasonably passable. Noël spent much of his time with the officers of the law, to whom he handed over the key to Balquidder's house, together with a suitably tailored account of my kidnapping. The law decided that it was not interested in my late husband's dealings with Balquidder, nor in Noël's.

It turned out that Bow Street already had a substantial file on Balquidder and they were more interested in the foreign registration of slave ships than in personal financial dealings. They were discreet, for many of the names in the pigeon-holes were well-known; as one officer told Noël, there were many who would now be sleeping a lot easier.

Bribery and extortion were Balquidder's main business methods and Aline was not the only woman to whom he had hinted at marriage in order to secure her co-operation. Noël had one short, unpleasant meeting with her about the matter. He came back looking grim. He didn't tell me what had passed between them, and I didn't ask; I was satisfied that any lingering attachment was now over.

A week after I had watched Balquidder slide into the icy waters of the Thames, his body was washed ashore. It was a relief to know that he was truly dead. I still, occasionally, have nightmares that he is returned, but they are fading.

One evening, as we were sitting in the drawing-room after dinner, Noël said, 'Emilia, I think I must go to Demerara myself.'

I was horrified. It was a long and dangerous journey. It would take six weeks at least and there were hurricanes in those parts. Now Balquidder was gone, what was the point?

'I must see for myself what can be done. You were right. I cannot condone slavery of another human being, whatever the colour of his skin.'

'But you'll be gone for months!' The ocean was so deep. Ships sank. If anything happened to him, how should I bear it?

'Nothing's going to happen to me,' said Noël, guessing my anxiety. 'Jem will be with me. I shall be sea-sick, I daresay, but that's nothing new. All the same, Emilia, I'll make arrangements with Mr Briggs for you to be Richard's legal guardian.'

Dear Richard was delighted at our engagement. 'You will really be my mama?' he kept saying.

'Yes, really.'

At last, after so many false starts, he and Noël came together, and I could see that this time, it would be all right. Richard liked to run up to Noël to be hugged, but he was touchingly careful of his father's bad leg and would sometimes stroke it gently.

'Poor Papa, is it getting better now?' he would ask anxiously.

Noël kissed him. 'It will get better when Spring comes,' he promised.

'I am ashamed of my neglect of him,' Noël confessed to me. 'I am sorry to have to leave him yet again, but it will be for the last time. Your father is adamant that we cannot marry until you are in half-mourning. If I leave as soon as it is safe for sailing, then I should be back by late summer. Perhaps you could have Richard at Tranters Court? It would do him good to be in the country and maybe your half-brothers could take him up a bit. He has been too much alone.'

This was not at all like the ending of one of my novels, I thought. There, the hero proposed on bended knee, the heroine blushed and accepted and wedding bells rang amid general blessing and good fortune. There were no messy loose ends and the hero certainly didn't absent himself for six months to the other side of the world. But this was real life and I had to agree. After all, it was I who had been so emphatic about the evils of slavery. Did I really want to be the sort of person who backed down as soon as her convictions involved some personal inconvenience?

I introduced Noël to Mr Robinson, and was pleased to see them getting on well. We talked, among other things, about Noël's forthcoming voyage to Demerara and Mr Robinson suggested that, if Noël considered writing an article or two about conditions on the plantations — anonymously, of course — then he knew of a couple of magazines which might be interested in publishing them.

Mr Robinson agreed to continue to be my banker until my marriage. I would have to come to London in due course, to deal with the proofs of The Mountfalcon Heiress and to deliver the manuscript of The Secret of the

Drakensburgs. Noël would be away and I doubted whether my father would act as my banker for such a reason.

Noël and I then went to see Mr Latimer, who congratulated us both on our engagement. He was obviously delighted that I was behaving sensibly the second time around — he and Mr Briggs would see to a proper marriage settlement, he promised. Noël insisted that I kept the whole of my fortune. 'I have quite enough,' he said, 'and Richard will have his mother's money, in due course.' It seemed that I would have to get used to being a rich woman.

Our little household in John Street broke up at the end of February, once it became safe for travelling. Miss Carver and Mrs Good were dismissed — though Noël wrote them both references and gave them five guineas apiece to tide them over. Personally, I didn't think they deserved anything, but Noël said that they had been deceived by Aline, just as he had. Mary, Hannah and Abel came up to Yorkshire. Mary went to Ainderby Hall and Abel, Hannah and Richard came with Noël, Mr Bagnigge and myself to Tranters Court. Hannah was now to be my personal maid, a promotion which gladdened her heart, and mine too. I felt I needed some allies in what I suspected would be difficult days ahead.

Abel was to help look after Richard, who was getting too old for a nurse, said Noël. Abel, we felt, was to be trusted; he had proved himself both faithful and reliable. Richard was delighted at the change.

Our arrival at Tranters Court was much as I'd expected. My father greeted me with his usual chilly reserve and thereafter made it clear that Noël and I must be chaperoned at all times — an irksome task which fell on poor Mrs Daniels. Even Noël, for all his tolerance, grew impatient.

'I now see how you came to elope,' he confessed.

'You're welcome to carry me off at any time,' I retorted. I couldn't stand my father's assumption that only constant viligance ensured my chastity.

'Meet me in the shrubbery after luncheon,' said Noël.

'Only if you intend to behave improperly!'

It was a late spring and chilly with it. Noël and Mr Bagnigge left for Demerara in April. I did not want to put an extra burden on to Noël, so I hid my tears and did my best to comfort Richard. I strove to be a civil, if not an enthusiastic, guest in my father's house.

I wish I could report that there was the obligatory affecting scene as at the end of

Miss Burney's *Evelina*, when her father says, '*Come hither, child, — rise Evelina, — alas, it is for me to kneel to you! — and I would kneel — I would crawl upon the earth, — I would kiss the dust . . .* ' etc. etc. But, of course, nothing of the sort happened, and, in truth, I would not have known what to do if he had. I would have been horribly embarrassed.

My father had aged. He now walked with a stoop and leaned heavily on his stick. His skin had become paper thin and white. It was plain that he found me difficult to deal with — I think he was still expecting to see the harum-scarum sixteen-year-old who had eloped, and a twenty-five-year-old daughter was something of a shock. He had tried, with only moderate success, to curb any expression of Noël's and my affection. It was obvious that I could no longer be sent to my room. I had grown up and now ran my own life. I was a woman of independent fortune. He had, perforce, to treat me as such.

Things became easier after Noël left. I remembered what Noël had often said about my father being too old to change, and tried to become more tolerant. I realized that it was I who had changed when I found myself smiling at one of his pronouncements, instead of going into an impotent rage. My father gradually ceased to be the ogre that he had once been.

My stepmother was surprisingly easy to deal with. In some ways she reminded me of Mrs Irvine, being sensible and practical and she adapted to my changed status far easier than my father. In fact, I came to enjoy her company and my apologies to her for my youthful behaviour were genuine.

'My dear Mrs Kirkwall, not another word, I pray,' she said at once. 'Let bygones be bygones.'

Unlike my father, she was intrigued by my books and I lent her *The Doom of the House of Ansbach*. She told me she thoroughly enjoyed it and, rather guiltily, passed it on to her sons. I then lent her *The Castle of Apollinari*.

I had misjudged her all those years ago, I realized. She had been about my age now when she married my father. Would I be able to do any better with a distraught ten-year-old child, I wondered? We began to talk, as women do, about this and that. I asked her advice on running a large house.

'My home in Edinburgh was merely a couple of rooms,' I confided. 'Soon I shall be mistress of Ainderby Hall and I do not know at all how I shall manage. If you would teach me while I am here, I should be truly grateful.'

* * *

What else is there to say? Richard's health improved and he became more confident and outgoing. Nobody at Tranters Court found him backward and his education came on by leaps and bounds. He went every morning to the curate's house for lessons and seemed happy and settled.

Noël wrote from Bonne Chance and we both realized that the estate would have to be kept for a few years yet. Mr dos Santos, the overseer, was dismissed and Noël found a more sympathetic young man of an Evangelical persuasion, to take his place. *This is an imperfect world and I can only do my best,* Noël wrote. *But I believe that Mr Gill will support my wishes and, though I can do little about the iniquities of the system, I can see to it that these poor fellows are treated as fairly as possible. I hate it, Emilia. I am ashamed sometimes to look them in the face. But I am a lone voice out here. The place to change things must be back in Britain.*

I wrote back encouragingly, relieved that we were now in accord on this, and, in due course, Noël sent Mr Robinson a couple of articles, written in a straightforward soldierly fashion, which added their mite to the anti-slavery debate. I was proud of him. I also missed him desperately and wrote long letters saying so. Noël's letters to me were half love letters and half accounts of what he was doing at Bonne Chance, illustrated with funny little drawings, usually featuring some episode in which he cut a ludicrous figure, such as the time he fell into the canal. He also wrote carefully printed letters to Richard, so that he might read them easily. Richard slept with them underneath his pillow and, I confess, there were times when I did the same with mine.

Noël and Mr Bagnigge returned safely in September. I shall never forget the moment when Noël stepped down from the carriage, looking bronzed and healthy and hardly limping at all. Richard raced down the steps and was lifted up in a hug. Then Noël put him down and held out a hand to me.

This was Tranters Court and we were a lady and a gentleman. We could not embrace in public. My father would been have horrified by any unseemly display of emotion. Nevertheless, just to see Noël's eyes — so startlingly blue in that tanned face — and to hear his voice, was enough for me. At least, so I thought for an hour or so.

Twenty-four hours later, enough was enough. It was pouring with rain and the shrubbery was out of the question. I tackled my step-mother.

'Mrs Daniels,' I said firmly, 'if you cannot arrange for me to be alone with Noël, I shall do something so shocking that my father will never speak to me again!'

She laughed. 'The colonel has forestalled you. After luncheon I shall send you to the conservatory to fetch my embroidery scissors. I daresay you will find what you want there.'

'Thank you,' I said, with real gratitude.

★　★　★

We were married quietly at the end of September.

I loved Noël, but I had avoided thinking about the more intimate aspects of marriage. Stephen had always been lukewarm in his pleasures and complained that I wasn't the shape he liked. I had felt awkward, ashamed and used. I was frightened that it would be the same, though I hoped that I wouldn't feel so used. The kisses and caresses Noël and I exchanged whenever we managed to evade Mrs Daniels's lax chaperonage, were one thing — at least I was dressed — bed was another.

Our honeymoon was a revelation.

'I had no idea it could be like this,' I said to Noël on our first night together. 'Are you sure it's legal?'

Noël laughed. 'Enjoyed it, did you?'

'You must know that I did.' I lay in the crook of Noël's arm and savoured the astonishing pleasure, the intensity of feeling and my unexpected responses.

Enough of that. The rest is between Noël and myself.

After our honeymoon, when Noël, Richard and I were settled at Ainderby Hall, I reminded Noël of my miscarriages and added, sadly, that I doubted whether I could give him children. I was relieved that he already had a son and heir. However, to my surprise, about five years after our marriage and long after I had given up hope, we had a daughter, Catherine, named after dear Mrs Beresford, and, a couple of years later, our little Emilia, known as Emma to distinguish her from her mama. They are the apples of Noël's eye. We have a plump, unpretentious Scotch nurse, who sings them Gaelic lullabies and tells them stories of selkies.

Richard was fourteen when Catherine was born, not quite a child, but not yet a man, and I was concerned lest he should feel displaced by her birth, as I had done when my stepbrothers were born. But I need not have worried. He liked having little sisters, he told me, they made him feel grown-up. He gave them piggy-backs, just as Noël used to when I was a child, and got Abel to repaint his old rocking-horse for them. Cathy and Emma think he's wonderful.

The Secret of the Drakensburgs, which came out in the second year of my marriage, broke new ground. I allowed Erminia to be in love with Sir Godfrey, even before she was certain of his affection and to express more realistic feelings. It was easily the most successful of my books, and ran through several reprintings very quickly. The critics, however, were divided. I had a number of reviews which said things like, *We cannot admire the lack of maidenly decorum shown by Erminia FitzUrse, and we hope that Mr Miller will see fit to return to the pure English heroines he has hitherto depicted so well.*

Noël sold Bonne Chance in 1817 to Mr Gill, the new overseer, who had proved himself to be a kindly and conscientious man, and had just come into an inheritance. The sugar was immensely profitable, but the investment had been heavy, and Noël barely broke even on the sale. We were both relieved to be free of it.

My last book was *The Prince of Zamanga* and it owed its inception to Noël's journal, kept expressly for me, whilst he was in Demerara. He had met a sympathetic plantation owner's daughter, a Miss Maria Davies, and she had painted several dozen watercolours to go with the journal, so that I might see what the plantation looked like. The book was my plea for the abolition of slavery.

It was about an African prince who was sold into slavery to a place called Essequibo, named after one of the rivers of Demerara. Originally, I had wanted him to fall in love with the plantation owner's niece, Mariana, and she with him, but Mr Robinson said that the public would be outraged.

Reluctantly, I altered it. However, I allowed Mariana and the prince some affecting scenes together and it was perfectly obvious to me, if not to my readers, that Mariana would have much preferred the African prince to the worthy-but-dull naturalist who gained her hand at the end.

Noël likes it the best of all my books. He says that he is impressed with the way I capture the heat and humidity of Demerara. I tell him, which is true, that his letters and journal helped enormously — and discussing customs and the country with him. But, most of all, I was helped by his affection and support. In many ways, it is as much his book as mine.

The book did not sell as well as I'd hoped and, after *The Prince of Zamanga*, I wrote no more Daniel Millers. Public taste was changing and I had no interest in the so-called, *silver-fork* novels of aspiring gentility that were coming into fashion. In any case, I no longer needed to escape from reality.

Instead, I wrote articles for the Anti-Slavery Movement and soon found myself with a wide correspondence. Victory is not yet won, but we are confident that it will happen soon.

At home, I turned my hand to writing stories for my children; proper stories, with real, naughty little girls and no moral exhortations. My publisher won't touch them. He says the public wants children's stories to have a high moral tone. Personally, I think high moral tone belongs in the waste-paper basket. Cathy and Emma agree with me — they like my stories. But, for the moment at least, they remain in manuscript. Perhaps their time will come.

Fast Boats
and
Rough Seas

OTHER TITLES IN THIS SERIES

Practical Motor Cruising by Dag Pike
ISBN 0 229 11827 5

Dag Pike takes motor cruiser owners
by the hand to show them the ropes of
practical motorboat handling and
management in harbour, on rivers
and at sea.

Marine Inboard Engines by Loris
Goring
ISBN 0 229 11842 9

A very practical book describing how
the various parts of both petrol and
diesel marine engines work, their
basic service maintenance for general
running and winter lay-up, and faults
that are prone to occur. The author
makes a distinction between the jobs
that can safely be done by the amateur
and those which should be left strictly
to the professional engineer.

Available January 1990

Fast Boats
and
Rough Seas

DAG PIKE

ADLARD COLES
8 Grafton Street, London W1

03767364

YT	YP	YK	YF 6/89.	
YN	YC	YW	YG	ML

Adlard Coles
William Collins Sons & Co. Ltd
8 Grafton Street, London W1X 3LA

First published in Great Britain by
Adlard Coles 1989

Copyright © Dag Pike 1989

British Library Cataloguing in Publication Data

Pike, Dag
    Fast boats and rough seas
    1. Motor cruisers. Seamanship
    I. Title
    623.88'2314

ISBN 0 229 11840 2

Printed in Great Britain by
Butler & Tanner Ltd, Frome

All rights reserved. No part of this publication may be
reproduced, stored in a retrieval system, or transmitted,
in any form or by any means, electronic, mechanical,
photocopying, recording or otherwise, without the prior
permission of the publisher.

Contents

Introduction

The sea is continually changing and this very change is the challenge. When you start to travel at high speeds on the water or you operate in rough seas, then you are faced with a situation which challenges your skills, often to the limit. It is an exciting world, where you live by your wits and by your fast reactions to rapidly changing situations.

I have spent over 30 years in both fast boats and rough seas, and I think that during every offfshore race or rough passage I have muttered to myself 'Never again!', yet I still go back for more. Fast boats and rough seas can be a tough and painful experience while it lasts, but when it is over the pain is soon forgotten in the warm satisfaction of achievement that comes from taking on a challenge – and succeeding.

The sea is certainly a challenge and it provides an environment like no other. It is the meeting point of wind and water, where the unpredictable can and often does happen. Waves are very irregular in shape and height and the so-called 'rogue wave' is waiting to catch the unwary. It is not an environment where you can relax for long, and you have to learn to read the waves and the weather if you are to cope.

Boats built for high speeds or rough seas have to be rather special. The prevailing conditions place high demands on the hull, on the machinery and on all the fixtures and fittings, so standards have to be high. There is no particular magic about the design of a racing vessel or a lifeboat, but close attention must be paid to the detail of every single item on board so that the risk of failure is minimised.

Failure of components is one factor that can get boats into trouble in rough seas. In fast boats, a failure can leave you rolling around in embarrassed silence, but in rough water you could find yourself in a situation which is starting to compound what might have been just a simple failure. Perhaps a compass light has failed at night which, in itself, is not too serious, but before you can find the torch, the boat swings off course and ends up broadside to a breaking wave. Any small failure causes you to relax your guard and the sea always seems to be waiting to take advantage of your misfortune.

A great deal of emphasis tends to be put on the boat, but the crew — and particularly the helmsman — is a vital element for the boat's safety in difficult or extreme conditions. The crew have to be fit to do their job and must have an environment in which they can work. The conditions on high-speed boats or on boats in rough seas can be very demanding indeed; yet much can be done to improve conditions by thoughtful planning of the working environment.

The human/machine interface is of vital importance, yet in many cases it receives scant attention. Seating, controls and visibility must all be considered in great detail, if the crew are to have a fair chance. Driving a boat in difficult conditions requires that the helmsman has everything in his favour, as far as possible, and that means a careful ergonomic study. This applies equally to the rest of the crew, whether they have jobs to do such as navigating or whether they are simply resting and waiting their turn.

In fast boats and rough conditions many of the conventional techniques for navigation cannot be used. It may be impossible to write or to use paper charts, so electronics are being introduced to provide vital navigation information. Here again, the man/machine interface has to be considered if the navigator is to have a chance to use the equipment properly.

So the story goes on. In the world of high-speed boats and rough seas nothing can be taken for granted. This is boat handling close to the limits, where the sea can be very unforgiving, where mistakes can have serious consequences and where experience can be a vital factor for success. The ability to predict the weather, with a much greater degree of accuracy than was previously possible, has perhaps made us a little casual about some of the normal seamanlike precautions, and also a little casual about boat design. The emphasis has tended to swing away from seaworthy hull shapes and seamanship, to an approach to power boating where speed and style rule, and the other traditional aspects of boating tend to take second place.

Fast Boats and Rough Seas is an advanced book on boat handling. In it, I have tried to distil 40 years of boating experience covering all aspects of high-speed boats and rough conditions. Whilst the speeds may be very different, there is a great similarity between a boat travelling at 100 m.p.h. and a boat running in 30-foot (9-metre) seas. The pressures on the boat and the crew may be close to the limits in both situations and although you may not operate at these extremes, I hope that you will benefit from the experiences described here.

1 Wind and waves

Wind and waves tend to rule your life at sea. We will look at the wind and its causes in Chapter 11 on weather, but here we are concerned with the wind and its effect on the surface of the sea. It is the wind which causes waves, and it is waves which form the surface of the sea over which the boat has to be driven. Whether you are in a power boat travelling fast or whether you are out in rough weather, the pattern of the waves has a profound effect on the behaviour of the boat, and so an understanding of the waves and how they are formed will give you a much better feeling for the way the craft has to be driven.

WAVE FORMATION

Waves and the way they are formed is an incredibly complex subject and even scientists are still arguing about some of the more detailed aspects. The subject can be presented using complicated formulae, but one's understanding is not likely to be any better for this. From a sailor's point of view it is much better to have a broad idea of the different types of waves and how they are formed, but as with most subjects there is no substitute for practical study; as a seafarer you ought to take every opportunity to observe the waves so that you have a better understanding of them. There is always something new to learn about waves, and this constant study will enable you to recognise when dangerous situations are developing, and also to develop that close affinity with waves which will enable you to anticipate their behaviour.

Although there is usually a predominant direction of travel when you look at any sea surface, if you look at the waves closely you will see that they tend to have a fairly random appearance. Broadly speaking, waves can be divided into five main categories, one or more of which will be present at any time except, of course, in a flat calm. These five wave types are *ripples, oscillation waves, pressure waves, translation waves* and the delightfully named *clapotic waves*. Apart from pressure waves, these wave types are generated by the wind, the diference between them being mainly how they are affected by other influences, such as shallow water or tidal streams. It is the way in which waves are modified by these other influences, together with combinations of different wave types, which produce some of the more dangerous and unpredictable seas found in stormy weather.

Before we go too deeply into this subject, let us look at some of the terms used to describe them. The *wave length* is the distance from the crest of one wave to the crest of the next. *Wave height* is the height from the bottom of the trough off the wave to the top of the crest, whilst the *period of waves* is the time it takes for two successive crests to pass a fixed point. Finally, the *frequency of waves* is the number of crests passing a fixed point in a given time. Another term that you will encounter is *significant wave height* and this is the average height of the highest one-third of the waves. Another aspect which is important, when it comes to boat handling on the open sea, is the *gradient* of the wave to the horizontal. Obviously, this gradient will depend on wave length and wave height, but it will also vary from the weather side to the lee side of the wave, and to a large extent it is all these variations in the gradient of the wave which make life interesting or exciting, as the case may be, for the driver of a fast boat in lively seas.

WAVE TYPES

If we return to the five different wave types, we can rule out ripples because they have little place in a book dealing with rough seas; they are simply the visible evidence of very light winds on the surface of the water. From these ripples, the sea grows into small wavelets as the wind strength increases, and these wavelets grow steadily into recognisable waves until there comes a point where the energy of the wind in creating waves is balanced by the size of the waves and a state of equilibrium is reached. It is easy to visualise that the wave has to be supported by a certain amount of energy, otherwise it will simply collapse and become a flat surface again. It is the pressure of the wind which supplies the energy to support the waves; waves generated in this way are called *oscillation waves* – the type which you normally meet at sea.

These waves give the appearance of a mass of water moving bodily forwards, but in fact this is not the case. If you watch any small object floating on the water, you will notice that it does not move forwards in the line of the waves, or if it does it only moves forwards very slowly; this is because the surface of the water tends to move under the influence of the wind. In fact, each water particle in the wave is moving in a circular path of small radius, which is one of the reasons for calling these waves oscillation waves. Once a wave train has been started by the action of the wind it would keep going for ever, if it were not for the internal friction and the surface tension of the water which gradually slow down the waves and cause them to lose energy.

The shape of an oscillation wave, if it could be completely isolated, would be found to be *trochoidal*. A trochoidal curve is a path traced by a point located on the circumference of a rolling circle, and waves of this shape have a steady curve which would be easy to predict and negotiate if it wasn't for the external factors which act upon it. One of these factors is the wind which exerts pressure on the back of the wave, tending to flatten this area, with a consequent increase in gradient on the front of the wave.

Given a calm sea and a steady wind from one direction, one would expect a symmetrical and regular wave train to develop. Such conditions rarely occur at sea, however. Even with an apparently calm sea there is usually a barely discernible swell — the remains of waves from a previous blow. Any increase in wind strength will produce waves with a different wave length to the swell and possibly from a different direction. These wave trains will intermingle and, in practice, one is faced with a sea which comprises several superimposed wave trains. The prevailing wind, once the waves have been fully formed, creates the predominant wave train. As the wave train generated by the prevailing wind increases, the other wave trains become less significant. Nevertheless, they

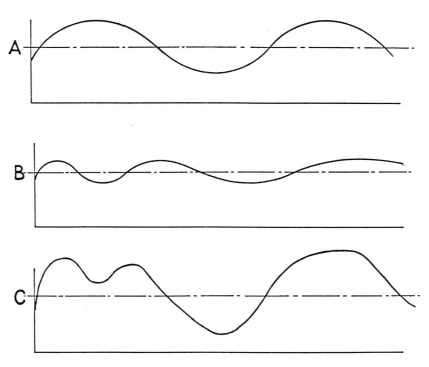

The combination of wave trains A and B produces the wave pattern shown in C. This accounts for the irregular wave patterns often found at sea.

remain and are superimposed on the predominant train, adding their height or depth to that of the predominant train when crests or troughs coincide. The implication of this is that the sea, instead of being a series of waves of regular height and length, becomes a series of troughs and crests of unpredictable sizes. If the various wave trains are all moving in approximately the same direction, as can be the case, a sea results which has a series of higher crests followed by a series of lower crests. This type of combination is probably the basis of the old theory that every seventh wave is larger than those before and after it. Such seventh-wave cycles can be caused by a shorter, steeper sea superimposed on a longer ground swell. Although the highest waves may not be limited to every seventh wave, there is no doubt that waves can vary in height in a fairly regular pattern. As well as producing higher waves at intervals, this feature can also produce relatively smooth patches where the combination of crests and troughs tend to cancel each other out.

CLAPOTIC WAVES

When two wave trains are travelling in different directions, the crests of the different wave trains will coincide at points other than along the wave fronts. This combination of the two wave crests will again produce a higher than normal wave, but this time the combination will take the form of a pyramid-shaped peak which is sometimes called a short-crested wave. Most seafarers will have come across these pyramid-shaped waves which can rise up alongside the boat almost out of the blue and which produce a frightening looking crest which disappears just as quickly as it appeared.

Fortunately, when different wave trains intersect, one of the wave trains is usually much superior to the others, so the chance of a combination of crests producing a very high peak is reduced. You are less likely to find violent waves of this type in the open sea, but there are situations where intersecting wave trains are the same height and these can produce particularly dangerous and vicious sea conditions. This occurs when a wave train approaches a vertical harbour wall or a cliff face with relatively deep water alongside. The waves are reflected from the face of the wall or cliff at an angle equal to that at which they strike it, and a 'mirror image' set of waves is produced. If the approaching wave train is parallel to the wall or cliff, then the reflected waves will also be parallel. If the initial wave train is at an angle of 45 degrees, then the reflected waves will also be at an angle of 45 degrees, producing two sets of waves which cross each other at 90 degrees. The seas formed by the interaction between the initial wave train and the reflected waves are called *clapotic seas*. They can be very dangerous for small boats, with wave crests rising up and breaking in a very unpredictable manner.

I have encountered these clapotic seas off exposed artificial breakwaters. They

A traditional lifeboat design in clapotic seas off Bridlington Harbour. Note the characteristic peaked shape of the waves, which are made more dangerous by the shallow water. (Photo: Arthur Dick, Bridlington)

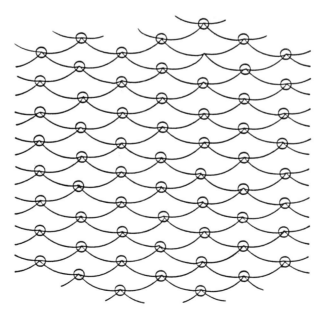

The interaction of crossing wave trains, the ringed areas denoting wave peaks, but there will also be 'holes' where troughs combine.

can be particularly dangerous because you tend to meet them just when you think you are reaching the safety of harbour. The waves in this type of clapotic sea have a viciousness about them which is rarely found in other types of wave, and very often you will find that the boat has little time to recover from negotiating one wave before it is hit by the next. In strong wind, these clapotic seas are to be avoided if at all possible, particularly when you may be tired at the end of a long passage and have less resilience to cope with them.

It is possible to predict where these clapotic seas might be found by studying charts. Any exposed breakwater will tend to reflect waves in this manner, even though the waves may be slowed, to a certain extent, by shallow water as they approach the breakwater. These reflected waves are less likely to occur from cliff faces because there is usually a mound of rubble at the bottom of the cliff which helps to dissipate the wave energy. However, I have encountered clapotic waves over a mile offshore, off the island of Hoy in the Orkneys. Here the cliffs are exposed to the full force of Atlantic gales, and the cliffs drop sheer. The resulting clapotic seas were very vicious, even though we were some distance offshore.

From this you will gather that waves at sea are anything but regular. It would be nice to think that you could just set the throttles to a comfortable speed and let the boat rise and fall over a regular series of waves, but life at sea is rarely like this. The seventh-wave phenomena will occur, and even this you could learn to live with if it occurred every seventh wave, but in fact these bigger and smaller waves come along at very irregular intervals and you have to accept that the surface of the sea is a very unpredictable place.

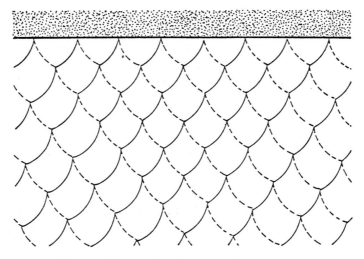

Clapotic waves reflecting from a harbour wall. The solid lines denote the approaching waves and the broken lines the reflected waves. Where these intersect, abnormally high pyramid-shaped waves can be expected.

I was once in the Mediterranean in a large 'deep-vee' boat and we had been travelling for over 2 hours into a head sea with the wind blowing around Force 6. We thought during this time that we had learnt to cope and had found a comfortable speed to match the conditions, when suddenly, out of the blue, along came two large waves which promptly picked up the boat and threw it down on its side, much to the discomfort of the crew. This encounter was severe enough to break the engine mountings on one of the powerful diesels, and it was a salutary warning not to take what looked like a predictable sea for granted.

FREAK WAVES

Figures issued by the National Institute of Oceanography indicate just how unpredictable waves can be. If you take the average height of waves passing a fixed point, then, statistically, one wave in 23 will be twice the average height, one wave in 1175 will be three times the average height and, perhaps the most alarming statistic of all, one wave in 300,000 will be four times the average height. These statistics, at first glance, sound very frightening. They are certainly worth bearing in mind when you are at sea in rough weather, but they need to be put into perspective.

First, the average height of a wave train is lower than you might think. There are many smaller waves well below the average height which do not register so readily in your mind when you are travelling at sea. You tend to judge a sea solely by the larger waves which you encounter, as these waves have a greater impact and you tend to forget about the smaller ones. Waves of twice the average height would probably include the larger waves which you tend to consider when estimating the height of waves at sea. This is why the significant wave height has been established as a yardstick, because it gives you a better indication of the larger waves which you might normally encounter in an average sea.

Second, if you take a wave period of 10 seconds, which can be fairly average in rough seas, then there are 6 waves a minute, 360 waves an hour, 8640 waves per day passing a given point. This means that the chance of meeting that one wave in 300,000, which is four times the average height, is fairly remote; particularly when you bear in mind that these waves tend to be transient rather than travel as huge waves over long distances.

As far as the seafarer is concerned these so-called freak waves are completely random, which means that they could be expected at any time. There are many tales of people encountering freak waves coming out of the blue, but I don't like the term 'freak wave' because it implies something which cannot be expected, and this is far from the case. Statistics show that these waves should be expected even though their occurrence may be random, and one must always be on the lookout for such waves in rough weather. It is a daunting thought that in a sea

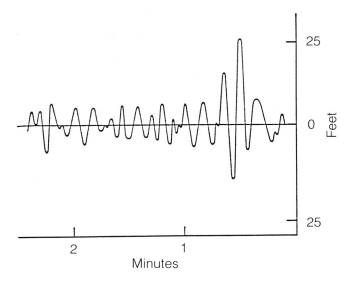

Wave recorder readings from the Daunt Light Vessel off Ireland, showing a 25-foot wave amongst waves which average a mere 10 feet in height.

with waves of an average height of 10 feet (3 metres), a sea which is 40 feet (12 metres) in height could appear with little warning, and this certainly confirms the need for concentration on the part of the helmsman. To be caught unawares by such a sea must be to court disaster, and rogue waves must certainly account for some of the vessels lost inexplicably at sea. The trace from a wave recorder installed on the Daunt Light vessel off the south coast of Ireland is proof of the existence of such waves. What is not recorded on this trace is what impact the passing of this wave had on the lightship, but obviously she survived to tell the tale.

The significant wave height which is used in forecasts is a close approximation to the estimate of the height of waves which an experienced sailor would make. Statistically, it is stated that if the sea is observed during the passage of 60 waves, the height of the highest wave which passes a given point will be 1.6 times the significant height. In 3 hours of observation, the highest wave is likely to be twice the significant wave height and this is another way of demonstrating the very variable nature of waves, even in what appears to be a regular sea pattern.

WAVE SIZE

What size of waves can we expect to meet at sea? There are many factors involved and we have already seen how the wave size can vary in an apparently regular sea. Wind strength, fetch, the depth of water and currents and tide all have their effect on the height of the waves. Obviously, the more sea-room there is for the wind to have its effect on the sea, the higher the waves are likely to be. The effective distance over which the wind has an effect on the sea is known as the 'fetch', and this is generally considered to be the distance to the nearest land to windward. The effect of fetch on wave height can be dramatically illustrated when a boat seeks shelter behind a headland. Suddenly the fetch is greatly reduced by the intrusion of the headland and the sea is consequently diminished.

Wind strength has a great effect on the size of waves too, but there is a time lag before the wind has its full effect on the waves' development. The Beaufort Wind Scale gives the size of waves likely to be encountered in the open sea for a given wind strength. For instance, a wind of Force 8 is likely to produce waves up to 25 feet (7½ metres) in height. However, as we have seen, this can only be a very approximate guide, and relates to the waves generated by the existing wind without taking into account any other wave trains which may be present and which, by combining with the predominant wave train, can produce larger waves.

Waves over 100 feet (30 metres) in height have been reported, and the prospect of meeting such a wave is daunting. Most reported heights are largely the result of guess work as it is very difficult to measure the height of a wave from a vessel. Wave-height estimates, even by experienced seafarers, tend to be on the generous

Force 12 in the North Atlantic. Waves here are estimated at 50 feet in height with very heavy breaking crests – no place for a small boat (Photo: Author)

side, and the largest height of wave recorded by a wave recorder fitted to lightships or weather-ships is around the 50-foot (15-metre) mark. This is the sort of wave height which might be encountered in mid-ocean, whilst close inshore in storm conditions wave heights are likely to be of the order of 20–30 feet (6–9 metres). Wave height alone is not the only critical factor which determines how dangerous a wave is. To determine the danger, the wave length also has to be taken into account so that the gradient can be assessed.

GRADIENT

The combination of wave height and wave length determines the gradient. A 20-foot (6-metre) wave with a wave length of 1000 feet (300 metres) will have a very gentle gradient, but more commonly wave lengths are of the order of 200–300 feet (69–90 metres) in the open ocean, and this related to a 20-foot (6-metre) wave gives a steeper and more dangerous gradient. A critical gradient angle of 18 degrees is estimated to be the point at which a wave becomes unstable. At this angle the wave can no longer support its own weight and the crest will start to break and fall to leeward. Although with a trochoidal wave the

A vertical wave front just about to break. Estimated height 25 feet. (Photo: Author)

slope gets steeper near the crest, the 18-degree angle is taken as the mean angle of the face of the wave. There are several factors which contribute to the steepening of the gradient of a wave, and as a breaking wave is probably the most dangerous type likely to be encountered by a power boat, it is worth considering in some detail.

Waves obviously do not travel as fast as the wind which creates them, and the speed differential between the wind and the waves increases as the wind speed rises. As the wind is exerting pressure on the windward side of the wave and there is an eddy or low-pressure area on the leeside, the pressure exerted by the wind increases towards the top of the wave, particularly if the wave is higher than the average of the wave train. This increase in pressure towards the top of the wave means that the top of the wave tends to move faster to leeward than the bottom; eventually, the wave will become unstable and the top will break to leeward.

This pressure difference caused by the wind is the main cause of 'white horses' which are found in winds over Force 4. These are not particularly dangerous as it is only the very top of the wave which breaks to leeward and the breaking water has very little strength and volume. This minor breaking of the crest temporarily relieves the pressure differences and the wave stabilises again. It is only in winds of around Force 8 or more that white horses really become significant and dangerous, but at this stage other factors start to intrude and affect the sea state. At this wind strength, the white horses lose their random behaviour and become a more regular occurrence. As soon as the wind decreases, the white horses disappear, although the waves remain, demonstrating that this is primarily a wind-generated phenomenon. At moderate wind strengths, the amount of water actually in motion as the wave breaks is small and presents little hazard to a small boat, but as the wind strength increases, the volume and depth of the breaking water increases so that in severe conditions it can easily overwhelm the boat.

EFFECTS OF TIDES

Waves also become steeper when the whole body of water is moving, such as in tidal streams or currents. The effect of currents tends to have a moderating effect on waves as the current is usually generated by a wind blowing in a steady direction across the surface of the water. Thus, generally, wind and current have a common direction which has the effect of increasing the wave length and consequently reduces the gradient of the waves. Tidal streams, on the other hand, reverse direction every 6 hours or so. When the tidal stream and wind have a common direction the sea conditions are moderated, but when they are in opposition there can be a marked increase in the severity of the sea conditions. Many of the world's most notorious stretches of sea are those where strong tidal streams run in opposition to the wind; areas such as Portland Race and Pentland

Firth off the coast of Britain have an awesome reputation amongst mariners.

Normally, when a wind is generating waves a state of near equilibrium is reached when the waves are of a height that can be supported by the prevailing wind. Now if the body of water is moving to windward, as it would be in a wind-against-tide situation, two effects are noticed. First, there is a slight increase in the apparent wind strength, resulting from a combination of the wind and tide speeds working in opposition. Second, the progress of the waves to leeward is slowed, and these two factors cause the wave length to shorten appreciably. Shortening the wave length whilst maintaining the same wave height increases the gradient and consequently the prospect of the waves breaking.

Wind-against-tide conditions are thus characterised by a short, steep sea. Even in relatively light winds this sea can become quite uncomfortable, and because the crests are arriving in quick succession it is very easy for the boat to get out of step with the waves, that is, not recovering from one wave before the next is upon it. In stronger winds the short, steep seas will break; for a small boat such seas are extremely uncomfortable, because of the steep gradients which cause excessive pitching or rolling. If the vessel should find its bow dropping, having just negotiated one wave with a breaking crest approaching from the next wave, a dangerous situation is rapidly developing in which the boat could easily be overwhelmed.

The short, sharp waves of wind-against-tide conditions. (Photo: Motor Boat & Yachting)

I encountered conditions like this in a comparatively narrow channel where the tide underneath us was carrying us rapidly through the channel. The wind was Force 8 on the bow and at the windward end of the channel there was an evil-looking patch of breaking water. Such was the turbulence in the seas in this wind-against-tide situation that on one occasion, as the boat rose to negotiate a wave which was about to break, the following wave broke over both the top of the wave in front and over the top of the boat. It was a nasty moment, with tons of water crashing over the deck, but fortunately, with a well-found boat, we survived that and the next series of breaking waves before the tide carried us clear of this dangerous stretch.

When the wind and tide are in the same direction, there is a flattening of the sea caused by the wave length being increased. Even in strong winds this can reduce the chance of breaking waves quite considerably. In some areas the difference in

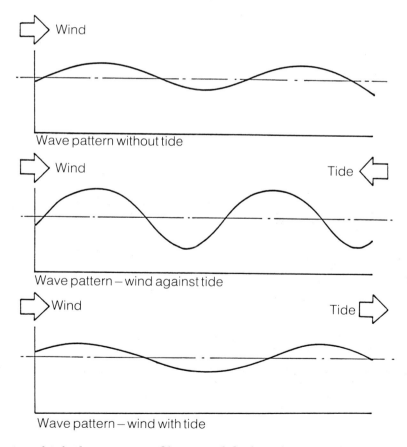

Wind

Wave pattern without tide

Wind   Tide

Wave pattern – wind against tide

Wind   Tide

Wave pattern – wind with tide

The way in which the wave profile is modified under the influence of tides or currents.

the sea conditions caused by tidal changes is very marked and this is worth bearing in mind when driving a powerboat in rough seas. Also bear in mind that the change from comparatively docile conditions to breaking seas can occur in a very short space of time, sometimes less than an hour. When you are out in a gale, wind-against-tide situations should be avoided as far as possible. Certainly, if a further ingredient such as shallow water is thrown into the equation, these areas should be avoided like the plague.

SHALLOW WATER

Shallow water is another cause of breaking waves. This is obvious when one looks at the surf breaking on a beach, but breaking waves can also occur on shoal patches where there may still be a considerable depth of water, certainly deep enough to navigate over safely in calm conditions. The cause of a wave breaking in shallow water is that the bottom of the wave or the trough, which can be some depth below the surface, is slowed down by its proximity to the sea bed. The top of the wave is still travelling forwards at its original speed and the initial effect of this slowing of the wave is a reduction in the wave length. This in turn increases the gradient, and eventually the wave becomes unstable and breaks.

In shoal water a wave tends to break in a very different manner to that in the open sea. At sea the crest runs down the face of the wave in a relatively gradual process. In shallow water, because of the slowing of the trough by the sea bed, the wave tends to 'trip over itself' and a near vertical wall of water is formed before the crest falls violently into the trough and the energy of the wave is translated into a strong horizontal energy with a strong flow of water. It is from this translation of energy into a breaking wave that the term *translation waves* originates. In shoal waters where the depth is such that the bottom effect may be felt but the waves do not break, this will be discernible by a shortening of the wave length and an apparent steepening of the gradient which can generate quite nasty sea conditions.

The depth of water at which a wave will start to slow and shorten is roughly equal to the wave length. As far as the change in the wave shape is concerned, the effect is barely noticeable until the depth of water is about half the wave length, but this still means that the shape and character of waves can alter in what is still comparatively deep water. There are reports of a noticeable change in wave character, even in water depths of 100 fathoms (180 metres) or more when deep ocean swells encounter this comparatively shallow water. Inshore you may find that a rapid change in the depth of water will cause a marked change in the behaviour of waves and you may be able to see this by a line of breaking waves over the change in depth.

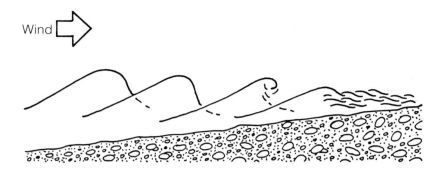

Breaking wave in shallow water. Here the whole wave rears up and breaks heavily with considerable violence.

ISOLATED SHOALS

A wave approaching shallow water will shorten and break in a reasonably predictable manner, but consider what happens when waves are approaching an isolated shoal. Here you would expect the waves to break on the windward side of the shoal and a comparatively calm area to exist on the leeside, with only the smaller waves being allowed to cross. Unfortunately this is not the case, as the waves passing on either side are slowed down close to the shoal, while those parts of the waves in deeper water continue at their original speed. The result is that the waves are refracted and alter their direction of travel, so that behind the shoal you can find the two sets of waves which have passed on either side producing a very nasty confused sea generated by the two crossing wave trains.

This same phenomenon of refraction accounts for the way that waves, which approach the shoreline obliquely, still appear to break almost parallel to the shore; the inshore end of the wave is slowed down, allowing the seaward end to swing shorewards relative to it. Such refraction along the shoreline can mean that, even though you are seeking shelter behind a headland which apparently cuts off the wind and thus reduces the fetch, you sometimes have to go a long way beyond the headland to escape from the refracted waves which will tend to creep around the point and enter the supposedly sheltered bay beyond.

We have already seen how refraction can produce a nasty cross sea with pyramid-type waves where the intersecting wave crests coincide. Such a sea is very similar to a clapotic sea, which can be vicious, and these seas lie in an area which at first glance could be expected to be one of relative calm. Herein lies a recipe for disaster. Waves can also be reflected by shallow water, and this means that if there is a shoal which is fairly regular in shape with its long axis parallel to the direction of the approaching waves, there could be reflected waves coming off this shoal and mixing with the approaching wave trains, to produce dangerous sea conditions where they would not normally be anticipated. In such situations it is easy to see how so-called freak waves could be generated, and why tales of experiences in rough seas almost invariably include references to freak or rogue waves coming from nowhere. If you analyse the situation carefully such conditions are predictable, and a careful study of the chart will show one or more of the factors which can lead to a distortion and increase in wave size and character.

COMBINATION CONDITIONS

We have looked at the various reasons for waves breaking, but it is perhaps rare for these causes to occur in isolation. All too often in coastal sea areas, two or more of these causes are combined, and certainly the more dramatic and dangerous sea conditions which might be experienced by power boats are caused by combinations of shallow waters and tides with odd areas of clapotic seas thrown in for good measure. These nasty sea conditions can be experienced where a tidal stream or current is forced into a narrow channel; in the Mediterranean, areas like the Straits of Messina between Sicily and Italy and the Straits of Bonifacio between Sardinia and Corsica are good examples of where

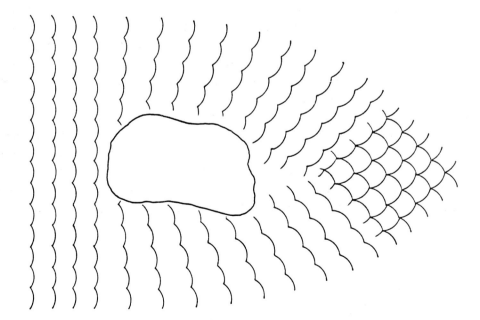

The refraction of waves around a shoal or island showing how a dangerous system of crossing waves can be found on the lee side of a shoal.

difficult sea conditions can be found. These are partly caused by the increase in wind strength through the narrow straits with high sides, but also by the compression of the tidal stream which increases its rate of flow and helps to generate nasty sea conditions. A similar situation can be found in Long Island Sound in the United States in the area called 'The Race'. A quote from the pilot book illustrates this point: 'The mean strength of the tidal streams through The Race is about 3½ knots. There are always strong tide rips and swirls in the wake of the irregular depths, except for about half an hour at slack water. The rips are exceptionally heavy during bad weather and especially when a strong wind opposes the tidal stream or when the stream opposes a heavy sea.' These are the types of area that you cannot always avoid, but here it is really a question of choosing your time to go through the channel to ensure the best conditions.

Probably one of the most notorious sea areas anywhere in the world is the Pentland Firth in Scotland. Here there are not only very strong tidal streams which run up to 8 knots through the firth, but the situation is complicated by patches of shoal water and the islands of Stroma, Swona and Skerries which obstruct the narrowing passage between the mainland and the Orkney Islands. If you add to this the ingredient of a strong westerly gale and heavy seas sweeping in from the Atlantic, then you have a recipe for some of the worst sea conditions which could be encountered by small boats.

At the western end of this channel is the Merry Men of Mey, a stretch of violently breaking seas stretching almost from shore to shore, whilst at the eastern end is the Bore of Duncansby which has a similar effect. Strong eddies and countertides can form behind the islands, and the seas here in gale-force winds can only be described as maelstrom conditions which could spell death to any small craft. It is a battleground for the elements and no place for a powerboat unless you choose your conditions very carefully.

I have already mentioned conditions off the Island of Hoy which is close to the Pentland Firth, and further north in the Shetland Islands off Sumburgh Head is a wild stretch of water, one of the famous 'roosts' of Scotland where the mighty Atlantic seas encounter tidal currents flowing off this headland. The battle of waves and tides is fought over an area of sea which can be up to 3 miles off the headland. I have been through this area in a lifeboat and it is certainly a very wild stretch of sea.

HEADLANDS

Headlands jutting out into any current or tidal stream tend to compress the flow and increase the speed of the stream. These headlands can also distort the flow. A prime example of this is found off Portland Bill on the south coast of England where not only is the tidal flow compressed round the headland to reach speeds of 6 knots or more, but there is also a large eddy formed behind the headland which creates a circular flow of the tide, the eddy returning to produce a very confused tidal flow in the lee of the headland. These conditions in themselves are enough to ensure that the sea is never still in this area and if you add the ingredient of a strong wind, then you have sea conditions which can rival the Pentland Firth in ferocity.

One of the interesting aspects of the Portland race is that if you keep very close inshore there is a 300-metre wide stretch of comparatively calm water even when the race is boiling outside. This passage can remain negotiable for vessels even in quite strong wind conditions, but you do need a well-found and reliable boat if you are to navigate such a passage successfully in rough weather, because any engine or steering failure would rapidly lead to disaster. These inshore passages are found around many headlands, provided there is an adequate depth of water, and can allow safe passage and save travelling many miles to seaward to clear the rough seas off the headland. The reason for such a calmer passage is probably due to the very much reduced tidal streams which can be found inshore, due to friction with the land; but there may also be a sheltering effect of the inside passage by the breaking water offshore. The violent breaking water in the race will dissipate much of the wave energy and prevent the larger waves moving inshore.

TROUGHS

When we consider rough seas or talk about seas in general we tend to think in terms of waves and their crests. This is no doubt because the wave crests are the parts which break and are the main danger area, but for every wave crest there must also be a trough and these can present an equal danger to small boats. In fact, in some cases the trough can present a greater danger than the crest if you consider that it is a 'hole' in the sea into which a boat can fall at about the same time as the crest may become unstable and fall into the same hole. Whilst you can often see the big waves coming some distance away, with troughs there is very little advance warning and the first knowledge you will have of a deep trough is when the boat is falling into it. Bear in mind that if one wave in 300,000 is four times the average height, then one trough in 300,000 is four times the average depth.

These wave troughs or holes, as they are often called, are really a hazard in areas where the waves have steep gradients and are breaking. I can well remember coming face to face with just such a trough when carrying out rough-weather trials in the Portland race. The boat lifted to what looked like a comparatively normal wave crest for the sea conditions at the time and then, to my horror, when we were on top of the crest, what appeared to be a bottomless pit opened up on the other side. (When you are in this situation there is no time to slow the boat down.) The whole vessel seemed to become airborne and then drop bodily into the trough with a tremendous crash, but fortunately we were in a well-found boat and we survived without damage. I can remember my feet actually leaving the deck as the craft dropped. However, this experience convinced me that deep troughs probably present a greater hazard to small boats than a breaking wave crest, largely because of the lack of warning of their arrival.

PRESSURE WAVES

Another type of wave which can arrive without warning and which we have not so far considered is the *pressure wave*. This is the wave created mainly by the passage of a large ship through the water. These waves can be felt up to a mile from the ship which created them, and whilst they take on the pattern of ordinary oscillation waves far from the ship itself, their danger lies in the fact that they can arrive unannounced; and being superimposed on top of the existing wave pattern they can cause some dangerous seas.

Perhaps the biggest danger with pressure waves lies in the fact that they can occur in calm or slight sea conditions when you are going along enjoying the sea and the sun; if you then suddenly hit a big wave it can create havoc. The problem with these waves exists primarily for fast boats, and if you see shipping passing nearby, then always remember the wave which can follow the passage of a ship. It could take 10 or 15 minutes to arrive, but arrive it will, and if you are not ready for it you can find your boat performing all sorts of unpleasant gyrations. Didier Pironi's fatal accident in an offshore racing boat in 1987 is largely attributed to the fact that he hit, at very high speed, the wash of a ship, his boat flew into the air and turned over, landing upside down. This should serve as a warning that, even in a slower planing boat, the risk of the wash from passing ships is still a potent factor, and is one of the reasons why you mustn't relax too much at the helm of a fast craft.

GETTING TO KNOW THE SEA

From this chapter you will see that waves can hold many nasty surprises, even in comparatively calm conditions. Knowing and understanding the sea is a prime requirement for advanced boat handling, either in fast boats or in rough seas, and once you know your enemy then you can learn to cope with all the unpleasant things it might throw at you. Reading about this in a book is one thing, but the best way to learn about the sea is to go and watch it in all its moods, and become familiar with the way it can change depending on the various influences that affect it, such as wind and tides. Watch the way in which a wave breaks when it has a long straight crest and then again when it has an irregular·crest with dips and peaks.

The sea is never static, and part of the attraction of handling a boat in rough seas or at high speed is the way you have to measure up to what the sea throws at you. Finally, remember that behind every wave crest is a trough, and if you are to drive your boat well then you have to learn to negotiate both the troughs and the crests, as we shall see later in the chapters on boat handling.

2 Hull design

Before the advent of GRP boats there were almost as many hull shapes as there were boats. GRP construction has brought about a certain standardisation in boat design, but even so there is still an enormous variety in powerboat hull design. One wonders why this should be, because surely some particular hull forms are better than others and, with experience, optimum hull forms should have been developed.

You have only to look around any marina to realise that, even with the limited standardisation brought about by GRP construction, there is very little consensus about the optimum hull form for powerboats. The deep-vee hull rules the roost and is by far the most popular, both for planing and displacement hulls. There is also a large number of what might be termed semi-displacement hulls in the powerboat market, as well as the more traditional concept in hull design which is related to the seaworthy displacement hull. To add to the confusion, there are concepts such as the trihedral hull and, at the exotic top end of the market, the high-performance catamaran. Within these broad categories there is an infinite variety in hull form with subtle differences in shape and concept – so there is still a great deal of individuality about boat design.

Part of this wide variation in hull shape is a result of the designer trying to match the shape to the particular requirements of the vessel, but there is a tremendous number of other factors which come into the reckoning. Some features of hull design bear the stamp of particular designers, rather like a trademark. For instance, when the deep-vee hull was first developed by Ray Hunt, back in the late 1940s, the design became known as the Hunt hull. Similarly, when the deep-vee was later refined and developed onto a long, narrow hull – with Don Shead being the originator of this concept – these hulls became known as Shead hulls but, of course, with time, other designers have developed the same idea even further.

Much of the variation in hull design comes from the fact that designers have to cope with a wide variety of parameters. Certain features of hull design, which we will look at later, affect the boat's seaworthiness; then again, if the hull is required to go very fast, this demands that other features be incorporated. The construction material used for the hull will affect the shape to a certain extent, and the need to incorporate comfortable accommodation in the interior also has to be taken into account. It would be nice to think that powerboats are designed to reflect the optimum in seaworthiness, speed and safety but, in fact, these parameters may often come some way down the list of priorities; and comfort in harbour and appearance can instead be the overriding considerations. The compromises that the designer has to make in producing an efficient hull design can be conflicting, and in designing a boat it is the job of the designer to decide, with the customer, the relative importance of the various design features, which may conflict, and then somehow produce a reasonably cohesive result.

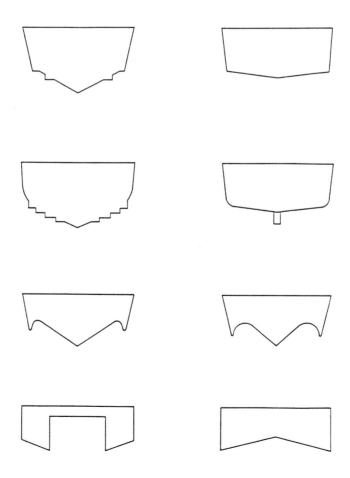

The wide variety of hull shapes which can be found on planing boats.

COMPROMISES

At one end of the design spectrum are lifeboats, which are designed almost without compromise. Here, a hull design has been developed to operate in rough sea conditions, and the traditional double-ended lifeboat hull with a pronounced sheer is the epitome of seaworthy design. However, even in lifeboat work, compromises are being made because speed is becoming an increasingly important factor in sea rescue, and modern lifeboat design is having to compromise on the ultimate in seaworthiness to allow higher speeds. Here the compromises are not just with hull shape and performance but also with the acceptance that, by increasing the speed, a greater emphasis is put on the skills of the person driving the boat; we look at this in Chapter 5.

At the other end of the spectrum is the offshore racing boat. Here again there is little room for compromise: the accent is on out-and-out speed and the hull is designed accordingly. There are areas of compromise, however, when you want to go very fast in waves. For this a design to cushion the wave impact is necessary, which means giving up something in terms of top speed to achieve the desired result.

However, with both lifeboat and offshore racing design, it isn't necessary to make the compromises required to provide comfortable live-aboard accommodation as well as the other features found on modern-day pleasure boats. With cruising boats the designer has to move away from the two extremes, and produce a hull shape which incorporates a large internal volume to give the maximum interior space. Whilst it is often considered that the designer of lifeboats and offshore racing boats has reached the peak of his profession by concentrating on these areas, in fact, the designer of a pleasure boat probably has a much more difficult task because he can be much less single-minded and has to find a solution amongst a much greater number of conflicting requirements.

HULL TYPES

Powerboats can generally be divided into three basic types, with the design speed being the main feature which decides the category. *Displacement* boats can operate at speeds up to about 10 knots and move through the water with the water parting at the bow and closing in again at the stern. In this way the hull creates a wave, the length of which is a factor of the length of the boat (the longer the vessel, the longer the wave length). A displacement boat cannot travel faster than the wave it creates, as it has neither the lift nor sufficient power to enable it to rise up over the crest of the wave at the bow. As the speed of the wave is directly proportional to its length, the longer a displacement boat is, the faster its theoretical maximum speed. The beam of a vessel can have a certain influence on the theoretical maximum speed, as a very narrow boat can slice through its bow wave, enabling the craft to travel faster than a beamier model. This was the way racing powerboats were made to travel quickly before the planing boat was developed, but such long narrow boats are not particularly seaworthy.

When a boat has an underwater shape which generates dynamic lift and the craft has adequate power, then it can rise bodily out of the water and ride over the wave created by its progress through the water. Once the boat is up and *planing* in this way, a much faster speed is possible and the limit of speed is then dictated mainly by engine power and the weight of the boat. The dynamic lift is provided by the reaction of the underwater surfaces of the hull moving against the water, and the ideal planing underwater shape – to give maximum lift with minimum friction – would be flat, rather like a plank of wood. However, such a shape lacks directional stability and it would also slam heavily in a seaway, due to the impact on the waves. Hence the designer had to make compromises which resulted in the deep-vee hull, where the underwater surfaces are angled. The angle of this vee from the horizontal varies greatly from boat to boat but reaches a maximum of around 28 degrees on racing boats. The angle of deadrise, as this is called, is one of the main areas of compromise in fast-boat design, with the maximum deadrise generally being used on high-performance craft to get the maximum cushioning effect in waves, whilst slower planing boats tend to have a shallower deadrise.

The third type of hull form is the *semi-displacement* hull which is another concept in compromise, aiming to retain some of the virtues of the traditional displacement hull in a planing-boat design. Instead of the hard chine hulls familiar to the planing boat, the semi-displacement hull has a rounded bilge, but these tend to have a much harder shape than that found in displacement boats. Many of these vessels feature a fine bow entry to help cushion the impact with waves, but this runs into flat surfaces aft to generate lift. A skeg helps to give directional stability and unless these boats are provided with very powerful engines they tend to come only partially up onto the plane, hence the generic term for them, semi-displacement.

FORCES ACTING ON BOATS

Before going into the finer details of hull design too much, it is worth considering the various forces which act on a boat in a seaway, because these can have a significant bearing on the way the designer reaches his compromise. First, there is the *weight* of the boat itself and this acts vertically downwards through the *centre of gravity* of the boat. The centre of gravity is fixed no matter what attitude the craft adopts and it is only when weights are altered on the boat, i.e. a water ballast tank is filled or fuel tanks emptied, that the centre of gravity alters its position. When weights are added, the centre of gravity moves towards the added weight and when weights are removed, it moves away from this point. If a bow ballast tank is filled, then the centre of gravity will move towards the bow and this will result in the boat being trimmed down by the bow. Empty the tank and the centre of gravity moves aft so that the bow will lift.

Balanced against the centre of gravity is the upward thrust of the *water* which is displaced by the hull. This force acts vertically upwards through the *centre of buoyancy*. The centre of buoyancy is the centre of gravity of the displaced water; as the water is homogeneous, the centre of buoyancy is, in fact, the geometric centre of the underwater shape of the hull. When the boat is at rest in still water, the centre of buoyancy acting upwards balances the centre of gravity acting downwards and the boat is in equilibrium.

Two events can alter this state of equilibrium, either a movement of the centre of gravity or a movement of the centre of buoyancy. As we have seen, the centre of gravity only moves if you move or change a weight on board the boat. If one of the crew moves from the centre line of the boat to one side, the centre of gravity will move in that direction, and this means that the downward force of gravity is offset from the upward force of buoyancy and a turning moment is produced which causes the vessel to heel. However, in heeling, the underwater volume of the boat changes shape and so the centre of buoyancy also moves until once again a state of equilibrium is reached. This situation applies in both the transverse and the fore-and-aft directions, although the effect is not so noticeable fore and aft due to the much greater stability which the hull has in this plane.

At sea the centre of gravity stays in virtually the same position, but the underwater volume of the hull is continually changing shape as waves pass under the hull and the centre of buoyancy moves accordingly. With the centre of gravity remaining constant, the change in the centre of buoyancy produces a turning moment as the centre of buoyancy always moves towards that part of the hull which is more deeply immersed, so the force acting upwards through it will tend to bring the boat back onto an even keel until the two centres are back in line again. In the transverse plane, the righting levers formed by the centre of buoyancy acting upwards and the centre of gravity acting downwards give the boat stability. Generally speaking, the fuller the transverse sections, the more stable the boat, as a small angle of heel will produce a comparatively large movement at the centre of buoyancy so that the boat will come quickly upright again. Another way to improve the transverse stability is to increase the vertical distance between the centre of gravity and the centre of buoyancy, so that when the boat heels a more powerful righting lever is produced. This is an area where designers need to compromise because with a strong righting lever, which usually results from having the centre of gravity too low, the boat becomes stiff which means it doesn't heel easily, but it will generally have a very quick pendulum-like rolling motion which can be very tiring at sea.

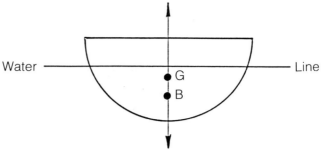

In still water the downward forces of gravity (G) is equal and opposite to the upward force of buoyancy (B), and the boat is in equilibrium.

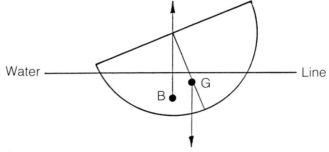

If the boat is heeled (B) will move towards the lee side, thus providing a moment to right the boat.

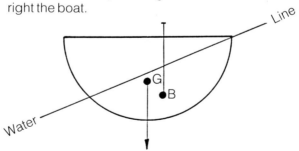

Similarly, when a wave approaches the beam (B) will move towards the immersed side, again producing a moment, which in this case will cause the boat to level.

The transverse action of a displacement boat in waves.

In the fore-and-aft plane, the boat is much more stable due to the length of the vessel compared with its beam. Here the problem is not so much to ensure sufficient stability, but to ensure that there is sufficient buoyancy at the ends of the boat for these to lift over waves and not go through them. When a boat heads into a wave the fore part of the craft becomes immersed which causes the centre of buoyancy to move forwards away from the centre of gravity, thus creating a lever which causes the bow to lift until the centre of buoyancy moves aft again as the wave passes and equilibrium is momentarily restored. If the bow is very fine, there will be a smaller shift of the centre of buoyancy with a consequent reduction in the lifting effect. This means that the bow could become very deeply immersed before it lifts and a fine bow increases the risk of the wave actually breaking on board. Most boats intended to operate in rough seas will have full bow shapes to generate sufficient lift to make sure that the bow lifts over the waves. However, this must not be overdone otherwise the boat will attempt to follow the exact contour of the wave, and this can produce a very uncomfortable motion because of the rather violent pitching which will result. This is an area where there are many different approaches, but one of the best compromises is a bow which is

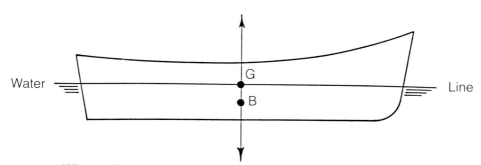

When a displacement boat is in still water the downward force of gravity (G) is equal and opposite to the upward force of buoyancy (B), and the boat is in equilibrium.

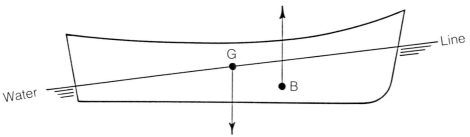

When a wave approaches from ahead (B) will move forward, creating a momentum which will lift the bow over the wave.

The longitudinal action of a displacement boat in waves.

fine on the waterline, to reduce the initial impact on the wave and then introduce a flare towards the deck, which gives a rapid increase in buoyancy as the bow becomes immersed. This flare also serves to deflect the water away from the boat and keeps down the spray.

When designing a boat, the designer cannot consider the bow shape or indeed any other part of the vessel in isolation. The important thing is to achieve a balanced hull so that a full bow shape would normally be balanced by a full stern shape. A particularly unhappy combination can be a fine bow and a full stern shape, because when a wave passes under the stern it will cause the bow to sink at a time when it should be ready to lift to the next approaching wave. This can be a problem in many planing powerboat designs when the boat has to operate at slow speeds off the plane, when the dynamic lift which usually keeps the bow up has been removed.

Because the boat is moving forwards the bow shape tends to be much more critical than the stern shape. This is particularly the case with planing boats where the transom stern is now almost universal. However, the stern shape can be more critical when operating in a following sea at displacement speeds when the waves are overtaking the craft. Here the canoe or cruiser stern is considered to be the ideal because the waves can flow smoothly past on each side. This hull shape is still retained on some traditional hull designs, but in general there is a move away from pointed sterns in favour of the transom stern.

A very full stern shape gives plenty of buoyancy in this area, which would cause the stern to be lifted by a following sea when operating at a slow speed. This, in turn, could cause the bow to bury into the sea; by so doing the bow provides a pivot about which the stern can swing. This is the classic broaching situation when the boat turns broadside onto the oncoming waves, and emphasises the need for a full bow shape to match a full stern shape so that the bow does not sink readily. A steeply raked stem reduces the chance of the bow acting as a fulcrum in this manner because it will have less grip on the water.

DISPLACEMENT HULLS

Generally speaking, a displacement boat, to be a good sea craft, requires a hull of generous proportions and smooth contours with no sudden changes of line. The traditional displacement boat is typified by the time-honoured fishing vessel or lifeboat concept whose hull is all curved with no sharp angles. The deck has an adequate sheer to give the boat high ends which reduces the chance of waves breaking on board at the bow or stern. A good draft is desirable so that the hull has a good bite on the water and is not easily deflected from its chosen course. This type of traditional hull was developed partly because of its good seagoing qualities, but also because it was adaptable to wood construction. With the

A displacement hull lifeboat operating in the Fastnet gale of 1979. (Photo: RNAS Culdrose)

advent of steel construction, many displacement boats incorporate a hard angular line sometimes with a double chine to smooth the contours. With GRP there are virtually no restrictions on hull shape and so designers have been able to introduce much more subtlety into hull shapes, but overall, as far as displacement hulls are concerned, they have been unable to produce anything that performs better than the traditional shapes.

With planing-boat hulls the designer certainly has a more difficult task because not only do these craft have to produce higher speeds, they also have to be capable of operating satisfactorily at slow speeds when they become, to all intents and purposes, displacement hulls. In many cases this slow-speed performance is overlooked in the need to achieve good high-speed performance, with the result that some planing boats are less than ideal for operating at displacement speeds in rough conditions.

PLANING HULLS

A planing hull differs from a displacement hull in that the weight of the boat is supported, to a large extent, by the upward thrust or dynamic lift created by the reaction between the forward speed of the boat and the horizontal water surface. When at rest the planing hull develops all its lift by displacing water, but as speed rises the dynamic lift is developed by the forward movement and as the boat rises, the lift generated by displacement decreases. For a given power, the hull will eventually reach a state of equilibrium where a combination of the dynamic lift and the displacement will balance out against the weight of the boat. At higher speeds there is more dynamic lift and less displacement, but on each occasion the point of equilibrium has to be reached.

Spray rails and chines

Introducing a vee-shape into the bottom of the planing hull greatly improves the stability of the hull. This directional stability is further enhanced by the fitting of spray rails. These are wedge-shaped sections applied to the hull in a

A motor cruiser being driven hard. The spray rails and chine layout can be clearly seen. (Photo: Author)

fore-and-aft line and, in addition to improving the directional stability, they also serve to peel the water away from the hull, thus reducing the wetted area and hence the friction between hull and water. This frictional resistance, or drag, is the main impediment to high speeds in planing boats, whereas with displacement hulls the resistance is virtually all created by the waves generated by the hull. Spray rails have a horizontal surface at the bottom edge which helps to generate lift and these have a stabilising effect on the hull to help prevent it 'chine walking'. This is when the hull wants to ride on the flat surfaces on either side of the vee, which is a form of instability. Designers have different ideas about spray rails; some carry them right aft, whereas others terminate them before they get to the transom.

To a certain extent, the layout of the spray rails will depend on the chine line, which is the angle between the bottom panels and the side panels of the hull. On earlier designs of planing boats the chine line tended to be kept very low, running virtually parallel with the deck line, creating a fairly full bow shape. On many modern boats, particularly those designed for higher speeds, the chine line rises up almost to join the deckline at the bow and the spray rails tend to follow this

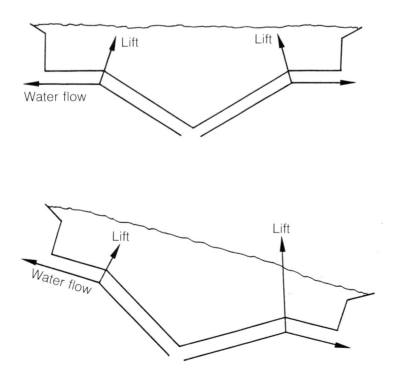

How the spray rails help to stabilise the deep vee hull by increasing the lift on the lower side of the hull when it is heeled.

same line. This raised chine line running up to deck level produces a steeply raked stem which tends to give the bow a good fine entry and gentle contours which can be beneficial when travelling into waves. The chine itself usually incorporates a horizontal surface to generate additional lift and to act in much the same way as the spray rail, but deflecting water and spray downwards and away from the hull. On some designs, the chine is even angled downwards to generate additional lift, and an extension of this concept is to create embryo side hulls and develop the hull form into that of the trihedral.

One of the aims of the trihedral hull is to pick up the bow wave and turn it back downwards again, thus generating additional lift and producing a boat which comes very easily up onto the plane and which can support considerable weight. The trihedral hull is a very practical shape, particularly for working boats where it gives a large deck area and good stability at rest, but against this has to be balanced the high impact loadings which can occur on the concave areas of the hull shape through wave impact. Trihedral hulls have proved popular in smaller sizes, but they are not aesthetically pleasing and have not gained popularity in larger sizes in the pleasure-boat market.

Forces on planing hulls

A planing boat, when operating in the planing mode, is affected by three main forces. The first of these is the force of *gravity*, which is exactly the same as in displacement boats and acts vertically downwards through the centre of gravity. The second is the force due to *buoyancy* and this acts vertically upwards through the centre of buoyancy. When the boat is planing, this force is much smaller than it would be in a comparable displacement boat, as the underwater volume is much smaller. As only the stern section of the vessel remains immersed in water, the centre of buoyancy tends to be well aft. The third force is that due to *dynamic lift* produced by the forward speed of the boat reacting against the water, and this force acts vertically upwards, concentrated at a point just aft of where the water surface meets the hull. Both of these upward forces tend to act through the aft part of the craft and to compensate for this the boat is designed with its centre of gravity well aft so that a balance is achieved. Normally the faster the design speed of the boat, the further aft will be the centre of gravity, since at these higher speeds both the centre of buoyancy and the centre of lift move further aft.

In a head sea, when meeting a wave, the forward sections will become immersed and this causes both the centres of buoyancy and lift to move forwards. As the centre of gravity remains in the same place, a moment will be produced which will cause the bow to lift to restore stability. As the bow comes over the wave the water will fall away and the bow will be unsupported, so that it will tend to drop into the trough if the boat is travelling relatively slowly. At higher speeds, the momentum of the boat lifting to the wave will be maintained, and for a short time

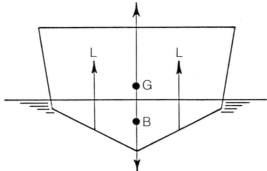

Transverse forces acting on a planing boat.
When the boat is on an even keel the lift factors
balance each other to keep the boat upright.

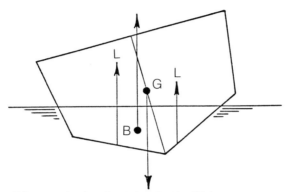

When a planing boat heels, the lift factor on the
lower side is increased, thus producing an
additional righting force in addition to that
generated by the movement of the centre of
buoyancy.

The transverse action of a planing boat in waves.

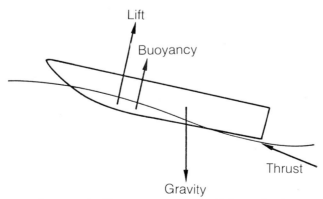

*How the forces on a planing hull vary in waves. When the bow is immersed
both the lift and buoyancy forces move forward, causing the bow to lift.*

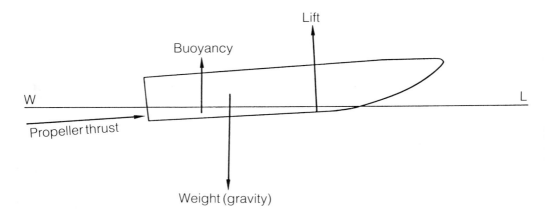

The forces which act on a planing boat. The upward forces of the lift and buoyancy balance out the downward force of gravity.

this momentum will compensate for the loss of lift as the fore part of the hull leaves the water. As the momentum dies away, gravity will take over and the boat will return to the water with very little change in attitude until the stern strikes the water — when lift will be produced, thus restoring the boat to its normal horizontal attitude.

With a planing boat operating in waves there is a constant change and balance of the forces acting on the hull. Because the waves themselves are continually changing in shape and form there will be very few moments when the boat is actually in balance; when these do occur they will be transient. With a planing boat the driver has certain controls such as the trim and flaps and the throttles themselves with which he can exert an influence over the lift generated by the hull; so whilst the hull design itself is important in achieving the correct characteristics, a great part of how a planing boat behaves at sea is in the hands of the driver and his use of the controls.

The throttles in particular are important and the speed at which a planing boat is travelling will influence the amount and effect of the dynamic lift. Push too hard in terms of speed and the vessel will fly out of the water on the top of a wave, putting great stresses on both boat and crew; with a planing boat the speed has to be matched much more carefully to the conditions.

Transition speeds
In rough sea conditions, the speed of a planing boat has to be reduced to the point where it may have to operate initially in the transition range between planing and displacement modes. These transition speeds will depend to a certain extent on the hull design, but they would normally occur at speeds between 10 and 20 knots, the same sort of speed range at which semi-displacement boats operate. In

*A semi-displacement hull pilot boat being pushed hard in difficult sea
conditions. (Photo: Author)*

general, this transition-speed range is not a particularly happy one for planing
boats, because the boat tends to adopt a rather bow-up attitude when it tries to
come onto the plane because both the dynamic and buoyancy lift centres move
well forward in this speed range. The reverse happens when the craft is coming
off the plane, and at this point the bow tends to drop before the buoyancy lift
moves forward to compensate for the loss of dynamic lift. Both of these situations
place the boat in a somewhat unnatural attitude and the average planing boat is
not particularly happy in this transition-speed range.

By contrast, the semi-displacement boat is designed to operate largely at these
speeds where it can be reasonably comfortable. The fine bow and rounded bilges
usually found on these hulls enable them to operate comfortably in the transition
mode as there is less reliance on dynamic lift, so bringing in or taking away this
factor has less effect on the trim of the boat.

Both planing and semi-displacement boats are designed to give their optimum
performance at the chosen speed ranges. However, in rough sea conditions, both
of these hull designs have to be able to operate in the displacement mode to
reduce the stresses on the hull. Here, some designs can be found wanting. Some
planing boats incorporate a reverse deck sheer which reduces the freeboard at
the bow, so that when operating at displacement speeds there can be a real risk of
the bow burying into waves before it picks up sufficient buoyancy to lift. With the
fine bow often found on semi-displacement hulls, the same thing can occur, and

in balancing the compromises in hull shape the designer has to move away from the more extreme hull forms which might give better performance at higher speeds but which could prove less than satisfactory at slow speeds. Another factor which can be overlooked with planing-boat hulls operating at low speeds is the lack of directional stability. With the bow sections more deeply immersed at low speeds, the hull tends to oversteer which can make life difficult when manoeuvring in harbour.

Leaning into the wind
Another feature in the design of deep-vee hulls, which is worth remembering when it comes to boat handling, is the way in which a deep-vee hull craft will lean into the wind when the wind is on the beam. This is caused primarily by the wind trying to blow the bow of the boat – which is out of the water – away, which means that a corrective helm has to be applied to keep the vessel on a straight line. This corrective helm makes the boat heel over slightly and causes the characteristic leaning into the wind. The situation can be compounded on a single-screw boat with the propeller reaction, which tends to heel the boat slightly against the thrust of the propeller. If the two heeling actions coincide, there may be a noticeable heel which can be quite alarming in certain conditions. This only applies to fast boats, but it can catch you unawares if you are unprepared.

CATAMARANS

In the offshore-racing world catamarans have operated with a considerable degree of success, although there has been little attempt to translate these high-performance catamarans into fast pleasure craft. Racing monohulls tend to reach the point where they become less controllable at speeds between 90 and 100 m.p.h. This is largely because there is so little of the hull left in the water that there is insufficient hull for the steering and other controls to react against, and the hull is close to the point of instability. The main advantage of the catamaran is that it extends this limit considerably because it rides on at least two points all the time. Most modern catamarans, in fact, use stepped hulls, which means that most of the time the boat is riding on four points which give excellent stability even at very high speeds. Helping the performance of the catamaran is the fact that *air lift* is generated in the tunnel between the two hulls thus reducing friction resistance with the water. In fine or even moderate sea conditions the catamaran can have a decided edge over the monohull as far as top speed is concerned, but in larger waves the pendulum swings in favour of the monohull with its more seaworthy hull configuration. Catamarans have also been used successfully at lower speeds where for day-boat use they offer huge cockpit space, but for general all-round work the monohull is usually a better proposition.

A modern racing catamaran which uses aerodynamic lift to reduce the wetted area. Note the cockpit canopies to give the crew protection. (Photo: Author)

There have also been some moves to use three pointers for very-high-speed work and these hulls also generate air lift which reduces resistance. In general, both catamaran and three-pointer concepts offer the possibility of better performance from the same power, but their construction is more complex with a consequent increase in cost and their use is only really justified where very high performance is required.

MONOHULL VARIATIONS

Even on monohull fast-planing boats there are many variations in hull form, the main alternatives being the long, narrow hull and the wider, fat hull. The former is generally used for racing and high performance, with the broader beam being used for cabin boats where the additional space in the hull has benefits in terms of accommodation. Certainly, as far as seaworthiness and operating at high speeds are concerned, the long, narrow hull has smaller flat surfaces to impact on the water and gives a better ride in this respect.

HULL STRENGTH

Whilst the shape of any powerboat is important, it is equally important to build the hull strong enough to operate at high speeds or in rough seas. Even today, after many years of experience with fast boats, most hulls used for high-speed work are heavily overbuilt, which is a good approach as far as reliability is concerned, but may detract from performance. Designers tend to rely on experience when specifying the scantlings of high-speed boats rather than a scientific approach, but experience is gradually pointing the way towards building lighter and faster craft.

Weight and stresses
Offshore powerboat racing is the proving ground for much of this experience, but light weight on its own is not always the best solution. A light boat will always fly out of the water much more readily than a heavy one and so weight can be a useful factor in keeping a craft moving fast in a seaway. When the boat is in the air it is not being propelled and therefore is slowing down. A heavier boat which can maintain contact with the water longer will always be able to go faster than a lighter one in wave conditions, and with increasingly powerful engines becoming available this is the route being adopted by many designers.

Stresses on a planing boat can be very great indeed, and there can be very high local stresses with much of the dynamic lift being concentrated at a point close to the forward point of contact between the hull and the water. Modern racing-powerboat hulls can be stressed to accept loadings of up to 80 p.s.i.,

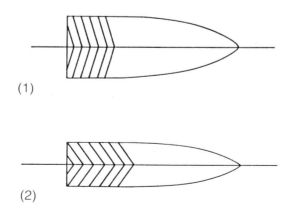

(1)

(2)

The planing surface of (1) a beamy boat and (2) a narrow boat. The beamy boat is a more efficient planing surface, but the narrow boat cushions wave impact better.

although the transient loadings on the hull could be much higher than this. However, they last for such a short time and are transmitted to other parts of the hull that the whole hull does not have to be stressed to absorb these very high-point loadings. The deep-vee hull of a modern planing boat absorbs much of the shock, provided the vessel lands squarely in the water, but all too often the boat will land on the flat surface of the hull vee and this can induce very high stresses into the hull structure. Fortunately, the hull is not completely rigid and slight flexing allows the hull to absorb these high shock loadings without damage. There is the temptation in some designs to introduce slight concave areas into the hull bottom such as might be found on trihedral hulls or on inverted spray or chine rails and here very high localised loadings on the hull occur if the boat leaves the water and re-enters. Most fast-boat hulls incorporate a slight degree of flexibility in the structure in order to help absorb very high shock loadings. The panel size between frames and stringers has to be kept as small as possible and the hull of a racing powerboat is built to absorb extremely high stresses.

STABILITY

Apart from strength, the other factor which can affect the safety of boats, particularly in rough seas, is transverse stability. Obviously, if a vessel is transversely unstable it will capsize, and most hulls, if inclined beyond a certain angle, will capsize. The transverse stability of most hulls is generally adequate until the deck becomes immersed. When this occurs, the centre of buoyancy does not continue to move away from the centre of gravity, so that the righting lever (which is a measure of the force which keeps the boat on an even keel) starts to get smaller. Also, when the deck level becomes immersed there is a good possibility of water being shipped on board, which adds weight and assists the capsizing movement. From this point on, the situation can rapidly escalate to the point of capsize, but most powerboats are stable up to angles of 60 or 70 degrees. This situation is therefore only likely to occur if the boat is operating in very rough conditions or if it becomes damaged. One design feature which obviously improves the stability is the provision of adequate freeboard, but this can add top weight to the boat which will move the centre of gravity. Again, a compromise is required and on some displacement boats this is achieved by fitting bulwarks. However, bulwarks are fine until water is shipped over them and then it tends to be contained on deck and can make the capsizing situation worse.

Another means of ensuring an adequate range of stability for a craft which will be operating in rough water is to prevent water getting below decks. This is not a simple problem on pleasure craft where cockpits and large open doors and windows are desirable features in fine weather. A door or window does not have to be completely watertight to keep out most of the water, but it certainly has to be strong. The pressures on a window when it is immersed are very great and toughened glass of adequate thicknesses in small panels in strong frames is required. Doors with their large surface area have to be adequately strong and so do the frames that support them. These are the sort of features that you should look for if you are going to operate a powerboat in rough seas. But what happens if you are out in really rough conditions and a breaking wave appears on the beam just at the moment that the boat is heeled away from the wave? With most vessels the righting lever, which is the force which brings the boat upright, increases the more the boat heels. Only when the deck level becomes immersed does the righting lever start to reduce and this usually occurs at angles between 40 and 60 degrees, depending on the design. Even after this the righting lever still exerts a positive force – but it is reducing in size, and how rapidly it reduces depends largely on the design of the boat and, of course, its watertight integrity.

Assuming that the superstructure of the boat is watertight and strong enough, the craft is likely to retain a positive righting level until it reaches an angle of perhaps 100 degrees, this angle very much depending on the shape and volume of the superstructure. Eventually, however, the righting lever will be reduced to zero and then become negative, which means that the forces of buoyancy and gravity are combining to capsize the boat from that point on. The boat, if it still remains intact, will probably find a stable position upside down.

Very few pleasure boats would survive the stresses of a capsize, and some form of material failure – such as windows breaking – would result. Modern lifeboats are certainly designed to survive such a capsize, and they are also designed to right themselves following such a capsize.

There are three ways of ensuring that a boat will self-right after a capsize, and one of these is to introduce into the design of the vessel a positive righting lever no matter what the attitude of the craft. This means that the designer has to ensure that the position of the centre of gravity in relation to the centre of buoyancy is such that one never overtakes the other to produce a negative righting moment. Another way to ensure self-righting is to move a weight, e.g. water ballast, when the boat is in the inverted position. This requires tanks and pipes and is far from an ideal solution. A third method, which has the merit of convenience, is to incorporate an inflatable air bag high up on the boat so that when it capsizes this air bag is either automatically or manually inflated and brings the craft upright again.

Self-righting is a primary requirement on lifeboats and rescue craft. But it is not just a question of producing a self-righting boat; conditions need to be such that the crew can also survive the capsize. Introducing such features into pleasure boats is neither required, nor particularly desirable, because it means giving up other design features, and in theory at least, pleasure boats should never find themselves in the type of survival conditions where self-righting might be necessary.

Stability tends to be discussed only in the context of when the boat is stopped. However, when a boat is moving through the water there are dynamic forces which come into effect which, in most cases, increase the transverse stability. This is particularly the case in planing boats where, if the craft heels over to one side, the dynamic lift is greatly increased on that side and rapidly brings the boat back upright again. Even on a displacement boat the dynamic forces have a considerable influence; therefore, provided it is safe to do so, a boat travelling at full speed is going to be more stable than one travelling slowly.

In a planing boat travelling at high speed, this dynamic stability accounts almost solely for the stability of the boat as there is so little of the hull in the water. A planing boat when stopped will often roll heavily because of the loss of the stabilising effect of the dynamic lift. The one dynamic factor which can have the effect of reducing stability is that generated by the rudder. When a vessel is on an even keel, the forces generated by the rudder tend to heel the boat slightly as well as steer it in the horizontal plane. When the boat is heeled, the forces on the rudder have a stronger vertical element, in addition to the horizontal steering element, so that if the wheel is turned the same way as the craft is heeling it will act against the righting forces. You can find yourself in difficulty as a result of this effect when running in a beam sea where the tendency is to steer away from a wave approaching on the beam; by so doing, you can increase the angle of heel just at a time when you don't want the boat to heel over. The rudder can have such an effect on stability that one manufacturer has developed a system which uses the rudder for stabilising the hull.

On slower boats, where there is much less dynamic stability, it is the hull shape itself which is responsible for most of the stability characteristics. A hull which is semi-circular in cross section will roll easily and with very little provocation, as very little water has to be displaced in order to alter the angle of heel. A deep displacement hull, on the other hand, has to move a lot of water around from one side of the hull to the other before it can roll, and this movement of water helps to damp the rolling. Skegs and bilge keels fitted to the hull have a similar damping effect, and bilge keels are often fitted for this specific purpose. These keels have to be built strongly as they are subject to very high loadings in a rough sea, but they can help to make life more comfortable on board.

Stabilisers can have the same effect and are remarkably efficient at reducing rolling. They are generally suitable for use on boats with speeds up to about 25 knots, but above this speed the resistance from the stabilisers becomes excessive. Moreover, above this speed, hulls tend to rely much more on dynamic stability.

One factor to bear in mind as far as slower boats in rough seas are concerned, is

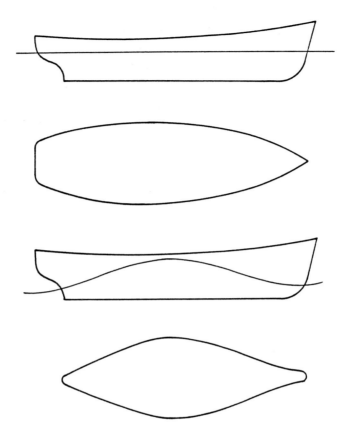

A displacement boat's stability is largely dependent on the water-plane area. At rest this is adequate but with a wave amidships it is greatly reduced, resulting in a considerable loss of stability.

that when a boat is perched on the crest of a wave its stability can be greatly reduced. This is because of the change in shape of the waterplane area, which virtually eliminates the stability generated by the ends of the hull. The stability could be nearly halved in this situation, and if the vessel is not particularly stable anyway, a dangerous condition could result. While going into a head sea, the waves pass the hull quickly enough for this transient situation to be of little consequence, but in a following sea a craft could be perched on the crest of a wave for some time, if it was travelling at a speed close to that of the wave. In this situation a boat has little stability, and turning the helm could create a heavy list which, if the cause is not appreciated, could lead to capsize. The moral of this particular dilemma is, of course, not to travel at the same speed as the waves; either go much slower or much faster.

There are a tremendous number of factors which have to be taken into account in the design of boats, both for high speed and for rough weather. The two are not incompatible by any means, and the modern deep-vee hull has proved itself to be a very seaworthy craft. With modifications, deep-vee hulls are now used for lifeboat work and have allowed excellent seaworthiness to be combined with good speed capability. However, it is not just hull shape on its own which will ensure survival in rough seas or performance at high speeds. Hull strength and construction are equally important, neither of which can be divorced from the handling of the boat, the reliability of its engines and all the other factors which go into the development of a seaworthy vessel. The design of hulls for high-speed or rough-water operation is a very complex subject. Hull designers tend to concentrate on the subtleties of shape, but at the end of the day it is every part of the boat and its equipment that come into play in bad conditions, and with the best hull in the world you won't get very far without the right engines and equipment to keep the boat going.

3 Controlling the boat

We have looked at waves and hull design and the way these two interact, and now it is time to consider the third factor, the controls on the boat and the manner in which the helmsman can make his contribution to the way the boat behaves at sea. There is a school of thought that suggests that all you have to do at sea is set the throttles to a comfortable speed, steer the craft and away you go, but if you want to travel at high speed or if you are operating in rough seas, then the helmsman's contribution to the way the boat performs is vital and the control systems are an essential ingredient in the boat's performance.

The controls provide the vital interaction between the helmsman and the boat and play an important part in both the speed and safety of the vessel. In displacement boats the helmsman has only the throttle and steering to use, but even here, the use of these controls, in an informed and skilful way, can help to nurse the boat through rough conditions. As speeds rise with the use of planing hulls, the range of control systems expands to include power trim, flaps and even ballasting, so that the helmsman has much more control and consequently has a greater proportion of the performance and safety of the boat in his hands.

This transfer of responsibility, from the boat to the helmsman, is seen particularly in lifeboat design. Traditionally, the heavy displacement lifeboat was designed to go through virtually any weather conditions, and the helmsman's skill was required more in terms of local knowledge for navigation than in skills for handling the craft. As speeds have risen in lifeboat design, so a much greater proportion of the safety of the lifeboat is transferred to the hands of the helmsman, as both the speed of the boat and the steering become much more important factors for survival in rough seas. This transfer of responsibility produces a much more efficient lifeboat, because of its higher speed, but it also means that the controls and indeed the entire steering position have to be designed to allow the helmsman to steer the boat efficiently in bad conditions; we will look at this aspect in a later chapter. Here we will look at the various control systems and analyse their effects on the boat's handling and performance.

STEERING

There are two distinct types of steering used on powerboats; which might be termed *passive* and *dynamic* steering. Passive steering is the traditional type of steering using a rudder to control the vessel; whereas with dynamic steering, the direction of the propeller thrust itself is used to provide steering. There is a significant difference between the two in terms of boat handling, particularly when manoeuvring in harbour and when driving a boat fast in a seaway.

Passive steering

The rudder acts by diverting the flow of water past the boat, which in turn creates a sideways thrust at the stern to alter the boat's heading. Because the rudder usually lies in the propeller slip stream, it can often be effective at very low speeds, because the slip stream causes the water to flow past the rudder blade and give a steering effect. This effect can be useful during slow-speed manoeuvring to achieve steerage way without much headway. Apart from this, the steering effect from the rudder will increase the speed.

On a displacement boat the speed range is not particularly great, and so it is not difficult to find a good compromise rudder blade area which is effective at both high and low speeds. On a planing boat the problem is more difficult because of the much greater speed range; the small rudder area which is adequate at high speeds, and which helps to reduce drag, is often less than effective at low speeds, and it is much harder for the designer to find a good compromise rudder size. One solution is to mount the rudder aft of the transom so that at slow speeds the rudder is fully immersed, but as speed increases so part of the rudder lifts out of the water, thus reducing the effective area and also reducing drag. This type of rudder is used mainly on surface propulsion systems.

On both planing and displacement boats which use rudders for steering there comes a point when the speed of the vessel is such that there is an inadequate flow of water past the rudder to maintain steerage way. On planing boats with their small rudders this speed could be quite high, perhaps around 5 or 6 knots, whereas on a displacement boat it will probably be around 2 or 3 knots, but much will depend on the prevailing wind and sea conditions which will determine the steering force needed to keep the boat on a straight line. This point, when the steering starts to lose its effect, should be recognised in rough-weather handling because it indicates a point when the helmsman starts to lose control of the craft, so speed should never be allowed to drop near to this point.

Most modern rudders are of the balanced type where a proportion of the rudder blade area is placed forward of the vertical pivot. If all the blade area is located aft of the pivot, then it requires considerable force to turn the rudder. This area of blade forward of the pivot in fact helps to turn the blade and a balanced rudder of this type produces light and sensitive steering. The balance can be quite critical because with too much area aft of the pivot the steering becomes very heavy, although it will self-centre easily, whereas with too much area forward of the pivot point, the boat will tend to oversteer and not hold its course well.

Dynamic steering
Dynamic steering is found on vessels fitted with outboard motors, stern drives, some surface drive systems such as the Arneson drive, and water-jet units. Here the actual propeller thrust is angled to provide the steering effect which gives a much more positive form of steering. The stern drive or outboard leg has a certain small steering effect, acting like a rudder, but it is the change of direction of the propeller thrust which provides the main effect. With this type of steering, opening the throttles and putting the helm over can give a pronounced steering effect even at very low speds. This can be useful both for manoeuvring in harbour and when operating in rough seas.

Over-enthusiastic throttle control in a small racing boat. Even using a foot throttle the margins of control can be quite small at high speed. (Photo: Colin Taylor Productions)

On high-speed boats, there can be dangers in using dynamic steering when the vessel leaves the water and 'flies'. The problems come when the boat re-enters the water because the first part to re-enter is usually the propeller. If the propeller thrust is angled to one side or the other, there will be a short period when this steering thrust has nothing to react against because the hull is still out of the water. This can put the craft into a dangerous condition of instability and is probably one of the primary causes of accidents to offshore racing boats. It is notable that in most cases where such a boat 'spins out', the crafts involved are fitted with stern drives or steerable surface drives. To a certain extent, the same situation could occur with rudder steering, but here the steering effect when the hull is out of the water is far less pronounced and is not so likely to have the same disastrous consequences.

Directional stability

Designers strive to give their boats good directional stability, which means that the craft will follow a chosen course without having to continually turn the wheel to hold it on course. A directionally stable boat can be a relaxing vessel to steer, but the designer must not overdo the directional stability, otherwise the boat becomes hard to turn. Like most things in boat design, a balance has to be struck and it is both the underwater and above-water areas, as well as the trim of the craft, which affect directional stability. On a displacement boat, a long straight

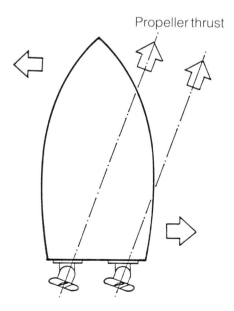

Propeller thrust

The mechanics of a spinout. With the propeller thrust off-centre, it has nothing to react against when the hull is airborne.

keel, sloping aft with a large deadwood, a cutaway bow and fine lines will add to the directional stability. The trim can also have a considerable effect, and trim by the stern normally improves directional stability.

On a planing boat the directional stability is helped by the spray rails and the vee of the hull angle which keep the boat in a 'groove', heading in the right direction. One of the problems with planing vessels can occur at low speed when a bow drops as the boat comes off the plane. This change of trim can rob the craft of much of its directional stability, making the boat very difficult to steer at low speed in a following sea, there is a good flow of water past the propeller so contribute considerably to directional stability.

The above-water parts of the vessel affect the steering by offering areas on which the wind can exert pressure. Here the difficulty can be to reconcile the behaviour of the boat in head and following winds. A large wheelhouse aft will help to keep the boat head in the sea in a head wind rather in the same manner as a steadying sail, but in a following sea the wind acting on this wheelhouse will reduce the directional stability, tending to make the boat yaw about. On many planing boats, where the bow is often clear of the water at speed, this can have an effect on the steering, but we will look at this particular feature later.

Steering in following seas

In rough seas good steering is essential, particularly on boats operating at displacement speeds. Because a displacement vessel can usually travel at full speed in a following sea, there is a good flow of water past the propeller so that the full steering effect is available. However, when a boat is travelling down the face of a wave and the bow immerses in the next wave, the craft takes on the attitude of being down by the head, which is equivalent to an alteration of the trim, and this can cause an almost complete loss of directional stability, particularly in boats where there is a deep forefoot and the waves are short and steep. Here you can find yourself winding away at the wheel trying to keep the boat on its course and the steering may often have little or no effect. In this situation the boat is approaching the classic broaching condition and it only needs the wave behind to start breaking to set the broach in motion.

When a wave is breaking, the water in the wave, instead of merely going up and down, actually starts to flow forwards in the direction of the waves. With the wave travelling faster than the displacement boat, this moving body of water will arrive at the stern of the vessel and start to flow past it. A rudder depends, for a steering effect, on water flowing past it from a forward to aft direction. If this direction of water flow is reversed, as it could well be when the water from a breaking wave flows past, then at best there could be a distinct loss of directional control and at worst the rudder could start having a reverse effect. I am sure that one of the major contributory factors in displacement boats broaching in following seas is

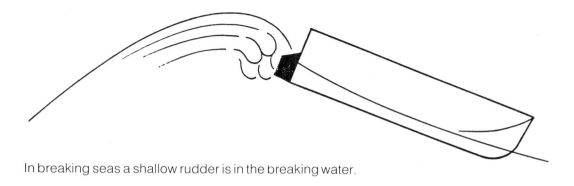

In breaking seas a shallow rudder is in the breaking water.

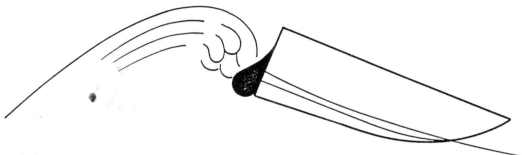

A deeper rudder will remain effective much longer because it remains in the static deeper water.

The effect of rudder depth on steering in breaking waves.

the fact that not only does the boat suffer a considerable loss of directional control in these conditions, but also the helmsman, by turning the rudder hard over to try to correct the way the craft is swinging, makes the situation worse because the water is flowing past the rudder in the reverse direction.

If this theory is correct, then the best action, if you find yourself in this situation, could be to turn the rudder in the opposite direction to the norm. I have never had the courage to try out this theory in practice, and I would hesitate to recommend it because it is speculation. One of the questions that has to be considered in this situation is: How far below the surface of the water does the flow of water from the breaking wave extend, and does it extend right down to where the rudder is working? My feeling is that this flow of water probably extends no more than 3 or 4 feet (about 1 metre) below the surface except in very large waves, which means that a shallow-draft boat would be much more liable to this loss of directional control than a deep-draft boat, where the rudder remains in good solid water and keeps its steering effect.

Certainly, in my experience, taking a deep-draft vessel through breaking seas on a bar, you feel very confident and maintain full steering control, even though the breaking waves are rushing past the stern. There is no feeling of loss of directional control as there is when operating in a shallow-draft boat in the same conditions. You are much better off operating boats with dynamic steering in these conditions, because you can quickly improve the steering control by opening the throttle to increase the thrust. In a planing boat, of course, you would be using the speed potential of the boat to either overtake the breaking seas or at least keep in a position on the back of a wave clear of the breaking seas astern.

Emergency steering

Steering is vital to the control of the boat and any steering system must be engineered to the highest standards to give the right degree of reliability. Not only must there be no chance of steering failing, but also there must be a chance of any loose objects getting mixed up with the steering levers or control rods to jam the steering. It is surprising what can come adrift when a boat is bouncing around in rough seas or at high speed and loose objects should never be left near the steering gear.

If the steering mechanism itself should fail, then it is often possible to fit an emergency tiller on the squared end of the rudder stock. Many boats are now fitted with this facility, the tiller being inserted through a removable plug in the deck. If this quick solution to a steering failure is not available, then you will have to resort to trying to lash the tiller to the rudder stock using, as the starting point, the short tiller arm which is usually clamped round the stock of the conventional steering.

The loss of steering on a twin-screw boat is not so serious because you can always steer with the engines, running one engine at a steady speed and varying the speed of the other to achieve the steering effect. On a single-screw boat you have a much more serious problem on your hands and here you will have to resort to trying to rig a jury rudder or perhaps towing a strong bucket or drogue astern and try to gain steering from this.

If the boat is fitted with flaps, these can be used for emergency steering and this can be quite effective at higher speeds. You simply lower the flap on the side towards which you want to turn and the drag from this flap turns the boat. Such a steering system would enable you to get back to harbour, but it would not be effective at slow speed in harbour, and you would probably have to end up by getting towed in.

Steering and transverse trim

When the wheel is turned, the turning thrust from the rudders or the propeller acts on a point low down or even below the hull. At this point, there is a sideways thrust acting on the hull and this thrust will tend to heel the boat as well as steer

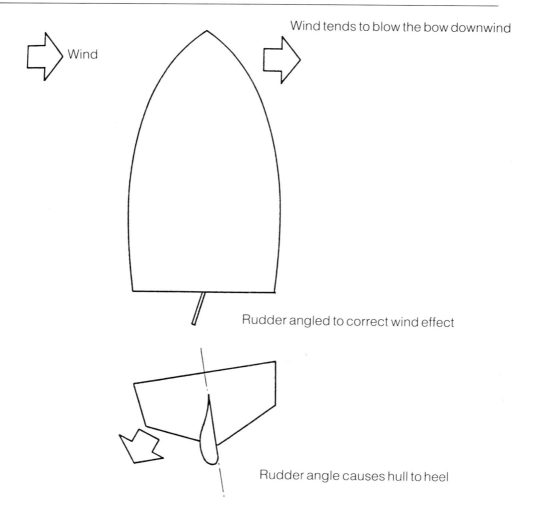

Wind

Wind tends to blow the bow downwind

Rudder angled to correct wind effect

Rudder angle causes hull to heel

The way a deep vee hull heels into the wind. The wind tends to blow the bow off course. This is counteracted by the rudder, which in turn causes heeling.

it. It is this secondary action of the steering which accounts for the way a powerboat leans into a turn in a very comforting manner. This heeling into a turn is less noticeable on displacement vessels where the steering thrust is usually higher and the forces involved are less.

In a beam wind, the wind acting on the bow of the boat will tend to blow it off the wind, so that a bias has to be introduced into the steering to maintain course. This steering bias has a component which tends to heel the boat, which is the reason why most fast craft tend to heel into the wind when it is on the beam. On single-screw vessels where the reaction to the propeller turning also tends to heel the boat, these forces will combine to heel the boat a considerable amount when the wind is on the port side, but will tend to cancel each other out when the wind is on the starboard side.

THROTTLES

The traditional approach, of simply finding a comfortable speed and letting the boat take its course, has to be changed if you want to get the best out of a vessel at high speeds or in rough seas. Not only do you have to match the speed to the conditions, but more subtle effects can also be achieved by careful throttle control; the throttles probably represent one of the most important elements when it comes to boat handling.

The theory of matching the speed to the conditions (fast boats or rough seas) still holds good, but the point that has to be remembered is that the conditions themselves are continually changing and therefore the speed also has to be continually changed to match these conditions. If you remember the chapter on waves, you will recall that there is a tremendous variety in the size and shape of waves. A constant throttle setting, which can cope with all of these variations in wave size, will have the boat running at less than its optimum speed for most of the conditions, whereas if you read the sea ahead and assess the oncoming waves, then you can match the speed to each wave in turn. This is the way that

These unpredictable sea conditions require delicate use of the controls in order to maintain high speeds and comfort. (Photo: Author)

high speed is maintained in offshore racing boats, but the same approach can be used in displacement boats in rough seas. Here, nursing the craft over each wave greatly reduces the stress on the boat and the crew, and also enables much better progress to be made.

Apart from the direct effect of speed and waves, the throttle can also have an effect on the trim of the boat. On a displacement vessel, if you open the throttles you will notice that the bow rises and the stern sinks in a fairly immediate response. This change of trim can be used to adapt the trim of the craft to match that of an oncoming wave so that the boat lifts more readily to the wave. Closing the throttle allows the bow to drop and you can use this to good effect as the bow comes through the crest and adapts to the downward slope. On a planing boat this change in trim, when you open and close the throttle, can be even more pronounced and can be used to particularly good effect in rough seas.

We have already seen the effect that opening and closing the throttles can have on steering, by giving an immediate thrust, and this demonstrates that you should not consider controls in isolation. The importance of the throttles in controlling the boat is often overlooked when it comes to the position and even the design of the throttles, and for boats operating in critical conditions good throttle control is vital.

A normal throttle installation on a powerboat comprises a single lever incorporating both gear and throttle. The first part of the movement in either direction engages the gear and further movement of the lever results in opening the throttle. Such systems are convenient when manoeuvring in harbour but are less efficient when operating in the open sea, when you will rarely or never use your gears but could be using your throttle continuously. By incorporating gears and throttles into a single lever, the range of lever movement which controls the throttle opening is reduced and this makes the throttle much less sensitive. It also means that the lever-movement range that you use at sea is placed well forward, often where it is difficult to reach and exercise sensitive control.

Much to be preferred for fast boats and rough conditions is the use of separate throttle and gear levers. This means that the throttle levers have a good range of movement for sensitive control and they can be placed in the optimum position for easy use without having to consider the requirements for the gears and astern movement. Offshore racing crafts have had separate levers for a long time and it is interesting to see that there is now a move towards separate throttle levers in many high-performance powerboats. This type of installation is equally valid in displacement boats.

Foot throttles
Some smaller racing boats, where the crew are seated, use a foot throttle. Such a foot throttle is similar in some respects to that used in a car where it is possible to

achieve very sensitive control. The same sensitive control can be achieved in a boat because it is possible to move the foot under close control using the heel as the fulcrum and steadying point. An additional benefit of such a system is that it leaves both hands free to control the steering wheel or operate the other control systems such as power trim and flaps. There is a lot to recommend foot throttles for all types of powerboats, fast and slow, but they do demand a well-designed seating position and there can be disadvantages when manoeuvring in harbour. Here it requires a degree of coordination between foot and hand to get the boat moving at the right speed and in the right direction, but a great deal of harbour manoeuvring is done using only the gear control with the engines being kept at idle.

FLAPS

Flaps are hinged plates mounted on the outside corners of the bottom of the transom. They are often called trim tabs, but this tends to confuse them with power trim and, in this book, the term flap will be used throughout to avoid confusion. Flaps are usually operated by hydraulic cylinders; in the raised position they are flush with the bottom of the boat and they can usually be lowered to an angle of between 10 and 15 degrees. Flaps are only fitted to planing boats and are only effective at speeds above 15 knots or so.

Use of flaps
Flaps are used to trim the boat and can be used in several ways. When both of the flaps are lowered together, then the stern of the vessel is lifted and the bow drops accordingly so that, used in this way, the flaps alter the angle of trim. This might be done to get the boat operating at a more efficient angle of trim to achieve higher speeds, but they are not usually very effective in this way because the flaps introduce additional drag to the hull which tends to balance out any advantage gained by the improved angle of trim. Where flaps can be much more effective when used together like this is in head seas, when they help to keep the bow down, thus reducing the chance of the craft flying off the top of a wave. Trimmed down in this way, the boat remains 'glued' to the water in a much more positive way, which allows higher speeds to be maintained in rough conditions.

Used individually, flaps can adjust the transverse trim of the boat. If the port flap is lowered, then the port side of the vessel will lift and vice versa. The flaps are used individually in this way to keep the boat on an even keel and this can be particularly important on a deep-vee hull, which needs to stay upright in order to get the full advantage of the cushioning effects of the hull shape. If the boat is heeled over on one side all the time, then it impacts on the flat surface of the vee to give high shock loadings. This can be the case particularly when operating in a

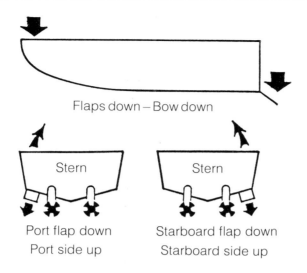

Flaps down – Bow down

Stern

Stern

Port flap down
Port side up

Starboard flap down
Starboard side up

TOP: *Putting both flaps down brings the bow down.*
BOTTOM: *Adjusting one flap controls the transverse trim of the boat.*

beam wind, and in this situation the weather flap is lowered to bring the hull upright and improve the comfort of the ride.

When the flaps are used individually in this way, their effect cannot be considered in isolation. One flap lowered affects the steering, creating drag which pulls the boat round to the side on which it is lowered. This means that with one flap lowered the steering has to be biased in the opposite direction to balance out the drag, so when you adjust for the trim in this way you will need to have two or three attempts at it in order to get the correct balance with the steering. Lowering even one flap also has an effect on the fore-and-aft trim and this effect will also have to be watched for when making the adjustments.

Flaps and fuel consumption
With boats operating in the 15–25 knot speed range, the trim of the craft can have a considerable effect on fuel consumption. In this speed range the boat is probably not completely on the plane, and therefore tends to operate in a somewhat bow-up attitude which is not the most efficient attitude for the hull. By lowering the flaps the hull can be persuaded to adopt a more efficient angle of trim, which in turn can allow the throttles to be brought back a little to give improved fuel consumption whilst maintaining the same speed. By lowering the flaps even at comparatively low speeds the boat can have a more comfortable ride in rough seas. Flaps can be particularly beneficial in this way on semi-displacement hulls which tend to run with a bow-up attitude anyway. Using flaps can give the vessel a much better and a much more efficient ride.

Flaps represent one of the most versatile controls on powerboats and can offer benefits at any speed above 15 knots. They are very versatile in their application and it is well worth spending a lot of time checking out the effect of flaps on a particular hull when used individually and in tandem.

POWER TRIM

Power trim is the ability to alter the vertical angle of the propeller shaft which in turn alters the angle of the propeller thrust. A secondary effect of this alteration is that it can vary the depth of immersion of the propeller. Altering the angle of the propeller thrust can be used to adjust the trim of the boat and the depth of immersion is used to improve the efficiency of the propulsion, particularly when surface-piercing propellers are used.

The adjustment to the drive leg, whether it is an outboard or a stern drive, is done by means of an hydraulic ram which moves the leg in or out. When the leg is right in, close up against the transom, the thrust from the propeller is angled slightly downwards, away from the transom, which generates a slight upward push against the transom, tending to lift the stern and drop the bow. As the leg is jacked out under the influence of the hydraulic ram, the thrust becomes horizontal and then starts to point upwards, exerting a downward thrust on the transom and tending to lift the bow. It is normal to keep the drive leg right in when bringing the boat up onto the plane or when turning at speed. In these two

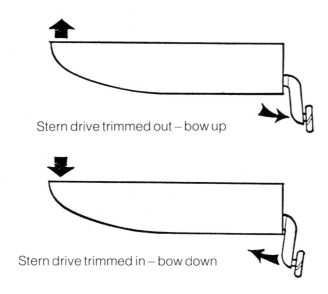

Stern drive trimmed out – bow up

Stern drive trimmed in – bow down

The effect on the longitudinal trim of the boat of trimming a stern drive leg.

situations with the drive leg in, the propeller is in its most deeply immersed position and it gets a good bite on the water to generate thrust. When coming up onto the plane, the thrust pushing the bow down helps slightly to counteract the normal tendency of the hull to rise as it comes onto the plane and helps to give the boat a smoother take-off.

As speed rises, so the drive leg is jacked out and this has the effect of raising the bow slightly, which alters the angle of attack between the water surface and the hull. With the bow raised, there is less of the hull in the water giving less drag, which in turn imrpoves performance. By also bringing the propeller close to the surface, jacking out improves the efficiency of the propellers because the top blades are working in disturbed water as this water comes away from the drive leg and it is primarily the bottom blades which do most of the work. Bringing the propeller close to the surface puts it into a semi-surface-piercing mode which helps improve efficiency. The ideal line of thrust for maximum efficiency is horizontal and if you find that the boat goes faster with the leg jacked right out, then this probably means that the drive leg needs raising vertically. We will look at this aspect later when we discuss setting up the boat.

Surface-piercing propeller drives
With Arneson drives and with some high-performance stern drive units, the propeller is designed to operate in the fully surface-piercing propeller mode. Here the drive is raised at speed so that the hub of the propeller is approximately level with the water surface. This keeps only the bottom blades of the propeller in where there is solid water without any interruption to the flow, and removes the resistance generated by the propeller shaft and its appendages. Adjusting the shaft angle with these propellers has much the same effect as it does with stern drives and outboard trim, but there is one added bonus from being able to trim the shaft angle with these units. Surface-piercing propellers are not particularly efficient when operated fully immersed because there is greatly increased resistance from the propeller and the engine tends to become overloaded, preventing it from reaching maximum power as the boat comes onto the plane. With fixed surface-piercing propeller drives on heavily loaded boats, it can be quite a problem getting them in the plane until the water starts to break away from the transom and the propeller operates efficiently, but with these adjustable trim drives, the drive can be jacked up to get the propeller working in its surface-piercing mode at an early stage of the speed range.

BALLAST

Both flaps and power trim offer means of adjusting the longitudinal trim of the boat at high speed within certain limits, but an alternative which is used on some boats is to have ballast tanks. On high-performance racing craft, ballast tanks are often fitted in the bow with filling and emptying controlled by dashboard levers which lower a water pick-up into the water flowing off the transom. By filling a bow ballast tank in this way the centre of gravity is moved forwards and this helps to prevent the bow lifting out when it hits waves. Ballast tanks are particularly effective in a head sea and, in addition to the change in trim which they give to the hull, the extra weight added to the hull also reduces the tendency of the boat to fly off the top of a wave.

Ballast tanks can be fitted in any part of the hull to increase the weight of the boat and to adjust the trim when operating in heavy seas. There is no doubt that the additional weight taken on board can help to improve both the ride and comfort in heavy weather conditions, but the benefits rarely justify the additional cost and complication. On some powerboats the fuel can be used to adjust the trim, and means are incorporated into the fuel system to allow fuel to be transferred from one tank to another. Rather than have a transfer system, trim can be adjusted in the longer term simply by drawing fuel from forward or aft tanks as appropriate to adjust the weight distribution in the hull to suit the sea conditions. It is only a really valid proposition on longer passages and, as a general rule, fuel would be taken from aft tanks when operating in a head sea and from the bow tanks when operating in a following sea.

COMBINING THE CONTROLS

As we have already seen, there is an interaction between the flaps and the steering and, in a similar way, the various controls on the boat have to be used in a coordinated way to achieve the best results. For instance, in a head sea you want to keep the bow down, so you transfer weight towards the bow if this is possible, put the flaps down and trim the drive leg in. This will have the

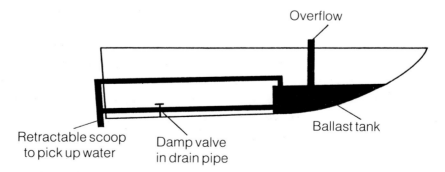

Overflow

Retractable scoop
to pick up water

Damp valve
in drain pipe

Ballast tank

Diagram of the layout of the filling and emptying arrangements for a ballast tank.

effect of keeping the bow down, but will also have side effects; the flaps will add to the resistance and bringing the drive leg in may reduce the efficiency of the propeller. You may be able to accept the added resistance of the flaps because of the benefit of reducing the boat's flying off the top of a wave; bringing the stern drive leg in also has the benefit of giving the propeller a better bite on the water in these conditions where you will perhaps be looking more for comfort than the ultimate in performance. In these head seas you will be looking to keep the craft glued to the water as much as possible. Although it looks very dramatic when the boat flies out of the water, it is, in effect, very inefficient because the propeller is not driving the boat in that condition, and life can be very uncomfortable for the crew and there is also a heavy stress on the vessel and its machinery.

In a following sea the boat will probably still be overtaking the waves although at a slower pace, and here you will want to keep the bow up to a greater degree because it will also try to fall into the trough as you come over a crest because the lee side of a wave is quite steep. Here you want buoyancy and lift at the bow to prevent it driving into the next wave as it plunges downwards. For this you will keep the flaps up and the drives out and if there is a bow ballast tank you will keep this empty, but you will need to find a balance that suits the sea conditions and the speed because you also want to stop the boat flying as it negotiates the crest of the wave.

In beam seas it is the interaction between the steering and the flaps which will be your main concern. The steering can have a considerable effect on transverse trim at high speeds, and transverse trim can be particularly important in beam seas where you want to try to maintain a level ride.

Added to this trimming of the boat is the way in which the throttles can also be used to adjust the trim in the short term. They are the only control you have which can be adjusted quickly and are your primary defence against the wide variations which can occur in wave height, shape and form. Even the steering can have a part to play here because the higher wave peaks tend to be transient and cover a small area, so that it is sometimes possible to drive round them if you see them in time.

From this you will see that when you are driving a fast craft you have quite a number of controls to help you get the best out of a situation, and it is only the skilful driver who will manage to find the right combination of controls and adjustments to match the prevailing conditions. This is a skill found in the top offshore racing drivers, and whilst driving a pleasure cruiser at speed may not demand the same skills and concentration, getting the boat trimmed and adjusted properly can make life on board a great deal more comfortable – so it is worth taking the trouble. Even on a displacement vessel, skilful driving can improve the ride and make things safer.

In rough seas skilful use of the controls can become much more vital, and concentration is equally important in order to help the boat negotiate the worst of the seas. Because the boat is generally travelling at much slower speeds in these conditions, perhaps even at displacement speeds, many of the controls will be much less effective, and it is then that you have to place much greater reliance on skilful manipulation of the throttle and steering controls.

FUTURE DEVELOPMENTS

You will have realised by now that one of the most important aspects of powerboat control is trim and keeping the movement of the bow under control. The use of the throttle can achieve this to a certain extent, but to give a better response, some boatbuilders are looking at the possibility of fitting fast-reacting flaps linked to automatic-sensing devices. It is not difficult to fit fast-reacting flaps; all that is needed are large diameter hydraulic cylinders with powerful pumps so that the response is almost immediate. The control system is more difficult and there are two possibilities. One is to use accelerometers to measure the rise and fall of the bow and the other is to use change-of-trim indicators. Neither of these devices quite achieves the desired result because, ideally, the flaps need to be set to the correcting angle before the boat meets the oncoming wave. However, because of the quick response of the flaps, it is still possible to achieve beneficial results by such an automated system, which applies flap angle in proportion to the anticipated acceleration or change of trim. In this way it should be possible to achieve a smoother ride, particularly in a head sea, and with a well-written computer program it should be possible to anticipate the flap setting, based on the experience of previous waves.

Another system being considered is the interaction between flaps and rudders or steering, so that it is possible to control the heeling or banking of the vessel into a turn. Often when turning a planing boat, it heels over to the point where the flat side of the vee is parallel to the water surface which can give rise to some very heavy slamming, often making it difficult to control the boat during the turn. Controlled banking, by combining the steering and flap control functions, could help to overcome this problem and, similarly, the same interaction could be used to help maintain the boat on an even keel when travelling in a straight line.

Automation of the power-trim control has already been introduced by one major stern-drive manufacturer, but this was linked to engine r.p.m. and was not particularly successful. It is much more important to link the power trim to boat speed, and an automated system which does just that has been introduced in the United States. This system has to be set up manually so that the relationship between speed and trim is optimised for the particular boat, but once this initial setting up has been carried out, then the trim adjusts automatically to match the boat speed. Manual fine-tuning is still possible after the automatic system has performed the initial setting and as you usually have your hands full with throttles and steering when the vessel is coming up onto the plane, this automatic system at least sets the power trim close to optimum until you have the chance to fine-tune it.

This move towards automation can offer considerable benefits when operating in a seaway, when so often you find yourself without hands free to operate the flap and power-trim controls; certainly, you can rarely adjust them so that they have immediate effect in changing circumstances. Automation has a lot to offer in this respect, but there is still quite a long way to go in developing the correct interactive control systems and sensors and, perhaps more importantly, developing actuating systems which respond fast enough for the controls to have the desired effect.

4   *Displacement hulls and rough seas*

In this chapter we'll be looking at boat handling in rough seas. In very rough conditions planing boats will come down to displacement speeds, so this chapter will cover both hull types. The common factor is that they are all operating at displacement speeds, i.e. below 10 knots. Whilst the displacement hull is primarily built to operate at these speeds, the planing boat is very definitely not, so in a later section we will look at the particular problems of handling planing vessels at slow speeds in stormy seas.

When trying to define rough seas, the best solution is to consider them as sea conditions where you can no longer just set the throttles and let the boat take its course. Instead, you have to start reducing speed or even operating the throttles to negotiate the boat through the waves. Much depends on the size and construction of the vessel as to what will constitute rough seas, but in general we are talking about sea conditions generated by winds of Force 6 or upwards.

HEAD SEAS

A displacement boat works in a comparatively small speed range. When operating in a head sea the main thing to do is find a speed at which the boat runs comfortably. Even in quite rough seas it is possible to find a speed where the boat will lift over the wave and drop down the other side without too much discomfort to the craft or the crew, provided the boat is strongly built. This question of matching the speed to the conditions is the secret of operating in head seas, provided the waves have a normal gradient and a wave length which allows the boat to operate without any undue change in attitude.

When a displacement boat is driven hard into a head sea, the bow will lift to the wave and at the crest the bow then becomes unsupported as the wave crest passes aft. In this situation, the bow will drop to restore equilibrium before lifting once more to the next wave. The problems start in a short, steep sea when the bow may not have time to lift to the next wave, particularly as the stern will still be raised under the influence of the wave which has just passed. A slower speed will give the

*A powerful displacement lifeboat drives through breaking waves in
conditions in which a cruiser would have to be nursed very carefully.*
(Photo: *Pim Korver Film*)

boat more time to adjust to the changing wave profile and will thus help to make
the motion easier.

If the vessel is driven too hard in a head sea, then there is a real danger of a wave
breaking on board as the bow is forced through, rather than over, a wave. With
solid water breaking on board in this way there is a risk of structural damage
because this water has surprising weight and force. In this situation, the most
vulnerable part of the boat is the wheelhouse windows, although having said this
I have never experienced these windows breaking, despite seeing tons of water
crashing down on the deck on many occasions. In a boat with a fine bow there is a
greater risk of the bow burying into a head sea because it has less buoyancy.

When you are trying to find a comfortable speed for operating in particular
conditions, it is important to take care that you maintain sufficient speed to give
steerage way. At a slow speed the response of the helm will be slower and the bow
could fall quite a way off course before the corrective action on the rudder starts to

A small displacement cruiser burying its bow into a head sea. (Photo: Hydraulic Research Ltd)

have effect. If, at this time, a wave should rise and strike against the weather bow, then the slow rudder response could mean that the boat will be knocked round – beam on to the sea – before any corrective action has a worth-while effect. In this situation, opening the throttles is one way to get a fairly immediate improvement in the steering effect, and this can bring the boat back on course quickly without any rapid increase in momentum. The safe minimum speed to maintain steerage way will vary from boat to boat, but it is unlikely to be less than 3 knots and will be more with craft which have small rudders. The risk of being knocked off course is greatest with a breaking wave where the water is actually travelling towards the boat and exerts a considerable force on the bow.

If the sea conditions reach the point where the boat is having to be forced hard, in order to maintain steerage way in the deteriorating conditions, then the time has come for you to start nursing the boat over the waves. This is when you can use the throttle to good effect. By opening the throttle as the wave approaches, the bow of the boat will lift and the burst of engine power will also improve the steering effect at this time. As the bow lifts to the wave, the throttle should be

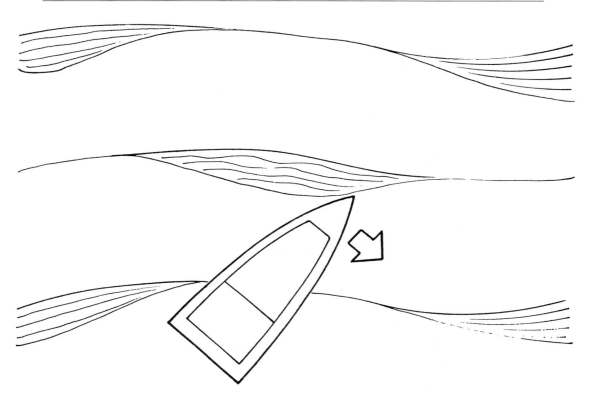

Breaking waves on the bow can cause the boat to swing beam on unless there is good steering way.

eased off before the bow punches through the crest. Easing the throttle will cause the bow to drop slightly, thus reducing the tendency for it to fall heavily into the trough. You then have to be ready to open the throttles again as the next wave approaches.

By using this throttling technique reasonably comfortable progress can be made to windward. You can feel nicely in control of the boat and you will be well prepared if a larger than normal wave comes along. However, this type of operation does require considerable concentration, because there is always the risk of being caught out of step by the irregularity of the waves and you always have to keep your eyes open for that larger than normal wave.

BEAM SEAS

Running with the wind and sea on the beam in moderate seas has the disadvantage of discomfort, due to the heavy rolling which is likely to occur. In these conditions, full speed can generally be used on a displacement boat without any real problems arising, because the boat is lifting bodily on the waves and the bow and stern have little movement in relation to each other. However, occasionally, you can find the boat dropping off the edge of a fairly steep wave front which can be both uncomfortable and a little frightening, so, as the beam seas start to get rougher, you have to take more care.

Running with the sea on the beam exposes a large area of the boat to the approaching waves and in rough seas this can make the craft vulnerable. The transition from what is an uncomfortable beam sea to a dangerous one will depend a great deal on the type and characteristics of the craft, but once the waves have started to break then you need to watch your step more carefully.

There are two main problems with beam seas. First, as the waves become steeper, the boat will try to adjust to the tilted surface of the sea and, consequently, will heel to quite a large angle. This in itself is not too serious, provided the range of stability of the boat is adequate, but you have to remember that the wind will also be pressing on the windward side of the boat and tending to increase the angle of the heel. The second problem is more serious and occurs when breaking waves are encountered. This means that the surface of the water is moving bodily to leeward and can exert very great pressures on the windward side of the vessel. These pressures are resisted by the still water on the leeside which produces a turning moment which could develop to the point where the boat will capsize. In these conditions you also have the risk of seas breaking on board, because many displacement boats have reduced freeboard amidships. These breaking seas could fill a cockpit or other deck openings which makes your predicament worse, so that there will come a time when operating in a beam sea is not the optimum way to go.

Fortunately, a wave rarely breaks along a long front, but tends to do so in patches so that, with anticipation, it is possible to avoid breaking waves in beam seas. This means watching the sea ahead carefully and anticipating which part of the wave crest is going to break, and then, either reduce speed to let the wave break in front of the boat, or turn into or away from the wind so that you pass behind or in front of the breaking crest. Even in moderate breaking seas you can make life a lot more comfortable on board by this method of avoiding the largest of the waves and steering round the uncomfortable-looking crests. In moderate seas you don't have too much to worry about if you get things wrong, but once the seas start to break then the stakes become higher and you have to be much more cautious.

If, when in a beam sea, you are faced with a situation where a wave which is about to break is bearing down on the boat and it is too late to reduce speed, then there are three alternatives. You can maintain course, hoping that the boat will cope; you can head into the wave; or bear away from it. A lot will depend on the type and capabilities of the boat, but the best action would normally be to turn

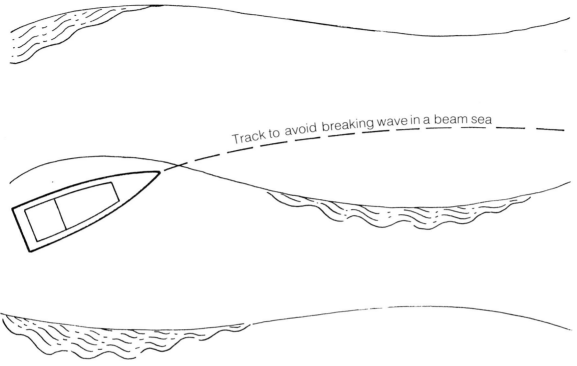

Dodging areas of breaking waves in a beam sea.

away from the wave, because this has the advantage of buying time and it will also reduce the impact of the wave on the boat which is then moving away from it. The breaking crest often rolls only a limited way to leeward and you could escape the breaking water altogether by this action. If you do turn away from a breaking wave in this fashion, then open the throttles wide, both to get the maximum steering effect and also to keep your distance from the breaking crest as long as possible. If you choose the opposite course of action and head into the wave, then reducing speed will probably be necessary to reduce the impact of the wave.

One point to notice when running in a beam sea is that you will often see the waves approaching on the quarter starting to break. You may think yourself very lucky that you keep missing these breaking waves, but they are, in fact, caused by the wash of the boat combining with the approaching wave to create an unstable wave which consequently breaks when otherwise it would not have done so.

FOLLOWING SEAS

Running before a heavy following sea has the reputation of being the seaman's nightmare, conjuring up visions of broaching, capsizing or being swamped.

Much of this fear stems from sailing boats, where running before a sea is virtually the only action left under extreme conditions. There is no doubt that running before a following sea has its dangers, but provided they are recognised, they can be compensated for and the dangers can be minimised.

At first glance, it would appear that running before a sea and travelling in the same direction as the wind and sea would be a far safer course to take than battling against the waves. However, a boat is controlled by the steering and needs a good flow of water past the rudder to be effective. If you find the water flow reduced or even reversed because a breaking wave is overtaking you, then you will have much less control of the craft, or control could be lost altogether, and it is this factor which presents the major hazard in a following sea. An average open sea wave will be travelling at somewhere between two and three times the speed of the average displacement boat so it will take some time to pass onto the boat. When the crest of the wave is approaching the stern, this face of the wave is the steepest part and the bow will be pointing downwards towards the trough. In this position, gravity will exert a downward pull on the boat, combining with the thrust from the propeller, into an increased forward motion down the slope. Similarly, when the boat is on the back of the wave with the bow pointing upwards, it is, to all intents and purposes, going uphill and the speed will be correspondingly reduced. These involuntary increases and decreases in speed can be controlled to a degree by opening and closing the throttle as the circumstances dictate, and unless the waves are breaking it should be possible to retain adequate control over the boat.

In a breaking wave, the surface water is moving forwards in the direction of travel of the wave at a speed slightly in excess of the speed of the wave. This forward movement of the breaking crest is transient, starting as the wave crest becomes unstable and ending when the wave has reached stability again. The behaviour of a boat in a breaking following sea will depend, to a certain extent, on the position of the boat in relation to the crest as it breaks and on the design of the vessel itself.

If the wave rises up and starts to break immediately astern of the boat, then there is a real danger that the breaking crest will fall onto the craft. This is more likely to be a problem with the type of heavy breaking wave found when waves approach shallow water, rather than the open-sea breaking wave which tends to have a more rolling type of crest. One thing in favour of the boat at this stage is that the downward angle of the boat on the forward surface of the wave will help to increase the speed of the craft, and might even enable it to accelerate away sufficiently to escape the breaking crest. If not, the crest, in falling, will accelerate and take the boat with it, which will also help to increase the momentum, particularly if the boat has a large transom stern which faces the oncoming rush of water. With double-ended boats with a canoe stern, the theory is that the

Running before a heavy following sea. These are conditions where you need to head into the sea in order to appreciate what it is really like. (Photo: *Author*)

pointed stern divides the oncoming water and allows it to pass safely along each side of the boat.

So here we have a craft which is accelerating under the combined influences of the rush of breaking water at the stern and the downward slope of the face of the wave, and all would probably be well if the boat could just keep accelerating in this way. However, the time comes when the bow of the boat starts to bury into the water as the stern is lifted by the rush of water. This means that the bow starts to act as a pivot and also starts to put up considerable resistance to the forward rush. It is at this point that the risk of broaching occurs, with the bow trying to stop and the stern trying to swing to one side or the other under the influence of the rush of water. This strong turning effect can turn the boat broadside on in the classical broaching situation. Once broadside on to the sea, the turning moment reduces, but is then replaced by a capsizing moment similar to that which can be found in a beam sea. Even if the boat escapes this particular situation, it could well find itself vulnerable to the next wave which comes along, because it is unlikely that it will have recovered in time and achieved the steerage way neccesary to cope with the situation.

We have already seen how a deep-draft vessel with its rudder well immersed should still retain steerage control in this following breaking-sea situation, whereas the shallow-draft boat could be much more vulnerable. The hull design

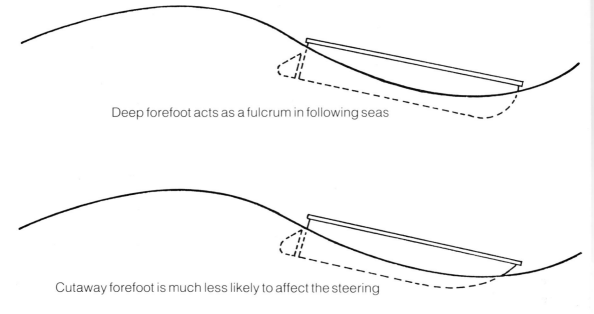

Deep forefoot acts as a fulcrum in following seas

Cutaway forefoot is much less likely to affect the steering

The effect of bow shape on a boat's behaviour in a following sea.

of the boat also has a bearing on its behaviour, and a boat with a sharply angled forefoot is likely to create a pivot point more readily than one with a cutaway forefoot. A transom stern also makes the boat more vulnerable.

If you find yourself in this situation with a breaking wave approaching at the stern, there is not a great deal you can do, other than try to keep the boat absolutely square onto the sea for as long as possible. This will demand concentration and hard work with the steering wheel, although the rudder could become virtually ineffective in these conditions. As a general rule, you will want to open the throttle as wide as possible to try to run from the breaking wave or at least reduce its impact, and to retain steerage control for as long as possible. This will also have the effect of lifting the bow to a certain extent and it will also help to reduce the impact of the wave at the stern.

When running before a following sea which may be large, but is not breaking, you would normally want to use full throttle so that you maintain steering control and try to keep pace with the waves as far as possible. In these conditions you may notice that the waves astern are starting to break, but this is again usually the influence of the wash of the boat combining with the crest to cause it to break. This can be a significant problem when crossing a harbour bar in a following sea, and I have seen quite harmless-looking waves suddenly rear up astern when crossing a bar. It seems that the extra disturbance caused by the progress of the boat is enough to turn the waves into an unstable form, although in theory these breaking waves which are assisted by the wash should not cause you any problems, even though they present a frightening picture if you look astern.

When running in front of a moderate following sea which is not breaking, there can still be a considerable change in the trim of the craft as a wave passes underneath. Here you notice this change in angle more than you would in a head sea because the wave takes longer to pass under the vessel, giving it longer to adapt to the angles of the different faces of the waves. You will often notice that when the crest of the wave is passing underneath the boat suddenly feels rather unstable – this is due to the fact that because the boat is only supported amidships, rather than over its whole length, its stability is considerably reduced at this point. This is a fairly transient situation and stability is rapidly restored as the wave passes; but if you should find yourself running at a speed close to that of the wave, this period of instability could last for longer, and it might be sensible to consider reducing speed to allow the wave crest to pass more quickly and thus reduce the periods of instability.

One problem found on many boats when operating in a following sea is that the visibility astern is not as good as it might be. It helps a great deal to have a good view astern and on each quarter as well, but many boats lack this facility.

With a well-found vessel underneath you, running before a heavy following sea can be a very exciting experience. I have travelled down the Irish Sea in a 48-foot (14½-metre) lifeboat on a wild night when the wind was blowing up to Force 10. The first hour or two were quite frightening as we became used to the conditions, but once we had gained confidence that the boat was adequate for the job, we could revel in the excitement of rushing like an express train down the face of a wave, or so it seemed, and then watching out, through the windows in the top of the wheelhouse, for the next wave approaching from astern. I think an unnecessary dread of following seas has been built up amongst the small-boat fraternity, but you certainly need a sound boat before you start taking chances in a following sea, or indeed in any rough sea.

If you are out in conditions where the sea is starting to become rough and you are running before it, you can find yourself in quite dangerous conditions because you have been unaware of just how bad things are getting and because, to a certain extent, you are running in harmony with the sea. The lack of impact of the waves in a following sea can lull you into a false sense of security and it is a sensible precaution to stop every now and again, turn round and head into the sea, just to see what conditions are really like. It might be frightening to realise just how the waves are building up, but it is better to be frightened in this way than to be caught out unawares.

PLANING BOATS AT DISPLACEMENT SPEEDS

If you are operating a planing boat at displacement speeds, then you could find yourself more vulnerable than you would be in a displacement boat in the same conditions. There are two reasons for this. First, if you are at the point where you have to slow down to displacement speeds in a planing vessel, then conditions are probably becoming quite bad anyway and, second, a planing boat is not running at its optimum at displacement speeds, both in terms of hull shape and of control.

In terms of hull shape, planing boats tend to have fine bows and full sterns, which is not necessarily a happy combination in rough seas. At the bow there can be a lack of freeboard if the boat has a reverse sheer. This, combined with a fine bow, gives a lack of buoyancy in this area which can mean that the bow buries readily into both a head sea or a following sea. The craft is also much lighter and probably more affected by wind, so that you may find it more difficult to maintain steerage way at low speeds in a planing boat because the bow will tend to be blown off to one side or the other. This situation will be exaggerated because the rudders are always smaller and are therefore less effective at slow speeds, although on

This motor cruiser is running downwind at 18–20 knots in Force 6 conditions. Head to wind it could rapidly be reduced to displacement speeds. (Photo: Motorboats Monthly)

vessels fitted with outboards or stern drives, where the propeller thrust is used for steering, a good steering effect can usually be maintained at low speeds.

A delicate hand will be needed on the throttles at displacement speeds because a small movement of the throttle can produce quite a large variation in the speed. However, you can use this to good effect when you want to nurse the boat through the waves and you will probably use the throttle a lot more on this type of boat, short bursts on the throttle being used to help maintain heading and to help lift the bow to approaching waves.

The tactics of operating a planing boat in rough conditions can often mean that, rather than reducing speed when you are operating in a head sea, you should look for an alternative heading for the boat where it can still be operated at higher speeds. For instance, whereas a planing vessel may well have to slow right down in a head sea, it can still maintain good speed in beam seas or in following seas particularly, and this could well be a safer course of action to take, rather than running the boat at displacement speeds. Much will depend on where you are heading and what your options are, but fast speeds in a following sea can often be safer than for a displacement boat operating in the same conditions, because the fast speeds allow the craft to dictate its position with respect to the waves.

SURVIVAL CONDITIONS

When you get to the point in a head sea where perhaps even the slowest speed, in order to maintain steerage way, is still too fast, or in a beam or following sea where you feel you are losing control, then you are entering the phase of what might be termed survival conditions where, rather than trying to make headway in any particular direction, you are just intent on surviving. In these conditions, the object is to find a course and speed at which the boat is most comfortable and will allow you to ride out the storm provided, of course, that you have adequate fuel and sea room.

In these conditions, the sea on the beam or astern can make the boat vulnerable to heavy breaking waves. The bow of the vessel is designed to take the impact of waves more than any other part, and so if you are going to heave to and go into the survival mode, then having the sea on the bow is probably the safest course. However, in a head sea, the situation will arise when the speed needed to maintain steerage way is too fast for the prevailing conditions but, fortunately, there is still one option left open. This is to put the boat on a course with the sea on the bow, which has the benefit of increasing the effective wave length so that a better speed and thus better control can be maintained. With the wind and the sea about 30 degrees on the bow, it should be possible to maintain a better speed than when going directly into the sea, yet this angle is still small enough for the bow to be turned quickly into the sea if a big breaking wave is seen approaching. With the sea 30 degrees on the bow, you have the option of two different courses and, indeed, if there is a need to make progress to windward, perhaps to seek shelter, then you can often make better progress by tacking to and fro across the wind and sea, rather than heading directly into it.

In very rough sea conditions, there have been cases where boats have been left to their own devices, and have survived. However, for each survival experience we read about, there must be others which have not survived and, because no one lived to tell the tale, it is not known what course of action was taken. Certainly, with sailing boats, it is often suggested that the best rough weather tactic is to down all sails and let the vessel drift. However, there are very basic differences between sailing boats and powerboats. The former are much more stable, to the extent of being self-righting, and usually have a far less vulnerable superstructure, which makes them better able to withstand the impact of waves. A powerboat which is left to its own devices will lie either beam-on or stern-on to the sea, which is not the best heading to lie in, in terms of survival, and I would certainly hesitate to recommend this as a course of action to take in extreme conditions.

Another option is to use a sea anchor, which keeps the boat lying head to wind and sea whilst not making any progress, and this seems to be a desirable situation when all else fails; it could also be a useful course of action if you have engine or steering failure. However, whilst the theory of using a sea anchor is all very well, in practice it is much more difficult to construct and use effectively and, even if you have the materials on board to make one, it is not likely to bring immediate salvation.

The business of surviving extreme conditions in a powerboat will ultimately depend a great deal on the particular situation. In the short term, I am convinced that the best survival technique is to drive the craft gently into the seas, nursing it over the waves, and using the controls to best advantage. The problem comes when fatigue sets in and you lose concentration. It only needs a momentary lapse of concentration to put the boat into danger. Powerboats are rarely far from land and shelter, and the obvious tactic, if you find yourself caught out in bad conditions, is to nurse the boat in towards shelter. If you are faced with the prospect of a long period at sea, then the time has come to experiment a little to see how the vessel behaves on different headings, and even to see how it behaves with the engines stopped. If you carry this out while you are still comparatively fresh, you will be in a better position to appreciate the risks and benefits, and hopefully you will find a course which keeps you out of trouble.

SPEED AND SAFETY

While this chapter is primarily about displacement boats, when we talk about survival conditions and safety it is worth considering the effect of speed on safety. There is a natural tendency, when you meet a big wave or when the boat is being thrown around in a beam sea, to close the throttle. It is a natural instinct, but it is not always the right solution to the particular problem.

I have seen people suddenly encounter a big wave and their natural instinct has been to close the throttle. This in turn causes the bow to drop and, whilst you might reduce the impact of the wave on the boat, you often end up disappearing in a great welter of water and spray because the boat has gone into the wave rather than over it. In this situation, the right course could well have been to open the throttle to force the craft up and over the wave. In fact, the boat will gain very little momentum in the short term if you do this, but the change of trim will be beneficial. If you find yourself in this situation, where you feel that this is definitely not the right approach, then it could well be that your average speed through the waves is too fast, and you will not have any margin of error left to cope with the big wave when it comes along.

In the same way, following seas are not for the faint-hearted and if you have the power and speed in a planing or semi-displacement boat, you will be able to overtake the waves and then be in a much stronger position to survive in really bad conditions. You don't necessarily want to overtake the waves, but what you need to be able to do is to dictate your position in relation to the waves, so that you can sit on the back of a wave until it breaks in front of you and then drive over it with comparative safety. This aspect will be looked at in more detail in Chapter 6. Much the same applies to vessels operating in a beam sea when the use of speed can be beneficial rather than harmful.

In all this talk about handling displacement boats in rough seas and the use of power and speed, you will have noticed that there are very few hard and fast guidelines to follow. Experience so often will indicate the obvious course to take in any particular situation and it is very much a case of weighing up all the factors — the weather forecast, the sea conditions, the boat you are in, the sea room, and all the many variables which have to be taken into account. You have to weigh these against the various controls that might be available and their effect on the behaviour of the craft. Whilst so much of the response to conditions will be largely instinctive, if you understand fully what is happening to the boat and the influences acting on it, you will be in a much better position to cope with any given situation. Don't be afraid to experiment, because so much of what happens in rough conditions is a matter of trial and error. Try not to push yourself to the limit, because then you will have little left in the way of reserves to cope if things do become even worse.

5 Boat handling – planing hulls

As we have already seen when you get up to planing speeds, you have more control options open to you when it comes to boat handling, both in rough seas and when it is fairly calm. This gives you the chance to exercise better control over the boat, but at the same time it puts more responsibility for the handling of the vessel in the hands of the person driving it, so that fast boats call for more skill and experience if you are going to get the best out of them.

You could ignore some of the controls, such as the power trim and flaps and even to a certain extent the throttle, but by adopting this approach you will certainly not get the best out of the boat. In calm seas you will not achieve the same speed as you might if you had fine-tuned the boat to get the optimum performance; whilst in rough seas you are likely to get a much more uncomfortable ride, which is neither fair on yourself nor the boat.

SETTING UP THE BOAT

Setting up the boat so that it runs in the optimum trim is a twofold operation. First, there are the basic parameters built into the design. In most cases these will be pre-set and you will have no chance of adjusting them. It is only with outboards, stern drives and some types of surface drive that there is the possibility of making adjustments, such as raising the height of the drive shaft and, on a twin-engined boat, adjusting the toe-in. These parameters can be adjusted at the dockside or in the boatyard, but once set they are normally left well alone unless there is a major problem with the handling of the boat.

The height of the propeller is important if you want optimum speed. Ideally the thrust line from the propeller should be horizontal and on a horizontal line with the centre of gravity. However, in this position, there would not be a clear flow of water to the propeller and a compromise has to be made. With outboards and stern drives, the normal manufacturers' recommendation is to have the cavitation plate, which is located above the propeller, in line with the bottom of the transom. With a vee hull, the centre of the drive leg at the cavitation plate should cross the line of the bottom of the transom. This setting would be suitable for comparatively slow planing boats, but on faster boats it is normal to raise the drive at least an inch above this setting, which brings the propeller slightly into the surface-piercing mode and should improve the performance. On racing boats, particularly with outboards, this setting could be much higher; of course, with some stern drives, which are designed for use with surface-piercing propellers, the propeller hub comes in line with the transom. This line is the normal setting for all surface-piercing drives, although on those where the propeller is mounted some distance behind the transom, the propeller may be even slightly higher to allow for the water rising slightly as it comes away from the transom.

It is only on outboards that the propeller height can be adjusted and there are hydraulic systems which allow this to be done. In general, however, the height is adjusted by a degree of trial and error and then locked in position. The limiting factor in raising the propeller height is that of getting the boat onto the plane but cavitation plate heights of 2–3 inches (5–7½ centimetres) above the transom line can be used successfully on high-performance craft. On boats with other forms of drive, the designer has to fix the height during building, but there is a limited adjustment available by the power trim.

Toe-in is the setting of the drives in relation to each other. Rather than have two drive shafts absolutely parallel, better performance can be achieved by angling the shafts in towards each other very slightly, so that the thrust from the two propellers tends to interact and meets some 20 feet (6 metres) or so astern of the transom. The toe-in angle will normally be a matter of 3 or 4 degrees and this

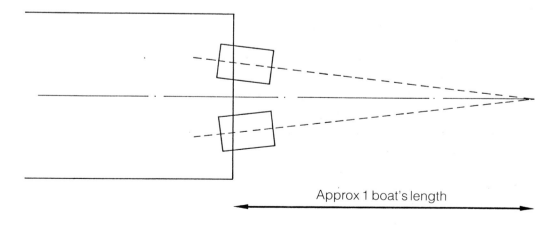

Approx 1 boat's length

Setting the toe-in of twin outboards or stern drives to give more efficient propulsion (angle exaggerated in diagram).

is usually set by experience, although it is possible to fine-tune the setting by adjusting the tie rod that links the two engines together, and then carrying out a series of runs over a measured distance to see whether there is any increase or decrease in performance. For this testing, every other parameter on the boat must remain exactly the same if you are to gauge the very slight differences which result from setting up the toe-in correctly.

Transom wedges

Another form of permanent adjustment found on some planing boats is to incorporate a wedge into the hull surfaces at the transom. This wedge has an effect rather like a permanent flap and is usually only required on slower types of planing vessels, where it permanently adjusts the trim of the hull to bring it to a more optimum angle at the normal cruising speed of the boat. To a certain extent, incorporating a wedge in this way means that the designer has got his sums wrong, although with many modern planing boats, where the same hull can be used in a wide variety of different speed ranges, fast hulls which are operating at slower speeds can often benefit from fitting such a wedge. If you find that the craft permanently needs to run with the flaps down to get better performance, then fitting such a wedge might be of benefit; but on faster boats it is unlikely to be required unless the boat permanently points its bow to the sky.

Power trim and flaps

When you take over a high-speed craft you will normally only be concerned with two settings which you can adjust at sea. These are the power trim and the flaps, and in setting up the boat for calm or slight seas, then only the power trim should be necessary. The easy way to set the power trim is to have a sensitive log on board and, keeping the throttles at a fixed setting, you adjust the power trim and watch the effect on the speed. When the speed rises to a maximum, the power trim is at its optimum setting. In doing this, the engine r.p.m. will also vary, particularly as the power trim lifts the propeller partially out of the water, and you will have to watch that the engine r.p.m. does not exceed the normal limits. If you do find yourself moving into this area, it could be that the boat needs a larger pitch propeller; we look at propellers in more detail in Chapter 9.

When you are setting up the boat in this way and you find the optimum setting in calm water, remember this setting on the power-trim indicator, so that you can return to it at a later date when the boat may be operating in rougher seas and it is difficult to sense the effect of power trim quite so readily. Generally speaking, when the boat is running in waves, you will want the power trim in a little to help keep the propeller well immersed. (In these conditions you will probably also be running at slower speeds when equally you want the power trim in a little.) In rougher conditions, when you are forced to slow down quite considerably, it is normal to bring the power trim in almost completely and this is where the flaps will also start to come into play.

When running in calm water at high speed, it should not be necessary to use the flaps, except to trim the boat upright if there is a beam wind. It is worth experimenting with the flaps in these conditions and if you find the performance improves, then the craft is not trimmed quite to its optimum and you might consider fitting some form of permanent wedge. Normally the drag from the flaps will slow the boat down and have a detrimental effect on the performance, even though it could, in some cases, improve the trim.

To set up the vessel for rough weather when you are going into a head sea, have the flaps down and if you have a ballast tank have this filled as well, so that in this way you try to keep the boat close to the water and it will have less inclination to fly off the top of a wave. Of course, bringing the power trim in can also help to keep the bow down, which should enable you to travel at higher speeds in a head sea when the going gets rough.

Flying the boat looks spectacular but it is not good driving – it puts heavy strain on both hull and machinery, and re-entry almost inevitably slows down the boat. (Photo: American Dream *Offshore Racing Team*)

USING THE THROTTLE

Once you have set the boat up, then your primary means of control is the throttle. By varying the propeller thrust with the throttle you will have already seen how you can raise or lower the bow, but the throttle also has a vital role to play in the speed at which you impact approaching waves. This speed of approach, to a certain extent, determines whether the boat will fly off the top of a wave or not. Although it looks very spectacular when a boat does this – and most of the pictures of offshore racing show craft behaving in this way – it is not an efficient means of progress, because every time the boat flies off the wave the propeller comes out of the water and ceases to drive the vessel forward. To a certain extent this is a safety device, but if you wait until the boat is actually leaving the water before the power is cut in this way it is too late. What normally happens is that the boat has a fairly abrupt change of trim, and when it re-enters the water it does so in an ungainly way and it takes some time before equilibrium is restored and the boat starts to run at speed again.

Unless the sea gets too rough, it is possible with a deep-vee hull to get it up and running so that it stays virtually at a level trim despite the impact of the waves which try to upset the trim. Much will depend on the wave size, but if your boat is trimmed properly it can run virtually across the top of the waves with the control of the attitude of the boat being exercised solely by the use of the throttle. The biggest problem with this is actually getting the vessel up into this situation, and it does mean that you may have to negotiate several waves rather uncomfortably as the boat builds up speed, and then levels out and starts to move at high speed.

Getting a craft trimmed in this way is a real joy and the boat really sings as it flies along. It requires careful setting up, using the power trim and the flaps and then, finally, the throttle to keep the balance, as passing waves have varying influences on the hull. When you get a boat up and running in this way, it is possible to make very rapid progress to windward even though the waves can be

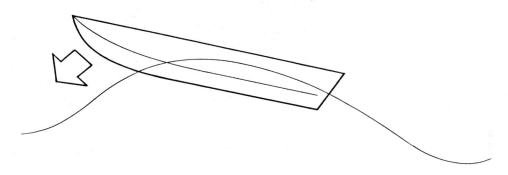

Boat punching through a wave crest leaving the bow unsupported.

quite large. It does require some degree of courage to take the bull by the horns and get the boat up into a situation where you can take advantage of this.

This type of boat control is what really sorts out the top throttlemen in offshore racing, and it enables them to get the vessel moving at a much faster pace than lesser mortals can achieve. When the boat is in this situation the throttleman has to watch every wave, because there is always the risk that a bigger wave than normal will come along and upset the delicate balance of the boat. A good throttleman will read the waves and concentrate very closely on each one as it approaches, adjusting the throttle almost by instinct as the craft meets the wave, so that the bow slices through the top without the wave imparting too much lift, allowing the boat to continue on an almost even keel.

This type of throttle control is equally possible with motor cruisers and I have even used it with one of the largest deep-vee hulls built at the time, an 85-footer (25½ metres). This 85-footer was going through a Force 7 gale in the Mediterranean with a very vicious, short, steep sea being whipped up, and I found myself continually easing back on the throttle to give the boat a more comfortable ride. By the time we were down to 15 knots and faced with the prospect of a long haul into harbour, I remembered how in these types of

A fast boat in a rough sea. Vladivar *lands after flying off one wave and is at the correct angle to meet the next one. (Photo: Motorboats Monthly)*

conditions racing boats would get up on top of the waves and really make good progress, and I wondered whether the same would happen with this large boat. It took a fair amount of courage to wind the boat up and open the throttles and we suffered a few nasty bangs as we hit the first two or three waves, but soon after the boat really got up on top and, with the flaps down, away we went, travelling at close to 30 knots in conditions where I would never have thought it possible for a boat of this type.

When you are running a boat in this way, total concentration is necessary because you are keeping a very delicate balance between all the factors acting on the boat, and if one gets one element out of step you can find the boat flying through the air to land very hard, and then you have to go through the whole process of getting the vessel back up onto the plane again. One of the major ingredients in trying to keep a boat up and running in this way is to use the throttle very delicately. The tendency, when you see a larger wave approaching, is to bring the throttle right back to reduce the impact between wave and boat, but in most cases only a slight reduction of the throttle setting will be needed. This will not change the trim of the boat too dramatically and you will find yourself making much better progress. This is one of the reasons why I favour throttle controls separate from the gear lever, because then you have a much wider range of movement which allows for the more sensitive control necessary for this type of driving.

HEAD SEAS

We have already covered most of the aspects of head-sea handling in this process of setting up the boat and using the throttle. Getting the boat up and running on

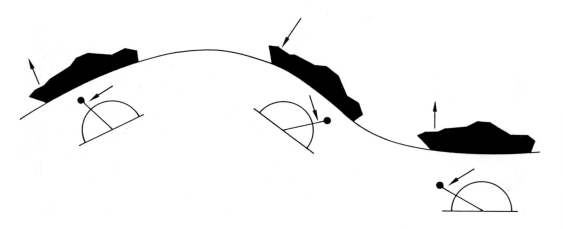

Throttle control when operating a fast boat in waves.

the tops of the waves is all very well when you are racing, but you are much less likely to take these sorts of chances with a cruising boat, which is less well designed to cope with the heavy impact which can result if things get out of hand. It is also unlikely on a cruising craft that you can maintain the necessary level of concentration for any length of time, and very often the visibility from the steering position is not good enough to enable you to read the waves easily. Reflections on the windscreen, and even the windscreen itself, if it has been sprayed with water, can greatly reduce your ability to read the waves ahead.

In these conditions, you will be more likely to find a throttle setting at which the boat runs comfortably and let the boat do the work. In moderate seas you can often make good progress in this way and, certainly if you are on a long passage, this takes a lot of the tension out of driving and makes for a comfortable life. In moderate conditions you could even set the autopilot and have a nice gentle cruise, but always, in a planing boat, you must remember the wide variety of shapes and sizes of waves that you will meet at sea. If you do decide to set the throttle in this way, then the speed at which you are running must leave an adequate margin for the boat to ride comfortably over larger than normal waves without danger or too much discomfort.

If conditions start to deteriorate you will find yourself easing back on the throttle, because the motion of the boat will soon indicate whether you are

A planing motor cruiser up and running at a good trim angle in difficult sea conditions (Photo: Motorboats Monthly)

pushing things too hard. Fortunately, with most modern fast cruising craft, the weak point in the boat (which generally starts to complain first) is the crew itself and this is a good safety factor. If the boat does start to fly off the top of waves, then you are obviously pushing the vessel too hard and easing off the throttle should find a more comfortable speed. When conditions get to the point where it is difficult to find a comfortable speed and still keep the boat on the plane, then you are faced with two options. The first, as described, is getting the boat up on the tops of the waves and really concentrating with the throttle, so that you can still make good progress into a head sea. The second is to ease back and come off the plane and operate the boat in the displacement mode. If you have any doubts about your capabilities, then the second course of action is the wise one to adopt.

The whole secret of fast-boat driving into a head sea is to match the speed of the craft to the conditions, and the throttle is the main control that you will work. Obviously, you may get benefit from adjusting the flaps to help keep the bow down and normally if you find yourself reducing speed, you will almost certainly want to bring the power trim in, which will also help the balance.

BEAM SEAS

A fast craft in beam seas can be quite an exhilarating ride. If you want to make rapid progress in waves, then you have to concentrate hard, and even in beam seas it is necessary to read the waves ahead all the time, otherwise you can find yourself caught out and have several unpleasant moments. It would be easy if the waves came at you in a regular pattern; then it would simply be a question of the boat lifting over the wave as it passed underneath and dropping down into the trough in a nice rhythmical way. However, waves are far from regular and you become very aware of this when you run in a beam sea. It is easy to find yourself with a wave suddenly presenting what appears to be a near vertical face as the boat approaches, and then equally quickly that wave seems to disappear and you drop into a trough. The boat can suffer some quite heavy impacts dropping off waves in this way, but you can avoid much of this if you use the steering and throttle controls to good effect.

If you watch the waves, particularly in a beam sea, you will notice that some are considerably higher than others, some having gentle gradients, others having steep gradients and with peaks and troughs; very rarely do you get a long wave front. It is quite easy to see where the flatter areas of sea are and, by using the throttle and steering, you can often steer around the worst of the waves which tend to be localised peaks. It is surprising how comfortable a ride you can have if you drive the boat in this way. However, there is no doubt it needs quite a lot of concentration and a sensitive hand on the throttle and steering. It is often difficult to get good steering control in these conditions because you only have one hand on the steering wheel, and it can pay to concentrate on just one of these controls – normally the steering wheel – so that you can really use this to good effect.

You will certainly make better progress if you concentrate solely on steering, because the tendency when you do use the throttle will be to slow down rather than speed up, so by keeping the throttle set and using only the wheel you will avoid this temptation.

With the wind on the beam you will find that the boat will steer off the wind much more easily than trying to steer it into the wind; this will be your normal course in taking evasive action. Having said that, when you steer off the wind the wave is still coming towards you, so you may have to steer further off to actually miss a particular wave. By steering into the wind, on the other hand, you will get a better chance to let the wave pass across the bow and run into the smoother water behind. Each wave is different and you will have to make your assessment of each at the time. One point to remember here, as far as navigation is concerned, is that if you keep turning off in the same direction you will, in effect, be steering a course quite different from that which you had previously set.

Even when the wind is not exactly on the beam and you may be steering a course 30 or 40 degrees into the wind, you can still adopt this same technique of driving the boat through or round the lower parts of the wave to make good progress. These are tactics that you can adopt even in quite rough seas, but as the seas get rougher the consequences of making a mistake become greater and you will need to concentrate that bit harder. It can be a very exhilarating ride, but you must always be aware of the risks you are taking and the consequences of getting out of step with the waves.

Mention has already been made of the way in which fast boats, particularly those of the deep-vee type, lean into the wind under the influence of the rudders. This is obviously most pronounced when you have the wind on the beam, i.e. when you are operating in beam seas, and it is an aspect that you have to take into careful consideration. Obviously, if there are flaps fitted to the vessel then you can level the boat up so that it runs true, but even then, if you are using the steering to avoid the worst of the seas, whichever way you turn will cause the boat to lean. This is one of the primary causes of an uncomfortable ride in a beam sea. It will particularly be the case if you take the option of pointing the bow up into the wind to avoid a nasty sea ahead, and there is always the risk here that the boat will land very heavily on one flat side of the hull. You will get this effect whichever way you turn, and the only way to avoid it is to use the steering gently so that you don't upset the transverse trim of the boat too much.

FOLLOWING SEAS

Running before a following sea in a fast powerboat can be exciting. Not only can you often employ full throttle in this situation, but you feel that you can do so with comparative safety, because your speed of encounter with the waves is much slower than with a head sea. The speed at which the waves travel is determined by their wave length, so that smaller waves will be travelling at 12–15 knots and the larger waves, perhaps those generated by a Force 5–6 wind which you can find inshore, may be travelling at around 18 knots. Certainly, in coastal waters you are unlikely to find waves travelling at more than 20 knots unless, of course, they are swells where the wave length can be considerably longer and the wave travels faster accordingly, but these waves tend to have a very gentle gradient which is unlikely to impinge on your progress. With a moderate-speed planing boat, you will be overtaking these waves, perhaps travelling at twice the speed of the waves, so that your period of encounter allows the boat to recover from each wave in turn, without any dramatic change of attitude of trim. At higher speeds the speed of encounter obviously increases, and once you get up to the fast offshore racing speeds around 70 or 80 knots then, even in the following sea, you find the boat behaving virtually the same as it would in a head sea, because the speed of encounter with the waves rises rapidly.

This then means that there are two very diferent techniques for handling fast boats in following seas. At the slower speeds, say up to 30 knots, it is often possible to simply set the throttle and let the boat take its course whilst still making rapid speed downwind. Much will depend on the size of the waves and their speed of travel. One of the problems you will find is that as the craft climbs up the back of the wave it tends to lose speed because it is, in effect, climbing uphill, and then when it gets to the crest it tends to sit there for a moment until enough of the bow projects over the steeper leeward face of the wave to cause it to drop with a quite sudden change of trim. This all tends to happen in slow motion. Relatively speaking, with the boat on the crest of the wave travelling little faster than the wave itself, there is a marked change in attitude as the boat drops down the leeward face of the wave, and at the same time suddenly accelerates. This acceleration is under the impetus of the throttle and the force of gravity. In rough conditions, and depending a great deal on the speed and type of the boat and the speed of the waves, you could find the bow of the vessel burying quite heavily into the next wave in front. Certainly, with a boat with a full bow, you will find the impact of the boat into the wave can be quite harsh, giving a very uncomfortable motion.

There are two remedies in this situation if it becomes uncomfortable, which is likely if the wind and waves start to increase. First, if you have the potential, you can increase speed which will have the effect of reducing the time that the boat

Running before a breaking sea in a fast, rigid inflatable. The passage of the boat through the wave tends to drag the wave crest behind it. (Photo: *Author*)

spends on the crest of the wave, thus reducing the dramatic change of trim at the crest. Second, if you don't have the potential to increase speed you can reduce it so that in fact you tend to ride with the bows on the upward slope of the wave, virtually keeping pace with the wave. If the wave should disappear in front of you or break, then you can open the throttles and accelerate over it. This will give you a slower and more comfortable ride, and is the tactic to adopt if you find the sea conditions starting to rise to the point where you feel you ought to nurse the boat. Sitting on the back of the wave in this fashion also requires a fair degree of concentration. A bigger wave may come up behind you which could well be travelling faster than the boat and you could have a potential broaching situation on your hands, unless you recognise it and accelerate away.

At higher speeds, say 40 knots and above, you treat the following sea virtually as a head sea – although there is a difference which has to be taken into account. You drive the boat, by opening the throttles, up the windward side of the wave in the same way as you would tackle the leeward side of the head sea, and whilst you are unlikely to burst through the crest as you would in a head sea, at least the boat

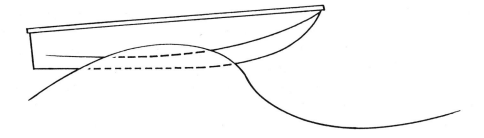

Driving through a following sea can cause the bow to fly just as it would in a head sea.

tends to come off the crest without too much change in attitude, because the momentum of the boat keeps the bow up even though it is not supported by the wave. In this situation you are more likely to fly the boat than you would in the head sea, because the leeward side of the wave is steeper. However, the wave is travelling more slowly and if you get things right it should be possible to keep the propeller immersed on the leeward side of the wave, except for a small jump as the craft comes over the crest. As with so much of boat handling at high speeds, it is a question of matching the speed to the conditions, particularly if you are simply intent on a comfortable ride while still making good progress. At the higher speeds found in racing boats, to all intents and purposes, you treat the following seas as you would a head sea, giving a burst on the throttle to lift the bow as you approach the wave and then cutting the throttle before you burst through the crest, hopefully landing comfortably on the other side.

In rough conditions, say Force 7 or upwards, then running in a following sea in a planing boat can be one of the safest means of progress, provided, of course, that you have a sound and reliable vessel. You can still make rapid progress in this direction, at least travelling roughly at the speed of the waves, simply by sitting on the back of a wave and waiting for that wave to collapse or break before driving onwards. It is not really a wise tactic to adopt if you have a long way to travel because you will soon get tired and lose concentration. As already stated, concentration is the name of the game because mistakes could get you into trouble.

The same technique can be used if you are entering harbour when there is breaking surf on the bar and you have to drive the boat in through this with the wind and sea behind you. In many situations such as a harbour entrance would be untenable for a displacement boat because of the risk of broaching and losing control as the waves overtake you. In a planing boat you are much more able to dictate your position in relation to the waves, and here you can keep the craft riding on the back of a wave as you go in. If the wave breaks, then you drive over it to place the boat on the back of the next wave in front and so on until you are through the broken water. It requires nerve and concentration and this is not the time when you can afford to have anything go wrong with the boat, but it is a feasible way of tackling breaking waves.

In following seas one of the problems you can encounter is a certain loss of stability, particularly when you are travelling at lower planing speeds, say around 18 or 20 knots. Here the dynamic stability of the hull, generated by the boat moving through the water, will be much less and it will be further reduced if you are in breaking water where the water is moving ahead. You will find this aspect most noticeable when you pass through the crest of a wave where the inherent stability of the hull is also reduced. This can cause the boat to lean over, so that if you do fly it at this stage it could land very heavily on the flat of one side of the hull. Whilst such a loss of stability is not likely to be dangerous to the point of capsize, it can make handling the boat more difficult. Once again, it is a question of using the throttles at the right time to increase the dynamic responsibility and to get the bow up as you come through the crest of the wave if you feel this sort of instability developing. This will be apparent by the rolling of the boat and by sloppiness in the steering. As so often with a high-speed craft when you get to this situation, the solution is to put on more power rather than to close the throttles.

In following seas the use of flaps and trim will depend a great deal on the speed at which you are travelling. Very fast boats, which virtually treat a following sea as a head sea because of their speed of advance, will tend to use the flaps and trim accordingly, the flaps being kept down if the boat is starting to fly unduly off the top of waves and the power trim kept in, in this situation. In more gentle seas the power trim can be trimmed out and the flaps kept up, and it is a question of finding the right balance at which the boat makes good progress.

At slower speeds you will generally want to keep the flaps up in order to give the bow as much lift as possible so that it doesn't drop off as you overtake a wave. At these slower speeds you will bring the power trim in for the same reason. Both of these controls have less effect at slower speeds anyway. Ballast tanks, if they are fitted, would normally be kept empty in following-sea conditions, except perhaps when racing at very high speeds when they could help to reduce the chance of the boat flying off the top of the wave.

VERY HIGH SPEEDS

At the very high speeds found in offshore racing, trim and flap controls are critical to fast progress. The aim should be to find a balance at which the boat rides level practically all the time with very little change of longitudinal trim, obviously with the drives trimmed out as far as possible to get maximum performance, but not to the point where the propellers leave the water readily and lose their propulsive effect. You should try to keep the propellers in the water at all times and, hopefully, also part of the hull so that the propellers have something to react against. At very high speeds the flaps only come into use when the sea conditions demand a reduction in speed or when the transverse trim has to be balanced. At the maximum speed of any boat, if the flaps are put down they may give a better trim, but this would be more than balanced by the drag created by the flaps; the solution should lie in getting the boat set up properly in the first place so that the flaps aren't necessary.

Ballast tanks are normally fitted in the bow simply to help keep the bow down when making rapid progress. However, the extra weight carried by filling the bow tank is also beneficial in as much as the vessel becomes heavier and is thus less likely to fly. By the same token, a heavier boat will be more effective in rough seas than a lighter boat, simply because the extra weight will make it less likely to fly off the top of a wave and thus lose a propulsive effect. However, in most cases the extra weight has a negative effect in reducing the top speed of the boat because, in general, racing boats are built to be as light as possible.

There has been a change in this philosophy, however, with the advent of very powerful diesel engines. One of the advantages of using diesel engines is that the offshore racing rules allow diesel engines of twice the capacity of petrol engines and there is no penalty for turbocharging. Modern diesel engines can produce close to the same power as their petrol engine counterparts, but since the rules allow twice the petrol-engine capacity, much more power is available which more than compensates for the extra weight.

There is little doubt that a heavy boat with higher power will be just as fast as a lighter boat with lower power, but the heavy boat will have a decisive edge in rougher seas and this is an approach to racing favoured by many. There is a snag in using diesel power in this way, however, because diesel engines are less responsive than their petrol counterparts and so throttle reaction is slower. This means that you have a less effective means of controlling the boat when operating in rough seas. Perhaps the big advantage with diesel engines lies in their improved safety because the extra weight of the boat keeps it 'glued' to the water much better. This means that you can generally push the boat much harder in bad conditions with all the controls remaining effective, whilst the lighter boat could become out of control, as has happened on several occasions in racing.

LOSING CONTROL

There are two main areas where racing boats can lose control and generate the potential for major accidents. First a craft can leave the water at an awkward angle, perhaps heeled over to one side through catching a wave crest badly or catching a wave crest which is very uneven. Once the boat leaves the water and is actually flying, there is no control left to correct the situation and events have to take their course. In general, the boat lands very heavily which in itself may not be too serious but this introduces the risk of damage, and under racing conditions introduces the prospect of the boat slowing right down, perhaps almost coming off the plane before the crew get their act together again. In this situation there is also the risk that the vessel, on landing, may hit the water very unevenly at high speed and in so doing could turn around rapidly end for end – to the great discomfort of the crew.

The second problem area occurs if the boat flies off the top of a wave at a good controlled angle, but where the complete boat (including the propellers and rudders) is out of the water. If the steering is moved during this flying interval then there is every chance, when the propellers or rudders hit the water, depending on how the steering is arranged, that they will generate a thrust at an angle to the forward motion of the boat. With none of the hull in the water to react against, the boat could again turn rapidly end for end. This situation is more likely to occur with propulsion systems where the propeller thrust is altered to provide the steering because there could be a much greater thrust reaction against the airborne hull than would occur with rudders.

The question of boats turning end for end in this way tends to be more prevalent with monohulls largely because, at the very high speeds which offshore boats are now capable of achieving, around 80–90 knots, there is little of the hull left in the water. The propeller thrust can take control when there is little or nothing of the hull to react against and the boat becomes unstable. A stepped monohull will be better in this situation because, at least, there will be two points of the hull riding in the water at any one time.

CATAMARANS

One of the reasons for the success of the catamaran in offshore racing has been the fact that it is basically operating in a much more stable fashion with the boat riding on four points, and it is better equipped to cope with changing circumstances. The aerodynamic lift generated between the two hulls of a catamaran also gives a degree of stabilisation and cushioning, so that when the craft is airborne it does indeed tend to fly to a certain extent, giving a better prospect of the boat landing in a stable attitude. However, against this is the fact that the drives on a catamaran tend to be mounted on the two sponsons. Because they are so far apart, if one drive or propeller should come out of the water there is a considerable turning effect generated by the other drive which can cause considerable instability. However, catamaran hulls do tend to have good directional stability, so that overall there is less likelihood of a catamaran swapping ends. Certainly, as far as racing results are concerned, the catamaran definitely has the edge in terms of speed, being capable of 100 or 110 knots with reasonable security – conditions in which the monohull is left floundering. However, the monohull has the edge in rougher seas and with the faster diesel-engined powerboats, there is not too much to choose between the two racing concepts except in nearly calm conditions, when the catamaran has the decided edge.

PROPELLER TORQUE

When a propeller turns and generates thrust there has to be a reaction against this thrust. Much of this reaction is, of course, the forward thrust which pushes the boat along, and there is also a considerable turning reaction because the blades are angled. On a twin-screw boat this turning reaction or propeller torque is balanced because the two propellers are contrarotating, but on a single-engined boat there can be considerable problems with this factor, particularly at higher speeds.

The propeller torque generally reacts against the hull so that you will find on a single-engined boat capable of 30 knots or more that the boat will always lean one way. With a right-handed propeller (that is, a propeller turning in a clockwise direction when viewed from aft) the boat will always lean to port, which can be balanced by using a flap. In general, you will find that such a boat leans over but not necessarily to the point of discomfort in reasonable conditions. Where you can find problems is running in a beam sea if the wind is also on the port side and causing the craft to lean. Here you then have a situation where the propeller thrust and the wind are both acting together. Even this you can cope with, although the ride may be a little uncomfortable because the boat will tend to lean

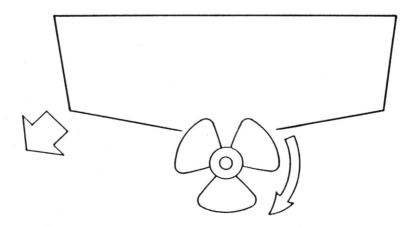

Reaction against the propeller thrust will cause the hull to heel.

on the flat of the vee rather than on the centre. Problems start when you alter course into the wind when you can find the boat heeling over quite alarmingly. I have experienced this a couple of times on sports boats when the vessel heeled over to an angle of 30 degrees or more. It is quite a frightening experience, but the solution is simple; either put the steering amidships (or even over the other way) or cut the throttle. This is the sort of situation that could be very unpleasant if it occurred when you were running in beam seas of any size. If you have flaps remember that you can correct it.

Even on twin-screw boats you can get problems with propeller torque, particularly if one propeller is out of the water and the other remains immersed. This will be a problem on monohulls rather than catamarans, but it could result in the boat heeling over to the point where, if it occurred when the hull is flying, it could have a pronounced capsizing effect on the hull and this could be one of the causes of the boat swapping ends.

CONCENTRATION AT HIGH SPEEDS

It will be evident from this chapter that you can't relax too much when you are travelling at high speeds. Apart from reading the waves ahead and driving the boat accordingly – which in itself can require considerable concentration – you also have to navigate and watch out for other craft and for floating debris which can be a real hazard to fast boats. If you get to the position where you feel very relaxed about the situation and think you don't have to concentrate, when watch out because you are liable to be brought down to earth very quickly.

You can keep up this level of concentration for a couple of hours or so, but after that you can find yourself making mistakes so it's sensible not to drive a boat for any longer period. Even at slower speeds in rougher seas concentration is necessary, and it is wise to swap helmsmen every so often to get a fresh approach. Normally the speed of a fast boat will enable it to get out of rough seas or bad conditions quite quickly so that the need for concentration does not generally present any problems. However, if you find yourself caught out with the prospect of several hours' hard driving ahead of you, then it is time to re-assess the situation and perhaps adopt displacement-boat tactics to give yourself a rest.

Alongside concentration comes experience, and this is something you need to build up. Rather than drive off blindly at high speed, virtually letting the boat do the work, the answer is to analyse everything that happens to the vessel whether you do it or whether the sea does it, and in this way you will quickly build up experience. It is this experience which will stand you in good stead if you find yourself at sea in deteriorating conditions when things can start to go wrong. It is only with this basis of experience, combined with concentration, that you will be able to drive a fast boat intelligently and competently.

6 Coping with extremes

In this book we are talking about operating boats at high speeds and in rough seas. This chapter is devoted to the latter because if you don't like the way things are working out at high speed you have an immediate remedy to hand – go slower. If the sea builds up to the point where you are unhappy, then you must look at what resources you have in order to cope. When things get really bad then it is time to go into a survival mode with the object of weathering the storm until things improve.

There are no magic solutions in these situations and your decisions will be based to a large degree on the type of vessel you are in, the nature of the conditions and your experience and ability to cope. In these extreme conditions, lifeboats are expected to cope and to have something left to help others in trouble. We can take a lesson from lifeboats and the way they operate, but it is to be remembered that much of the safety of lifeboats in rough seas is determined long before the boats actually put to sea. The boats are strongly built, their equipment is sound and the crews are well trained and fit. These are all prerequisites for survival in bad conditions and you would do well to heed this. You may not plan to be at sea in rough conditions, but there is always the risk of being caught out, and the prudent sailor will make some mental as well as practical preparations for this by ensuring that both he and his craft are in good condition for putting to sea.

When you are caught out in worsening conditions, the first thing to do is to make an assessment of the situation. What are the weak points in the boat and its equipment? Are the crew fit for the task ahead? Where is the nearest shelter and safety? Your first concern should be with the boat and where it might let you down. If it has large areas of glass you might be reluctant to push the boat into a head sea. If it has a rear cockpit, you might want to avoid the risk of a sea breaking over the stern in a following sea.

On the machinery side you will be concerned about the amount of fuel remaining and the reliability of the engines and propulsion, and auxiliary systems such as the electrics. In rough seas it only needs a small failure which, in itself, may not be too serious but which can start off a chain reaction of events

A lifeboat is designed to operate in extreme conditions. A motor cruiser operating in these conditions could suffer structural damage. (Photo: HMS Osprey, Portland)

which can lead to disaster. I remember coming across a boat at sea which was on fire in rough conditions, a pretty serious situation which had started because of a steering failure. The steering was a wire and pulley system. The wire frayed and then finally broke. Given time, such a condition would not have been too difficult to fix, but without steering the boat turned broadside on and was rolling very heavily. This made it difficult to effect the repair, but much more seriously, the rolling set the poorly secured battery sliding about, which eventually broke the main battery cable. The sparking which resulted started a fire and the single occupant was lucky to get out alive. This may be an exceptional case, but any failure will add to your worries. When you assess the situation, you should take all factors into account and if you are unhappy with any of them you should go into the survival mode earlier, which may allow you to press on to safety.

We have already looked at different methods of heaving to in Chapter 4. These all require the boat to be driven which means that you may have to spend long hours at the controls. There are alternatives and one is simply to close the boat down and leave it to its own devices. I don't think this would be my choice, but I know of several cases where powerboats drifting under their own devices have come through unscathed. The problem is that we tend to hear about the ones that made it rather than those which simply disappeared without trace.

Even when you are very tired, keeping some semblance of control is better than just letting the boat drift. If you have nothing to do, you tend to give up mentally and that is not a good state of mind for survival. In a strong displacement vessel you would probably get away with it, but in a light planing boat the chances would not be good.

You can drive the boat on a course which seems sympathetic to the boat and the sea, but the good skipper tries to keep something up his sleeve. There are the traditional methods of coping with rough seas, such as using drogues, sea anchors and oil. The use of this equipment is often bandied about, in talk of rough sea, but few modern-day skippers have experience of their use and fewer still used them in anger. They are certainly not the solution to all your problems, but they are worthy of consideration here.

DROGUES AND SEA ANCHORS

Essentially, these two devices give another means of exerting a force on the boat in a particular direction, and which the helmsman can use to control the vessel. Both use the movement of the boat through the water in order to exert the required pull, the main objective of this pull being to stabilise the boat in the required direction.

The drogue and sea anchor should not be confused. A drogue is towed astern of the boat when it is under power with the object of stabilising the steering and preventing the boat from sheering off course in a following sea. A sea anchor is used mainly from the bow, but could be used from the stern, when the engines are stopped and the boat is drifting, with the object of keeping the boat at the desired heading in relation to the wind and sea.

We have already talked about the problems associated with handling boats in following seas. Steering can become difficult because of the movement of water in relation to the craft and a broach could result. This occurs because the bow tends to act as a pivot point about which the stern can swing. The drogue exerts a pull at the stern of the boat, making the stern the fulcrum and allowing normal steering to be restored.

The drogue is towed astern and reacts against the thrust of the propellers. The faster the boat travels, the greater the pull at the stern and thus the greater the

*Towing a drogue. The main tow line is on the right through the stern
fairlead, with the tripping line on the left. (Photo: Author)*

stabilising effect on the steering. Full speed should always be used, but this in
turn demands a strongly constructed drogue to withstand the pull. The use of a
drogue enables a boat to operate in reasonable safety in heavy breaking seas from
astern which would otherwise be very dangerous. There are many factors which
affect the performance of a drogue and it is important to understand these. Bad
design or deployment of a drogue could lead to its not working effectively.

The stabilising effect of the drogue is obtained by the pull at the stern and is
primarily required when a wave is approaching the stern. For the drogue to act
properly it must be well immersed and this depends to a large extent on the length
of the drogue rope which is paid out. This in turn depends on the wave length; the
best rope length I have found is about 1½ wave lengths. This ensures that when a
wave is approaching the stern of the boat, the drogue will be pulling into the base
of the wave behind and not near the crest where it might pull clear of the water. If
the waves are short and steep, then 2½ or 3½ times the wave length might be a
better length. Too much scope should not be used as there is danger of the rope
becoming slack, which would allow the boat to run forward in a series of jerks

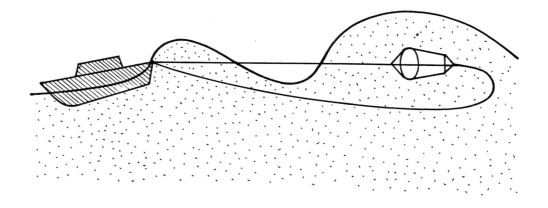

Streaming a drogue. The drogue must be well in the water when the maximum pull is required on the drogue line. There must be adequate slack in the tripping line to prevent accidental tripping.

putting undue strain on the gear, which could also jerk the drogue out of the water. The object should be a steady pull at all times.

The material and characteristics of the drogue rope also have a bearing on the behaviour of the drogue. The maximum pull exerted by the drogue could be in the region of 3 tons, so a strong rope is required. A rope which stretches unduly will act like a piece of elastic and cause the drogue to surge. A rope with little or no stretch will cause the drogue to jerk as it reacts to every movement of the boat. On balance, polypropylene is probably best for a drogue rope, although Terylene (Dacron) is an alternative.

With the pull of the drogue reaching up to 3 tons, it is imperative that the boat is fitted with a very strong post or bollard on which to make fast a drogue rope. The position of the post in not critical, but the position of the fairlead through which the rope is led is very important. For the drogue to work effectively, the pull exerted must be right at the stern of the boat, so that any attempt by the boat to sheer is immediately counteracted by the pull on the rope. The fairlead at the stern must fully enclose the rope so that there is no chance of its jumping out, and the rope must be carefully protected against chafe if the drogue is to be in use for any length of time.

The size of drogue required varies with the size of the boat. A diameter of 30 inches (76 centimetres) should be adequate for a 50-foot (15-metre) boat, reducing to 20 inches (50 centimetres) for a 20-foot (6-metre) boat. The drogue itself is constructed of heavy canvas in the shape of a cone with the forward or towing end held open by a metal hoop. Metal is used for this hoop to produce negative buoyancy and for the same reason the towing bridle is made from galvanised steel wire. The cone of the drogue is truncated, leaving a small hole which helps the drogue to tow in a straight line.

By fitting a tripping line to the drogue, recovery can be greatly simplified. A tripping line also enables the drogue to be streamed ready for instant use, but not pulling. When required for use all that is necessary is to slacken the tripping line and the drogue rope will take the weight. The tripping line is attached to the tail end of the drogue by means of a small bridle. The inboard end is led through a fairlead as far removed from the main rope as possible so as to reduce the chance of the two ropes twisting together. This is always a risk if the drogue should start to turn and it can make recovery very difficult as well as possibly reducing its effectiveness. For open-sea work the tripping line is best dispensed with, but for crossing a harbour bar, where the drogue may have to be tripped quickly, it is desirable.

A drogue works most effectively in craft with pointed sterns or with small transoms. The drogue will slow the boat down to a certain extent, but less than one would expect, something in the region of 1–2 knots. In these types of boats the moving water will be divided readily by the stern and pass on each side. In a boat with a wide transom this would not be the case and the moving water would strike the transom with considerable force, with the possibility of damaging the vessel or of parting the drogue rope.

A drogue is a rare item to find on boats today and few carry fittings suitable for handling a drogue, presumably because the owners never expect to be at sea in conditions where the drogue might be used. Their use enables a boat to run before a sea with a great deal more safety and confidence than otherwise. This facility could enable a boat to run for shelter where otherwise caution might dictate that the safest course would be to head out to open sea. A drogue, properly used, can also enable a harbour entrance or bar to be negotiated under rough conditions, which would otherwise be untenable. Such an operation should not be undertaken lightly, however, and it requires an intimate knowledge of the entrance, as well as a crew practised in the use and operation of the drogue. In spite of the heavy pull at the stern, a drogue does not prevent the boat from being steered.

The golden rule in using a drogue is to put it out before you think you really need it. If you think that the prevailing conditions demand the use of a drogue, the chances are that you should have it out. Do not wait until the boat has nearly broached once or twice before using the drogue: it may be too late by the time you have got it out. The aim should be to get the drogue pulling with a good steady pull, and almost invariably full speed should be used so that the maximum pull is obtained. Under these conditions it should be possible to steer a good straight course in a heavy following sea.

There is a great deal of similarity between a drogue and a sea anchor, but it is in their use that they differ. A sea anchor performs two purposes – one being to reduce the drift of a boat which has its engines or steering out of action and is being blown towards the shore or some other danger. When used for this purpose, the drift will not be stopped altogether, but it will be reduced. In a sense, one is buying time by using a sea anchor, in the hope that the defect can be cured or help can arrive in the time gained. The name of the sea anchor derives from its use in this manner.

The other function of the sea anchor, and probably its main function, is to enable the boat to lie at a desired angle to the wind when the engines are stopped, fuel is running low or the vessel is otherwise disabled. This is normally an emergency procedure, as adverse conditions can be better coped with by the use of engines and steering if these are available. The sea anchor is a second line of defence, but could come into its own if the crew become very tired in a prolonged storm, when their reactions and ability might be impaired.

With its engines stopped a boat will drift with the wind, the rate of drift depending on the strength of the wind, the area of the boat exposed to the wind and the area of the boat under water. Much will depend on the attitude the boat adopts in relation to the wind, i.e. drift is likely to be faster when beam-on rather than end-on. The sea anchor, by having a good grip on the water and being unaffected by the wind, can provide a reaction against this drift. Compared with a drogue, the speed of the boat will be relatively slow so that the sea anchor needs to be correspondingly large to exert a meaningful pull. The conditions under which a sea anchor is used can mean that the boat is exposed to breaking seas where the surface of the water is moving. Such a sea meeting the boat could result in sudden increase in the pull on the sea anchor. The size of the sea anchor should thus be balanced between these two requirements, so that a degree of resilience is introduced.

There are many ways of constructing a sea anchor and one similar in design to

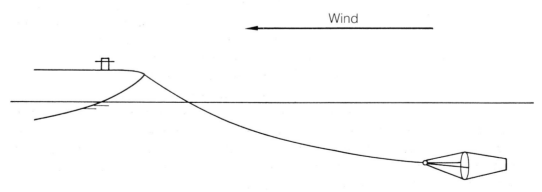

How a sea anchor is streamed from the bow of a boat to keep it head to sea.

a drogue is probably best. It can be constructed lighter than a drogue, as the stresses involved are much lower and, unfortunately, a drogue is unlikely to fulfil both functions, being too heavy and too small to act as a sea anchor. The drogue would probably sink to such an extent that it would exert little or no pull unless the drift of the boat was very rapid. I have used sea anchors which have been constructed like a parachute, with no stiffening hoop, and these have worked successfully with small boats. A similar type of sea anchor is standard equipment on inflatable liferafts and has the advantage of folding up very small and being easy to stow.

Very few boats carry a sea anchor as such, hoping that they will not encounter the conditions which will demand the use of one. It is possible to devise a makeshift sea anchor from materials on board. A canvas cover or small sail could be utilised if lines are tied to the corners to form a bridle. A plastic or metal bucket might do the job for a small boat. A strong line 10–15 fathoms in length should be used. It is a question of exercising ingenuity with the equipment available, but a temporary sea anchor is unlikely to withstand prolonged use due to rapid wear and tear. As a sea anchor is likely to be required in a hurry, there is unlikely to be time for lengthy construction.

A powerboat, when left to its own devices to drift, will usually adopt an attitude with its stern towards the wind. This is because the stern is more deeply immersed than the bow, and on planing boats where the stern gear projects below the bottom of the boat this will invariably be the case. The deeper stern offers more resistance to the drift of the craft and consequently the bow tries to drift faster than the stern by going downwind. However, the area and position of the superstructure and the hull have an effect on the final attitude. If there is a large area forward, the stern-to-wind tendency will be accentuated, but if it is aft, the stern will try to blow downwind, possibly cancelling out the effect of the underwater shape. Such a boat, left to its own devices, is likely to lie beam-on.

The sea anchor is normally deployed over the bow so as to keep the boat head to wind, but it can also be used to keep it at any desired angle to the wind. By attaching a second rope to the sea-anchor line and leading this to one side or other of the boat and adjusting the tensions, the angle of the hull to the wind can be altered. This system can be useful when the wind and sea are not running in the same direction and it is required to head into the sea. A fair amount of experimentation may be required to achieve the desired angle.

When lying to a head sea with a sea anchor out, there is always the risk of the boat being set bodily backwards when a breaking wave will overtake it. The boat is moved stern-first through the water and this can put a heavy strain on the rudder, particularly the large ones fitted to displacement boats. Apart from securely lashing the rudder amidships, there is not much that can be done to alleviate this problem.

The line attaching the sea anchor to the vessel need not be as heavy as that used for a drogue in view of the reduced stresses. A resilient rope such as nylon should be used to help absorb these shocks and reduce the strain on the boat. Chafe will be a major problem with the sea-anchor line. It should be well protected and the nip freshened at regular intervals. There is little requirement for a tipping line under normal conditions, but it could be of value if the boat is drifting ashore in breakers. By tripping the sea anchor, the rate of drift could be increased so as to get through the breakers as quickly as possible when conditions allow. This seems to be more of a theoretical requirement rather than a practical one, as I cannot envisage anyone using the tripping line under these rather desperate conditions.

STEADYING SAILS

Steadying sails used to be a common feature on motorboats of all types, but are now restricted almost solely to smaller fishing boats, and are used to keep a boat head to wind when lying to drift nets and to reduce rolling. The steadying sail is carried on a mizzen mast and the boom is sheeted tightly in amidships to prevent the sail from flapping. By presenting a larger area to the wind at the after end of the boat, the stern will tend to remain downward and the bow head to wind. In this respect it performs a function similar to a sea anchor but the stabilising effect is much less, and it is unlikely to be sufficient to prevent the bow being knocked offf the wind by a breaking sea. The best use of a steadying sail would be in conjunction with a sea anchor, where each would help reduce the limitations of the other.

The steadying effect of a sail is achieved by the lateral resistance offered by the sail area as the boat rolls, in a similar way to a bilge keel acting in the water. The position of the sails on the vessel is not critical from the steadying point of view, but the effect of such sails on the steering should be borne in mind. In a head sea a sail forward would make the boat very difficult to steer, and likewise a sail aft in a following sea has a similar effect. If there is a choice of positioning a steadying sail, it should always be placed downwind on the boat; this could help considerably in terms of control. However, the use of a steadying sail in a beam wind should be treated with caution in view of the effect that the pressure of wind on the sail can have on stability. Generally, though, a steadying sail can make life on board more comfortable under adverse conditions and this can have a beneficial effect on the endurance of the crew.

The drogue, the sea anchor and steadying sails are all means of exerting additional control on a boat. It is important that the nature of the control is fully understood, as misuse can produce very undesirable effects. The effect of using one or more of these items of equipment must be considered in conjunction with those of using the engine and steering, if these are available.

OIL ON TROUBLED WATERS

The universally proclaimed panacea for all desperate situations at sea is that of spreading oil on troubled waters. There is no doubt that the correct type of oil used under certain circumstances can have a beneficial effect, but this is limited and miracles must not be expected. The oil produces its modifying effect by spreading over the surface of the water and increasing the surface tension, thus reducing the chances of the waves breaking. Within limits, the thicker the oil, the greater the increase in surface tension and thus the greater the reduction in waves breaking. By thickness, I mean viscosity, not the depth of the film on the surface. A very viscous oil will not spread rapidly, however, so a balance has to be found between these two requirements. The recommended oil is an unrefined fish oil, normally supplied as 'storm oil'!

It is rare to find a boat carrying oil for the specific purpose of spreading it on the water, so that when the need for it arises the only oil likely to be available is either lubricating oil or diesel oil. Diesel oil is almost useless, but lubricating oil will have some effect. It is less viscous than the optimum and it will spread readily on the water, but its effect in reducing the breaking of waves will be less than fish oil.

Having obtained the oil, the next problem is how and where to spread it. It can be assumed that oil spread on the surface will drift down to leeward, as this will be the general movement of the surface of the water. Assuming that the objective is to reduce the breaking of waves in the area around one's own boat, then it is necessary to spread the oil to windward, so that by the time the waves reach the boat there is a good coating of oil on the water. This spread can only be achieved when either a drogue or a sea anchor is being used. The traditional method is to have a small block on the drogue or sea anchor, through which is rove a light line with an oil bag attached. This is a canvas bag stuffed with oakum into which the oil is poured. The bag is attached to the line and hauled out to the drogue where the oil spreads; the line and block enable the bag to be refilled.

It is presumed that this idea has some merit, otherwise it would not be standard equipment on ships' lifeboats, but I cannot help feeling that it was developed as a theoretical exercise and I cannot see it working practically. It is often difficult to get a drogue or sea anchor streamed properly and the complications of the extra line and block would increase the chances of the whole thing fouling up. Unless the boat was moving very slowly, the oil from a drogue would never reach the boat. From a sea anchor there might be some gain, but remember the size of the waves is not reduced, only the chance of their breaking.

I am doubtful whether the oil bag could distribute oil in sufficient quantity to have much effect. In my experience oil has to be distributed in fairly large quantities, say at the rate of 1 gallon every 5 minutes, for much benefit to be gained. If oil is used in this quantity, the amount normally carried would restrict its use to special circumstances rather than continuous use, such as when crossing a harbour bar or a tide race in a following sea, or when approaching another boat in trouble in bad weather. In these circumstances the oil would only be required for a short time, but if the conditions were critical the use of oil could make a justifiable improvement.

The technique would be to spread oil from downwind of the boat so that it would drift into the danger area. When this had the desired effect the area could be entered, possibly while spreading further oil. The initial spread of oil would only be effective if the tidal conditions were suitable. An ebb tide over a bar would be likely to carry the oil away from the bar faster than the wind would carry it in. In a tide race the same would apply, so in both of these situations, which are likely to produce the worst seas, the use of oil would be largely ineffective.

When using oil at sea, it must be borne in mind that a great deal of the oil will end up on the decks, making them dangerously slippery. It should also be borne in mind that it is an offence to discharge oil into the sea. However, there is unlikely to be much criticism if life-and-death circumstances are involved. On balance, though, you will probably have gathered that I do not think much of the idea of using oil in this way.

TOWING

Another emergency situation which you may have to cope with at sea is to tow another boat or be towed yourself. Even in calm seas, towing is quite a skilled operation if it is to work successfully for any distance. In rough seas it can be an operation fraught with difficulty and danger.

Being towed

This will probably only be necessary if you have an engine failure, so you will be lying dead in the water. This leaves all the manoeuvring to the other boat, but you can help by getting things ready and securing the tow at the first attempt.

You need somewhere to make the tow-line fast. Ideally, this should be a good strong central mooring post on the bow. However, a large number of modern powerboats lack this facility, although an anchor windlass would do, provided it is well secured to the deck. A tow-line puts more strain on the fittings than simple anchoring or mooring.

An alternative is to use the mooring bitts or cleats on each bow. On their own they would not be strong enough, but a bight of rope, doubled if necessary, around both cleats can make a good point to secure the tow-line. The bight should be long enough to pass clear of the bow so that there should be no problem with chafe on the bow roller (often a problem when using a central mooring post). If you are not happy with the strength of the mooring cleats or post, then you can take just a single turn of the tow-rope round the cleat and then lead the rope aft to a second cleat to help spread the load. Finding the right set-up for making fast a tow-rope is something you can do long before the need for a tow arises.

Towing another boat

Towing another boat is not something to undertake lightly. It calls for skilful manoeuvring and rope handling. The tow-rope is best passed to the other boat with your stern level with his bow. Manoeuvre close enough to throw the line across, using a lighter line for the initial contact if it is easier to throw. If the sea and wind conditions are difficult, you can float the line down to the other boat with a fender tied on the end to keep it afloat and make it visible.

At all times when passing the tow-line take care that the line does not end up round your propeller. The person handling the line on your stern should allow only just enough slack to get the line across and never allow a bight of rope in the water. When making the line fast on your stern you may find the same problem as on the bow of the towed boat; the solution is either a bridle between the two stern cleats or spreading the weight onto the bow cleats.

Take up the weight gently on the tow-rope and try to keep an even strain – not an easy task in rough seas. You should be able to find a speed at which both boats are comfortable with not too much snatching on the line. Adjusting the length of the tow can often help achieve a compatible motion between the two craft and if the towed boat still has steering, then it should try to follow your track. A position just on the quarter of the towing boat can be comfortable and heavy sheering about is to be avoided as it puts a great strain on the tow-line and fittings and causes chafe on the line.

Whenever securing a tow at sea wear a lifejacket and, if you have one, a safety harness. You are very vulnerable on the foredeck at sea, and falling overboard will only compound matters.

EMERGENCIES

To cope with an emergency demands foresight. One should inspect the boat imagining all the things which could go wrong, particularly the small things, and then decide what action to take to prevent the situation getting worse. The first thing to take into account is the stowage of all portable items of equipment. An item coming loose and sliding about can cause damage to both itself and the boat, but worse, it is liable to distract the attention of the crew from the job in hand. Have a bag easily available where any loose items can be stowed, and keep lengths of shock cord or rope within reach to secure things temporarily. The movement of a boat in a seaway can test even the best of stowages, and the most unexpected things can come adrift.

At night a torch should always be available and this can serve as a temporary compass light, as well as being used for checking around the boat. Checking should be done at regular intervals so that any chafe or loosening can be detected and the necessary action taken in good time. Checking should also cover the bilges, engine compartment and cabin so that any developing faults can be detected before they become serious. Most of the preventive work should be done in harbour, either in the building or fitting-out stages, or during maintenance. Once the boat puts to sea, there is relatively little that can be done to prevent emergencies arising, except to handle them intelligently and thus reduce the stresses as far as possible.

The crew must also take care and not expose themselves to unnecessary risks. An injured crewman can be as great an emergency as the loss of steering. It is very difficult to treat and make an injured person comfortable in a rough sea. The best that can usually be achieved is to lash the casualty in a bunk, as far aft as possible, and treat the injury, if possible. However, concern for the casualty's condition is likely to affect one's own judgement, thus leading to further emergencies. For a badly injured person it may be best to summon help in the form of a lifeboat or helicopter rather than risk further dangerous conditions.

Engine failure

Probably the most common type of emergency experienced by powerboats at sea is the failure of an engine. As is pointed out in Chapter 9, failure is usually caused by a fault in the ancillary equipment rather than by a mechanical failure of the engine itself. This being the case, the fault can often be corrected if there is time, and if you have the necessary equipment. On twin-engined boats there is no immediate problem provided sufficient speed and steering control can be maintained by the remaining engine. On a single-engined boat the position can be serious, and one is left with five alternatives, one or more of which can be used depending on what equipment is available on board.

The first alternative, and one which will inevitably be adopted initially, is to let the boat drift so that it adopts its own natural heading in relation to the sea. When drifting, the motion of the vessel can become fairly violent and is not conducive to effecting repairs on the engine. One also has to consider where the boat is drifting to, and this underlines the necessity of maintaining adequate sea room in a single-engined boat, particularly in rough weather. The motion of the boat can be reduced by hoisting a steadying sail, which brings us to the second alternative – hoisting sails with the idea of making progress as well as steadying the boat. It is difficult to improvise effective sails, even if suitable material is carried and a suitable mast fitted, so sails are really only a viable alternative if the boat was designed to carry them. Any temporary sails will only allow progress downwind, which the boat would be making anyway with the effect of the wind on the hull, but it might also be possible to gain steerage way.

A third alternative, and one which will reduce the drift of the vessel and bring it head to wind (thus making life on board more comfortable) is to use a sea anchor. The fourth alternative is to anchor. This, of course, demands relatively shallow water and under rough sea conditions would probably be used only as a last resort to prevent the boat drifting ashore or into dangerous breakers. The use of an anchor in rough conditions imposes considerable strain on the anchor, the cable and the craft itself. The anchor must have good holding power on different types of sea bed and the cable would need to be heavier than that normally recommended. The surging of the boat in the waves would cause heavy jerking on the cable with a consequent strain on the anchor post or windlass, unless the cable was well sprung with heavy chain. Chafing on the cable in the fairlead would also have to be watched carefully. Without a doubt, anchoring under these conditions must be considered to be a temporary situation only and you should be prepared for the line to part.

Before going further into this situation, it is worth looking at the fifth alternative, which would certainly be used in these conditions if not before. This is to use distress flares or a radio to summon assistance. Flares are only effective when seen and the supply on board will be limited, so use them with discretion and when they are likely to do the most good. At the first sign of serious trouble, it is worth letting off one flare, particularly if near the coast. It is amazing how many people look out to sea from the shore, and with the public becoming better educated in these matters, a distress signal is usually recognised for what it is and the necessary action initiated. It is unlikely that an engine failure in the open sea will be immediately serious from the boat's point of view, but look ahead and summon help in good time.

Drifting ashore

Let us return to the situation of drifting ashore. If the anchor holds for a while, at least you have bought time with the hope that help will arrive. In the meantime, prepare for the worst and decide on a course of action. If the coastline is steep and there is little likelihood of the anchor catching hold before the boat reaches the foot of the cliffs, then your position is very serious and your only hope would be to reduce the drift as much as possible to give more time for help to arrive. The liferaft or inflatable dinghy should be inflated ready for use, but it is probably better to let the boat take the initial impact on the rocks, as it will offer more protection for the crew. It is only after the boat starts to break up that you should consider abandoning it. I shall refrain from offering further advice. I lack personal experience in this situation but would hope that personal survival instincts would take over. Individual circumstances could vary widely, and to cover them all would need a separate book.

Drifting ashore onto a beach in rough seas does not offer much more hope of saving the boat, but the prospects for the crew are much brighter. There is a better chance of the anchor holding enough to get organised for the final beaching. The crew of a shallow-draft vessel have a better chance, as the boat can drift closer to the shore without grounding. Here the technique may be to let the boat drift ashore through the surf on a sea anchor. This should keep the boat head to sea sufficiently to prevent a capsize, but the surf is liable to break on board and cause damage.

Another way would be to slacken the anchor line to let the boat pass through the surf, head to sea. This would demand either a short area of surf or a long anchor line. Alternatively, the anchor line could be hauled in short until the anchor starts to drag. The drag on the anchor would be sufficient to keep the boat head to sea while she drifts in stern first. Both of these techniques demand that one of the crew is on the foredeck tending the anchor line and this could be dangerous once the boat enters the surf and waves start breaking aboard.

One further way of negotiating surf would be to leave the boat anchored as securely as possible outside the surf, while the liferaft or dinghy is slacked through the surf on a line made fast to the boat. This method may be better if the boat has a deep draft and is liable to ground in the middle of the surf, but it does depend on having a long line available. The slacking of the line from a tender could be difficult as liferafts and dinghies are not usually fitted with points around which a rope could be tied. To try to hold the rope by hand could be hazardous in heavy surf. For this exercise a liferaft would appear to be more suitable as there is less chance of being washed out of it in heavy surf.

An emergency at sea in bad weather can be very frightening, but with forethought the effects can be minimised. It is obviously better to direct your efforts to prevent anything going wrong, but if it does, then at least have some means on board to be able to do something about the situation. Thinking and analysing possible courses of action in such situations will put you in a much better position to cope than if you are taken by surprise.

7 The human element

In previous chapters we have talked about the controls – how to use them and their importance. The controls represent the point at which the crew interface directly with the boat – what might be termed the human/machine interface – and you will have already appreciated that a great deal of the safety or speed of the boat lies in the hands of the person driving it and the way they concentrate and judge what is going on around them. This human/machine interface is critical to the way in which a boat is driven, and yet in so many pleasure powerboats and, indeed, even lifeboats, the control positions leave much to be desired. This is the great neglected area of boat design, perhaps because the designers and builders of powerboats often have little practical experience. I suspect they are trying to make too many compromises in the design of pleasure powerboats, and in making these compromises the area that inevitably seems to suffer is the control position. As boats often spend a vast proportion of their time tied up in harbour, it is easy to see why builders and designers have other priorities.

The job of the helmsman is to assess the many factors which affect the boat and the boat's reaction to them; and to take appropriate action using the primary controls of wheel and throttle as well as the secondary controls (where fitted). A larger than normal wave, or one with a breaking crest in rough seas, can arrive with very little warning and a critical situation could develop quite rapidly. When travelling at high speed, situations can change incredibly quickly and the helmsman has to be equal to the task. Concentration and observation of the sea are the main qualities required in a helmsman, both in rough seas and at high speed. Relax and you can be caught off guard with disaster only a short step away. You only have to relax your concentration for a short time and that could be just the moment when a larger wave than normal comes along and you quickly find yourself in trouble.

It is not always easy to maintain the required level of concentration, particularly when the boat is moving violently and the crew are taking a considerable pounding, as is often the case in a fast craft, particularly under racing conditions. Life can reach a very low ebb, as it can when operating in rough seas, even in a displacement boat. It is possible to switch off from the pain and discomfort to a certain extent, but inevitably it will affect your concentration; therefore, much of the thought which needs to be put into the design of the control position has to be geared to making the crew comfortable and enable them to operate the controls freely and easily. Finally, they must be given clear visibility all round the horizon so that they can see what is going on outside and react accordingly.

SEATING

Ships and boats are probably the only form of transportation left where the person controlling the vehicle still remains standing. In cars, trains and planes the driver always sits and there is a very strong case for adopting the same solution on boats, particularly those operating at high speed or in rough seas. If you are standing in a boat which is being tossed around at sea, then you are certainly not in full control of that vessel; you will end up using the steering wheel as a handhold rather than a control which is clearly unsatisfactory. Because you have to hang on, trying to locate yourself in the boat, you will not always have a hand free to operate the throttles, and your control will lack the smooth cohesive movements necessary for good boat control.

Seating, then, should be considered a must (although the standing position found in many offshore racing boats is an acceptable second best and you will probably be able to absorb the high shock loadings better by flexing your legs), because the thickly padded shaped backrests locate you securely in the boat to a large degree. I am firmly of the opinion that a well-designed seat can do the job just as well and give you a more efficient position from which to drive the boat.

The helmsman's seat must be strong and well-braced. The weight of the human body can be magnified several times because of the movement of the boat, and the seat must be strong enough to take these high loadings. Padding does not need to be soft and luxurious; indeed, soft padding is often not suitable because under high loadings you tend to bottom out through the padding. It is much more important for the padding on the seats to be able to absorb the high shock loadings without bottoming, which generally demands a fairly hard foam. Preferably, this foam should be of the slow recovery type so that the seat does not have a spring return motion which can be uncomfortable when you are bouncing around at sea. The seat should be a reasonably tight fit around the hips and around the shoulders so that it helps to locate you in position, and armrests or a deep bucket-type seat help to locate the lower part of your body on the seat. A headrest is useful provided it is adjustable; one with side pieces that partially wraps around the head can stop some of the uncomfortable motions which allow the head to be thrown from side to side.

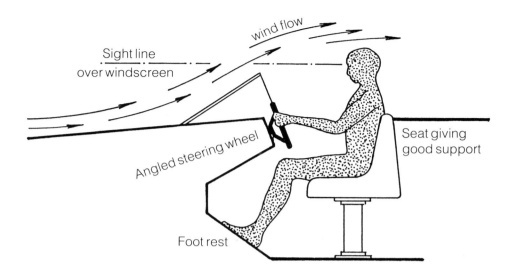

Points to look for with an open steering position.

Seat belts

To suit different occupants the seat should be adjustable, rather in the manner of a car seat. The idea is that the seat should anchor you firmly in the boat, allowing both hands to be free to operate the controls. One further refinement to help safeguard you is to fit seat belts, which can either be of the lap single strap type or with a full harness over both shoulders. The latter is preferable because then you can completely forget about holding on, which leaves you much freer to concentrate on using the controls properly. Apart from the good control which seat belts offer there is also the safety aspect to be considered, because they do prevent you from being thrown about the boat and injuring yourself if you get your handling wrong. They also offer protection in the event of sudden deceleration, for instance, if the bow suddenly buried into a wave at high speed. The benefits of fitting seat belts are applicable to both displacement boats operating in rough seas and fast pleasure cruisers. We will look at the requirements of high-speed racing boats a little later under the aspect of safety.

Matching the seat must be a good footrest because this allows you to use your legs to brace your body against the movement of the boat. Even if you are strapped in, a properly angled footrest gives a good feeling of security and, like the seat, the footrest itself should be adjustable for maximum comfort.

Crew seating

So far, we have talked about seats for helmsmen so that they can control the boat, but similar adequate seating should also be available for everyone else on board. It is no good the helmsman being comfortable and able to drive the boat hard if the rest of the crew have to hang on like grim death. Certainly, there is a need to provide a matching co-driver's seat, similar to that of the helmsman, to enable the co-driver to navigate or operate the electronic navigation instruments with both hands. For the rest of the crew, it shouldn't be a matter of taking pot luck and making do with what seats or standing positions are available. Most sports cruisers are inadequate in this respect, with few handholds provided, and I have yet to see one fitted with seat belts. Yet such seat belts could at least provide a reasonable means of the crew securing themselves when the boat is thrashing along and it would give them a chance to relax just a little, instead of having to take their pleasure with their knuckles white. Even in lifeboats and workboats which often operate in rough seas, whilst good seating may be provided for the helmsman and perhaps one other crew member, very little thought seems to have been given to what the rest of the crew have to put up with, and it is worth remembering that a boat is only as good as its weakest link – and that weak link could well be one of the crew who gets thrown around the boat because he has not been holding on tightly enough when the boat has lurched.

If seat belts are fitted on a boat, and I am strongly in favour of them, then it is a good idea to place some padding on the lap strap and around the shoulder areas to reduce the possibility of chafe, because remember that you are being thrown up as well as down and you may have to wear the belts for a considerable period. You will notice that I haven't talked about sprung seats. In general, I am not in favour of them, largely because they tend to damp out only one frequency, and you can encounter many different frequencies of bounce on a boat. My experience with sprung seats is that there will be times when you find yourself going up in the seat when you should be going down, resulting in an uncomfortable ride which can accentuate the movement of the boat rather than damp it out.

STEERING WHEEL

We shall now consider the controls in relation to the helmsman and his seated steering position. For effective steering, the wheel is best mounted at an angle of about 30 degrees to the horizontal. This is somewhat similar to the way a steering wheel is positioned in a truck, enabling you to sit comfortably with your knees under the wheel. The wheel can then be turned by pulling on the rim giving you good control. In many cases the wheel is placed at a steeper angle, rather like the steering position in a car, which is fine provided you can sit comfortably at the wheel and the wheel is placed so that it comes readily to hand. The criterion should be whether you can turn the wheel easily, and in my experience the flatter wheel angle gives better control and comfort. A vertical steering wheel is certainly not recommended because it is almost impossible to get your knees underneath it and yet this traditional type of steering-wheel position is still found on many fast boats today. This is probably a case of designers trying to emulate the steering position in racing boats, where the wheel is often vertical to match the stand-up steering position, but it is very uncomfortable when you are seated.

Steering wheels on high-speed craft today still have the traditional wooden spokes around the rim. These are really totally unsuited for both fast boats and for those operating in rough seas. The risk of getting clothing caught in the spokes is very real, apart from the fact that it is difficult to use this type of traditional wheel effectively if you want good steering control.

GEARS AND THROTTLES

The typical engine and gear control fitted to a powerboat is the single lever type. Earlier when we were talking about controls, I recommended fitting a separate throttle and gear control to achieve a more effective range in the throttle movement, which in turn allows you more delicate control. Whatever type of throttle control you have, the important thing is to have it positioned so that you can use it effectively. This may be stating the obvious, but I have found very few high-speed boats where the throttles are well positioned – and the same applies to most slower boats. Ideally, the throttle should be positioned so that you can operate it while still resting your arm, allowing the elbow to act as a fulcrum; in this way you can achieve much more delicate throttle control. This may mean constructing some form of armrest behind the throttle-control box, but some outboard manufacturers have introduced a padded armrest into the throttle-control box itself, which is a very enterprising development. This type of armrest is harder to engineer when you have a twin-engine control box, but it is not impossible and it is the only way in which you will obtain good throttle control.

The other important aspect is to angle the throttles so that the range of throttle which you use most of the time in the open sea (that is, from full-ahead back to the idling position) is located in the most convenient position for easy use. So often you see throttle boxes mounted horizontally, which means that the forward section of the movement which you are most interested in is placed ahead and away from you. With this type you can only operate very coarse control which is far from ideal when controlling a fast boat in waves. Ideally, the fully open position on the throttle lever should be about 30 degrees forward of the vertical and the idle position should be about 30 degrees aft of the vertical; in this way you should be able to maintain delicate throttle control.

A foot throttle is by far the best type of throttle control on a powerboat. As with car driving, it gives you very delicate control and, as a bonus, it leaves you with both hands free, either to concentrate on the steering or with one hand to operate the trim and flap controls. If you have one hand on the wheel and one on the throttle lever it is necessary to give up one or the other if you want to adjust the trim or flaps, which is never a very happy situation. The foot throttle gives you excellent control provided you are well located in the seat, but whilst it is suitable for use in the open sea it does throw up a few problems when you are manoeuvring the boat in harbour, although here you do tend to be more interested in the gears than the throttles.

FLAP AND POWER-TRIM CONTROLS

There are many different types of controls for these units and very little consensus about what is best. Flap controls can be push buttons or joystick-type levers or even simple switches. Power-trim controls can be flick switches incorporated into the throttle lever or on the dashboard or, again, push buttons. Lack of any consensus about what is best probably reflects the fact that none of the systems is particularly good, and if these controls are to be effective there is much room for improvement, both in the type of control and its location.

Certainly, as far as power trim is concerned, the flick switch mounted on the throttle lever is excellent and it means that you don't have to take your hand off the throttle to use it. However, the disadvantage with this system is that it is mainly suited to single-engine installations, although at least one outboard manufacturer has produced a practical twin-engine version. On twin-engine boats, both the power-trim controls tend to be used together, so perhaps it wouldn't be impossible to link both units into a single switch and operate the two units in unison. They would need to keep pace with each other and you could get into a mess if one moved faster or slower than the other.

None of the dashboard-located controls for either flaps or power trim is particularly effective. This is partly because they are often located so that you can't get to them easily, and partly because of the lack of logic in the way the controls are engineered. The push-button type are probably the easiest to use and I would favour the top button of the pair being used to lower the flaps or push the power trim out and the bottom button to take them up or draw them in. Whatever type is fitted, the control for each unit should be located close alongside its partner so that you can operate both in unison with two fingers.

There is plenty of work to be done to improve these controls and the automatic system mentioned earlier is one way out of the dilemma. Another solution, found on some smaller racing boats, particularly those with a foot throttle, is to mount the controls on the steering wheel so that they can be used by thumb pressure without taking your hands off the wheel. This is effective, but it does require careful engineering if the electrics are to stay waterproof. Certainly, the use of a foot throttle is one step towards being able to use the flap and power-trim controls effectively because at least you have one hand free to operate them.

DASHBOARD LAYOUT

A dashboard that looks like something out of *Star Wars* certainly impresses your neighbour in the marina, but it is unlikely to enable you to get the best out of your boat at sea. I have already mentioned the need to be able to concentrate and read the waves ahead, and you won't be able to do this effectively if your attention is constantly diverted by a glittering row of dials in front of you. Most of these dials relate to the engine-monitoring systems and you really don't need them right in front of you, because I guarantee that if something goes wrong with the engine you are unlikely to notice it on the dials first.

If you must have engine dials then mount them away from the steering position where they can still be monitored from a distance, perhaps by another crew member. A much better solution to the question of engine monitoring is to have audible alarms fitted so that if anything goes wrong your attention is immediately alerted to the problem. This then clears much of the clutter from the dashboard leaving just the two r.p.m. indicators and perhaps a log and compass to tell you what is going on. The compass should be mounted as high as possible so that you don't have to divert your eyeline too much from the horizon outside to the compass inside. The compass should also be mounted as far from the helmsman as is reasonably practical, provided of course that you can still read it, so that you don't have to change your focus too much from the sea outside to the compass inside.

With the advent of electronics in the form of position-finding systems, radar and possibly electronic charts, the time is approaching for a serious look at dashboard layouts on power boats. If you are both driving and navigating the boat, as is often the case on a pleasure boat, then having this sort of information in front of you is much more important than engine instrumentation, but it does need to be built in the optimum position which will demand some degree of cooperation from the designer and boatbuilder. At present, most electronics are simply bolted on where there is a convenient space, with very little attempt at integrating these systems into the dashboard. This will have to be done if electronic instrumentation is to gain the attention it deserves, and if it is to provide information for navigation at high speed in a sound and sensible way. In general, screens such as radar or electronic charts should be mounted reasonably low with the screen angled back at the top by about 20 degrees. Care must be taken when positioning them to ensure that they are not sensitive to reflections from windows, etc. The ideal types are those where the control panel and the display can be mounted separately so that they can both be put in the optimum position. You will see in Chapter 8 how just two screens, radar and the electronic chart, can give you virtually all the information you need to navigate a powerboat in almost all conditions. This will be the way ahead for the future, but it seems that in the meantime we will have to make do with very much second-best in terms of dashboard layout.

VISIBILITY

Visibility for the steering position, as we have already stated, is very important if you are to be able to read the sea, but this is another contentious area which receives less attention than it deserves. With an enclosed wheelhouse you have no alternative but to look through the windscreen; if this is the case, then the windscreen and the dashboard layout should be designed so that the reflections on the screen are kept to a minimum. Light-coloured surfaces on the area immediately below and behind the windscreen can reflect badly on it, particularly when the sun is shining, which makes it very difficult to read the sea ahead. The situation is made worse if the windscreen is of the smoked-glass type now commonly being fitted to many powerboats to improve appearance. Reflection can be a major problem with this type of screen and the only real solution is to paint the area below the screen matt black so that nothing reflects from it.

Whilst designers tend to concentrate on the view ahead and make sure this is reasonably good, the view to the side and particularly to the stern is often less than adequate. The view to the side may not be too important, but you certainly need to be able to see astern in case there is another boat overtaking you, but equally to watch what is happening to the seas behind. This is particularly the case with displacement boats which are moving slower than the waves, but it is just as important on a fast boat because there will often be craft faster than you at sea, which will come roaring up astern just at the moment when you might take it into your head to alter course across their bow.

At night the problems of visibility become much worse because the darkness outside the screen tends to reflect every light on the inside. Where lights are necessary these should be red or orange which will not affect your 'night vision' too much, but lights should be kept to a minimum. This is another good reason for moving as much of the instrumentation as possible from the dashboard. What lights you have should be capable of being dimmed and this applies particularly to the compass light so that you can select the optimum level to match the prevailing conditions.

WINDSCREENS AND WIPERS

Windscreen wipers are always a problem with an enclosed wheelhouse or where you have to look through a windscreen; and finding an effective wiper to work in the marine environment, at a reasonable cost, is a problem which has not really been solved yet. Even when the wiper is effective, there is often the problem of smearing because of salt spray on the screen and, if you take your boating seriously, then a really effective wiper linked to a good system for washing the screen with fresh water should be considered a must. Visibility is so important when driving a fast boat, and the fact that it is sometimes reduced to a small area cleared by the wiper is not conducive to good boat handling.

With an open boat or a boat fitted with a flybridge, you have the option of an outside steering position and this immediately gives you better visibility, although as always you come up against problems and compromises. If you want shelter from the wind and spray, then you have to look through the screen and you will encounter the same problems as with an enclosed wheelhouse. Ideally, you should be able to look over the windscreen to get a clear view ahead; a well-designed screen will allow you to do this, whilst still offering protection from the elements. This is the best situation of all but it is rarely achieved, and what often happens is that you find the top rail of the windscreen is placed just at the height of your eyes so that you find yourself straining either to look over or under it, which is bad for concentration. A seat with height adjustment may get you out of this predicament, but then you may also run into problems with the position of the various controls if you have this flexibility.

HANDHOLDS

Even though you have comfortable seats to secure you properly there will always be times when you need to move around the boat and this will emphasise the need for good handholds. If you are going to move about on a fast boat, handholds are an absolute must to prevent people being thrown around, and even on slower boats correctly positioned handholds can do a great deal to ensure that the crew have a comfortable journey. Positioning handholds needs experience and you can really only work out where to position them when you are at sea, when the ideal positions will become fairly obvious.

Handholds can be grouped into two categories: those which are virtually the size of a hand and can be bolted onto convenient surfaces, and the vertical type, which run from deck to deck head, and are very useful for moving around in the wheelhouse, although they are not very welcome when you are in harbour. However, it is possible to locate the latter type close to tables or seats where they won't get in the way in harbour; they can often make up for their inconvenience in harbour by their usefulness at sea. A third type runs along the deck head, although these are less useful at sea than might be imagined.

Handholds can also be useful outside when you have to move around the deck. One of the weak areas on most sports boats is the lack of handholds for the people occupying the rear bench seat, which makes them particularly vulnerable if an overambitious driver makes the boat fly around. Without handholds it would be very easy to lose one of the crew overboard. Handholds rank with dashboards and control layouts as the big areas of weakness in any boat design for high speeds or rough seas.

THE CREW ENVIRONMENT

Creating the right environment for the crew is one aspect of fast boating or rough-sea operation, and is a factor in the design and construction of the boat. However, the mental and physical aspects of the crew also have to be considered, because both fast boats and rough seas impose quite severe mental and physical strains on a helmsman and crew which will bear closer examination.

Mental strain comes from the need to concentrate and from fear and apprehension of the boat entering what is basically 'the unknown'. When conditions get really bad in rough seas there is always the desire, however slight, to give in and not fight any longer. Different people have different mental approaches at sea in rough conditions and it is difficult to generalise. Certainly, my prevailing feeling in these conditions is a firm resolution never to go to sea again, but this resolution implies that I am going to survive and have the chance to go to sea again, so at least there is some hope in this thought. If conditions get really bad, the important thing is never to give in and let events take their course – no matter how bad they get! There is always some action you can take even in the worst of storms and the fact that you can occupy your mind in trying to find a solution can often prevent the onset of panic. There are many remarkable stories of survival at sea and these generally show that the survivors didn't give up easily. However, to approach a storm at sea in this manner requires quite a lot of willpower, so you need to save some of your mental energy to work out what is happening to the boat and to find solutions to the problems.

Physical strain comes from the need to locate yourself against the motion of the boat and, if you are at sea for a long time, also from the lack of sleep. Good design, and particularly good seating, can do a great deal to reduce the physical strain. If you have to stand up and hang on in a boat which is moving in a seaway, this can be exhausting to the point where you literally fall asleep on your feet. Ideally, there should always be at least two people on the boat capable of handling it confidently, so that periods at the wheel (and the concentration needed) can be relatively short. People who reign at the helm for hour after hour because they

The cockpit of a racing boat with well padded slots to locate the crew. Note the navigation information all prepared beforehand and the electronic compass dial in front of the normal magnetic compass. (Photo: Author)

feel that they are the only person on board capable of handling the boat are a danger to both themselves and the crew. They are not likely to be either physically or mentally capable of dealing with an emergency should it arise.

Physical strain from the continual pounding of the boat, particularly in a fast boat in racing conditions, can have a considerable effect on your mental ability. I estimate that in these conditions your mind is only working at around 50 per cent of its normal capability, the other 50 per cent being used trying to handle the pain and bruising received from the physically demanding conditions. Under racing conditions you can stand this for 2 or 3 hours, but in rough seas you might have to put up with it much longer and you have to recognise the drain on your mental ability which is taking place, and realise that you must think out decisions very carefully and try not to rush into any hasty actions.

When a person is tired and exhausted, there is a great desire to take risks if the risks will reduce the time of exposure to the rough conditions. A situation can arise when there is a safe harbour close at hand, but where the entrance could be very dangerous if attempted under the prevailing conditions. The temptation to try to get in out of the storm will be very great, and under these conditions it is quite easy to convince yourself that the dangers at the entrance are much less than they really are. You will only find out that you have got things wrong when it is too late, and this emphasises the need to take a long, hard look at any strategic decisions which you may take at this time. While crossing the Atlantic in *Virgin Atlantic Challenger II* fatigue was a major problem, and it was for this reason that I had a back-up navigator on shore monitoring all my decisions, just to make sure that I didn't make any silly mistakes.

Fatigue is a combination of both mental and physical tiredness and it is probably the greatest danger when you are out at sea for any length of time. Drugs are available which can reduce or rather postpone the effects of fatigue, but the idea of using these doesn't appeal to me and I don't have experience of them. The danger in using such drugs would appear to be that you rarely know how long the bad conditions are likely to last, and the effects of the drug could well wear off long before you reach harbour. You could therefore be in an even worse state once the effects of the drug have worn off. Much the same thing can be said for using alcohol in these conditions. A tot of whisky or rum will give a quick uplift when you are cold or tired, but this is short-lived and the ensuing depression can make you much worse in the long run. It is a fallacy to think that alcohol can keep you going and it certainly has no place in fast boats, nor is it recommended in rough seas.

FOOD AND DRINK

Food and drinks of a milder kind are very important, not necessarily because of the nourishment they provide, but for the rise in morale which they give. The availability of food and drink is some indication that circumstances have a degree of normality. It is difficult to arrange cooking facilities on board powerboats suitable for use in rough conditions. Tins of self-heating soup or even vacuum flasks made up before the conditions get bad can obviate the need to brave the rigours of the galley and help to keep you going. Microwave ovens are a possibility for heating precooked food under difficult conditions.

CLOTHING

Good and adequate clothing can help considerably in reducing the physical strain, by keeping the crew warm and dry. What you wear will depend a great deal on personal preference and even when you are shut up in the warmth of a wheelhouse at least one person should be equipped to go outside in a hurry if something goes wrong. It makes a great deal of sense to wear adequate clothing at all times and if you are in an open boat when conditions are bad, then remember that a great deal of your body heat is lost through the head and some sort of hat or covering can help a great deal.

SEASICKNESS

Seasickness is probably the most debilitating affliction which can affect both your mental and physical capabilities. Different people have different tolerance levels towards the motion of the boat. For me, it is the pitching motion of the boat which tends to bring on seasickness. One of the prime causes of seasickness is that your brain is receiving different messages from your eye and from your balance organs in the ear. It has difficulty in reconciling these differing messages and consequently sends a trigger signal to the stomach; hey presto, seasickness. I find proprietary seasickness tablets very effective provided they are taken in good time, but the transdermal type, which looks like a small sticking plaster placed behind the ear, is even more effective because the chemicals can still be absorbed even while your stomach is in something of a turmoil. Seasickness is no laughing matter and it is important that the skipper recognises any members of the crew who are affected because they will be more vulnerable and may need watching carefully.

SPEED PROBLEMS

In offshore racing, even when speeds are up to the 50-knot mark, life-jackets and crash helmets are mandatory. This makes a great deal of sense because boats tend to be pushed harder than normal when racing, and in this situation things can go wrong so the life-jacket and helmet offer a degree of protection. However, they are far from being the total solution where safety is concerned, and events have demonstrated that at higher speeds simply wearing a life-jacket and crash helmet is a long way from being adequate protection.

The latest thinking for very high speeds is that something more akin to car safety is the right approach. The crew should be strapped in with a full harness and should wear life-jackets and crash helmets. Additionally, the area around the cockpit should be suitably strengthened and protected in order to give the crew a chance of survival when things go wrong. The concept of building a safety cell is valid and its value has been proved in practical experience. However, this type of protection is far from being acceptable in all circles and the real truth is that there is no type of protection which is going to be satisfactory in all types of accident. The disadvantage of a safety cell with its protective or fully enclosed cockpit is that you then have to look at the waves through the windscreen, which can reduce your ability to read the waves and, of course, it also makes getting out more difficult. The next stage is then to fit oxygen supplies in case the boat capsizes and the crew are trapped underneath. Perhaps 'worst of all is the false sense of security which this type of safety cell brings. It means that crews may well drive their boats closer to the limit and thus be more vulnerable to an accident in the first place. At the end of the day, one of the safety problems is that there are a considerable number of inexperienced drivers whose enthusiasm outweighs their expertise. With boat speeds continually rising, the need for experience in boat handling is the best guarantee of safety.

The same applies, to a lesser degree, in the slower boats used for pleasure. Modern sports boats and even cruisers are now capable of speeds up to 60 or 70 knots in some cases, and at these speeds the crew can be very vulnerable to accidents. The major problem with high-speed craft is that everything can be perfect one minute and then the next minute things can go badly wrong with very little warning. It is sudden unrecognised changes in sea conditions which can cause inexperienced drivers to be vulnerable and where accidents can happen. To a certain extent the same applies in rough seas, and whilst protective equipment such as life-jackets and crash helmets should be required wearing in fast boats of any type, the real answer to safety is experience and concentration.

8   Navigation

There is a great deal in common when navigating at high speed and navigating in rough seas. Both circumstances create conditions in which many conventional navigation techniques are not possible. You cannot write easily, you cannot put lines on the chart and plot positions easily, and it is extremely difficult to use such equipment as hand-bearing compasses and RDF. These difficulties occur at a time when accurate navigation can be more critical than normal and the navigator comes under considerable pressure. If you add to this the fact that in many cases you need both hands to hold on with and that the continuous movement and battering can dull your brain – making even thinking a difficult operation – then you have a very challenging environment for navigation. At high speed the navigation problems are compounded because of the time factor. Putting your position on the chart is not a great deal of help if you are going to be over a mile away from that position by the time you have it on the chart. With navigation you are always much more interested in where you are going than where you have been. That's history and it's what lies ahead that is important for safe navigation.

It all adds up to a situation where navigation can become quite a hit-and-miss affair and you may take more chances than necessary in a situation where there are already difficulties and dangers. However, there are techniques which can make navigation at high speed and in rough seas a comparatively safe operation. These can be divided into two distinct areas: eyeball navigation and electronic navigation, and ideally the two should be used side by side to check one against the other.

EYEBALL NAVIGATION

Eyeball navigation is largely a question of looking out to recognise what you see of the land or navigation marks, and relating these visual clues to what you ought to be able to see when you refer to the chart. Many people call this type of navigation, pilotage. Inherent in any eyeball navigation is a great deal of planning and

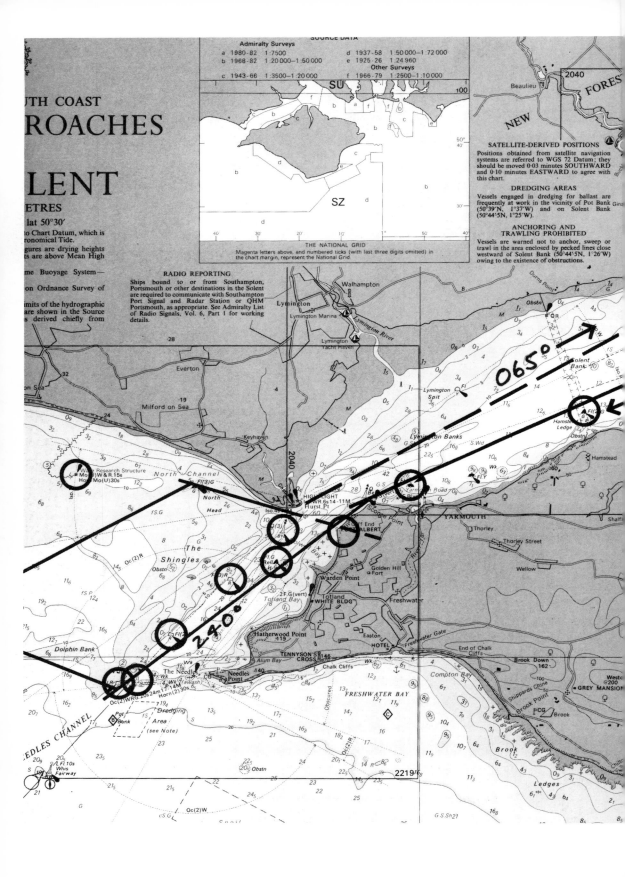

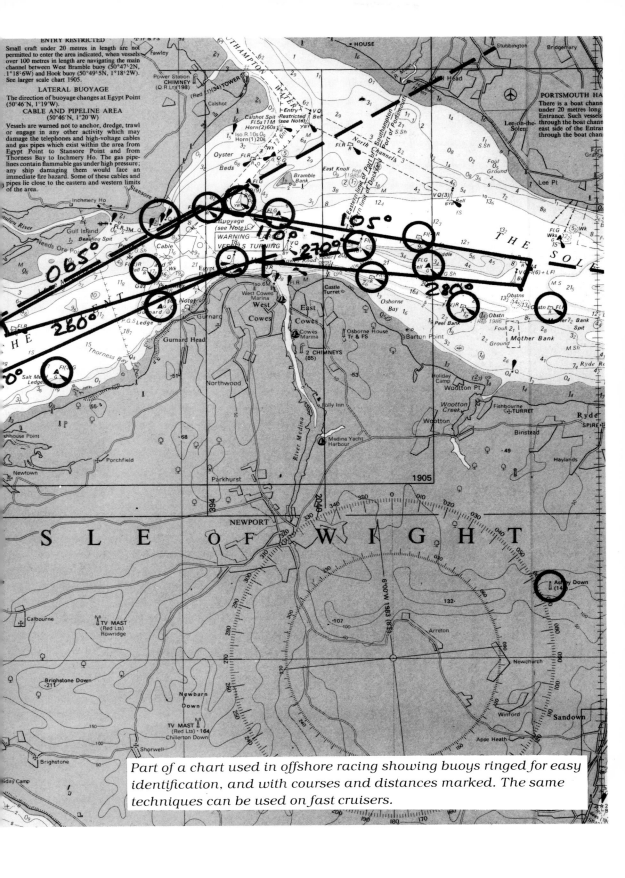

Part of a chart used in offshore racing showing buoys ringed for easy identification, and with courses and distances marked. The same techniques can be used on fast cruisers.

preparation before you leave harbour, so that you have all your courses and distances worked out between the various points through which you want to pass. In this respect it is rather like a form of waypoint navigation, but instead of latitude and longitude positions you have buoys or headlands or other navigation features which you pick up and identify before altering course.

The basic preparation for eyeball navigation lies in getting out the chart when you are in harbour and drawing lines connecting the points through which you want to pass. From these lines you measure the course and distance, applying necessary corrections such as deviation and variation, and then jot these down on a piece of paper or in a notebook. At sea you want the chart laid out in front of you with the courses marked on it, then each time you pick up a waypoint you refer to the notebook for the next course and follow that to the subsequent waypoint and so on. If you know roughly the speed you are travelling at you can relate these courses to time, and then simply by reference to your watch you can work out roughly how far along a particular track you are, and how much time there is to go to the next waypoint. These calculations can be done mentally without too much difficulty, but it is not impossible to use a calculator in difficult conditions, particularly if it is secured to a firm surface so that you can use it one-handed.

Such a basic system is fine in theory, but it offers little in the way of checking the route being followed, until you pick up the next waypoint. The main problem is that you won't have much idea what to do if you don't pick up that waypoint when you expect to. This is where you have to do a lot more detailed planning and preparation, and if you study the chart closely you can usually find buoys or other marks along the route of the course which, when you sight them, will give you some idea of whether you are progressing along the desired course. There is a wide variety of these clues if you study the chart carefully and, apart from the obvious ones such as buoys or beacons, you could use church spires on shore or transit marks, even waves breaking along the edge of a sandbank.

On their own, each of these clues may not be very much help, but if you start relating them to each other then you can follow your progress down a particular track without too much difficulty. It is a good idea to ring all these features on a chart before you set off; this will serve to jog your memory as you progress along the track. You should be able to check your position surprisingly accurately by this method, but the chart will give you some idea of the margins of safety that you can allow on that particular route, and hopefully you will be able to narrow down the possible errors in the position as you start to close the waypoints. When you go out of sight of land or other features, then you will have to rely on dead-reckoning.

These are the techniques used in offshore racing navigation and they can be valid even at very high speeds, although trying to find and identify a turning mark such as a buoy at speed can be a pretty tense affair. You may have less than a minute between the time you sight the buoy and perhaps less than half a minute by the time you have identified it before you have to alter course around the buoy, which doesn't give you much time to decide what action to take. You can relieve this anxiety period, to a certain extent, if the buoy is close to land. In this case, you may be able to extend the course line on the chart beyond the buoy to the point where it crosses the land and see if there are any identifying features in the background which will give you a guiding point to steer towards before you actually sight the buoy. A prominent hill or a chimney could provide this clue. Even if it is not on the direct line you can still use the offset heading of this prominent point to give you a pretty good guide to find the turning mark.

These tactics are equally valid in rough weather where visibility for something like a buoy may be very limited by large waves, although you may be able to see the land in the distance fairly clearly. At the much lower speeds involved you will have more time to measure the situation and, at both high speed and in rough seas, it is helpful if you get used to judging distances because this in itself can give you a clue to your position. If you know how far you are off a coastline, this is a good guide to position. Such distance estimation can also be useful when rounding a headland where there are offlying rocks. If you are relying on this estimation of distance, then obviously you don't want to cut your margins too fine and you must make adequate allowances for any errors that might creep in. Distance judging is something which does need practice before you start to rely on it.

With eyeball navigation, the biggest challenge comes in trying to find an isolated mark, perhaps a buoy, which marks an isolated shoal or rock. You will have taken off the compass course from the chart accurately, and hopefully be steering that same course accurately. This means that in theory you should go straight to the waypoint, but particularly in rough seas it is unlikely that you will be able to steer an accurate course, and the greater the distance you have to run between one checkpoint and the next, the greater the error is likely to be. One way to overcome this is to introduce a dogleg into the course to pick up an intermediate mark for a position check, so that the distances steered between marks are halved. This means that there will be less room for error and there will be a good chance that the isolated mark will be found within the limits of your visibility.

Helmsman's bias
One of the main reasons for error in trying to steer a course is helmsman's bias. Most people steering a powerboat bias the course one way or the other unintentionally. In a fast boat this bias is usually away from the direction of the wind, so that the bow tends to swing to leeward and probably just comes back onto the course when swinging to windward, the result being that a course may

be 5 or 10 degrees off the desired one. Few helmsmen will admit to making this error and the only way to identify it is to watch the steering closely óver a period of time to see what happens. In rough seas it will probably be the waves which will introduce the bias, but once again the tendency is to turn away from the waves, rather than into them.

Although the helmsman's bias tends to be logical in this respect, you can't bank on it, and I have seen people do exactly the opposite and steer into the waves rather than away from them. A 5 degree error on a 50-mile course can be enough to ensure that you miss the point you are looking for at the end of the course.

You can identify the steering error and apply a correction to compensate for it. However, if you then run the appropriate distance and still don't pick up the mark, you don't really know which way to turn to look for it. This is where second-stage navigation comes into play and a good navigator will always have something up his sleeve to redeem the situation. So much will depend on the particular circumstances, but one way to resolve this problem is to introduce a bias into the course before you set out, so that you know that the course is taking you very positively to one side of the mark which you are trying to find. In this way there will only be one direction in which to turn when you have travelled the required distance.

The same technique can be used when making a landfall. Rather than aim directly for a headland, which if you are too far out to see you may pass altogether without seeing it, aim inland from the headland instead so that you will be sure of seeing some part of the coastline before you reach the headland. You must be careful about adopting this technique; make sure, for example, that the coastline on which you are making your landfall is clear of isolated rocks or sandbanks. By adopting this technique you are aiming for perhaps a 5-mile long stretch of coastline as opposed to the pinpoint of a headland, which gives you a much better chance of finding it.

Similarly, you might want to aim for the buoys marking a channel rather than the fairway buoy at the entrance to the channel, because then there will be a much better chance of sighting one or other of the buoys and identifying it. It goes without saying that if you do this you must make sure that you won't be making your landfall on sandbanks or rocks outside the channel, so it is necessary to make a careful study of the chart around your destination point in order to identify the good areas on which to make a landfall. It will all be part of your preparation in harbour because you won't be able to do much of this planning once you are out at sea, unless of course you are prepared to stop the boat and work things out.

One of the difficulties in using courses and distances is that your speed at sea, both when you are travelling at high speed or in rough water, may vary over a particular course. Ideally, of course, you want to keep the speed constant so that

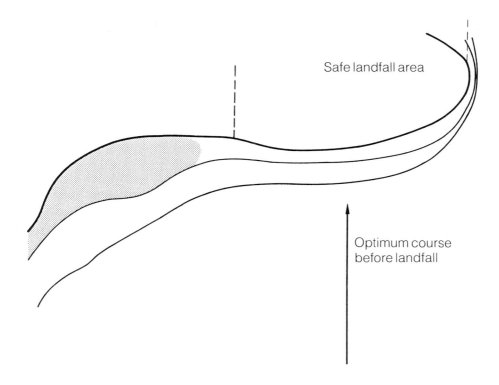

*The chart will show areas of clear coastline where it is safe to make a
landfall in fog. This is better than trying to aim direct for the headland.*

it makes your calculations easier, but inevitably changing sea conditions will
force you to decrease speed at times, and you must learn the art of averaging the
speed to get some idea of how far you have travelled. In a displacement boat, the
log will give you a fair idea of your speed and the distance travelled, which relieves
you of the need to do too many calculations, but remember that a log may not read
as accurately in rough seas. At high speed, logs are notoriously inaccurate and
here a much better way of judging the speed is by your engine r.p.m. You can
relate engine r.p.m. to speed by carrying out a series of runs over a measured mile
at different speeds.

Alternatives
Another aspect to consider in your planning and plotting before you leave is a
variety of alternative courses and destinations. Conditions may change when you
are at sea and this may mean a change in tactics which we will discuss later. It is
much easier to plan an alternative course when you are in harbour than to try to
do so on a boat tossing at sea. I know from offshore racing experience that you

have to spend a tremendous amount of time planning and plotting the route and looking at all the options and alternatives, because in racing the last thing you want to do is to stop and work things out. Probably 90 per cent of the planning and preparation you do before a race is not needed, but the problem is that you don't know which 10 per cent you will need until you are out there, so you have to go through the whole routine.

Night navigation

Night-time brings its own share of problems, because in these conditions it is very difficult to estimate distance. Identifying flashing lights can also be difficult because they may disappear behind waves, or in a high-speed craft you may miss some of the flashes as the boat bounces. If you are approaching a flashing buoy in a fast boat, it is extremely difficult to tell just how far off you are, and suddenly you find yourself right on top of the buoy, which can be quite a disconcerting experience. The answer in these conditions is to take things a little more gently and give yourself more of a margin to play with. It is not advisable to try to cut too many corners at night. Eyeball navigation does allow you to keep going at high speed or in rough seas under many circumstances, but as we have seen, errors can creep in and it certainly keeps you on your toes until you have found and identified the next waypoint.

ELECTRONIC NAVIGATION

In most cases eyeball navigation is adequate for coastal runs in clear visibility, but it doesn't leave a lot to spare if things start to go wrong. A much greater feeling of security can be obtained by using electronics for navigation, and there is no doubt in my mind that modern electronics have a great deal to offer boats operating not only at high speed, but also in rough seas where the information they provide can bring a great deal of reassurance. Modern electronics are becoming increasingly reliable and able to stand up to the pounding of boats operating in these demanding conditions. Used intelligently, electronics can provide all the information you need for safe navigation to fairly close margins.

Installation

If electronics are to be useful in these conditions, you need to take a great deal of care and planning in their installation. It goes without saying that the power supplies and all the wiring should be installed to the highest possible standards, but equally the equipment should be very carefully positioned around the navigation area so that it can actually be used in difficult conditions. This may sound like stating the obvious, but few motor cruisers have a wheelhouse layout which takes into account the needs of electronic equipment, so that these have to be installed where there is space available rather than in the optimum position for easy use. At high speeds in particular, even pressing buttons can be quite a difficult operation, and with some of the small keyboards on modern electronic equipment it is very easy to press the wrong button through involuntary movements of your hand. The keyboard needs to be positioned so that you can brace your hand against part of the boat whilst using your finger to press the button; in this way you can obtain accurate results. A handhold in front of the keyboard is a useful feature because it enables you to hold on as well as press the buttons, but even just having somewhere to rest your hand is usually adequate.

The trunnion type of bracket which is often used to support electronic equipment is pretty useless in fast boats and would be equally so in rough seas. A much better solution is a mounted electronics panel which gives a much tidier looking installation as well as one which is easier to use. Keyboards should be placed where they are within easy reach when you are seated. On some of the larger equipment, such as radar and electronic chart displays, the keyboard and the display require different positions for optimum use. Units fitted with remote keyboards are much to be preferred because each part can be placed in the best position. One of the best arrangements I have found for using keyboards in rough conditions is a portable keyboard which is secured on the dash panel by high-quality Velcro. When required for use, it can simply be pulled off the dash and held in the lap with one hand while you press the buttons with the other. An even better refinement of this arrangement is to have Velcro on your trousers so that you can secure the control panel while you operate it with one hand, leaving the other hand to hold on with.

Even when the helmsman is navigating it is possible to develop an effective layout by careful planning. If you take your electronics seriously and want to get the best out of them, then planning the installation is just as important as selecting the correct equipment.

Position finding

Position-finding equipment normally gives a read-out in latitude and longitude. On its own it is pretty useless information because it only has relevance when it has been plotted on the chart. As we have already seen, plotting on the chart at speed is a difficult or impossible operation, so the only way to use electronic position finding in these conditions is by waypoint navigation. To a certain extent the techniques are rather like the ones you use in visual navigation, except that you pinpoint the position you want to arrive at by its latitude and longitude and, of course, you receive constant updates as to your position in relation to the waypoint as you proceed along the course.

With waypoint navigation, it is once again a question of plotting and planning your route before you set out from harbour, noting the latitude and longitude of the various points you want to pass through and feeding these into the electronic position-finding system. From that point on, provided you give the equipment the right instructions, it will not only give you a continuous read-out of your position in latitude and longitude but, more importantly, it will also show you the course to steer to the next waypoint and the distance. Perhaps even more useful is the cross-track error which shows you the distance you are to the left or right of the track you wanted to follow. From this it is very easy to develop a mental picture of just where you are in relation to where you want to be.

The main systems for position finding are Loran C and Decca Navigator, the former being in use in North America and the Mediterranean, whilst Decca Navigator is primarily a northern European system. Decca Navigator may eventually be replaced by Loran C in northern Europe, but this is unlikely to happen before 1992 at the earliest. Both Loran C and Decca Navigator are susceptible to various errors which have to be taken into account, and it is probably unwise to rely on the accuracy of either of these systems to less than a ¼ mile. This is generally adequate for most navigational purposes because by that time you have picked up your target position visually (whether it happens to be a buoy or a headland); you can then use the visual navigation point to check against the electronics. With any electronic position-finding system it is an act of faith on your part as to whether you are obtaining the right information; so if you have to place a great deal of reliance on electronics, then it is wise to have at least two systems for confirmation. Even two systems are not always adequate because if they show different readings you will not know which one to believe, so the only real solution is to have at least three systems and then take the position given by the majority. This may sound extreme, but it is the way aircraft navigate and it is the only solution for close to 100 per cent reliability. It was also the philosophy I adopted in Virgin Atlantic Challenger where I had to rely totally on electronics.

Satellite navigation using the Transit system is adequate for navigation at speeds below 10 knots, and would thus be suitable for use in rough seas. On faster boats it is totally inadequate, because the positions are only produced every 60 to 90 minutes and the interval in between leaves too much to chance at these speeds. A new satellite navigation system, Navstar GPS, is scheduled to come into operation in 1990, and this will provide continuous position fixing in much the same way as Loran or Decca Navigator, but with a consistently high degree of accuracy and without being affected by weather conditions or other errors. Such a satellite system, when it becomes fully available, will obviously be the ideal solution for both high-speed and rough-sea work, and it is anticipated that the price of receivers will drop to become comparable with those for existing electronic position-finding systems.

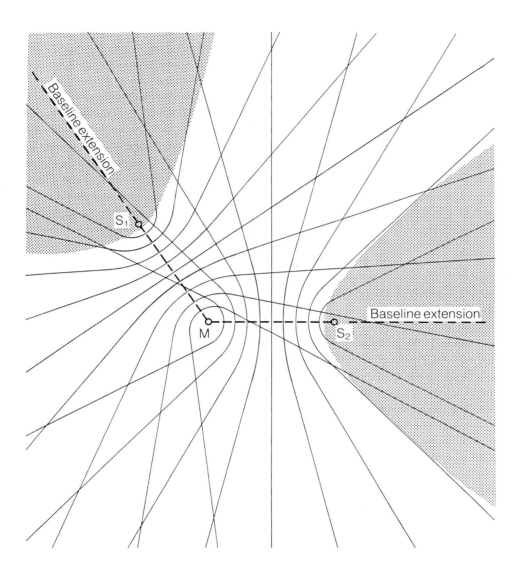

The master and secondary transmitters and the pattern of position lines they generate. The areas where the position lines cross at small angles will not give accurate positions. This is worst at the extensions of the base lines joining the transmitters (shown shaded).

Electronic charts and plotters

If you do need to plot positions on the chart from these electronic receivers when you are at sea, then the easiest way is to have a latitude/longitude grid drawn over the chart. This will enable you to plot the position, without the need for parallel rules or dividers, with sufficient accuracy for most navigational requirements. Even then, for high-speed work, there will be a delay in the plotting, and one way to overcome this is to link the position-finding system to an electronic plotter or chart display. This gives a real-time presentation of the navigation situation. Plotters are an interim stage towards electronic charts; they simply relate the position to a latitude/longitude grid on the display, which shows the route you want to follow and the track you are following. The electronic chart goes one stage further by showing the coastline and, on the more sophisticated models, soundings and navigation marks so that you have a complete navigation picture. When linked to the position-finding equipment, into which a route has been programmed by means of waypoints, this route will be displayed on the electronic chart as the course you wish to follow. The present position will normally be shown on the display by means of a flashing cursor and the track you are following will also be shown, so that you have a complete real-time tactical presentation of the situation which can be seen without the need for any hand work. Ideally, such an electronic chart display should also be linked to the compass, so that a heading marker emanates from the present position shown on the display to show you where you are going in relation to the land or other navigational features which are shown.

Radar presents a somewhat similar plan display of the navigational situation and the ideal way to arrange the chart and radar display is alongside each other, with both of them north-up and on the same scale so that a direct comparison can be made between the two. In this way you can quickly identify buoys on the radar screen by comparing them with what is on the chart. It also allows a direct comparison between the chart and the other radar coastlines so that you can quickly identify features on the radar. Targets on the radar not identifiable on the electronic chart are thus likely to be other ships. With these two displays you have the whole tactical navigational picture in front of you, which makes an excellent presentation for navigation at high speeds. With a layout like this I have navigated with considerable confidence at 50 knots with visibility less than ¼ mile in congested waters.

Radar

Radar on its own is a very useful navigational tool because it is probably the only piece of equipment which shows what lies ahead – and that is what you, as a navigator, are primarily interested in. Once set up, it requires virtually no attention and is thus ideal for use in both bad conditions and at high speeds. In these situations you can carry out what would be the radar equivalent of visual navigation, by setting the heading marker to pass clear, or close alongside (as appropriate) headlands or buoys, as these features are picked out and identified. As far as collision avoidance is concerned, small-boat radar still leaves a lot to be desired, because it is not always easy to work out the course and speed of other vessels; however, we will look at this further under fog navigation.

Radar does have limitations, and it is important to appreciate the presentation shown on the display. The radar scanner sends out a beam as it revolves, and this beam is reflected back from targets, which are then translated into marks on the display. The beam is equivalent to your standing on the boat and turning round through 360 degrees; you are only viewing things on the horizontal plane, even though they are presented on the map-like display as though it was a bird's eye view. From the horizontal viewpoint one target can easily be hidden by another, so you may not see it until it is no longer obscured. Of course, in rough seas, the waves can intrude between the scanner and the target. In heavy seas there is also a considerable reflection from the waves which themselves present radar targets, and so there will be a lot of clutter on the screen around the centre point. In rough conditions this can extend for a mile or more and obscure other small vessels. Rain and snow can also obliterate other targets on the radar screen to a certain extent so radar has to be used with a degree of caution, but as a navigational tool it is excellent, provided you don't take too much for granted.

Small-boat radars tend to have a wide beam angle of between 4 and 6 degrees so that any target coming within the span covered by this beam angle will appear on the screen as one target. This means that an island which is separated from the shore in reality could appear on the screen as linked with the mainland, because the radar beam cannot differentiate the gap between. This can be quite disconcerting. I found this to be the case on a trip round Ireland where we were using radar to pass through a narrow passage off a headland, between a headland and an island. The actual clear passage did not show up until we were less than a mile away, and it took quite a lot of faith in navigation to be convinced that it actually existed.

Quite often sandbanks and broken water will show up on the radar screen and this can be quite useful, particularly at night, in giving early warning of tide races and other disturbances. You should not ignore unexplained targets ahead because these may well turn out to be disturbed water of some sort, and this early warning can be vital to negotiating the waves safely.

The latest modern daylight-viewing radars are excellent for both day and night use and eliminate the need to peer into a hood, doing which can be awkward and can cause seasickness, particularly on a fast boat. Although having the appearance of being a delicate instrument, modern small-boat radars are fairly robust and seem to stand up to the punishment of pounding at sea, although I

Piecemeal installation of electronics on a fast cruiser. It would be much better if the dashboard design allowed for integrated installation. (Photo: *Author*)

did find that the scanner itself did not stand up to solid green water when a boat I was driving was overtaken by a particularly vicious breaking wave.

I have already mentioned that modern electronic equipment is fairly robust and seems to survive well in the hostile environment of fast boats and rough seas, but if it is possible, when mounting the equipment, to position it so that the printed circuit boards inside are vertical rather than horizontal they will have a better chance of survival. Flexible mounting of the units should be avoided as these mounts tend to damp out only a portion of the range of vibration frequencies which exist on a boat at sea, whereas the vibration on a powerful boat can cover a wide range of frequencies. These flexible mounts sometimes make the situation worse and, indeed, can make the screens almost unreadable due to the induced vibration. Vibration tends to be the enemy of electronic equipment and in my experience it is mechanical rather than electronic failures which occur as a result. On our Atlantic crossings, the electronics were made more rugged by securely locking all the nuts, bolts and screws inside the equipment so that nothing could come loose; after this precaution everything survived pretty well.

When you are selecting electronic equipment for the high-speed or rough-sea environment, try to choose models which have simple controls and operating procedures. You won't want to get the handbook out to refresh your memory at sea since many items of equipment, particularly position-finding systems, have complex controls which are unnecessary and produce redundant information. All you are really interested in here is position, course and distance to the next waypoint, and cross-track error; these should all be single function buttons when the equipment has been programmed and set up. In my opinion most current electronic equipment is very poor in design, as far as practical usage is concerned, and there is little logic in the controls and the way they operate.

Echo sounders
Whilst on the subject of electronics we mustn't forget the all-important echo sounder, which has a vital role to play in difficult conditions because it gives an

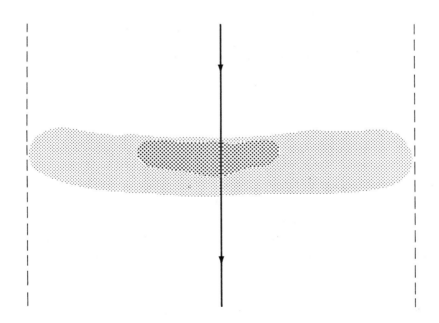

Shoals detected on the echo sounder can be a useful check on position.

independent check on your navigation. It is not always easy to get an echo sounder to work in rough conditions because of the aeration under the hull, and at high speeds they seem to be very reluctant to give good readings. However, you should be able to get an echo sounder to work up to about 30 knots, provided the transducer is placed in the optimum position on the hull. The readings you obtain will be particularly valuable when making a landfall in poor visibility. The depth of water shown on the sounder, when related to the chart, can give a continual check on your position, which is particularly valuable when nearing the coast.

FOG NAVIGATION

In fog there are a whole new set of navigation problems to overcome. One course of action is to place a great deal of faith in your dead-reckoning navigation until the object you are looking for looms out of the fog. Here the echo sounder can provide some reassurance that all is well. The alternative, if you have electronics, is to place almost total reliance on them. But in either case you are stretching your faith to a large degree and you will not have the normal back-up which is available in clear-weather navigation. Added to this problem is the risk of

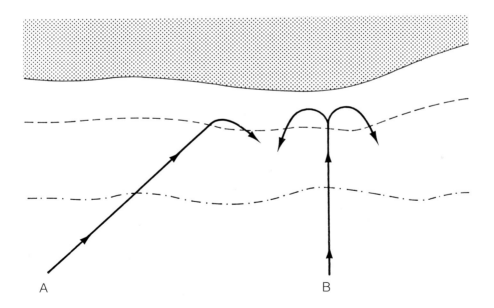

When making a landfall in poor visibility it is better to approach at the angle shown in A. Approaching directly, as in B, means having to turn through a greater angle if sudden shoaling is detected and you are unsure which is the safest way to turn.

collision with other vessels as you wander around in the fog. Navigation in fog at high speed is only something to be undertaken if you are extremely well prepared and experienced.

The dead-reckoning navigation techniques used in fog are very similar to those which will be used in any other situation, except that on a fast boat they have to be done mentally rather than by plotting on the chart because of the difficulty of doing the chartwork. Once again, preparation will stand you in good stead, but when you are making a landfall make sure that you aim for a good, clear stretch of coastline where you will always pick up an identifiable feature as you approach, even if you are off course in either direction. When making the actual landfall the echo sounder is vital to give you warning of shoaling water. Here it is better to approach the coast at a tangent rather than at right angles, because if something looms up in front you will know immediately which way to turn to avoid the problem. You will also have a small angle to turn through to head out to sea again. If you approach at right angles you face the dilemma of not knowing which is the best way to turn; you need to turn a full 180 degrees to get onto a reciprocal course.

Radar is the premier instrument for use in fog and it also has the benefit of being able to be used both for navigation and for collision avoidance. Navigation techniques are similar to those that you would use in fine weather, although you will perhaps be more cautious because in fog you are relying almost totally on the radar. As far as collision avoidance is concerned, if there is other shipping around, then it is common sense to travel at a slow speed – certainly at a speed which allows you to stop in at least half the range of visibility. If you can travel fast, then to a certain extent you have an advantage because your speed will usually be considerably greater than that of other vessels. To a large degree you can steer round them if you treat them as almost stationary objects. However, it does require experience to assess the situation and a more cautionary approach would be to slow down as you approach radar targets and navigate carefully, altering course only when you have a visual sighting. You have to be particularly careful here with other small boats which may not show up clearly or which may only show up at short range on the radar. You must never assume that the water ahead is clear just because nothing shows up on the radar.

A useful tactic to employ in poor visibility is to keep out of shipping lanes, which means keeping inside the direct line between headlands if you are coasting, and keeping just outside buoyed channels where the buoys mark deep water for shipping. There is usually sufficient water outside the buoys for small craft to avoid having to mix with the big boys. This tactic will reduce the chance of collision with shipping but you still have to watch out for other small craft. In general, in fog, your approach should be cautious rather than adventurous.

TACTICS

Apart from just knowing where you are and where you are going, as a navigator you also have to consider tactics for any particular situation. In rough weather, for instance, you should assess the merits of various places you could go for shelter, or the harbours that are available in order to escape from rough seas. In navigation at high speed, the shortest distance between two points is not always the fastest. A form of tacking, similar to that used by sail boats going into the wind, can often allow you to make faster progress, which will compensate for the greater distance covered. Similarly, you can often find more sheltered water by tucking in behind a headland or going into a bay, so that you get a more comfortable and faster ride over a longer part of the voyage. As in offshore racing there are a number of similar tactics that you can employ to enable you to go faster, but you will only be able to use them if you have done all the preparation beforehand and have all the options in mind. This means that when you are doing your planning and preparation for the race or for rough conditions, you will visualise as you look at the chart what the effect would be on sea conditions with the wind coming from different directions. You can plot a series of alternative courses which would take best advantage of any particular situation. Even sandbanks can offer shelter from an offshore wind and it can be beneficial to pass inside them.

I remember a Round Britain powerboat race when there was a strong wind just on the port bow during the long exposed leg from Land's End to Fishguard. By altering course about 20 degrees to starboard the ride on the boat was a lot easier, and we were able to make better speed because the wave length was effectively increased. There was the added advantage that as we approached land we reached sheltered water more quickly that we would have on the more direct route. We were then able to make very good time for the last 40 miles which enabled us to lead the fleet into Fishguard.

You should be constantly alert to possibilities like this which can be used equally well whether you are cruising or racing. The whole idea is to give the boat, its machinery, and crew a comfortable ride and in doing so you will also give yourself a better ride and be much more able to assess the conditions and take advantage of opportunities that occur.

In rough seas, this type of assessment is especially important because, as a general rule, you will be trying to get out of bad conditions as fast as you can. Whilst the boat may have a better ride by running downwind and you may be able to make better progress, bear in mind that harbours downwind are likely to be exposed to the full force of the seas and the entrance to these harbours might be difficult or even impossible to enter. Heading up to windward may be uncomfortable in the first instance, but if you are approaching land in this direction, the sea conditions will steadily improve as the fetch of the waves reduces, so that a rough passage to start with will be compensated by smoother waters later. Part of your planning and preparation, if you are going out in stormy seas or if you are caught out, should include an assessment of all the ports and harbours which are available to you, what their tidal conditions will be when you get to them, and the type of sea conditions you can expect at the entrance, so that you can make a worth-while judgement of the various options which are open to you. Skill and experience will come into this assessment because there are no hard and fast rules which you have to follow; you must judge each case on its merits.

Preparation, as we have seen, is the secret of success for navigation both at high speeds and in rough weather. Once you are out there you are fairly limited as to what you can do because of the motion of the boat. Even if you stop to work things out you will certainly not have the best conditions in which to make an objective assessment. This means that most of the navigation has to be carried out before departure in order to reduce, as far as possible, the workload when you are at sea. Preparation should cover a wide variety of possible eventualities so that as the navigator you will not be caught out.

Electronics offer the possibility of much more precise navigation at high speeds, but at the current state of development they do not entirely meet the requirements. However, electronics are improving almost daily, and it is anticipated that within the next few years specialised equipment for high-speed work will be available so that the navigator will be almost entirely dependent on electronics, whether he is travelling at high speed or in rough seas.

9 Engines and Propulsion

The engines and propulsion systems are everything to a fast boat, and are equally important in rough seas because you certainly need reliability. Anyone who has been at sea in a powerboat when the engines have failed will remember only too vividly the awful silence that follows such a failure. Careful installation and careful maintenance are important for any boat operating close to the limits at sea because the stresses and strains are very high.

PETROL OR DIESEL?

Before we go into details of installation and the standards necessary for reliability, let's first consider the engines themselves. The choice will lie between petrol and diesel engines and, whilst both will give adequate performance, the type of engine will have an effect on the handling. Petrol engines are generally used when high performance is required. The good power/weight ratio of petrol engines helps generate good performance in high-speed craft, but just as important is a quick response to the throttle. This fast reaction is needed when driving a boat fast in waves. In the chapter on handling you will have seen how the throttles are important in controlling the vessel in such conditions, and the fast response of petrol engines enables you to respond quickly to the changing pattern of waves.

Apart from the added weight found with diesel engines, there is also a slower response to the throttle because of the extra mass of moving parts in the engine. However, modern lightweight diesels are coming close to petrol-engine performance in some highly tuned versions, and the gap between the two types of engine is narrowing, although it still has some way to go.

In rough seas a diesel engine is generally to be preferred because it is not vulnerable to damp or water penetration in the same way that the ignition system of a petrol engine can be. As sea there is something very reassuring about the steady beat of a diesel engine, and the fact that diesels are used almost invariably for lifeboat work is an indication that they are well suited to the rough sea role.

However, in terms of reliability, there is little to choose between the two engine types. In recent years ignition systems on petrol engines have been greatly improved to stand up to the rigours of fast boats and, in general, you can expect a reliable performance from both types of engine.

ANCILLARY SYSTEMS

Where engines do become vulnerable is in the ancillary systems such as fuel, electrics, cooling and exhaust. Unlike engines which are produced in large quantities, thoroughly tested and carefully designed, these ancillary systems tend to be installed on something of a one-off basis, therefore they have not been through the same intensive testing and evaluation. On production boats these systems will have been reasonably well tried, but even so, on many modern craft the standard of installation still leaves something to be desired when the corrosive marine atmosphere and the motion of the vessel put them to the test. The type of installation standards we are talking about cost money. Boatbuilders often tread a delicate path between reducing costs and maintaining an adequate level of reliability. They, or you, may not be able to afford racing or lifeboat standards, but as long as you are aware of quality and standards you can at least watch for any deterioration in this area.

ENGINE BEDS

Boat engines can be subjected to high stresses, particularly in fast boats which may leave the water and re-enter heavily. The resulting forces can exceed 10G momentarily, putting a heavy strain on the engine bearers. Whilst flexible engine mounts are fitted on most pleasure boats to reduce noise and vibration, these are not found on racing boats or lifeboats. If you plan to drive your craft hard, then flexible mounts are not a good idea, but most boats have them fitted for comfort. If you have flexible mounts on the engine, then all the connections to the engine also have to be flexible and this includes fuel lines, electrical systems, the cooling system, the exhaust and the propeller shaft. Even with a rigidly mounted engine it is a good idea to have flexible connections in many of these fittings, as the additional movement found in flexibly mounted engines does put all these connecting links under some degree of stress, and this is often where a failure can occur.

FUEL SYSTEMS

As far as fuel systems are concerned, the main object here is to supply clean fuel to the engine. The fuel tanks should be strongly constructed with adequate baffles to prevent the fuel surging. One of the biggest problems with fuel tanks is securing them adequately. They can represent quite a large weight in the boat, and high stresses due to the movement of the vessel can put considerable strain on the mounting points. Filler pipes for the tank should be mounted outside the boat on deck so that any spillage during re-fuelling doesn't enter the craft. The breather pipe for the tank should be of adequate size to allow rapid filling, but should also be rigged so that water cannot be forced back down the pipe. Breather-pipe outlets are often fitted on the side of the boat and they are best positioned along the edge of the deckhouse or in a similar position where they are less likely to come in contact with water.

Water will often find its way into the tank through condensation; you can avoid this by keeping the tank full. A small sump in the bottom of the tank will allow any water build-up to be drained off, although in most boats access to the bottom of the tank is virtually impossible. This is why a water trap is fitted in the fuel line to the engine so that any water will be filtered out here. Dirt also has to be removed, and it is surprising how much collects in fuel. The water trap usually incorporates a filter, so that from this point on only clean fuel finds its way to the engine.

On a twin-engine boat each engine should be supplied from a separate tank, with a crossover line controlled by valves so that either engine can be operated from either tank. This makes the system more complex but it does mean that if you have contaminated fuel in one tank you can still keep the engines running. Fuel lines are normally made from copper piping, and are well secured and protected from sharp edges. Where flexible sections have to be incorporated, such as in the link to the engine, the fuel line here should be of the wire braid protected type. The whole system must be engineered to the highest standards if you are to avoid problems at critical moments. Incorporated into the system should be a shut-off valve close to the outlet from each tank, so that if you do have a fire in the engine compartment you can prevent the fuel from reaching it. These valves should be readily accessible from the deck level and not tucked away in the bilges where you can't get at them in a hurry.

The fuel represents one of the largest changing weights in the boat. If there is more than one tank placed fore and aft then the fuel can be used as a means of trimming the boat by drawing from one tank or the other, as appropriate. Normally the tanks are located around the centre of gravity, so there is little change of trim as the fuel is used up, but in a vessel which carries a heavy weight of fuel, use of the fuel for trimming the boat could be advantageous.

Although fuel tanks are normally constructed from metal, an innovation as far as lightweight tanks are concerned is the use of a foam core surrounded by a rubber skin, which in turn is mounted in a box constructed from lightweight materials. These type of tanks were used on the two *Virgin Atlantic Challengers* and worked very successfully and certainly seemed to stand up to very heavy punishment. Another possibility is the use of flexible tanks, but it is not always easy to secure these adequately and they are not particularly suitable for fast or rough-sea boats.

THE ELECTRICAL SYSTEM

Electricity and water should never mix; if they do it is the water which always wins. This means that with any electrical system the first priority has to be to keep the water out. There should be no cost-cutting in the electrical system because on a high-speed craft, or when you are in rough seas, the whole atmosphere in the boat becomes damp and any weaknesses will quickly appear. Any wiring or electrical fittings which might come into contact with water in any way should be fully waterproof; there really is little area for compromise here. The wiring system needs to be very carefully engineered to prevent any movement of the wires which could eventually lead to breakage. This applies particularly to the heavy battery cables, as a failure here is not covered by fuses. The heavy current involved could cause sparking which, in turn, could rapidly cause a fire. On a

Engine systems need to be of the highest quality to cope with high speeds and rough seas. (Photo: Author)

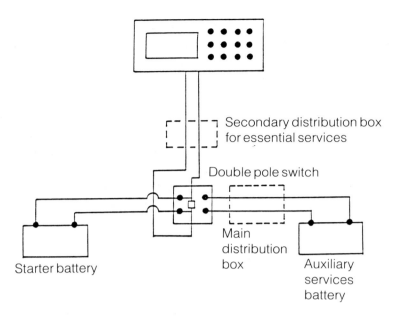

How to rig an alternative power supply from the starter battery for electronic position finding equipment. The double pole switch allows the alternative battery to supply the essential services.

petrol-engine boat, a failure in the wiring could stop the engine, and whilst you might be immune from this problem on a diesel-engine boat, this doesn't remove the fire-risk danger.

Batteries are the heart of any electrical system and their location and securing are of vital importance. Heavy-duty batteries are normally used on boats and because they represent a considerable weight they must be securely clamped down. Any movement of the battery could soon lead to an electrical failure in rough weather, so the securing system must be very positive; ropes and elastic straps are not adequate.

The electrical system on modern craft can be fairly complex, so the system is divided into various circuits which are protected by fuses. Some of the electrical circuits are vital to the operation of the boat, such as the supply to the navigation lights and possibly the navigation equipment and radar. One possibility here is to have an alternative supply for these items supplied from a separate battery with a changeover switch conveniently located to bring in the supplementary circuit to maintain these vital services.

As well as the fuses in the system many items of equipment, particularly electronic equipment, have their own internal fuses. If an internal fuse blows it can often mean a major dismantling job just to get at it and, whilst there is not much you can do directly about this, a secondary fuse of a slightly lower value could be placed outside the equipment and would probably blow first, and would be much easier to replace. Although fuses are still widely used, circuit breakers are a much more convenient way of protecting circuits on board, and modern types are very reliable and positive.

The dashboard is an area where there is considerable wiring congestion, and on open boats this must be protected from water which could find its way down behind the instruments and into the wiring. It is not unusual to find an ignition-circuit fuse located somewhere at the back of these wiring panels, and it is sensible to have easy access to the back of the dashboard panel so that you can solve any problems in the electrical spaghetti located behind it.

On twin-engine boats the electrical circuits should be kept separate as far as possible so that you have an alternative available. A paralleling switch which links the two batteries can help with starting when batteries are low. It pays to have some understanding of the electrical circuit in the boat and what options are open to you if things go wrong, because trying to sort out electrical circuits when a failure occurs in rough seas is something of a nightmare unless you have spent some time thinking it through beforehand.

COOLING SYSTEMS

The cooling system for the engine is another area where people often seem to take chances, little realising that the sea-water section of the system is just as vital to the security of the boat as the hull itself. With this system being open to the sea, any failure will allow sea water to enter the hull, with fairly dramatic consequences. The weak point in the cooling system is always the flexible hoses which tend to deteriorate with time, and you must remember than on a fast boat the pressure in the sea-water system can be quite high when the craft re-enters the water. All flexible pipes should be secured with double stainless-steel clips, and it is a good idea to make it an annual routine to replace all flexible pipes and check out the rigid pipes at the same time. Seacocks and filters are incorporated into the system, but seacocks are often placed where they are almost inaccessible and would be the first part of the system to be under water if there were a leak. Because of this, they are often ignored, and so tend to seize up. It is a wise boat-owner who checks out the seacocks at regular intervals because lives could depend on them.

EXHAUST SYSTEMS

The exhaust system also tends to be part of the cooling system because most modern exhaust systems are either water cooled or water injected. Water cooling tends to be restricted to racing boats where the exhaust pipe has a double wall through which water circulates and is then ejected at the stern. The more commonly used system is water injection whereby water is injected into the rear end of the exhaust manifold, where it turns downwards before it connects into a flexible rubber hose running to the transom. This water injection serves the dual purpose of cooling the exhaust gases, so that they don't attack the rubber exhaust pipe, and reducing noise.

With such a system any failure in the cooling water will mean that the exhaust system loses its water injection, and in a very short space of time the exhaust gases will set fire to the rubber, which in turn will burn through and you will have a fire on your hands. This sort of thing is likely to happen quicker than the consequent rise in the temperature of the engine cooling-water circuits, and the first warning you may have is smoke coming out of the engine compartment. Few people realise the vital role of cooling water in the exhaust system. In my opinion a flow indicator in the cooling-water circuits should be a vital part of the system. When connected to an alarm it will give immediate warning that the cooling-water flow has broken down. Apart from this, the only safe answer is to check everything at frequent intervals and replace any suspect items.

INSTALLATION

As far as the general installation is concerned, there should be adequate space in the engine compartment to allow for maintenance, otherwise it might not be carried out. If you have problems at sea you also want to have reasonably easy access, therefore the engine hatches should be designed so that they can not only give access to the engine compartment, but also offer some protection from flying spray or even waves. This means that sideways opening hatches are probably the best bet, but the general trend now is to have a hatch at the rear end so that it opens to give access from the cockpit. If you have any influence on the design of your boat, then bear in mind the possible need to have access to the engines at sea and try to position the hatches accordingly. Another feature which might be valuable is to incorporate a window into the engine hatch so that you can see inside without having to open the hatches. However, the chances are that you will never be looking when things go wrong, so a properly engineered alarm system is the best protection you can hope for.

OUTBOARDS

With outboard motors the whole machinery package is carefully contained in a single unit which is thoroughly tested, and modern outboards have a good reliability record. However, the fuel and electrical systems are still carried outside the engine and have to be engineered to the same high standards. If portable outboard fuel tanks are carried they have to be very carefully secured, preferably on an absorbent mounting, to help withstand the pounding shock, and they must also be well secured against any movement. The battery and electrical system must be engineered to the same high standards as found in other engine installations. Of particular concern are the mounting bolts which secure the outboard to the transom; these should be checked at intervals for tightness because they are subject to very high stresses, particularly with powerful outboards, and only the special high-tensile bolts should be used for this purpose.

PROPULSION SYSTEMS

Now we come to the complex subject of propulsion systems. As far as displacement boats are concerned, the conventional propeller shaft system is still widely used. The propeller is the most critical part of the whole engine/propulsion package, because this is where the power of the engine is transmitted to the water and any inefficiency in this area will show up in the performance of the boat. Being a thoroughly tried and tested system, it is generally very reliable, although the stern gland will need inspection as will the bearings in the P or A brackets when the boat is out of water. Most of the latter type of bearings are water lubricated and depend on getting a good flow of water to keep them running, so it is important to check that the water inlets for the bearing are always clear and not blocked with barnacles.

We have already seen that the only way you can control this type of propulsion system is by increasing or decreasing the speed of the propeller which limits the trim options on a fast boat. The trend in powerboat design is to move away from this system which is primarily for displacement boats. However, it is still used on some planing boats, and here the line of thrust from the angled propeller shaft has to be balanced in the hull design. Conventional shaft arrangements lack the possibility of propeller angle control found on other systems, and there is the other disadvantage of not being able to get to the propellers easily if a rope becomes entangled with them.

Stern drives

The most popular type of propulsion system today is probably the stern drive which is widely used on production and racing boats. With the drive taken through two right-angles it is a complex system, but one of the major benefits is the easy installation of these systems on production boats. From the efficiency point of view the stern drive also scores because the shaft line is parallel to the bottom of the boat.

Twin installations are normal, and lately we have seen triple installations on production boats. Indeed, some racing craft are fitting quadruple stern drives. These multi-engine systems, whether they are stern drives or outboards, are a handful as far as the controls are concerned, and they need careful engineering if all the throttles are to be usable with one hand and if the trim controls are to be usable at high speed. Power trim is almost universally available on stern drives and large outboards for fast boats, with the power trim changing to power tilt beyond a certain angle. This gives you the benefit of being able to bring the leg clear of the water to change a propeller at sea, or more likely to clear ropes or other debris fouling the propeller.

Surface-piercing propellers

Some stern drives used in racing are designed to run with surface-piercing propellers. Before we look at any of the alternative drive systems now available on the market, it is worth looking at these surface-piercing propellers which are the basis of most of these new drive systems. The theory behind the surface-piercing propeller is that, with a conventional drive, perhaps a stern drive or even a straight propeller shaft system, the top blades of the propeller are not performing much useful work, because they run in the turbulent slipstream from the propeller support brackets and the shaft or, in the case of stern drives, the stern-drive leg itself. This means that it is the bottom blades which really push the boat along. The designers of the first surface-piercing propeller systems reasoned that since this was the case, why not take the top blades out of the water completely and have just the bottom blades in the water? This would create a more efficient propeller drive by removing all the appendage drag caused by shafts and drive legs which upset the water flow to the top half of the propeller.

With the first type of system employing this surface-piercing idea the propeller shaft emerged from the hull at the bottom of the transom, with the propeller attached directly to the end of it. This was contained in a step built into the transom of the hull, so that the top of this step reduced the large amount of spray being thrown away by the top blades of the propellers that were out of the water. One disadvantage of this fixed-drive system was that there was no trim adjustment, although it still forms the basis of some of the more sophisticated drive systems which are now appearing on the market.

Sonny Levi was one of the early developers of surface-drive systems of this type. He has now carried the concept forward into the Levi drive, which has a fixed drive and propeller but is contained in a bolt-on unit which also provides a mounting for the rudder and the engine exhaust. In the Levi drive, the engine exhaust comes out immediately in front of the top blades of the propeller which helps the water to break away from these blades. This allows the engine to turn more quickly, developing more power and getting the boat onto the plane more quickly. The rudder is semi-circular, fitting around the propeller so that it gives a very good steering effect at low speeds, but only the tip of one arm of the semi-circle is in the water at high speeds, thus minimising the drag. The Lancing drive and one or two special drive systems developed for racing boats also use similar fixed-shaft arrangements, which means that the propeller height has to be worked out carefully at the design stage because there is no means of adjusting it once the drive unit is bolted on.

These types of drive systems have the benefit of simplicity and easy installation, but the lack of adjustment can cause problems. A step towards resolving this problem was introduced in the Buzzi drive which incorporates a limited angle universal joint at the transom. The shaft angle can be adjusted from this point onwards but only when the boat is out of the water, with the angle being adjusted by inserting spacers between the shaft-supporting brackets and the outrigger which supports the whole drive system. This allows the shaft angle and propeller height to be adjusted to its optimum during trials, but after that it is locked in place; this is a good compromise for many applications. Certainly, this system has been used very successfully in offshore racing.

From this point on we go into more complex drives which incorporate hydraulic power-trim systems, so that the shaft angle can be adjusted when the boat is underway, rather like the power trim on a stern-drive leg. The foremost drive system using this method is the Arneson drive, but a somewhat similar system is the Kaama drive. The difference between the two systems is largely a matter of where transfer gears are incorporated into the system in order to drop the drive line down from the engine shaft to the propeller shaft so as to keep the latter as low as possible on the hull. In the Kaama drive these gears are incorporated in the drive itself, whereas in the Arneson they are incorporated in a transom-mounted gearbox. With both these drives operating with surface-piercing propellers it is possible to raise the drive when coming onto the plane to allow the engine to develop full power, and then slowly immerse the drive as the boat is on the plane. At low speed the propeller can be fully immersed to give good manoeuvrability and it can be raised for shallow-water operation.

Another advantage with these drive systems is that because the propeller shaft is on a universal joint which allows power-trim adjustment, the same universal joint can be used to give a steering effect by swinging the propeller shaft from side to side under the influence of hydraulic rams. This means that many of the benefits of a stern drive are available and the same drive unit incorporates both power trim and steering.

Contrarotating propellers have been tried for some racing boats, but the first production application of contrarotating propellers is in the Volvo Duo-Prop stern drive. Such a system requires more extensive gearing and double shafts, but the contrarotating propellers do give higher efficiency and are particularly

Technodrive contrarotating surface drives – probably the most complex system on the market today. Note the engine cooling water pick-up at the bottom of the rudder. (Photo: Author)

suitable for translating the power of a diesel engine to high-speed boat performance. Volvo claim something like a 10 per cent increase in efficiency, both in top speed and in thrust, from this propulsion system.

Another drive manufacturer using contrarotating propellers is Technodrive, who produce what must be the most complex drive system for a powerboat yet developed. Not only does this drive unit incorporate power trim and power steering, but the contrarotating propellers operate in the surface-piercing mode and the drive unit also incorporates the reduction gears, the engine exhaust, the rudder and the water pick-up for engine cooling. The latter is mounted at the bottom of the rear-mounted rudder, the last point of the boat to leave the water if it flies, the theory being that cooling-water flow is maintained to the engine until the last possible moment. These drive units have yet to prove their capability in high-performance boats, and whilst they may be correct in theory the mechanical complexity hanging on the stern of the vessel will not appeal to everyone.

Many of these drive systems place the propeller 3 or 4 feet (about 1 metre) behind the transom of the boat, which effectively increases the overall length of the boat. Outboards are being placed on frames which move the engine further aft to give the same effect. In any fixed system like this, it is not always easy to get the propeller height exactly right first time and some form of adjustment is a desirable feature because the boat will be operating over such a large speed range. This adjustment gives the flexibility and control needed to try to optimise the drive for the particular conditions. Whilst with stern-drive units the power trim tends to alter the angle of thrust from the propeller rather than actually raise or lower the propeller, outboards can now be fitted with a hydraulic jacking system which physically raises and lowers the whole outboard, thus allowing the propeller height to be adjusted when underway.

Propeller height is increasingly critical for top speeds. Whereas for cruising boats it is usually recommended that the cavitation plate of the outboard or, for that matter, the stern-drive unit, is placed on a level with the adjacent point of the transom, for high-performance applications the cavitation plate could be raised to 4 inches (10 centimetres) above the bottom of the transom, which virtually means that the propeller is operating in the surface-piercing mode. The problem here is that the propeller may have very little bite on the water at slow speeds. There can also be difficulty in getting the boat onto the plane, particularly when it is heavily loaded with fuel, so the hydraulic jacking system available for outboards does have some merit, particularly for boats which may be required to operate efficiently at both high and low speeds. As speeds rise above the 50- or 60-knot mark, the drive system has to be more and more optimised to produce the ultimate in top speed. This can often be achieved at the expense of low-speed performance, which can make such high-performance boats less attractive for pleasure use, but providing sufficient power is available it is possible to make these craft quite attractive.

One question which has caused some concern with propulsion systems which incorporate both steering and power trim is: what happens when the boat leaves the water and then re-enters with the steering off-centre? With speeds up to about 70 knots this was not found to be particularly critical, but once speeds rise above this point, then unpleasant things can start to happen. The first part of the boat to touch the water when it re-enters will, in most cases, be the propeller, and as this is usually still under power at this point it will generate a thrust when it hits the water. If this thrust is off the centre line of the boat, then it will introduce a turning moment to the hull from which there is no directional stability of the hull to react against. When the hull itself hits the water microseconds later, this thrust is already in action and tends to generate a violent turning moment on the hull. The result is that the boat spins out with often disastrous consequences.

Although steerable drive units are used a great deal on very high-performance racing boats, the mechanics of spinning out in this way do not appear to be clearly recognised, even though most of the boats which have suffered this type of accident have been those with steerable drive units. Certainly in one case the Arneson drives have been modified to remove the steering element from the drive in order to provide what is thought to be a safer system for very high-speed operation. My feeling is that as more experience is gained then there will be a general return to rudder steering, such as that found on most of the fixed drive systems.

Another problem at very high speeds is the consequences of losing power in one of the drive units, or even having a damaged propeller through striking debris. On a monohull, where the drive units are placed close together, the consequences of this will not be too serious but on a catamaran, where the drives are wide apart, loss of one drive unit could be a similar cause for the boat to spin out.

As speeds in racing continue to rise, so this problem of transmitting the power to the water will continue to tax designers. The fact that there are so many alternative systems demonstrates the lack of consensus of ideas, but there are very definite moves towards using drive systems which do not incorporate steering into the propeller shaft and I think this is a trend which will continue. Equally, the need to have power trim for the drive system is becoming more and more important as the drives need to be optimised for very high speeds, but also have to be suitable for getting the boat up onto the plane. This is a complex area of development, particularly when some of these modern drive systems are being asked to transmit close to 1000 h.p. Indeed, the Arneson drive is probably the only unit of its type which is capable of transmitting power outputs up to 5000 h.p.

Water jets
The idea of water-jet propulsion is appealing, but since the passage of water through the jet increases the friction resistance, these drives have yet to match propeller efficiency. However, the gap is closing and one advantage of the water jet is that the thrust acts horizontally and close to a line through the centre of gravity of the boat so there is no turning moment to affect the trim. There is concern about the loss of propulsion in rough seas when the intake comes out of the water, but I have not found this a problem.

Even in rough-water work the drive flexibility offered by some of these modern drive systems can be useful because it enables you to keep what is essentially a very high-speed propeller immersed in the water to give good acceleration at comparatively low speeds. This is another valid reason for having power trim on a drive which is designed for high speed because it makes the drive system much more usable at displacement speeds.

As far as propellers themselves are concerned, the use of surface-piercing drives has led to the development of some complex propeller designs. Whereas the norm for fast craft a few years ago would have been a 3-bladed propeller, the trend

A cruising propeller (top) and a cleaver propeller (bottom).

now is towards 4- or even 5-bladed propellers. Some larger boats have even used 6-bladed propellers for very high speeds, but remember that in the surface-piercing mode only half of these blades are doing work. With an even number of blades there is a risk of vibration as the blades enter and leave the water at the same time, and a good compromise in this high-speed performance area is the 5-bladed propeller which gives a much smoother drive. The propellers themselves have to be very strong for surface-piercing work because each blade is alternately transmitting high power and then transmitting nothing, possibly several thousand times a minute.

The cleaver-type propeller is generally favoured for high-speed work, the name cleaver being derived from its sharp leading edge and blunt, virtually square, trailing edge. High-speed propellers are now invariably cupped at the trailing edge to increase the speed of the water flow as it leaves the propeller blade and runs aft. The design for these very high speeds is still very much a matter of judgement or perhaps even guesswork, as it is very difficult to analyse the water flow of propellers turning at these speeds.

10 Equipment and fittings

A powerboat is more than just a hull and engines. There are many fittings and pieces of equipment which transform a boat into an efficient machine and enable it to operate safely. Many of these items of equipment are required (from a safety point of view) to help you when things go wrong. Others help you to operate the boat more efficiently so that you derive more pleasure from being at sea.

SAFETY EQUIPMENT

When operating at high speed or in rough seas your safety margins are reduced and you need to pay careful attention to safety equipment. The chances of having to use the equipment are greater and not only do you need to consider what equipment you should carry on board, but you also need to give some thought as to how it might be used in different types of emergencies.

DISTRESS SIGNALS – RADIO

There are a number of internationally recognised distress signals, such as flying code flags and hoisting shapes, but nowadays there are two main methods of attracting attention if you are in trouble. One is by firing distress flares and the other is to use the radio. Without doubt, the radio is the most efficient way of attracting attention because not only can you indicate that you are in trouble, but you can also give your position and you can indicate what the trouble is so that the appropriate help can be sent. If you have an injured man on board, then it might be appropriate to have a helicopter to lift the man off, whereas if you are drifting ashore with engines stopped you probably need a tow, although the situation could equally demand a helicopter to take you off and leave the boat to its own devices.

Both VHF radio and MF are suitable for sending distress messages. On VHF radio Channel 16 and on MF 2182 Khz are monitored by shore stations and coastguards. Most radios have a single switch system to put them on to the distress frequency. Because of its emergency role, it is sensible to take a great deal of care when installing the radio so that hopefully even in conditions of near disaster, it will continue to work. There are two vulnerable areas with radios, one is getting water over the electronics unit and the other is the antenna becoming damaged. Protecting the radio from water is a good idea, but even better is installing a waterproof set; these are now available in VHF form, but not yet in MF form. It is certainly preferable to mount the radio below decks, although with some modern radios the control panel is waterproof and can be mounted in the cockpit. As far as the antenna is concerned it is possible to carry an emergency back-up antenna which can be rigged if the main one becomes damaged; this is probably the best way of ensuring reliability.

A good back-up for the VHF radio is a portable set and these are available in waterproof form; thus you can take the radio with you if you do have to abandon ship. An alternative means of summoning help is the EPIRB (Emergency Position Indicating Radio Beacon), which is a small portable waterproof unit operating on aircraft distress frequencies. When switched on these transmit a distress signal, which can be picked up and on which rescue helicopters can home in. The latest types of EPIRB also transmit on frequencies which can be picked up by orbiting satellites, thus increasing the chances of the signal being received on shore. Some also transmit a vessel identification signal. Whilst EPIRBs are a useful back-up, a VHF radio is better if your boating keeps you close to the coastline.

DISTRESS SIGNALS – FLARES

Distress flares are an effective means of summoning help, but are only suitable if the help is within visual range. By far and away the best type of flare is the parachute rocket which rises to a height of over 1000 feet (307 metres) and then descends under a parachute, so that there is a much better chance of its being seen. You need to carry about six of these flares so that you can fire off a couple at the onset of an emergency, while keeping the others to indicate your position if you see any passing vessels or if you drift close to the coast. Firing them all at one go is a panic reaction to an emergency situation, and leaves you with nothing left if this first signal is not seen. The trouble with flares is that there is rarely any method of acknowledging that they have been seen, so you just have to sit it out and pray that someone somewhere has seen your distress signal.

Alternative types of flare are: the hand flare which is ignited and simply held over the side of the boat, and the smoke flare which is ignited and either hand held or thrown into the sea where it belches out clouds of thick orange smoke. Both are only effective at short range, and so the parachute flare is a much better bet even in daylight. With smoke flares, the orange smoke disperses very quickly with the wind. If you use either smoke or hand flares, always make sure you hold or fire them to leeward because they can spew out hot sparks which could set light to something on the boat and compound your problem.

Carrying flares is one thing, but learning how to use them is another. Many yacht clubs or coast guard stations organise demonstrations on how to use flares. You certainly can't afford to be trying to read the instructions on the side of the flare on a dark night when you are in a dire situation. Flares should be stowed in the wheelhouse where they are ready to hand for immediate use. Indeed, there is a lot to be said for having a 'grab bag', with items such as flares, portable radio, food and drink and perhaps some warm clothing, so that if you have to abandon ship in a hurry then you can take these items with you in one grab.

LIFERAFTS

Abandoning ship should be considered as a last resort. There are many cases on record where a crew has been lost after abandoning ship whilst the boat itself has survived. So stay with your boat while it still floats, except of course in the case of fire which can force you to abandon ship very rapidly. Exactly when to take to the liferaft is a difficult decision to make, particularly if the boat is drifting towards an inhospitable shore. In this case, abandoning the boat should only be considered after the anchor has been used to try to stem the drift. In this situation the liferaft would offer the advantage of being washed inshore, but you still have to negotiate the surf or rocks on the shoreline. In these desperate situations you can only make what you consider the best decision at the time and there is little in the way of rules to guide you.

Perhaps the best yardstick by which to judge your actions in this type of abandon-ship situation is to do anything which will buy you time. The more time you can spend on board your boat preventing it from drifting inshore or from getting into more serious trouble, then the more chance there is of someone observing your plight and coming to your rescue. Try to avoid taking hasty action in the panic of the moment and, if you possibly can, try to think things out carefully and rationally.

So the liferaft is very much the last resort. Even so, it is better than nothing and it should be stowed on board where it is readily available, particularly where it is well protected so that it won't get washed overboard or damaged just at the time when you might want it most. The liferaft painter should be firmly secured to a strong point; never rely on holding the painter in your hand, otherwise in the excitement of abandoning ship you could easily let go after the liferaft is inflated. A knife is fitted on the liferaft to cut the painter once you are all on board, but even when you are in this situation it sometimes pays to keep the painter attached, at least up until the last possible minute because this will help to stop your drift. I am always faintly amused by the instructions on the liferaft which say 'Pick the liferaft up and throw it overboard'. A six-man liferaft which would be carried on a normal motor cruiser is quite heavy, and trying to handle this on a boat tossing around at sea is quite a struggle, so bear in mind when deciding the stowage of the liferaft that it should be somewhere where you can easily release it and get it over the side.

In addition to the 'grab bag' you should try to put as much other equipment as possible into the liferaft, such as warm clothing, portable radios, flares, torch and anything else that might be useful. Whilst there are minimal stores inside the liferaft pack itself, anything extra that you can put inside could help survival.

The liferaft should be sent for inspection once a year. Few people are aware of just what is inside the liferaft container, so before sending it for its annual inspection it is a good idea to inflate it and see what it is like by climbing inside it. Check with the service agent before doing this because there may be an extra charge for servicing if the liferaft has been inflated, but at least you will have some idea what to expect if the time comes when you do have to abandon ship.

LIFEJACKETS

If there is a chance of you entering the water, either voluntarily or involuntarily, then a lifejacket should be worn. In some countries such as France it is mandatory to wear a lifejacket when you are at sea in a small boat, but in most countries the choice of wearing a lifejacket is up to the individual. Certainly if you have to go out and work on deck for any reason, or you get caught out in bad conditions, then a lifejacket should be a necessity. If you get to the stage where you might have to abandon ship, then all the crew should have their lifejackets on.

There are a number of different types of lifejacket ranging from the buoyancy aid, which is more like a waistcoat; the fully inflatable lifejacket; the partially inflatable lifejacket; a lifejacket with full inherent buoyancy; and finally, what I would term the racing lifejacket, which has full inherent buoyancy and a comprehensive harness system so that it stays in place even if you hit the water at high speed.

In fast boats, this latter type is the only one that is really suitable because all other types are liable to cause you some sort of injury if you hit the water at speed. The main problem is that they don't have a fully effective harness to keep the lifejacket in place, so it could end up by strangling you. The racing type of lifejacket not only offers you good protection if you should enter the water at high speed, but it also provides very effective padding if you lose your grip and get thrown around in the boat when it is moving at speed. The trouble is that lifejackets of this type are not particularly comfortable to wear for any length of time.

Perhaps the best compromise is the fully inflatable type of lifejacket which can be worn continuously, and which is least likely to damage you if you enter the water at speed. The problem with this type is that the wearer has to be conscious when he is in the water, so that he can inflate it either by oral inflation or by means of a built-in gas bottle. A good alternative is the buoyancy aid, particularly the waistcoat type. These offer protection against the movement of the boat, but their disadvantage is that they wil not float you face-upwards in the water and are not so effective in terms of support as is a full-blooded lifejacket. Whatever type of lifejacket you adopt – and to a degree it is one of personal choice – at least try the lifejacket in the water, so that once again you will have some idea what to expect when you are faced with an emergency.

Personal lifelines do not have much place aboard a motor boat, partly because at any speed over 8 knots the sudden jerk on the line, as you enter the water, can cause you injury. If you do go overboard from a power boat on the end of a lifeline, you could end up close to the propeller, which is not a particularly happy experience; you are much better drifting away from the boat. Lifelines are best for sailing boats where there might be some difficulty in manoeuvring the boat back to a person in the water; this problem doesn't really exist on a powerboat if one of the crew goes overboard. Much more important is to have a lifebuoy (with a light) which can be released very quickly if somebody goes overboard to give that person something to hold on to and to help indicate their position.

FIRE EXTINGUISHERS

The engine compartment on a powerboat should have a form of automatic fire extinguisher which both detects and hopefully extinguishes a fire in this area. There is the type which does this automatically, but these can be less than effective because the air supply to the engine is not shut off automatically, so that the extinguishing gas may not be fully effective. The alternative is to have a detector which sounds an alarm at the steering position with an actuating switch which can be used to start the extinguisher manually. This at least gives the helmsman time to stop the engines and possibly blank off the air intakes before firing the extinguishing gas. Remember you only have one chance to put the fire out with these fire extinguishers, so don't be in too much of a rush to use the extinguisher without first thinking about what you are doing.

As far as the rest of the boat is concerned, there should be a fire extinguisher placed in each compartment, preferably just inside the door so that you can reach it without having to actually go into the compartment which is on fire. On a powerboat fire extinguishers should be capable of being operated with one hand as you might need the other hand to hold on. They should be of the type which has a trigger to control the extinguisher, rather than the type which works continuously once the knob has been pressed. I know from personal experience how frightening a fire is at sea and how quickly it can force you into abandoning ship. One of the major problems on modern boats is fumes from burning upholstery (or possibly from the electrical installation if it is an electrical fire), and these fumes can often prevent you from getting to the base of the fire and extinguishing it. You need to be very careful about these fumes because they can render you unconscious.

BILGE PUMPS

Bilge pumps are an important safety feature, although there is something of a dilemma with their installation. Bilge pumps are quite adequate in coping with a small ingress of water, perhaps if you ship a sea on board and some of it finds its way below, but they are rarely adequate in coping with any large inrush of water, such as if you had a hull failure. The best way of deciding on the capacity of bilge pumps is to have pumps which can cope with a failure of the engine cooling system, which is probably the worst type of accident in which they are likely to be effective. The size of bilge pump necessary to cope with a hull failure would be so large that it would need to be driven by the main engine. It would also be completely out of proportion to the risks involved.

Electric bilge pumps are certainly the most convenient way of keeping the bilges dry. To be effective in an emergency, the batteries which supply the pumps should be mounted reasonably high up in the boat so that they won't disappear

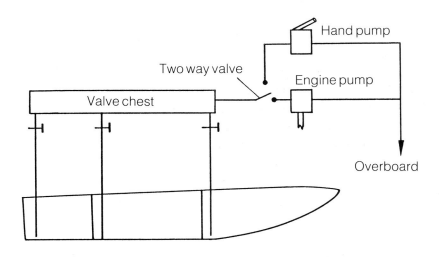

A bilge pumping system which can cope with a number of different compartments and allows the use of both hand and mechanical pumps.

underwater in the early stages of the problem and cut off the power supply. At least one hand pump of good capacity should also be fitted, and with this combination of electric and hand pumps you should be in a position to keep the water flow under some sort of control, until you can get to the seacock or reduce the flow of water which is coming in. In this sort of situation it is easy to visualise why it is not very effective to have the seacock placed in the bottom of the boat, because it will be the first to go underwater. An extension lever up onto the deck, to allow you to operate it from above the waterline, is well worth considering.

One of the problems with water coming into the boat is actually discovering that it is coming in. The first thing that may indicate trouble is either when the engine stops or when the boat becomes sluggish because of the weight of the water in it; by that time you could have a major problem on your hands. The best way of detecting leakage is to have an electric bilge pump with an automatic switch. Place the outlet from the bilge pump in a place where you can see it clearly from the steering position so that any water coming from the outlet will give you an early indication of trouble and a chance to cope with it.

ANCHORS AND LINES

An anchor is essential safety equipment, as well as a useful item if you want to anchor in a quiet cove and not rush around at high speed all the time. Remember, when selecting the size of anchor and line, that this is an item of safety equipment, so you will want an anchor which will hold the boat in difficult sea conditions and in strong winds. A rough guide to suitable anchor weight is 1 pound (0.45 kilogram) in weight for every 1 foot (0.30 metre) length of the boat. This is only a rough guide because different types of anchor have different holding powers. Much will also depend on the type of line – whether this is all chain or a combination of chain and rope. The former gives the anchor better holding power because of the increased weight and because the chain will lie more horizontally on the sea-bed. However, it is more weight to carry on board and it is not always easy to find good stowage for the chain on a fast boat.

As far as anchors go, the type of anchor which stows easily on the bow, such as the Bruce or the Danforth, are the popular types in use today on powerboats. In most cases they are stowed in the bow roller which also acts as a lead for the anchor line. To keep the anchor in this position it needs to be stowed very securely and not have any movement at all. Many modern cruisers have an electric anchor windlass which makes it much easier to use chain over the full length of the anchor line. With an electric anchor windlass the control of the whole anchoring operation can be carried out from the steering position, particularly when the anchor is self-stowing into the bow roller. It makes a convenient installation, but do make sure if you have an electric capstan of this

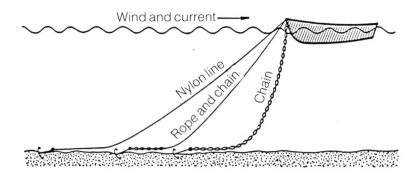

Wind and current

Nylon line

Rope and chain

Chain

How the weight of the anchor line varies the way in which the line will lie.
Chain is best because there is more spring in the line but a combination of
chain and rope is a good compromise.

type that it can also be used to let the anchor go even when there is a power
failure.

Using the anchor or being taken in tow are likely to be the only times when you
have to go up onto the foredeck of the boat at sea in rough conditions, and some
sort of protective railings around the foredeck are useful. These railings should
be strong enough to take your weight; indeed, fragile railings are more dangerous
than not having any railings at all.

COMPASS

Getting a compass to work adequately at high speed or in rough seas can be quite
a problem, and you do need to consider both the type of compass and its
installation quite carefully. Many manufacturers now recognise the problems of
compasses at high speed and are producing high-speed versions of the standard
magnetic compass. The difference between these compasses and the ordinary
compass is that they have a much higher degree of damping. This prevents the
compass card swinging about wildly, but of course it also tends to make the
compass less sensitive to helm adjustments.

If you use one of these compasses, then it is best to mount it as far forward as
possible from the steering position and fairly close to eye level, so that you don't
have to change your line of vision or your eye focus too much when switching your
eyes from the sea ahead to the compass. The helmsman needs to keep his eye on
the approaching seas and on the compass alternately, and if you can achieve this
by a quick movement of the eyes to check on the course being steered, then it
won't break your concentration on the sea ahead and there will be less chance of
your being caught out. Compass lighting is important, and this should be of the

red or orange type so as not to be too distracting at night. Ideally the lighting shoud be variable in strength so that you can match it to the conditions.

A viable alternative to the normal magnetic compass is an electronic compass. These work by having a fluxgate which senses the earth's magnetic field through a pair of sensing coils and translates the tiny induced currents in these coils into heading information. The advantage with this type of compass is that the sensor unit can be mounted on the boat where there is little or no magnetic influence – perhaps on the mast or in the accommodation – and the fact that the display can be produced in a variety of forms so that you can select the type that best suits your requirements. The options open to you are a digital display, a normal compass display with a 360-degree dial, or a simple pointer. More sophisticated displays also have arrows indicating the way in which the wheel should be turned to bring the vessel back on course. I have found that one of the best displays for steering is digital, provided of course that it has large figures. With this type of display it is very easy to steer the course accurately once you get the feel of it, but a good alternative is a pointer working over an expanded scale which gives good sensitivity. With some of these pointer displays the course to be steered is pre-set so that you don't actually have to read numbers when you are steering the course, but simply keep the pointer on the centre line, which makes it easier to read the display at a quick glance.

These fluxgate compasses still work on the earth's magnetic field and need correcting in the same way as a normal magnetic compass. Some of them are advertised as self-calibrating and for this you have to swing the boat through 360 degrees at a steady rate of turn; the compass then shows what the errors are on specific headings. It is a nice concept in theory, but in practice it is essential that the boat swings at an absolutely steady speed to get reliable results and this is not always easy to achieve. Certainly, you need to do several turns and compare the results before you can feel confident about relying on them. Even with this self-calibration, the compass should still be set up by a compass adjuster to check that there are no serious errors and if necessary apply correcting magnets.

The self-calibration system really serves as a convenient way of checking the compass, and there is no doubt that fast boat compasses do change their deviation errors after a heavy battering at sea. Of course, this self-calibration only finds the deviation; you still have to apply the variation as you do with all magnetic compasses. Another point to remember is that compasses are subject to magnetic influence from other items on the boat. This magnetic influence can pass through fibreglass and wooden bulkheads, so check what is behind and around the compass in all directions to make sure you have no portable items which might affect the readings.

WINDSCREEN WIPERS

Visibility from the wheelhouse is vital at high speed or in rough seas, and wipers have an important job to perform. Go only for the best quality of wiper because if you do ship water on deck the wipers have to cope, and I have seen the more fragile type simply bend and buckle under the stress of solid water. The need for quality is reflected by many of the wipers on the market, which makes them expensive but more suitable for the job. Windscreen washers are also useful to help remove salt which can stick to the windscreen in light spray. This helps prevent the smearing which can be a real problem in these conditions and can render the outside world almost invisible. Special coatings are also available for applying to windscreens preventing the water from adhering to the screen. My experience is that these are very good and certainly help to keep the windscreen clearer than would normally be the case. With these coatings you can still use the windscreen wipers and they are certainly worthy of consideration for the serious boater.

The other options to the windscreen wiper are the clear view screens, but my experience of these is that whilst they are very effective, they give a very limited view out of a small portion of the windscreen and are not really suitable for fast boats. Windscreen wipers should be fitted to all the front windows of the wheelhouse, because you need to see in an arc around the boat and not just a limited view ahead. Another point to consider is the problem of condensation on the inside of the screen which can also impair visibility. Here, a duct for warm air to the bottom of the windscreen can be a great help in reducing condensation, or even a small electric fan ducting air in from outside may do the job. Either is better than trying to keep the condensation down by wiping continuously.

TOOLS AND SPARES

At sea you have to be self-sufficient and it pays to have a reasonable tool kit on board. There is nothing more frustrating than finding a problem with the engine or other systems and not having the tools or equipment on board with which to repair them. You don't need anything complex in the way of a tool kit, but it should include a wide variety of tools such as spanners, screwdrivers, pliers, adjustable spanners and perhaps a hacksaw and one or two simple woodworking tools. With these tools you need some spares and equipment, apart from dedicated spares such as bulbs and fuses, to meet all on-board requirements and perhaps also water-pump drive belts and similar engine parts. You also need a good selection of general-purpose repair equipment such as hose piping, worm drive clips, nuts and bolts, screws and some pieces of metal and plywood.

Plywood panels and similar fittings can be useful if a window breaks, or even if you have to repair damage to the hull, if you should be so unfortunate. With a little ingenuity you should be able to cope with a whole variety of problems with such equipment. It is worth checking around the boat and thinking about how you would cope with any particular problems which might crop up when you are out at sea. If you think about potential problems in this way, you will be much better prepared to cope with them if they should happen – but remember that such preparation is no real substitute for making sure that everything is in tip-top condition before you leave harbour.

Other essential items to add to this tool kit are a couple of waterproof torches and lengths of rope, elastic cord, shackles, etc., to serve as lashings should any item of equipment come loose. The aim should be to be as self-sufficient as possible since the chances of finding help when you need it at sea may be very poor.

TENDER

If you carry a tender on board, then you will need to look very closely at how you stow this. The battering a boat takes at high speed can make a tender quite a liability and it is often difficult to stow it adequately. In rough seas, a tender can be more than just a nuisance and my recommendation for boats operating in either of these situations is that you have an inflatable tender which can be deflated and stowed away so that it won't become a liability when the going gets tough. If you stow the dinghy in davits at the stern, a favourite position, you will find it virtually impossible to stop it from moving slightly, and the continual movement is likely to cause wear and chafe and eventually damage. The other options are to stow the dinghy on the foredeck which makes it very vulnerable, and it will probably reduce your visibility too.

It is possible to adapt an inflatable dinghy to substitute for a liferaft, but think carefully before you take this step. If you do adopt this alternative make sure the dinghy is fitted with a portable canopy, because one of the biggest problems if you have to abandon ship is the risk of exposure in a small open dinghy. The liferaft canopy greatly reduces this problem so for the same reason you need a canopy on the dinghy. Gas bottle inflation for the dinghy is also valuable so that you don't have to set to with a hand pump before you can abandon ship. Using the dinghy in this way is a possible alternative, but think it through very carefully before you abandon the idea of having a dedicated liferaft.

The important thing to remember with all the equipment and fittings on a fast boat is that you must go for reliability. When you are in bad conditions and the windscreen wiper packs up, it can put added pressure on you at a time when you could well do without it. Or perhaps the compass light may fail at night, which is why you need a torch close at hand. These are the sort of things which can and do go wrong at sea and the best way to cope is to try to anticipate the things that might go wrong, and then have the equipment and facilities on board to deal with them if they do. Only the best will really do when you are travelling at high speed or in rough seas and there really should be little compromise in terms of quality. However, the best quality in the world will only work if the equipment is carefully installed or securely stowed. Only then will you be able to go to sea with confidence, and have the peace of mind which can bring enjoyment and exhilaration to rough seas or fast boats.

11   Wind and weather

When you go to sea in a powerboat, the weather tends to dominate much of what you do. As well as the effect of wind on the sea surface in generating waves, you will also need to know how the weather will affect visibility, and of course if you are going to sea for pleasure, then things like rain will be of considerable importance. An understanding of the weather patterns and the way in which the weather develops and changes are of prime importance to you, even in these days of sophisticated weather forecasts. You need to be on intimate terms with the weather, so that you get the feel of the whole weather pattern; in this way you will understand the changes that are occurring and will be able to use them to your advantage.

Weather forecasts are normally very accurate, but in many cases they are far too general to meet your specific requirements. They tend to lack an element of precise timing, which can be very important when you have to make decisions about the weather. Forecasts of weather more than 24 hours in advance can be quite vague and therefore may not be of much use in providing the information you need to plan a voyage. Good information is available in the form of weather charts printed in newspapers and on weather-fax machines, but you need an understanding of the weather systems and how they work if you are to benefit from these charts.

TIMING

Timing is perhaps the key to understanding the weather. A forecast may tell you that the wind is going to swing round in direction at some time during the afternoon, for example, but from your point of view it may be important to know whether this will happen in the early or late afternoon. The difference in timing could considerably affect your strategy, whether you are at sea for pleasure or perhaps caught out in rough seas. If you are racing, or travelling at high speed, you need to know exactly when the conditions are going to change as forecast, and it is in this element of timing that the forecasts tend to be vague. The reason is mainly that forecasts cover quite a large area, so the timing will be different in different parts of the area covered. However, all is not lost. You can, to a certain extent, work out the timing of changes by observing the weather patterns, particularly the onset of clouds and rain. These will give you a good clue as to the behaviour of the wind, which tends to dominate your actions at sea.

FRONTAL SYSTEMS

Weather changes tend to revolve around frontal systems. If you consider how a depression develops you will see that primarily it involves a cold front and a warm front. A depression is an area of low atmospheric pressure formed from a mixture of cold and warm air which revolves in an anti-clockwise direction, spiralling in towards the centre. Warm and cold fronts radiate out from the centre of the depression. If you know where a depression is located and the positions of the fronts within it, then you should have a pretty good idea of what the wind *direction* is going to be. Isobars represent the differences in atmospheric pressure over the area of the depression, so if you know how close (or how far apart) the isobars in a depression are, then you can also work out what the wind *strength* will be. This is the way weather forecasters work when producing their forecasts. The weather forecasters will predict the movement of the depression and the movement of the fronts which make up the depression; this information forms the basis of the weather forecast you receive over the radio.

Using these forecasts as a basis, you may want to introduce a more precise element of timing into the equation. The way to do this is to pinpoint the movement of the fronts in relation to your position. Cold fronts, warm fronts and occluded fronts (a combination of a cold and warm front) each have their own characteristic cloud and weather patterns; it is these which can provide the clue to what the weather in your particular locality is going to be. They can also give a much better idea of the timing of events.

Warm fronts

A warm front is formed when the warm air in a depression starts to overtake the cold air. Cold air is heavier and therefore lies closer to the sea surface. In a warm front the warm air lifts above it. This uplifting of warm air over cold air takes the form of a gentle slope when you see a cross-section of the front, as shown in the diagram on page 172. Because this is a fairly gentle slope, the mixing of warm air and cold air takes place over an extended area; it is this which is responsible for the extensive cloud cover which is associated with a warm front. Cloud is formed when water vapour in the warm air condenses as it comes into contact with cold air.

The first warning of the approach of a warm front will normally be very high cirrus cloud. This is light and feathery and could be as much as 500 miles ahead of the point where the front is in contact with the surface of the sea. As the front approaches, the cirrus cloud is followed by more dense cloud, which gradually gets lower. As this is happening a light drizzle will start, and as the point where the front is in contact with the surface approaches the rain will become heavier, the cloud will get lower and you will know the passage of the front is imminent.

The rain in a warm front is persistent rather than heavy, although there will be heavy rain close to the point where the front is in contact with the sea surface. In a very active warm front thunder storms can occur in this area of unstable air. In a weak warm front there may be little or no rain, although the changes in cloud pattern will be similar, the clouds being generally much lighter.

Although the rain may be a nuisance, what you are more concerned with, particularly if you are caught out in the strong winds which are sometimes associated with a depression, is the change in wind direction when a front passes through. In this situation you need to identify the signs of the approaching front. As the very heavy rain approaches, denoting the passage of the front itself, you will know that shortly afterwards you can expect the wind direction to change. In the northern hemisphere this change in direction will mean that the wind will

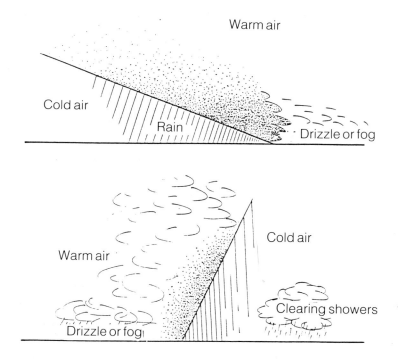

Cross-section of a cold front (top) and warm front (bottom), showing the type of weather which might be expected as the front goes through.

veer, i.e. swing in a clockwise direction, so that, if the wind was previously south-westerly, as the front passes it will become westerly or even north-westerly. This change in wind direction will tend to be more noticeable the closer you are to the centre of the depression. The wind will not change suddenly; it may take an hour or two, and you will see the wind changing at the same time as the weather conditions change. From heavy rain, the weather will change to a light drizzle or perhaps even fog.

Cold fronts

A cold front tends to follow a warm front, is less predictable and can take a variety of forms. Instead of the gradual build-up associated with a warm front, the arrival of a cold front is often announced by strong squalls of both wind and rain and by high, towering clouds. A cold front tends to be more dramatic in this way because the gradient of the front as the cold air is pushing underneath the warm, moist air is much steeper. The point at which the front meets the surface tends to be the most active part of the front and will be the first part that you see as the cold front approaches. Instead of the continuous rain associated with a warm front, the weather pattern of a cold front is usually made up of short, sharp showers and squalls. Sometimes the cold front can be very active as cold air is pushed ahead of the front into the warm air, creating considerable disturbance. Cold fronts may also produce line squalls – a line of very dark cloud usually associated with very heavy rain showers, and even waterspouts.

As a cold front passes, the heavy rain showers will gradually die out, to be followed by the characteristic high cloud and then hard, cold, clear skies. There may still be isolated showers, but as the sun comes out you will have the characteristic clear skies of the calm after the storm, although, in fact, the wind can still be blowing quite hard. However, you will know that the worst of the depression has passed and is moving away from you so there should be a gradual reduction in wind strength. In addition, as the cold front passes the wind will once again veer in direction; in fact, the wind change at this point can be quite dramatic, and you should take this into account if you are caught out in these conditions.

In general, cold fronts tend to be much more difficult to identify than warm fronts before the change in wind direction associated with the front has occurred. In other words, it is quite easy to anticipate the wind change which will occur with a warm front because you will have seen the front building up, whereas with a cold front the wind change will occur very close to the time you recognise the front. Weaker fronts of both types may not have the rain which is normally associated with frontal systems, although they will still have cloud, but these weaker fronts are not normally associated with strong winds so they should not create too many problems.

Occluded fronts

A cold front will normally travel much more quickly than the warm front which is in front of it, catching up with the warm front. When this happens, the warm air between the two frontal systems is forced upwards, and the cold air moves into the space below. This is called an occluded front and it is generally characterised by heavy continuous rain. The occluded front is usually slow moving, so the rain tends to be persistent, but you can take consolation from the fact that the development of an occluded front tends to denote that the depression is weakening and filling, and the passage of this front is not likely to bring about any dramatic changes in wind strength or direction.

Frontal systems are normally associated only with the equatorial side of a depression and are rarely found on the polar side. This means that, if the centre of the depression passes to the south of you when you are in the northern hemisphere, you are not likely to experience any sudden changes in wind direction, although the wind will gradually back or swing anti-clockwise as the depression passes through. The weather in this section of the depression is normally much more settled and stable, except when you are comparatively close to the centre of the depression.

WEATHER PATTERNS

In this study of frontal systems we have taken a depression in isolation, but life is not usually as simple as that as far as the weather is concerned. You have to consider each depression in relation to the high and low pressures of the whole weather pattern; frontal systems can stretch from one depression into an adjacent high pressure area and then link up with the next depression. Each feature of the weather system will affect adjacent systems, and there is always the risk of an unpredictable, sudden and dramatic change in the weather, sometimes on a very local basis. This is more likely to occur in the summer months, when temperature differences between land and sea can influence the changes.

Secondary depressions

One of the situations which develop with little or no warning is the formation of a secondary depression along one of the fronts associated with a primary depression. All depressions are formed along the line of a frontal system, and the development of a secondary depression of this type should not come as too much of a surprise. Secondary depressions are normally associated with a very active cold front, particularly when local variations in temperature can provide the necessary impetus to start the circulation of the secondary depression. Such depressions can develop very quickly, hence the lack of warning and the difficulty

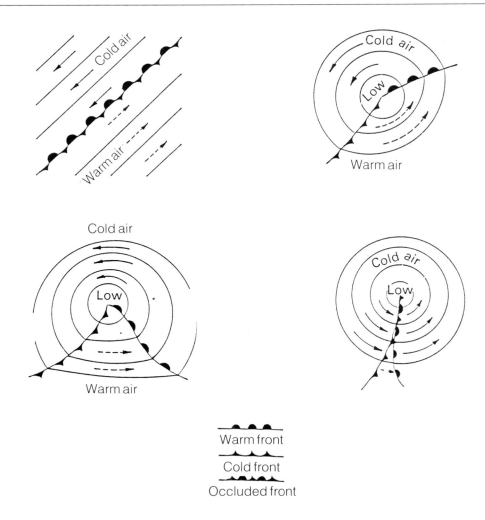

Warm front

Cold front

Occluded front

The development of a typical depression in the northern hemisphere.

in forecasting them. They can also become very intense, sometimes overshadowing the primary depression. The Fastnet gales in 1979 were the result of a secondary depression forming along such a front. This type of quickly developing weather pattern causes many of the situations in which small boats can get caught out in bad weather. Forecasters have difficulty in keeping track of these developments, particularly when they occur over the sea, where weather reports may be sparse. For anyone at sea in a small boat the only way to detect such unwelcome changes in the weather pattern is to keep an eye open for very active weather patterns, particularly those associated with cold fronts, and also to keep a close eye on the barometer.

A barometer may not work very well on a powerboat, particularly when the boat is pounding at sea, causing the needle to flicker. But any sudden drop in pressure should immediately arouse your suspicions as this denotes a rapid change in the weather situation. You will still have the problem of identifying the future weather conditions, however, and by the time you *have* identified them you may well have been overtaken by strong winds and rough seas, anyway. Secondary depressions are usually fast moving, which means that the wind direction may also change quite rapidly. In any situation such as this you must obtain weather information from every possible source. Try to find out exactly what is happening to the weather pattern and then plan your tactics accordingly.

WEATHER TACTICS

The tactics you adopt, whether you are travelling fast in moderate conditions or are caught out in a slower boat in rough seas, depend a great deal on knowing what the weather, and particularly the wind, is going to do. Forecasters, if you can speak to them directly, will probably be able to put a very accurate timing on changes in weather conditions as they apply to your particular area. If you have a particularly critical operation, such as a race or an unavoidable need to cross an area of open sea, then a discussion directly with the forecaster is highly recommended, if you have access to one. Otherwise you should try to work out the changes that might occur during your projected passage from the forecasts and then plan accordingly.

When you are out at sea, either in a fast boat or operating in rough seas, to a certain degree you have to negotiate with the wind and the seas in order to make progress. There are a variety of tactics that you can adopt, depending on the conditions, and certainly in a fast boat the shortest course is not always the quickest. Part of the planning and preparation before you leave harbour should be to look at the alternatives that are available, particularly in the light of the prevailing forecasts, although it is best not to make too many hard and fast decisions until you get out there and see what the conditions are actually like.

On a fast boat, head seas are probably the most difficult conditions to contend with because of the speed of the encounter. You may find it beneficial to put the wind 30 or even 40 degrees on the bow, so that in effect you 'tack' across the sea, reducing the speed of encounter. This should enable you to maintain a higher speed, but of course you are following a longer route. Out in the open sea such a tactic may not be particularly beneficial unless it enables you to keep the boat up on the plane in conditions where, if you were heading directly into the sea, the conditions may dictate that you have to come down off the plane. Such a tactic can be of great benefit when you are coasting and find that the direct route from one headland to the next takes you straight into the sea. This can produce a long, uncomfortable trip across the bay; the alternative of routeing into the bay and following the coast can prove very attractive. As you round the first headland, you can head up for a point on the shore, perhaps about half way round the bay, and this will have the effect of putting the sea about 40 degrees on the bow (or perhaps even more), allowing you to make good progress. By heading into the bay you also have the benefits of a reduced fetch and shelter from the wind but, by the time you approach the coastline in the apex of the bay, you will be in comparatively sheltered water and this will enable you to increase speed, as you will follow the coast to the next headland. This is certainly a tactic to adopt in racing if the sea conditions start to look nasty, and it is equally useful for a cruising vessel wanting to maintain a reasonably high speed. It is easy to calculate on the chart the extra distance you will have to travel; you then need to balance this against the increased speed you will be able to achieve to see the benefits of this course of action.

In a fast boat there will often be benefits from heading into sheltered waters – this is a well-recognised tactic in racing. You may find sheltered water behind a

Portland race with the smooth inshore passage inside the race in the distance. (Photo: HMS Osprey, Portland)

sandbank, where the side of the sandbank takes the full impact of the waves and leaves comparative calm on its leeside. Headlands will also give a degree of shelter, but here you must watch out for the refraction of the waves as they come round the headland. This can create a surprising amount of disturbed water on the leeside, so it is often far better to keep close inshore in this situation, provided that there are no offlying rocks or other dangers. In rough seas, the same tactics are applicable, although of course if you are travelling at lower displacement speeds you are not likely to save too much time by going the long way round a bay. However, if you are looking for comfort it can have its attractions.

On a slower boat in rough weather you will be much more concerned about any changes in wind direction because these could have a significant effect on your tactics. This is really why you need to understand the weather. In a fast boat, your speed will usually allow you to run for shelter if the weather takes a turn for the worse provided, of course, that you are keeping a weather eye open for the changes. Fast boat operations can also bring new dimensions to weather changes. If you are heading towards the approaching fronts, then the whole weather pattern will be accelerated. A front may be travelling at 20 knots; if you are travelling at 30 knots towards it then the fronts will pass through quickly, rather like a speeded-up film. Travelling in the same direction as the front you will remain in almost the same part of the weather system, or even slowly overtake it.

In the same way that a fast boat can dictate its position in regard to the waves in a following sea, so it is possible for a fast boat to dictate its position in regard to the weather, because it has the ability to take advantage of short-term changes in the weather. But remember that the sea does not always drop as quickly as the

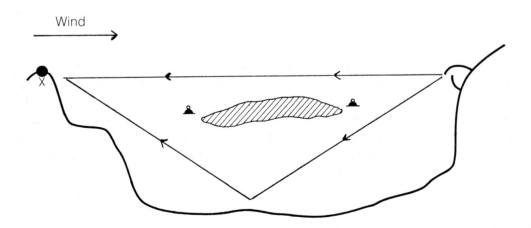

'Tacking' inside a bay; the longer route could be faster in adverse wind conditions.

wind. In many cases you can outrun the weather if it turns nasty, assuming you have enough fuel and sea room. Certainly, with a fast boat I have found that it usually pays to go out and have a look at the conditions out at sea rather than sitting in harbour listening to gloomy weather forecasts.

One often hears of people telephoning the local coastguard station to get a report on conditions outside the harbour rather than looking for themselves, and they have then received a very depressing report. There is no harm in doing this but, remember, the coastguard gets no medal for encouraging you to go out when conditions are marginal, and they sometimes add a point or two to the wind strength. Another factor to bear in mind is that the coastguard station is often high up, where the wind strength will be greater than at sea level. The forecaster has to give what he considers to be the highest wind strength that will occur, and most of the time the wind will probably be a point or two less. I am not suggesting that you disregard all these warnings; rather, you should take the trouble to look for yourself – after all, you will be the person out there therefore it is your responsibility.

Seeking shelter
From the weather charts and forecasts you will get some idea of the wind and how it may change. When a depression goes by and its centre is to the north of you, then the wind will veer. If you are in the northern sector of the depression with the centre to the south, then the wind will tend to back. These are only general rules, however, and if another depression is following close behind the first, the veering of the wind may only be temporary and you could quickly find the wind going back to where it was.

It is important to bear in mind the possibility of these changes in wind direction, particularly if you are looking to seek shelter under the lee of the land. With a wind change of 45 degrees you could find yourself in an exposed anchorage which was previously quite well sheltered. This sort of change will have a bearing on your tactics; one of the most important things to do is to keep an eye on the wind direction all the time. Any changes should be viewed with suspicion, particularly if you cannot relate them to the forecast changes; they could mean that the weather situation is changing unpredictably. You also have to bear in mind that you will often find a temporary change in wind direction around headlands and along coastlines, particularly where there are cliffs or where there are high hills in the background affecting the air flow. The wind will also tend to follow the line of a straight stretch of coastline if its overall direction is within 20 or 30 degrees of the coastline direction.

Remember when planning your tactics that it is not just the wind itself which can cause problems; indeed, it is primarily its effect on the surface of the sea in generating waves. Wind against tide adds a whole new dimension to the state of the waves, and around headlands and other areas where there are strong tides you can find some very vicious sea conditions which are totally out of proportion to the conditions which would be found in the open sea with the same wind conditions. When seeking shelter you have to bear in mind the refraction of waves around a headland, which can disturb what would be a quiet anchorage as far as the wind is concerned.

When you go to sea in a powerboat, the weather has a profound influence on both your progress and your safety. You need to get an intimate feel for the weather conditions and be able to assess the sort of sea conditions that you might expect, despite the fact that the forecast tells you what the wind strength and direction will be rather than the sea conditions. The fetch, the tide and the land all have an influence on the waves, in addition to the primary influence of the wind.

I am a great believer in going out to see the conditions for myself if they appear

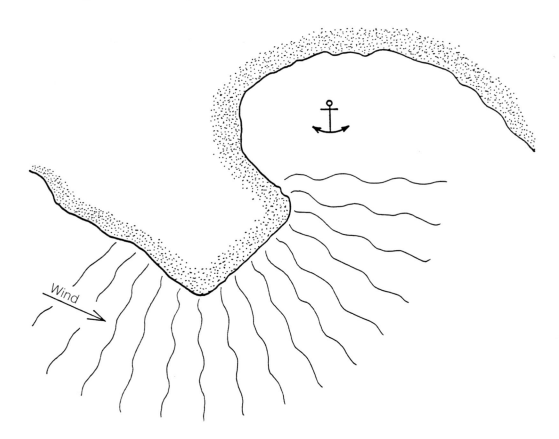

Waves can be refracted round a headland to make an apparently secure anchorage uncomfortable.

to be marginal from the forecast. So often, I have found that weather forecasts tend to be on the cautious side, giving higher wind strengths than those actually existing, and many times I have gone out on a marginal forecast only to find conditions more than adequate to make a passage. However, if you do this you must be prepared to turn back if you don't like what you see outside. You also need to be experienced enough to be able to make a decision about the conditions, bearing in mind that they could deteriorate as you make progress along your route. The answer is to find out about the harbours or shelter available along the route, so that if things turn nasty you can run for shelter. If you are committed to a long passage across open sea, where little or no shelter is available, you definitely need to have the weather and sea conditions on your side – indeed, you should build in a margin for safety. This all adds up to negotiating with the weather, and to do this you need experience. However, if you spend all your power-boating time being extra-cautious you will miss a great deal of the fun and adventure of going to sea. The element of fun and adventure has to be balanced against the risks; you are really only justified in going out to sea in marginal conditions if you have a sound boat, sound equipment and sound machinery so that there is no risk of equipment failure. If you have a boat of this calibre, you have excellent prospects for surviving a gale out at sea, although I guarantee that if you do find yourself in these conditions, life will not be particularly comfortable. However, at the end of the journey you will feel a great deal of satisfaction in having proved both yourself and the boat in difficult conditions.